Lore Bringer

Other books by Miller Lau

Talisker
Book One of The Last Clansman

Dark Thane
Book Two of The Last Clansman

Lore Bringer

Book Three of
The Last Clansman

MILLER LAU

To Pam – lodsa love & hugs

POCKET
BOOKS

LONDON · NEW YORK · SYDNEY · TORONTO

(Debs)
xxxx

First published in Great Britain by Pocket Books, 2004
An imprint of Simon & Schuster UK Ltd
A Viacom Company

1 3 5 7 9 10 8 6 4 2

Simon & Schuster UK Ltd
Africa House
64–78 Kingsway
London
WC2B 6AH

Simon & Schuster Australia
Sydney

A CIP catalogue record for this book is available
from the British Library

ISBN 0 7434 4083 8

Typeset in 10/12.5pt Melior by
SX Composing DTP, Rayleigh, Essex

Printed and bound in Great Britain by
Cox & Wyman Ltd, Reading, Berkshire

Acknowledgements

I'd like to thank those people who saved my life and my spirit, thus allowing *Lore Bringer* to be written.

A big, hearfelt 'thank-you' to Lincoln County Hospital Oncology: Dr Eremin, Mr David Valerio, the *amazing* chemo nurses – sorry, couldn't quite work the friendly vampires into this one – I'll see what I can do later – also, the lovely rads team – Team three rocks!

And to all the wonderful, inspirational women I have met, laughed with and cried with over the past two years – the BC Beauties: Dawn, Jasc-Anne, Wendy, Janice, Murphy, Anna, Teresa (Terri), Lizzie, Kim, Jenni, Joyce, Sno, Kath . . . too many to mention really, but angels every one; a mere thank-you seems inadequate somehow but consider yourselves group-hugged!

On the professional front my thanks go to everyone at Earthlight (and now Pocket Books) for their patience in awaiting this, the last book of the Last Clansman.

In memory of Juana – teaching the angels to salsa – and Rozy, wherever you are, in our hearts always.

Prologue

Tall he was, blue-eyed like the Fine from the southern lands. To see him in battle was to rejoice in the spirit of the Fine – Duncan Talisker, named Worldwalker by the Sidhe. With him came a new Seanachaidh for the land, Alessandro Chaplin. Together, they sewed the seeds of hope and pride in a place which had been reduced to darkness and fear . . .

The Corrannyeid had moved across the land of Sutra like a plague. At first as unremarked as those few blemishes that might stain the skin of a doomed victim, and then, as the people travelled through the forests of Or Coille for the Gathering, killing in such numbers as to be no longer denied. Dark shadows whose method of murder was to assimilate themselves into their victim's form and then rend it apart from the inside.

And even the Gods had abandoned the Fine although it was one of their own number who had raised this hellish army. Corvus, the Raven King, it was whose black malice almost destroyed us all.

It has been told that Talisker had another ally – when he fought in battle he was taken by a red tide of berserker rage and then, some say his soul would split apart, although scholars disagree on this, others would say it was his shadow – whichever, this other being would fight beside Talisker, never leave him unguarded

1

for a moment. None knew from whence they came but both Fine and Sidhe are in agreement that they saved the land of Sutra, first from Corvus' dark hordes and – years after – from the machinations of Jahl, he who would be Thane and God at the expense of all else . . .

And none can tell where they went, for what use are heroes any more when there are no battles left to fight? Perhaps Talisker died in his bed, an old, lonely man unremarked and unloved or, perhaps, the ether claimed him and he rides again in other worlds beyond our ken. Perhaps. There are those amongst the Fine who believe the time will come again when our need and our wishes bring Talisker and his cohorts alive . . . and he will come back to us once more.

Extracted from *History and Legends of the Fine*
by Lachlan 'Whitesnake' Donall

Chapter One

The stars were the same. Weren't they?

Yiska stared upwards but the stars failed to comfort him, obscured as they were by the colourless bulk of clouds heavy with snow. Snowflakes touched on his cheeks and lashes but failed to melt as the temperature of his skin had fallen, and been stung into freezing numbness. He could no longer feel his feet and his fingers were passing through the same recognisable state of tingling, he gripped his blanket more tightly around himself glancing back towards the road where he knew the comfort of his hire-car awaited him.

No one would know if he didn't do this thing – this crazy, senseless thing – which defied all his rational instincts. No, that wasn't quite true; *he* would know and he would have to look Rodney in the eye and lie to him.

As if to confirm this thought, Yiska realised he had begun the dance; his lips were moving, reluctant words dropping into the silence, hot beads of instinctive defiance from deep within his throat. His feet were moving also as if some puppet-master had taken hold of him, possessed him already with the spirit of his ancestors. The steps were tiny, shuffling, making a small hollow in the snow where his feet compressed the frozen whiteness. Realising the stupidity of doing a Ghost Dance in such a petty, reluctant manner – after glancing around once more to check on the emptiness of the landscape – Yiska raised his voice which drifted and danced like warm smoke amongst the snowflakes, suitably haunting.

As soon as he committed himself to the act Yiska knew it was the right thing to do. He knew that nothing would happen – the dance would be merely symbolic, satisfying his uncle that the spirits which were troubling him would be laid to rest. The likelihood of lying successfully to Rodney would have been as likely as achieving any end result here in the middle of a snow-swept Scottish field in the dead of night . . .

. . . and it seemed clear to him why people referred to this time as 'the dead of night'. At this time, the earth had lost its heat, the air was still and cold, the cicadas had stopped singing. It would be three hours before the questing fingers of the sunrise would touch the low slopes of the Chuska Mountains to the west. Before that, the desert floor would already be ablaze with heat and light. Now though, the distant mountains were a dark, jagged outline against the night sky, the stars, a sharp brilliance, like diamonds.

In the tiny cluster of houses behind where Michael walked, a few portable generators hummed, the only thing to break the silence apart from the distant 'yip yip' noises of a family of coyotes.

'Sicheii.' He called out when he saw the dark outline of his uncle against the brilliance of the stars – although he used an affectionate term of 'Grandfather'.

4

'What are you doing out here? It's cold. You haven't even brought a blanket.'

'Stop fussing, Mike. I'm old – my blood is thin . . .'

'Yeah, so that means you have to keep warm, Sicheii, not colder.' Michael stood beside him now, having climbed the small hillock where Rodney had gone to admire the view. He lit a cigarette, the orange flare of his lighter suffusing his tired features in warmth. After taking a deep puff he offered the cigarette to his uncle who shook his head disdainfully.

'I thought they would have persuaded you to give those things up in med school,' he sniffed.

There was peaceful silence as both men surveyed the view, or rather, the lack of it. In the desert there were few lights. From this vantage point the only sign of habitation was far off to the north-west where a dim orange glow amongst the foothills of the mountain marked the location of the mill which was lit up at night. The view was really the sky.

'See there,' Michael muttered. 'I can see the Pipe – Pleiades . . .'

'The whites call it "The Plough" you know . . .'

'Yeah, I know. So, what are you doing out here, Sicheii?'

Rodney sighed. 'I have been dreaming Mike. Strange dreams. When I was younger, I used to set great store by my dreams as the Elders taught me – but now, I sleep the sleep of an old man. Usually what I dream, I forget by morning. But these, are different.' Rodney sat down on the edge of the hill, so Michael followed suit.

'Why?'

'They are so clear. So vivid. The things I am seeing . . .

5

they don't even relate to the Dinéh. Even if they mean something to someone, why would they be sent to me? What do I know about Scottish warriors, swords or battles? What do . . .'

'Whoa, back-up! Scottish warriors?' Mike was grinning, his voice incredulous. 'You're right, how could you dream about this stuff if you know nothing about it?'

Rodney shrugged. 'I know plenty now. The dreams are not short-lived, they stay in my mind. Do you know they used long fighting spears just like the Apache? But they didn't carry them on horseback, the foot soldiers used them from the back of their battle-lines. I have seen many things in my long life – but men being impaled . . .'

Michael was still fascinated by the mere idea that his uncle should be having such dreams. He laughed. 'Are they all wearing tartan?'

The older man ignored his flippant question. 'There is possibly only one thing I recognised,' he muttered almost to himself. 'One of the warriors changed shape into a huge eagle – right there at the edge of the battle – he soared above them but I lost sight of him in the clouds.'

Michael's tone became serious, understanding that his uncle was deeply troubled by this. 'It doesn't necessarily mean anything, Sicheii,' he said quietly.

'Yes it does, Mike. I have dreamt of a Skinwalker. I will die soon.'

And so the dreams of an old man had brought him here; with a new given name and the Ghost Dance shirt which had belonged to his great-grandfather on his mother's side, who had been a Shoshone. *Sicheii* had been uncharacteristically laconic about the suitability of both the shirt and the dance, shrugging his shoulders and spreading his hands in a vague gesture. The Dinéh had never commonly practised the Ghost Dance but, as Rodney pointed out, it was difficult to know what else to do at this stage as the intent of the spirits was unknown. Either a blessing or a curse might be inappropriate and anyway, if the dance proved true, Yiska would be immediately in touch with the spirits. Yiska knew the old man was prevaricating, unwilling to get the local Medicine Man or Hand Trembler involved least word spread that he was losing his mind, but he had offered to come as he was planning to visit friends in Europe after his brief Scottish sojourn.

There was nothing in the field which at first glance might distinguish it from any other except a squat stone marker of black granite in one corner, almost covered by the snow. It said one word; 'McLeod.' When he found it and squatted to rub the snow aside, a dark unease had gripped Yiska's stomach. He had no idea if the stone marked a grave site or not but as soon as he had read the single word the moorland and the fields seemed less empty, more . . . sentient.

Time passed. Bands of snow ridden clouds shuffled across the night sky, the elusive stars peering from between them. He had been dancing for hours. The dance had possessed him in the truest sense, pulling and twisting at the passage of time so that Yiska moved as if contained within his dreamstate. His voice was tired, his lips frozen and cracked where the warm air of his breath passing over them had burned the skin away. Towards the east the first uneasy light of a snow-packed dawn touched the sky . . .

He realised that he could not stop dancing. Panic seized him deep within his chest, his breathing became tighter, hotter even as he turned his palms upwards to greet the dawn and turned around in a slow circle. The dance was slow – inexorable – *surely* he could stop. He could just stop. Right?

Okay, okay I'm stopping . . . now.

But his lips still moved – although his chanting was merely an incoherent whisper – and his feet still shuffled in tired, tiny movements. Maybe he would somehow *know* when to stop. Rodney had not warned him of this; of the hypnotic power of the dance. He was beyond cold now and he knew hypothermia was a likely occurrence.

This is ridiculous. Are you waiting for permission from the spirits?

Although his mind was unaware of planning a deliberate act of sabotage Yiska tripped over his own feet and crumpled onto the ground. For long moments he lay there, his thoughts as blank and formless as the landscape around him. Eventually, a quiet realisation came to him that his position was more precarious than when he had been upright, dancing. He had to move while he still had the strength.

'Hey. Hey you . . .'

The voice came from behind him cutting through the muffling thickness of the snow. Groaning quietly Yiska

8

tried to rise and managed to raise himself up onto his elbows.

'Hey . . . you all right, laddie?'

It's gonna be good explaining this to the locals, he thought wryly. 'Yeah, I . . .' He managed to flip himself over, which was difficult as his legs were completely numb and he had to rely on his upper body strength. He peered into the gloom and his frozen features managed to contort into an expression of dumb amazement. 'What the . . .'

Only a few feet away stood – what had Rodney called them? – a Highlander, a Scottish clansman. Everything Yiska knew about such men he had learned from Hollywood, but he was sure they were meant to be more, well, tidy. The man's kilt was a dull green with only a single stripe woven through it – not tartan at all – and it hung in chaotic swathes of fabric, weighted down by divots of mud and snarls of twigs. He had long red hair which looked like it had never seen a comb. Most worryingly, Yiska's cold-blasted mind belatedly realised, the man was translucent – he could see the snowflakes drifting through his form.

'Ah dunno what yer lookin so surprised fer,' the man scowled. 'It's no like you've been tryin' tae attract mah attention fer the last five hours or anything.'

Yiska must have looked blank as the ghost leant in towards him and said almost companionably. 'Ah wouldne sit in the snow like that if I were you, laddie . . . freeze the arse off ye . . .' he grinned. 'So, what d'you want? I canny do like three wishes or anything mind.'

Yiska stood up, his eyes fixated on the ghost the whole time. This hadn't been the plan; do the dance, sprinkle the herbs, go home. For a long moment he simply stared until the stranger flinched uncomfortably.

'Kin ye speak?' he frowned.

'Yes, I . . .' Yiska gathered his thoughts. 'I am Yiska Talloak – I come from the Navajo Nation in Arizona.'

'Arizona?' The ghost frowned.

'It's in America.'

'Ah, the New World.'

'Sure. Look, can you come and sit in the car? I think I'm in danger of hypothermia – freezing my ass off . . .'

'Car?' the ghost looked confused for a moment, then nodded, 'yeah, I remember cars.'

It was Yiska's turn to look confused. 'You do?'

'Oh aye. Ah've been back before, ye ken.' He began to walk across the snow towards the perimeter of the field. Yiska watched for a moment, noting that the ghost left no indentation or mark on the pristine white blanket. 'You comin', then?'

Once in the car it all seemed so much worse. Yiska was dizzy; he wrapped himself in the tartan travel rug from the back seat and tried to stop his shivering which became uncontrollable as his body fought to generate heat. When he glanced at the passenger seat the ghost was sitting there, staring around with a kind of benign fascination on its craggy features. There was a faint sickly smell wafting from the direction of his new acquaintance and Yiska wondered dimly if it would get worse when the car heated up – not that he cared really. He started the engine and switched on the heater.

'So, are ye goin' tae tell me what it is ye want?'

'I'm not sure really,' Yiska muttered through gritted teeth. 'It's to do with my uncle Rodney – he's been having these strange dreams and he's troubled by them. He saw this field and the marker in his dreams also . . .' Yiska explained the whole thing to the ghost as if it were the most normal, rational conversation in the whole world, his voice sounding flat and muffled within the confines of the car whilst outside the snow continued unabated.

By the time he had finished recounting Rodney's dreams the ghost was looking extremely agitated. Yiska was too tired to care. As the warmth eased back into his limbs he felt the pull of tiredness and the reassuring thought occurred that perhaps his companion was the result of his fevered imagination. He knew he was safe and warm in the car and his blankets and sleep seemed to call him like an undeniable siren.

As he drifted into a warm doze he heard the ghost say. 'We'll need some help on this . . . sounds like big trouble . . .' and then, 'By the way, mah name's Malcolm McLeod. But folk caw me Malky . . .'

24th, 2nd Trine, 1265

What can I tell you? My hands are trembling as I write this journal, and I am not given to fear. I am an intelligent man, and perhaps my intelligence is the source of my fear. For I have the wit to realise that what has transpired this night bodes ill for many but perhaps most of all for me. And yet, I cannot quell my excitement and I know that, despite my trepidation, I will make the journey to power as if it were my one true destiny . . .

But I am getting ahead of myself; let me try and make

order from the chaos of the night's events . . . I was sitting in my quarters in the luxurious southern tower of Durghanti. We were still making changes from the time when the Fine had control of the city and many of the furnishings were on the grand, somewhat vulgar style of the Fine – but I must admit, it was a cosy place, a fire burned in the massive grate and my cheeks were already flushed, whether from the warmth or the wine, I do not know. It could equally have been tiredness; the Fine were planning an uprising soon, we knew from our spies, and I had spent most of the day with the Emperor trying – completely in vain – to persuade the vapid old fool into a pre-emptive strike on Ruannoch Were.

Now I was relaxing, resigned to the stupidity of my Emperor but still confident that any uprising would be easily dealt with. The superiority of the Shoreth forces were beyond question. Anyway, I was reading; in my quarters there were piles of books left by the previous occupant, they covered many subjects and ranged in size from mere pamphlets to massive tomes. Most were tattered, their pages eaten away by dampness or worms, but a few were still readable. The one I was poring over with such interest told of the history of the Fine – it seemed bizarre to me that their so-called history should contain much that was obviously apocryphal – their Gods, for example, seemed to figure in their history as if they were . . . well, real. Their heroes appeared from nowhere and affected the course of the nation before disappearing into obscurity again. Perhaps what intrigued me most was that the Fine did not appear to know who had built their greatest cities – Soulis Mor in the north – so far impregnable but ultimately to be a *target in the Shoreth conquest – and Ruannoch Were. The cites we had already taken, Durghanti and Kamala Sev, had been built by the Fine but the former two were a mystery. Indeed, the writer asserted that they could not be built again because the techniques used to build them were unknown to the Fine craftsman. Let me say that I have never seen Soulis Mor but Ruannoch Were is indeed a marvel of engineering – it is built on the bed of a lake to start with and . . .*

. . . but I digress. I was tired and so the wine was making me unusually giddy. Perhaps I started to doze, I'm not sure . . . anyway, I dropped the book and of course the sound brought me to myself again with a start. I cursed as I picked it up, the spine was broken and a clump of pages had broken away from the binding. Then I noticed something had fallen from the back cover – had it simply been tucked in there or more deliberately concealed? I know not, but given the nature of that paper I am inclined to think it was hidden.

I was stupid. I'm not ashamed to admit it; I am a warrior, not a cleric or some sorcerer. I possess the most brilliant military mind of my generation but I do not think in any mystical way. When I saw that there was a pattern drawn on the page which had been beautifully decorated and embossed with thick gold lettering, I held it up to better catch the light and began to trace the shape with my finger as I read aloud – struggling with an obviously archaic version of the Fine language.

I know, I know, stupid. But there we are. The symbol was similar to a snake, twisted into an unlikely contortion, at the end of the complex twist it held its tail in its own mouth – I believe I have seen similar symbols before representing eternity, but I cannot remember where. With fateful synchronicity, I finished reading at the same moment my finger reached the end of the shape. It began to glow. For a second I thought perhaps it was just a reflection of the firelight against the golden ink, but then the thing caught fire in my hands. I dropped it to the floor with a curse and, standing up, began to stamp on it to kill the flames before they caught on the rug. When I stopped my zealous little dance, it had gone. Not burnt up – I was sure of that – there were no ashes or charred pieces to be seen, just a blackened outline singed into the rug.

I was annoyed, I must confess; the rug had been given to me by the Emperor after the fall of Kamala Sev – originally it had been in the Great Hall there. I had no water to hand so I tipped the remains of my wine into the pile lest there were any smouldering remains.

That's when I heard the laughter, cruel, mocking, capricious. In that moment, an astute man might learn all he needed to know about the person – thing – making the sound. It was certainly enough to put me on my guard so, just before I turned, I drew the blade which was hanging on the back of my chair.

The laughter continued, as if the idea that I might attack was risible indeed. And when I saw the source of the laughter absolute astonishment stayed my hand for precious seconds when I should have simply dispatched the creature.

It was a . . . a creature. Small, no more than two feet high, a strange, mottled mixture of brown and green, its wizened little body resembled a man only in that it had *its limbs in the same locations. Its face was equally wrinkled and, even contorted as it was by supposed merriment, was easily the most hideous visage I'd ever seen; the mouth full of tiny, pointed teeth, its nose sunken, almost vestigial like a bat's, but worst of all were the eyes – motes of coal dark light which showed no fear at the tip of my blade. Oh, perhaps I should also mention the smell – the stench was almost overpowering, a heavy, fecundity like rotting flesh which filled the room to the very rafters. My eyes were watering.*

'What – what manner of creature are you?' I asked. It was a rather pointless, rhetorical question, it could only be a demon or an imp of some kind.

The being ignored my question and began to regard his own horrible body with the kind of fascination which suggested he was unfamiliar with it himself. He held his skinny, claw-like fingers in front of his face and flexed them experimentally. I don't think he liked what he was seeing.

Finally, he spoke. 'Oh, joy,' he said. The voice was nauseating, a rasping, unpleasant sound. He glared at me as if I was to blame for something heinous. Then, 'You not . . .' a pause as if struggling to remember something. 'You not a Fine are you? What world is?'

'Sutra,' I replied. 'And I am a Shoreth. We have conquered most of the Fine cities.'

'Con-kerd?' He began to laugh again and capered up and down with glee. He was obviously no lover of what could only have been his creators given the nature and language of the spell. 'Killing many?'

'Yes, many,' I agreed, somewhat bemused.

'More left?'

'Yes. They still have possession of two cities,' I began to explain – although I must confess the smell was beginning to make me feel sick and light-headed. I sat back down in my chair my eyes still fixed on the creature. There was a pause as he watched me closely but when he spoke again, I was surprised at his choice of subject.

'Murderer you.'

'What? I am a warrior – I have killed many in battle, yes.'

'No. Not just in battle. Blood on hands.' He nodded towards my hands as he spoke so I looked also. There was indeed blood on my hands, although it could only have been some sorcerous trick of the imp. I let out a low cry of amazement.

'Eda,' he said. The word came out of his foul mouth as if it was a meaningless sound but he looked at me intensely.

'Yes.' There seemed little point in denying it; my mouth was dry as ashes and my mysteriously bloodied hands shook. 'She was my wife.'

Eda had married me for political reasons, ambitious as she was beautiful. Our short marriage was tempestuous and vile – she despised me and, the more effort I made to win her, the harder her contempt became. She could not forgive the fact that I was a career soldier, had imagined I would resign my position and become a politician, one of the Emperor's rich, indolent councillors . . .

All my reminiscences were over in an instant, of course; I met the imp's gaze as steadily as I could. 'It *does not grieve me to kill,' I said. 'People's souls are their own responsibility. Death can come for any of us at any time. Their readiness is not my problem.'*

'Sometimes souls are . . .' again, the slight pause as he searched for the words. ' . . . broken. Shattered.' Before I could think of a suitable reply to this somewhat philosophical remark, the imp began to behave in a disconcerting manner; it flung its hands up before it and started to mutter some bizarre words. I could feel the hair on the back of my neck standing up and I decided within a split second – relying on my warrior's instincts – that the time for discourse with the creature was at an appropriate end. Tightening my grip once more on my sword I stood up again and ran the vile thing through where I hoped its heart might be.

It looked at me in confusion and I, not understanding why my thrust was not fatal, lifted it up on my sword like a spit pig. It slid down the blade making a strange gibbering noise as I walked towards the fire. But it was by no means dead.

'Wait, wait . . . Zarrus. I can give power. Much power.'

I must confess that what actually stopped me from flinging it into the flames in that instant was the fact that the thing knew my name. I realise that seems irrelevant in the face of what it had already observed about the murder of Eda, but to hear one's name spoken by the creature was even more unnerving. Instead of dropping it in the fire, I stood it on a chest next to my chair. 'Speak,' I commanded.

He looked darkly at my sword, still impaled in his chest and I obliged and withdrew it. There was no sign of any blood or injury.

'We. We can kill many. Become ruler, Emperor . . . God.'

'That's treason,' I said without thinking. Then I stared at the creature more closely. 'God?'

'Hmm. True'

'H-how?'

'First, we raise a special . . . army. But, must trust me. Must help me.' The last word came out worryingly solicitous; 'meeee.'

'How?' I repeated.

'Say yes.' He appeared rather excited; his ears, which I had hardly noted before, were moving up and down in a slightly repulsive manner.

'Huh?'

'Say yes!'

'Yes.'

Letting out what must have been a whoop of joy, the creature stood upright on his spindly little legs. I sensed I was in danger but there was no time to do anything about it and my weapon had already proven useless. Launching himself forward, he leapt towards me – the horrific vision of his scaly slimy wasted body and the rows of glinting teeth will be imprinted on my memory forever – instinctively I raised my arms to fend off his attack but nothing happened. Or rather, there seemed to be no impact. One moment he was there and the next . . .

There was a sound, I later realised on reflection; a wetness sound. At first though I gazed around the room somewhat stupefied, and for a few moments at least I was willing to put my weird little visitor down to being a dream; a side effect of the tiredness and the wine. I sat *back down in my chair rather heavily and, as I did so, my night-robe fell open to the waist. I let out an involuntary wail of terror.*

I was just in time to see the tip of a scaly, pointed brown tail disappear into the skin of my belly.

I knew him now. Sensed his power, his directionless hatred and his searing ambition. He was in me.

By dusk, over seven hundred Fine lay dead in the field. Smoke and sparks drifted lazily across the valley from the north as the smell of burning wood and flesh mingled in the still air. No wind blew to clear the fug, so the smoke gathered in pockets along the lea of the hillside and clung close to the ground as if to blanket the dying.

The general surveyed the scene with little emotion. It was a victory of sorts he supposed, but when the opposition was so pitiably disorganised it meant little; and he had lost over two hundred, perhaps as many as three hundred men himself. The Fine may have been unequal in battle but they fought with a passion that the Shoreth would be hard pressed to find within themselves. He had watched as they charged his horsemen on foot with massive pikes held before them – surely they must have known that once the wood splintered, they would be defenceless against the second wave of riders, on foot against a mounted foe. Yes, they must have known, *surely* someone had thought things through . . . but there was precious little evidence of this.

The uprising must be crushed, he thought. He turned

his horse around, back towards the encampment. General Vezul found himself anticipating some warmed wine and perhaps some small morsel of food when he arrived back. Although he had not eaten since the previous night, the smells of battle always turned his stomach for a couple of days.

He rode back towards Durghanti, his eyes slitted against the glare of the setting sun. Along the path his men were crucifying as many of the dead and wounded as they could manage. It was the only way Onrir would receive their souls into the afterlife, as they were Godless creatures as far as Vezul could tell. He had given orders to only release the souls of those who appeared in command or carried weapons of status. He knew making this distinction was difficult for his men, the Fine were strangely without much sign of rank or leadership.

A strangled cry rang out into the still air, swiftly followed by a curse. Vezul did not look at the prostrate man whose agonies were being further exacerbated by iron nails. *He does not understand the honour I do him.*

Behind him, the rays of the sunset tinged the smoke with red and a hush began to descend on the carnage which had been the battlefield as the wounded succumbed to their plight or were dispatched by his soldiers. It was a strange quiet, one which he recognised from many previous battles; later, there would be celebration perhaps, but now, only a crushing soul weariness was felt by the survivors. Vezul knew he was lucky to be able to rest. Already, his limbs felt heavy and his eyes tired as adrenaline drained from his system. The thought of his own rooms in Durghanti seemed the luxury of kings but only served to remind him how close the Fine had come to reclaiming their lost city.

He was woken just before dawn. His footman, Jorrd was shaking his arm in a frantic motion. 'General . . . General . . . Sir . . .'

'All right, Jorrd,' he snapped. 'What's wrong?' The room was still in darkness although a faint, pre-dawn light was filtering beneath the shutters.

'I don't know, sir. They've sent a horse for you. To take you back to the field, sir . . .'

Vezul frowned. 'Who? Who ordered this?'

'It's just some soldier, sir. I don't . . .'

'All right, Jorrd. I'll see to it. Just pass me my cloak.'

It had begun to rain. Outside the air was fresh and earthy, few people were moving around. Vezul sourly acknowledged the salute of the nervous looking young soldier who had obviously galloped up the hill to find him – the flanks of his roan were steaming in the chill.

'Who sent you, lad?'

'Lieutenant Dirark, sir.'

Vezul said nothing else. It didn't surprise him – bright young officer though he was, Dirark seemed incapable of decision making in the field. He spurred his horse forward, whilst silently cursing his junior for disturbing him but knowing it was merely a consequence of command.

It took only a short time to reach the ridge where a few of the officers were gathered in a strangely vulnerable looking huddle. The rain was deceptive; Vezul's cloak and breeches had already soaked through and his mood had not improved any. He reined in his horse and snapped down at Dirark without dismounting.

'What's going on, Dirark?' He almost bit back the words when the younger man raised his face to look up at him. The expression there was one of stark fear and while he may have been indecisive, Dirark was no coward.

'L – look, sir.' He pointed back toward the battlefield and Vezul walked his horse forward to survey the scene once more. The gloom was lifting as a reluctant dawn painted the valley in forgiving silver light. The smoke had cleared away and . . .

'I don't see . . . what . . .'

His lieutenant had come to stand by his horse but even as he spoke, the realisation hit home to Vezul and he muttered a whispered curse.

'It's the bodies, sir,' Dirark said. 'They've vanished. All of them.'

It was coming again. Nausea. It hit the pit of her stomach like a brick wrapped in fun fur. Effie bunched her legs into a tighter foetal position and opened her mouth instinctively to vomit without opening her eyes. Realisation of what she'd done was instant as the warm rush spread across her pillow and into her hair. No words seemed adequate for her misery so Effie groaned, an equally sick, heartfelt sound.

She tried to open her eyes but they were sticky, crusted with sleep; the chaotic mess of her apartment, filtered through her lashes, appeared as bright flashes and bars of colour, reminding her of her own paintings.

'I could be dying,' she thought. The pain made the thought seem prosaic, undramatic. *'It was a bad "e". I could die . . .* Still, she felt unable to move even though the sick was stinking and seeping into the pillow. She remembered the club, the thrumming of the music, the endless, mindless noise; and the boy. Some smiling arrogant boy giving her the tiny pill as if it were a breath mint, as if it were nothing, no big deal. *What else had he given her? That stuff – that date rape stuff?* She had no idea, but the slow realisation was dawning that if she didn't move soon, she would be in real bad trouble. She was really cold.

Again, his face flashed across her thoughts; a pleasant face, attractive in a rather feminine sense, but there had been something . . . something about the curl of his lips and the assurance in his gaze. A dull wave of anger flooded through her and the boy had at least done her one favour, as the emotion motivated her to move. Snapping her eyes open she pitched herself deliberately off the side of the futon.

She landed in a cold pool of yet more vomit and her arm slipped out from beneath her sending her crashing into further indignity on the carpet. 'Ah, yuck . . .' she wrinkled her nose, her eyes watering again in disgust and fear. *How much could one person vomit, for chrissakes?* A pain surged up through her stomach as she struggled to get onto her hands and knees. In the calm, distant part of her consciousness which was watching with some bemusement, she noted that she was wearing a camisole and knickers so at least she had managed to undress and get into the bed in the first

23

place. The question of whether or not she had been alone and accomplished the task unaided still nagged her, but she had more pressing things to consider.

'Ahhh,' she heard herself making the sound as she arched her torso into a cat-like stretch. *It must be bad*, she thought, expressions of pain in an empty room were like unsolicited laughter; things had to be very bad or very funny.

Her vision was still swimming as she moved toward the orange blur of the easy-chair; the phone was just there, on the table, she should phone an ambulance. But what then? She could get into trouble. They would accuse her of . . . stuff. She stopped her slow-motion crawl and retched again but there was nothing left to vomit so it was just sore and dry. How long was it taking her to reach the chair?

'Fuck,' she said quietly. Her voice sounded frightened. There was a sound then. She couldn't quite identify it at first; it was quite sweet, repetitive . . .

'Miss Morgan? Miss Morgan?'

Police. Oh god!

'Go away,' she quavered, vaguely aware of the stupidity of calling out. She was nearly at the phone now. Grabbing hold of the edge of the seat, Effie attempted to haul herself upright. She failed as the leather cushion slid towards her and, losing her momentum, she fell back into a sitting position on the floor. Making a desperate attempt she grabbed for the phone and managed to knock the handset to the ground. Picking it up she cradled the cold plastic against her forehead as she tried to collect her thoughts.

'Are you in there? Effie Morgan? I can hear . . .' There

was a pause as if the person was considering giving up. *Maybe it's not the police.*

'Look I need to talk to you urgently . . .' He had a funny voice, an accent she couldn't quite place.

'Go away.' The nausea came again – this time her gut had found some reserves of liquid. She stared down at the newly wet handset distantly, wondering if she could still dial through the vomit. It seemed funny. Messy. She giggled weakly.

'Are you all right?' The voice again. Accompanied by banging on the door.

'No,' she said it too quietly. He wouldn't hear her. The banging came again and she watched in slo-mo the way the wood of the door flinched against the hinges with each bang. '*No . . .*' Darkness bloomed in the centre of her vision; a poisoned but not unwelcome flower. She was blacking out. 'NO!' She tried to say it loudly but the sound . . . the sound was taken from her as her breath failed.

As she woke, chill air played against the skin of her forearm; the kind of chill which presages snow, wet cleanness. Someone had opened the window – Effie sniffed – good idea, the flat stank of sick. Pulling the covers up to her chin, she opened her eyes.

A tall, extremely good-looking man was standing at the sink in the corner of her little bedsit staring somewhat incongruously at the floral pillowcase he was washing. *He's* . . . Effie frowned, trying to gather her thoughts, and felt somewhat cheated to still be so vague – thought she was better. But she was still seeing things, surely. He was an Indian, an American Indian . . . *no, get it right, Euphemia,* a Native American. He was wearing really dinky gold rimmed glasses which seem to glow against the warm pallor of his skin.

He turned towards her, sensing her scrutiny, and smiled a broad white smile. *God, he's gorgeous.* Suddenly aware and vulnerable, she shrank further into the quilt, bending her knees in front of her.

'You're a very lucky young woman, Miss Morgan,' he said. His voice was warm deepness but she detected a note of accusation there. *Did he know about the drugs?* She glanced around the room which this complete stranger was in the midst of clearing up; it was wrecked. Worse, she wasn't sure if she was the guilty party, maybe it had been . . . the boy. She groaned. 'So. What? You're my father now?'

Ha. That's funny. He'd never care enough to wash my . . . she glanced at the soapy fabric in the stranger's hands. *Oh no. Not those.* The Native American pulled a prim expression. *Strange. You'd think a gorgeous hallucination would be more fun . . .*

'I believe the word you're grasping for is "thanks,"' he said. 'It's possible I just saved your life.

'Yeah. Right. Let's not get carried away here.' She shifted uncomfortably in the bed. *Someone's taken the pillow away. Oh yeah . . .* she remembered.

'Studied chemistry, have we?'

'What?'

'Do you know what those trashy little pills can do to your liver?' He strode over to the futon and handed her a mug of hot, black tea. 'Here, drink something.'

She scowled but took the mug from him. 'What's going on here? Who the hell are you?'

'My name's Yiska. And the way I see it, Effie Morgan, you owe me a favour.'

It was always when she heard a storm that she remembered; beneath the cold shriek of the wind or the driving blasts of the snow, for Ferebe, there would always be the promise of warmth – the rich comfort of her father's voice. It was the night she met Storm.

'Do you know how many are left?'

Her own voice was young and high pitched, she was barely seven summers. 'Not many, Father. But Mama has told me that one day, a special one will come . . .'

And it was special. In the warm, rank smelling cave of crumbling chalk, the newborn calf lay nestled against its exhausted mother. All around the boundary of the enclosure the *Sanah*, whose job it was to look after the well-being of the creatures were jubilant, slapping one another on the back and sipping celebratory drinks of dremsi to keep themselves awake. The labour had been hard and long, Ferebe heard one of them tell her father; most of the *Sanah* had been here for two days, unwilling to miss the birth.

Ferebe stood with her chin resting on the perimeter wall looking down into the pit. She felt tired and strangely flushed, having come into the warm caves from the bitter weather outside – a storm which people would later say was an omen. She could hear the wind howling around the base of the chalk cliffs and rattling against the massive double door through which the mammoths and riders rode forth. But in here it was quiet, people were talking in hushed, deferential tones.

It was a great fortuitous night; a white mammoth had been born – *the* white mammoth.

Only, it wasn't really white for the moment, still bloodied from its birth, it lay curled within the arch of its mother's legs, its breathing shallow as if it was asleep, but from within the mess of coarse hair and drying blood, a beady blue eye was fixed on Ferebe.

'Hello,' she whispered. 'Hello, hello . . .'

'It's very weak, sir,' she heard one of the *Sanah* tell her father. 'It may not survive the night. Should we wake the Emperor?'

'No. Not yet. Not if it may die. Why wake him for such ill news?'

Die?

'You can't die,' she whispered to the stricken creature, 'you've only just arrived.'

The watching blue eye blinked at her and Ferebe felt a rush of sadness, incomprehension and fear. *It's telling me!* she thought. *It's showing me its fear!*

She looked around for help, for someone to explain to. *It's frightened – stop saying it's dying. It can hear you . . .* But there was no one who was not engrossed in conversation – they may have been talking *about* the new arrival but they were not paying him any direct attention. As a seven year old, Ferebe knew the feeling well. She smiled sadly down feeling tears pricking at her eyes. 'Don't be afraid, little Storm . . .' *What did mother do when she was afraid?*

General Vezul was deep in conversation with the Chief *Sanah*. The man was arguing, not without reason, that prophecy foretold the *birth* of a white mammoth which

28

would ensure six generations of peace and prosperity after a great conflagration, but it did not say that the creature would survive – only that it would be born. There was no reason to assume its survival and therefore, the Emperor should be woken immediately. If the calf were to die in the next few hours, the Emperor would be justifiably angry to have missed seeing the creature alive. Vezul nodded his head gravely, considering the man's argument whilst dusting the wet snow from his faintly steaming cloak.

'I suppose you could be right,' he began somewhat grudgingly.

'Sir, sir, look!' A younger *Sanah* was pointing down into the pit, an expression of bemusement and mild alarm on his face. All around the perimeter wall, the small clusters of celebrating *Sanah* fell silent in disbelief.

It was Ferebe. The child had climbed into the pit and now lay nestled against the calf, echoing the way it nested in the hollow of its mother's legs. She seemed oblivious to the blood of the newborn and its mother which was smeared across her arms and face. Stroking the damp coarse hair away from the calf's blue eye she was singing; her thin little voice echoing up from the pit and soaring into the cold reaches of the chalk ceiling.

'*Get her out,*' someone whispered frantically. Mammoths were unpredictable beasts at the best of times and there was no way of knowing how the new mother would react. The elder *Sanah* started forward.

'No.' Vezul gripped his arm. 'Look, she is calming them.'

And so it seemed. The calf's breathing grew steady,

more measured and its mother wrapped her trunk around both the calf and Ferebe, who continued singing. She glanced up at her father and smiled through the mess of her silver blonde hair which was stuck to her face by blood and mire.

'She will be a great *Sanah*,' the elder *Sanah* muttered.

'No,' Vezul shook his head, smiling fiercely back down to his daughter. 'She will be a great General.'

'Look . . . thanks . . . but I'm fine now. Honestly. You can go.' Effie smiled her sweetest, most confident smile at Yiska. *Oh no. A favour? We all know what that'll be . . .*

'Anyway, I'm . . . expecting someone.' She fidgeted with the lapels of her bathrobe fighting the desire to pull it tight across her chest, to hold it close and closed.

'Yes,' he seemed unperturbed. 'The police apparently. Or your dealer.'

'I'm not an addict if that's what you think,' she fumed.

'No. Of course not.' He said it with no inflection in his beautiful, rich-brown voice but she sensed his careful implication. Still, he made no move towards her and she was warily grateful for that. He sat down on the orange leather chair.

Back up. Back up . . . Effie's head was beginning to clear as the tea delivered a little kick of caffeine. *Whoa.* 'Shit. How do you know my name? What is this?'

Yiska sighed. 'Well, it's difficult to know where to begin . . .'

'Could you speak faster – could you get to the effing point?'

'We're not all on amphetamines, Miss Morgan.'

Ouch.

'Just hear me out and then, if you think I'm insane, I'll go. I promise.'

'Okay.'

'Right. My paternal uncle has had a series of dreams. Scottish type of dreams. Battles, people in kilts, *Braveheart* kinda stuff. He was worried, felt that someone needed his help. Someone sent those dreams to him.' He paused infuriatingly and sipped his own tea. 'We Navaho set great store by our dreams. Anyway, he sent me to Scotland, thought he could identify a place – which came in one of the dreams – by its landmarks. He asked me to do a Ghost Dance there, thinking that the spirit of one of our ancestors was trying to reach us . . .'

Jeez . . . 'And what happened? Did your ancestors contact you?' Effie tried to look interested.

'Not exactly, no . . .'

'Fer chrissakes! This is takin' far too long an' she disnae believe you anyhow. Jist look at her face!'

Effie felt herself go cold; completely cold down to her toes. Then hot. Her face was flushed, felt like it was on fire. Sweat instantaneously pooled in the hollows of the clavicle bones of her neck. A man had appeared . . . *yes, 'appeared' was the only word* . . . beside Yiska's chair. He was wearing a long green kilt – not a fancy dress kilt, but a real functional garment – he had red, kind of ropey, hair and was carrying a massive sword. Oh yeah, and she could see through him because he was a . . .

'. . . ghost? Nonononono . . . this can't be right. This is not good. This is *ungood*.' Her voice wavered slightly and she looked pointedly at Yiska, hoping that the ghost would simply vanish again once removed from her line of vision. 'You were right,' she garbled, 'I'm sorry . . . about the drugs I mean . . . make it go away.'

Yiska looked annoyed. It seemed he could see the ghost too because he frowned towards it. 'Now look what you've done. You've frightened her.'

'Look hen,' the ghost tried to smile encouragingly, showing a nasty expanse of gum, 'ah'm sorry like. But we've no got time tae mess around. We're looking fer Duncan. Duncan Talisker.'

'What?' The request threw her. It must be some weird paranoid shit. *Oh god, damage has been done to my brain . . .*

'You are Effie Morgan, right? Daughter of Shula Morgan who was killed by a de . . . serial killer?'

Effie was losing it completely now. Tears flooded down her cheeks and she felt a strangled sob trapped in her throat. 'No . . . yes, I mean. My mum . . .' she wiped her face on the sleeve of her dressing gown, 'my mum was killed in a car crash when I was young.'

The ghost narrowed his eyes. 'Is that what they telt ye? Well, ah'm no surprised.'

'M-make it go away!' The sob escaped her, making her voice a thin, pathetic wail but she didn't care.

'Oh very good Malky,' Yiska frowned. 'Yeah, very smooth.'

'Ah'm sorry like. I thought they'd tell her when she was old enough.'

'It's not like being told you're adopted or anything is it?'

'Do you know where Duncan is, hen? If no, what aboot Sandro? Alessandro Chaplin.'

'Uncle Sandro? He's not here.' She rubbed her eyes which were hot and itchy from the tears and looked back hopefully, but the ghost was still there.

'Oh.' He looked deflated. 'Well. I dinnae ken what tae do, Yiska. They're the only two folk who'd be able tae shed any light on yer premonitions.'

She was calming down a bit now. Granted, it was a bizarre kind of calm; a ghost and a Native American were in her living room and she was still mostly convinced that she was hallucinating. She realised then that the real burden of hallucinations might be deciding what was part of the hallucination and what was real. For instance, Yiska *might* have been real or he might be part of the whole thing. She *might* be entirely alone. In fact – and she felt her heart quicken at this thought – she might still be unconscious in a pool of vomit, lying over there by the leather chair. Maybe if she sank down under the duvet and closed her eyes it would all be gone when she really, *really* did wake up. 'Uncle Sandro's in Sicily with Aunty Bea,' she murmured. She closed her eyes and turned her face to the pillow, wiping her tears away as she did so.

There was a plastic sound in the background and then the purring of a dial tone near her face. Reluctantly, she opened her eyes again to look into Yiska's face. He didn't say anything though, just held the receiver of the phone demandingly. She groaned – the ghost was still there, she could see him behind Yiska's shoulder.

'Call 'im. Telly . . . telephone him, whatever it's called. Say Malky's here and he needs to find Duncan. It's urgent.'

33

Chapter Two

Catching crabs. Not Ferebe's idea of fun but then, it had its advantages. She sat on a large boulder, her feet pushed into the warm wet sand and squinted up the beach shading her eyes from the glare of the sun. A low level drumming like distant thunder was carried towards her on the wind. They were coming this way.

Beside her, the crabs she had caught in the rock pools with the tongs her mother had given her squirmed wetly in the netting bag, their violent reds and purple glinting in the light. Ferebe knew she could not sit here for too long or the crabs might dry out, but she really wanted to watch. She cast around and saw a shallow pool nearby; if she was quick she could put her catch in it – still in their bag – and nip back into her hiding position. She was wearing a grey dress and cloak and was sure the riders would not see her against the rock face. Quickly, she splashed over to the pool and dumped the bag unceremoniously in the middle, placing a heavy stone over the opening. Then she ran swiftly back to her place behind the rill of granite – just in time.

The officers rode into view, their silver breastplates glinting in the morning sunshine, their braided hair and black robes catching the wind. Their horses stretched out, heads down, enjoying the freedom of the beach after a long night in the stalls. The front riders began to stake out long poles in the sand for the trainees to tilt at with lances or swords; a red flag flew from the top of each, snapping in the brisk wind. Once they were set up, the riders began, in turn, to gallop at breakneck speed and attempt to capture as many red flags as possible; this was accompanied by much good natured jibing and cheering.

Ferebe was unimpressed by this. She had been riding all her life but many of the young soldiers were surprisingly inexperienced horsemen. Even as they gathered at the far end of their makeshift tilt a few of them fought to curb the excitement of their mounts. Ferebe would have been embarrassed not to be able to control her horse better, her father would have made sure of that. She thought most of them were pretty poor at the exercise, too, and their officer seemed frustrated by the lack of seriousness of his charges.

'You ride like a girl!' she heard him exhorting one of the officers who had put on a pathetic display. This annoyed her intensely and she tutted to herself.

'I can ride better,' she muttered.

She fell silent and watched with renewed, owlish interest as Felndar readied his mount. She had seen him many times, of course, since he had come to Kamala Sev with his brother to train, but she had never spoken to him. He was handsome and athletic, a bit like her father, and she knew that many of her friends had supposedly fallen in love with him. Ferebe had no time for such affectations; love was for those with little to occupy their minds, she felt. But her interest in Felndar was rekindled after she heard her mother and father arguing two nights earlier. Ferebe's Life-Day was to be this weekend, she had been twenty-two summers for almost a month and it was past time the Emperor (via her father of course) decreed her fate. For someone of her breeding and importance Ferebe was sure this would simply mean who she had to marry. The idea of marriage was a bit like toothache – it worried her intermittently and then subsided – but now it grew closer; she found herself wondering about the mysteries of such relationships, and realised they didn't frighten her as much as she had anticipated. Although she could not make out their voices clearly, during the argument her mother had definitely used Felndar's name. It came as little surprise; he was the top officer cadet, tipped to be a lieutenant and maybe even a general himself one day.

Ferebe stared with a kind of horrified fascination at the curve of his long, slim thighs which gripped his mount tirelessly. She could feel a warm flush in her belly and the sea breeze suddenly stung her face; discomforted by this she glanced back to the pool where she had flung her bag of red crabs.

'Oh no.'

They were escaping. Three of them, in a slightly comical line, were edging out of the pool. Without thought to her concealment or waiting to see how Felndar fared, she began to run towards the pool. She could hear the thunder of the horse somewhere behind her but so intent was she on her prize she didn't realize until the last possible moment that the rider was catching up with her.

Before she knew what was happening, Ferebe was plucked off her feet and flung over the withers of the horse. She squealed indignantly and kicked her legs against the animal which threatened to rear until Felndar managed to control it – turning it back up the beach and spurring into a gallop. The world was a flash of blue water and white sand and Ferebe cursed as she dropped her net bag. She could see Felndar's feet encased in leather and silver boots with spurs which she knew to be more decorative than useful. *Hope the salt gets in them,* she thought. *Serve him right.* She could also see the pommel of his sword which rested just below his hip.

Felndar reined to a halt amid his friends. Hoots of laughter and ribald remarks surrounded them. Ferebe could feel her face burning with indignation, the crashing sound of the sea and her heartbeat mingling in her ears.

'What have we here, Felndar? A comely little crab catcher!'

'Think I'll take her home for dinner,' Felndar responded. Without warning he smacked Ferebe's backside which caused more laughter. Ferebe cursed loudly and tried to wriggle off the horse but her cloak was caught in the filigree of the saddle. Exasperated, she reached out and used his leg for leverage, digging her nails in as she did so.

'Owww!' Felndar yelled. But there was little time for him to react, before he knew it Ferebe had pushed away from his horse and drawn his own blade against him. She stood grim faced, eyes blazing with fury. Felndar chuckled.

'Steady, crab-girl. We were just having some fun with you.'

'Fun!' she raged. 'Were you practising your wenching technique? I'm sure it's the only way you'd get a woman you . . . you worm.' She whipped the sword through the air before him the thin practice foil making a whistling sound. Instinctively she took up a fencing position and Felndar – reddening from the laughter of his companions – arched his brows.

'What's this? Know how to use that thing, do you? Been practising in the kitchen perhaps.' He slid off the back of his mount and stood before her, his arms open in a mocking placatory gesture.

'Arm yourself and I'll show you what I can do,' Ferebe growled.

'Come on, you can't be serious.'

'Frightened?' Actually, Ferebe was already regretting having drawn the blade but she wasn't about to let Felndar know that. It was the first time she had been able to inspect her future husband so closely and she realised he was probably five years older than her and about a foot taller. He had a disappointingly weak chin.

'Of a little girl? I don't think so,' he grinned and she had to admit he had a charming smile. 'I'll tell you what crab-girl, I'll teach you some swordsmanship if you teach me how to make crab soup.' He held his hand out almost absently and one of his friends placed a practice foil in it. Saluting with his blade he backed away from his horse to give himself room and the crowd of his friends moved with them in a nebulous circle.

'Come on then crab . . . ouch!'

'Stop calling me that!' Ferebe lashed out, a careless angry jibe but her long legs covered the distance with ease and she caught Felndar across the top of his arm. A thin line of blood showed through the white linen of his shirt and his expression changed in an instant from shocked surprise to darkening anger. His friends gasped aloud at Ferebe's first blood – *I've done it now,* she thought. *His precious honour will need to be satisfied.*

Felndar pressed forward in a frantic flurry of blows which, while they looked impressive, carried little weight behind them. *He's hampered by the fact he's fighting a woman,* Ferebe realised. Still the speed of the attack was mesmerising and she had little time to analyse her advantage.

'That was sheer luck, bitch!' Felndar cursed.

Ferebe kept her cool. 'Tut, tut, temper, temper.' She caught his foil on a downward strike and unbalanced it by moving the weight of her blade far up towards the handle – a trick her father had taught her – with a snapping motion she pulled the weapon from his hand and stepped in towards him. She had no dagger so she touched her index finger to his unguarded throat. 'My name is Ferebe Vezul,' she said quietly.

Felndar blanched. 'General Vezul's . . .'

Ignoring him, Ferebe turned to his friends who seemed both shocked and amused by the turn of events. 'Felndar and I arranged this little demonstration,' she smiled calmly. 'It teaches us two things: One, anger is not the same as courage and has no place in battle, and two, never, ever, underestimate your opponent.' She turned to Felndar and, holding his gaze steadily she made a light curtsey. He smiled a slightly unconvincing smile and inclined his head.

One of the crowd of friends began to clap and laugh. 'And never call someone crab-girl,' he chuckled.

'Indeed.' Ferebe smiled. The moment was past, Felndar would not lose pride through her actions. Without looking back at him she walked back up the beach to retrieve her bag, hoping that at least some of the crabs remained trapped inside. She studiously ignored the fact her legs were shaking. As she crouched down to examine the bag, Felndar grabbed her arm; he had followed her up the beach.

'Ferebe,' he said solemnly. 'I'm sorry for what happened. But the last woman to defend my honour was my mother when I was five. I don't need another mother.'

She regarded him coolly. 'If you were a better swordsman your honour would not need defending, Felndar.'

He looked as though she had slapped him. Dropping her arm he hissed a curse, turned on his heel and stalked back down the beach. Ferebe watched him go. *Well done. Nice start,* she chided herself. *Can't wait for the wedding night . . .*

Still, it could be worse, she considered as she watched him stride away. She liked the way he moved.

Winter sunlight filtered through the murky orange cloth of the blinds. Effie fidgeted in her chair and tried to concentrate on the discussion. Hospitals made her uneasy, or more precisely, medical people made her uneasy.

'So, what exactly is wrong with Mr Taylor?' Yiska asked. 'Is he here voluntarily or was he sectioned?'

The young doctor on the other side of the desk assumed a slightly smug expression and Effie decided she definitely didn't like him. 'We do *know* who he is. It would be counter-productive to encourage Mr Talisker's use of a pseudonym whilst he's undergoing treatment. Mentally, he has clinical depression. He's had treatment for that, Seroxat and ECT . . .'

Yiska looked surprised. 'You still do that?'

'Oh yes. It's very effective. Physically, we're not sure what's going on. Mr Talisker's immune system is dangerously compromised. His white cell count is only 1.1 at the moment.'

'That's almost neutropenic. Have you given him neuopogen shots?'

'No. We tend to wait until the WCC drops below one.'

'Have you tested for HIV?'

'We're not entirely stupid, Mr . . .'

'Talloak. *Doctor* Michael Talloak.'

'Oh. Well . . .' the young doctor grew defensive, started clicking the top of his pen for no reason. 'We've done many tests . . . you say you're family?'

Yiska nodded towards Effie. 'Miss Morgan is his niece.'

Effie smiled wanly. She was bored. 'Excuse me. I just need to get a drink,' she mumbled. She left them discussing Talisker's condition and wandered off down the corridor.

As hospitals went, the Royal Edinburgh wasn't too grim – perversely because it was mainly a Psychiatric Hospital. It was bright and clean and even smelt pleasant, although the faint waft of stewing vegetables could be detected from the kitchens; it reminded Effie of school dinners.

'Psst. Euphemia. He's in there . . .' Effie jumped as

Malky appeared at the end of the corridor. She wondered if the realisation that ghosts were real and she was being very personally haunted would get any easier over time.

'Effie,' she hissed, glancing around to check no one would see her apparently having a discussion with herself – they might keep her in. 'My name's Effie.'

She went over to the door that Malky was pointing to and peered in through the glass panel. Suddenly she was angry, nervous and angry at the same time. Her palms began to sweat and her throat dried up. It was years since she had seen Talisker at Uncle Sandro's house and she hadn't really paid him much attention. Now she wished she knew him better because he was part of the lie they'd told her. Malky had given her a little information about her mother's murder – although she was pretty sure he was holding back some horrible detail – and it seemed that Talisker had initially been implicated, although he was later cleared. But he *knew* about it, and Malky's assertion that her mum had been murdered by a demon was pretty off the planet, leaving a lot of questions unanswered. Mind you, she had to admit that since it was a ghost telling her this, perhaps anything was possible after all.

He looked ill. He was lying perfectly straight and still with his eyes wide open, staring into nothingness. Only the smallest movement of his chest belied the fact he was breathing. It was the whiteness of his skin which seemed the most shocking thing to Effie; she had never seen a corpse but she felt sure they could not be much paler. It was hard to estimate Talisker's age but his shoulder length red hair was streaked with grey.

'Are you goin' in, lass?' Malky asked gently.

'Yes. Are you coming?'

'I'll give you a few minutes first. Mebbe you want tae talk about your ma.'

Effie glared at the ghost, although distantly surprised by his tactfulness. 'Damn right I do.'

She crashed open the door and strode into the room. There was no time for pity or sympathy. Maybe this man had murdered her mother. She wanted answers, *now*.

'Talisker.' Her voice was like a whiplash but he didn't react or respond; just lay there as though held in some invisible brace. Effie strode over to the bed and bent down slightly so that her face was closer and not cast into silhouette by the light from the window. His wide blue eyes flickered across her features, a scrutiny Effie could almost feel like some tiny, dying insect. She snatched her sunglasses away from her face and, just as she was wondering whether he would remember her or not, he spoke.

'Who are you?'

'Don't you remember? Effie.'

'Effie?' his eyes widened in surprise. 'Effie Morgan?'

'Yes.'

There was a pause as he turned his head towards her with the slow motion deliberation of the chemically sedated. 'You look just like your mother,' he said.

She wanted to cry but she bit down angrily, stifling her feelings. 'I need you to tell me about her death, Mr Talisker. You were there . . . I need to know what happened.'

Talisker was suddenly gripped by a spasm of coughing, a dry racking sound. 'Do you want some water?' she asked. Without waiting for his response she poured him some water from the plastic jug which was on his bedside cabinet. He raised the head off his bed and took the cup from her without comment. His hands were cold. When he'd finished he regarded her for the longest time with his unsettling blue gaze. There was an *exhausted* quality to his eyes, she thought.

'Shula died in a car accident,' he said.

Ah. The party line. 'Really. What would you say if I told you I know she was killed by a demon?'

Maybe it was the drugs but his reaction was not what she'd hoped for. He frowned at her as if not comprehending what she'd said.

'A dem . . .'

The door opened and Yiska stood there with the doctor. 'I see you found your uncle, Miss Morgan,' he smiled.

'Yes, can we take him home?' Talisker said nothing but his gaze flickered back to Effie.

'It's up to Mr Talisker, of course. He is here voluntarily and can leave at any time. I'm perfectly happy to let him go since Dr Talloak has promised to supervise his care.'

'But I don't know . . .' Talisker began. He stopped, as Malky materialised between the two doctors in the doorway, his body apparently forming from a plume of mist. *'Malk?'*

'Hmm?' the doctor frowned. 'Is there something you want to tell me, Duncan?'

'Hiya Duncan. Are ye no well?' Recovering

44

surprisingly fast from the shock of seeing his ghostly companion Talisker looked straight through Malky, something which was easy to do.

'That's right, *Mike*,' Yiska smiled. 'Haven't seen each other for a while, have we?'

Talisker narrowed his eyes. 'Like never,' he replied quietly. 'Dr Smith, can I talk to my niece and . . . doctor, alone for a few minutes?'

Dr Smith smiled wanly, choosing to ignore Talisker's obvious confusion and the sudden tension in the room. 'Absolutely. It's an important decision, Duncan. Take all the time you need.' Dr Smith left, closing the door behind him.

'What's going on?' Talisker demanded. His words were slurred, which lessened their impact somewhat, but his eyes had lost some of their deadened look acquiring a harder, more wary expression.

'Duncan, we need your help,' Malky began. Talisker completely ignored him, it was as if the highlander wasn't there. Effie and Yiska exchanged glances.

'It's all right,' Effie said. 'We can see him too.'

'Who?' After his initial reaction Talisker had obviously decided denial was the way to go.

'Me, you bloody great lummox!' Malky seemed to be taking it personally. 'Jings, are the drugs affecting yer brain?' He sat down on the end of the bed and glared at Talisker as if challenging him to deny him again.

Talisker sighed heavily. 'All right, Malk. This had better be good.'

'Oh, cos you're so busy an' all.' Malky was peeved; he

peered into Talisker's face, the eyelids were drooping, heavy with sleep. 'Are we keepin' you up, like?'

'Sorry. It's the meds. I'm listening, honestly.'

'Right, well, ah think . . . well, ah think there's trouble in Sutra and . . .'

There was a strange, rusty noise as Talisker attempted to laugh. 'Sutra! Let me guess – you want me to go and sort it out? Worldwalker, last of my line, blah, blah . . .'

Effie and Yiska were unused to the rhetoric associated with Sutra, only Malky nodded in avid agreement.

'It's true though, Duncan. Sutra needs ye again.'

Talisker stopped laughing rather abruptly. 'Malk,' he said, 'do you know how many years will have passed in Sutra since I left it?'

'No.'

'I'd say about a hundred and eighty.' Malky looked crestfallen at this and Talisker addressed himself to Effie. 'And I don't know how you two were recruited into this but you don't understand . . .' his vision became slightly unfocused as he fought the effects of his medication. 'No one understands . . .'

'Yes, we do,' Effie prompted.

'No. How old do you think I am?'

'Well, you were at school with my mother and Uncle Sandro so, I guess about forty-six? Why?'

He shook his head. 'You're wrong. My body is at least a hundred and ten.'

'What!' Yiska breathed. 'That's madness.'

'Time does run differently there, right enough,' Malky conceded. 'But it disnae change the facts that Sutra – or someone in Sutra – is trying to find you,

Duncan. Yiska here, he's come halfway around the world, his grandfather has been havin' these dreams aboot . . .'

'Yeah, so how come I haven't had any dreams – like before when Mirranon was trying to reach me? How come you didn't come straight to me, Malk, instead of *them?*' Talisker frowned towards Effie as he said this. It seemed her unresolved anger towards him had cut through the blankness of his façade.

'Because I couldn'ae "see" you. Couldn'ae find your mind anywhere. Seems to me you've lost it in more ways than you think . . .'

'Is that some kind of joke?'

'Naw,' the highlander said mildly. 'Just making an observation.'

'I think you're all crazy,' Effie muttered. Suddenly she felt lost, out of her depth. Yiska seemed so sure about all this but then, perhaps he had some agenda. She glanced over at his calm features trying to fathom why he'd swallowed the whole story – perhaps, he was a journalist, this was some kind of entrapment. Maybe even a sick joke. 'I'm going. I'll ring Uncle Sandro and tell him I hooked you guys up.'

She walked towards the door feeling vaguely annoyed when no one tried to stop her from leaving. It seemed she had served her purpose. As the door closed behind her with a quiet click, she heard Talisker continue as if her leaving was no big deal.

'Sutra will be different now,' Talisker's voice was emphatic and cold, certainly unamused. 'Everyone we knew or loved there is long dead. There's no reason for me to go back there.'

'Yes there is,' Yiska said. 'Assuming it's all true and a way can be found. There's every reason. You're dying, aren't you?'

Tonight Ferebe was allowing herself to give in to girlishness. She had had a scalding hot bath after spending time with the Master *Sanah* cleaning and looking after Storm. Her father had also made the concession of allowing her to skip her weapons practice – which was a shame in a way, because she was learning a new skill with a crossbow – but she had to be ready for her Life-Day party.

Her silver hair (her mother's bane, being cut into a short bob which shaped into her face; so unfeminine, Elena lamented) had been brushed until it seemed to sparkle in the light. Elena had also wanted her to wear some hideous green dress but Ferebe had dug her heels in on that score; instead she wore a long, silver-grey straight gown which clung in all the right places and silver armlets on her upper arms. Her hands and wrists must be free of jewellery because her palm would be ceremoniously cut during the proceedings, just before she would be told of her future. It was a proud moment for Ferebe and her family and she had resolved herself not to bring shame on them by flinching when the blade was pressed into her palm. Her best friend had told her that it would hurt – it was like burning, she said – and some girls had been known to cry, but Ferebe was contemptuous of the very idea. Still, it didn't mean she wasn't nervous about it, she paced back and forth fiddling with her hair and changing her shoes several times. Eventually, she decided on her heeled boots, although they would not be seen beneath her gown they would give her a bit more height when she went to stand next to Felndar. She had seen him that morning and he had nodded curtly towards her without smiling – it seemed he was nervous also.

There was a knock at the door and her father came in. He stood there for a moment seemingly lost for words, then he smiled his approval. 'Seems you've grown, little Rebe.'

She knew this was as close as she might get to a compliment from her father so she flushed slightly, unused to praise. 'You look very . . . womanly,' he muttered. 'Here, I've brought you something.' He took his hand from behind his back. Ferebe laughed.

She expected a flower; and indeed, the General held a wild looking corsage of jasmine and ivy but also he held a chain-belt with an ornate, silver and horn dagger attached.

'You are a general's daughter, after all, Rebe,' he said awkwardly. 'Don't wear it if you don't want to. I mean, if you think it will spoil your gown.'

'No, no father, it's lovely. It will make me feel less like a stupid girl.'

He grinned at this – they had always had an understanding about Ferebe's rather wild nature. 'You're not a girl any more, Rebe – *Ferebe* – you're a woman. I wouldn't let your mother see the weapon belt if I were you, though.'

'No,' she agreed. 'I'll put it on just before I go down.'

'Good luck.' He turned to go and then turned back as if he had remembered something. 'Oh Ferebe . . .'

'Yes?'

'Never mind. I will talk to you after.'

She smiled at his departing figure – she felt she knew what he had wanted to say – he had never been very good at expressing his emotions. However, as it turned out, she was wrong.

It was summer, so dusk was late in the evening. The ceremony was to be held outdoors in the courtyard because it was so warm. An air of expectation and celebration pervaded the place; musicians played soft music and those parents and friends who would only be watching milled around drinking warmed wine and Dremsi. Ferebe joined the small crowd of nervous young women waiting for their names to be called. As she arrived, still adjusting the dagger her father had given her, two of the other girls turned and stared at her pointedly and then turned back giggling. Ferebe flushed angrily, they were Asta and Flis, the tall, effortlessly elegant daughters of some diplomat or other.

'Ferebe, you can't seriously be going to wear that?' They had obviously whispered about her attire and one of Ferebe's friends came over to her. She was pointing to the dagger and laughing but her tone was not unkind, more incredulous.

'I am,' Ferebe replied with quiet dignity. 'My father just came and gave it to me. I *am* a general's daughter, you know. You look beautiful by the way. Are you nervous?'

'Yes,' her friend lowered her voice. 'My mother has given me a compress of herbs to numb my palm, look.' She surreptitiously showed Ferebe a swatch of material which smelled like mint and moss.

Ferebe sniffed somewhat suspiciously. 'Is it working?'

'Yes, she said she used the same thing when she had her Life-Day.'

'Wonder how many of the others have stuff up their sleeve,' Ferebe muttered darkly.

'What?'

'Nothing. Never mind . . . Look, we're going in!'

'Be quiet, girls, and take your places,' someone called. They filed in and sat in rows of high-backed chairs situated to either side of the throne dais. The Emperor was not present, of course, General Vezul was officiating in his absence. He did not acknowledge Ferebe in any way but she felt a thrill of pride that her own father was to perform her Life-Day ritual. Afterwards, for some reason she remembered her illicit discussion with her friend as a last, stolen moment of her youth.

Despite the build-up and excitement, the actual event was fairly uninteresting to start with. Speeches were made and songs sung; Ferebe began to fidget slightly, gazing around the courtyard at the arrangements of foliage and flowers. A pleasant, balmy breeze was coming in off the ocean and the light from the sconces and candles gave the scene a gentle warmth. Her gaze drifted to Felndar a couple of times and, once, he glanced back, holding her gaze for a second and smiling faintly. She looked away quickly, embarrassed.

At last her father read out the first name; Alika Tresulet. Ferebe didn't know the girl but she felt a small stab of ire at the way she gave in to her nerves. As Alika knelt before General Vezul and held out her shaking left hand, palm upward, it appeared as though she would pass out. The General said something in a low voice – reassuring her, where he would have told Ferebe to pull herself together – and then pressed the blade into her palm. To her credit, she did not pull away or cry out.

Some of the others did. Ferebe's resolve grew in proportion to her nerves as the line of waiting girls grew shorter before her. When they had been given their mark, General Vezul would tell them the Emperor's decree; most of them were to marry and went to stand beside their newly assigned partners, usually looking smug. A few, especially promising students were given Life Orders to study or become Priestesses of Onrir.

At last Ferebe's turn came. She strode over to her father exuding a confidence she didn't actually feel. A few whispers reached her ears as people commented on her wearing of a weapon to the ceremony, but she didn't care. She smiled at her father and, kneeling down, offered him a steady hand.

In truth, it didn't hurt much, she had suffered much worse in training. It stung, that was all. She stared down at the tiny rush of crimson pooling in the cup of her palm wondering if she imagined the surge of warmth rushing up her arm. Protectively, she curled her fingers around it feeling a strange sense of anticlimax; maybe it would have been better, more memorable if it had really hurt. As she went to stand up again, still lost in this thought, she tripped on the hem of her gown. Her father reached out quickly and caught her arm to steady her. So he was still holding onto her as he made his pronouncement.

'Ferebe Vezul. The Emperor decrees that you become

an Officer in his Celestial Army. Your rank will be Lieutenant, First Class. Effective from midnight this very night. Onrir bless you.'

There was an audible gasp from the crowd followed by low murmurs of surprise. Ferebe was to become a high-ranking officer, the superior of the man who had been expecting to marry her.

'Father?' Ferebe whispered. She turned to look at Felndar, other people were staring at him too, watching for his reaction. His reaction was difficult to mask; his lips were slightly parted as if he too had gasped aloud, colour was rising in his cheeks – he was *insulted*, she thought. He saw her looking at him and glared back, a look of unconcealed fury. Then, he saluted her with slow, almost exaggerated deliberation and turned and walked out of the courtyard, the sound of his footsteps ringing out in the stunned silence.

'The Emperor has spoken, Ferebe,' her father pulled her arm so she leaned in towards him. 'You will be Felndar's superior officer. Perhaps in a few years . . .'

As Ferebe was the last to be presented, the musicians had started up again and people began talking loudly, either still expressing surprise or congratulating the other women.

'You could have warned him,' she raged, surprised at her own boldness.

'He'll get used to it,' her father said mildly. 'Aren't you pleased, Rebe? Your mother and I thought . . .'

Ferebe considered the turn of events for a few seconds. 'Yes,' she said eventually. 'I am pleased, Father. But I do not think Felndar will be a willing underling.'

'Perhaps you should go and speak with him then. It's never too early to get to know your men.'

Despite her father's advice Ferebe had little intention of following Felndar. Once she left the courtyard and was sure no one was watching her, she allowed herself to break into a run. She needed air, and space to think. As she passed the main bailey gates she saw a small group of waiting horses. Without much thought she mounted one of them and began to trot down to the beach, as she often did when she had to think.

Before her the sand basked in gentle silver light from the full moon; the tide was out about a mile from the headland but the light sparkled off the distant water and the sound of the waves made a gentle shushing in the distance. Somewhere in the dunes a nightingale sang, perhaps fooled by the brightness of the moon. Ferebe cared little for the serene beauty of the place; once she was on the flat she spurred the horse forward into a full gallop. The beast was reluctant at first until she cursed it out and slapped its flank, then it committed itself to the pace and she leaned forward into the slipstream of its neck revelling in the wind which buffeted her face and hair. The beautiful, oh-so-feminine gown was gathered up around her thighs – ripping in the process – and the cold air chilled her legs. She succeeded in her goal of stilling her thoughts; she had always found it impossible to think coherently whilst on horseback, the sheer physicality of the ride obliterated all else. The shock and confusion she felt was reduced to a hot, featureless roar in her mind which mingled with the snorting and breathing of her mount and distant sound of the sea.

It could not last for long, however, the frenzied charge could not be sustained. Horses were not keen on sand, and when they were halfway up the headland and the going became less firm, her mount shied. She reined in sharply and began to talk to the horse, making reassuring noises and patting his neck. As they slowed into a calmer walk, Ferebe noticed another rider ahead of her.

Although he was around half a mile distant, she knew it was Felndar. He sat his horse with his back rigid, bolt upright and even from where she was Ferebe could tell he was deep in thought and angry. Just as she was considering spurring her horse forward to talk to him, Ferebe noted someone – or something – else.

She knew at once the figure was not human, although it was human in shape and walked almost upright. It came from the shadow of the dunes, in the flattened colours bestowed by the moonlight and at this distance, it was difficult to make out many features. It was very tall, perhaps as much as eight or nine feet, and it was scantily clothed in tattered rags. The creature's upper torso was huge, out of proportion to its legs and hips, and this tilted it forward giving it a low, ambling gait. But there was something far stranger about it; there were sharp lines of blue light emanating from the creature's body – as if there were gaps or seams criss-crossing its flesh through which an inner light was shining.

All this, Ferebe noted in a second, but the most important thing was that it was moving fast, running up behind Felndar's horse and raising an axe.

'Felndar!' she shouted. 'Felndar! Look out!' As she shouted, two more of the creatures emerged from the shadows of the dunes, their strange blue light surreal in the darkness. She spurred her horse forward once more, continuing to shout. She saw Felndar glance back, but too late, his pursuer grabbed for the rump of his horse almost as though it intended to vault into the saddle but instead pulling down hard, succeeding in knocking the horse's legs from under it. Felndar went down, his horse screaming in terror. Ferebe screamed too, in helpless anger, as the other two creatures closed in.

Felndar was quick, though. He rolled away as he hit the sand, out of reach of the flailing legs of his horse and his attacker. Now the stricken stallion acted as a barrier between them. He drew his ceremonial blade which would be pitifully useless against such foes – Ferebe was doubtful that its edge would even be honed – and screamed a curse as the first creature lumbered forward and leapt over the horse's body to press its attack.

Ferebe was almost upon them now. But as she neared, she realised that she was as ill-armed as Felndar; worse in fact as all she had was the dagger her father had given her. She did not stop, though, it was too late for that, one of the creatures had seen her. It turned toward her; Ferebe felt her bowels turn to water as a wave of fear crashed over her – its face was hideously malformed and scarred. Behind it, one of its companions was staving in the head of the unfortunate horse with a boulder while the other continued to swing its weapon at Felndar who was fighting a defensive battle.

'Stay back!' he yelled. She ignored him. Her horse

was faltering, sensing the blood and fear of the battle –
kicking its flanks hard Ferebe charged the last hundred
yards or so to connect with the creature which had
turned towards her. As she reached it, she kicked out
hard and fast, the spiked metal heel of her boot making
a strange sound, as though it had struck rock, as it made
contact with the throat of her aggressor. However, her
ploy had brought her within arm's reach and he grabbed
hold of the back of her saddle, causing her mount to
deviate and lose momentum. Ferebe lashed out
desperately with the dagger, catching the creature's
forearm – again, the strange sound, the rasping a knife
would make if being sharpened. Although the creature
made a bellowing sound and let go of the saddle, there
was no sign that her weapon had cut him. Circling
around, she kicked out again, but this time he was
quicker, grabbed her foot and twisted it hard; there was
a crunching sound, swiftly followed by Ferebe's
scream.

She managed to remain in her saddle though and
cantered her frightened mount out of reach of her
assailant, a loud, sickened sob catching in her throat as
she passed another creature. It was still crouching
beside the dead horse, eating the flesh from its neck.
Steam was rising from the wound where the meat had
been ripped away by the creature in its feeding frenzy.
Ferebe had a split-second image as it looked up from its
feast as she charged past; blood was soaked down its
front and smeared across its bizarre face. The skin of the
strange being was shockingly blue-white and, in the
moonlight, the tracery of blood like a black latticework
on its face.

She carried on towards Felndar, everything seemed to slow, her heartbeat loud in the silence of her terror and pain. Felndar was going to be killed within the next minute. He had fought bravely, she knew, and the fact he was now running away was little reflection on his courage, purely pragmatic self-preservation; against the creature he really stood no chance of survival. The creature was faster though, covering the ground with long strides. The end seemed inevitable.

As she came abreast of Felndar, Ferebe reached out her hand, tightening her seat on her mount with her thighs.

'Grab on,' she yelled.

Felndar reached out as he ran, his hand so tantalisingly close it seemed she could feel his warmth. But their speed was mismatched; she was past him before he had time to grip. She turned her horse as quickly as she could just in time to see Felndar's aggressor pull its axe back for what was to be a chopping motion aimed at Felndar's neck.

She screamed in anguish and, without deliberate, rational thought, without aiming, she threw her dagger. It flew from her hand like a cold silver bird, straight and true, glinting sharply under the yellow moon. In the slow motion of battle which allowed her time for disconnected thought, she realised that it was as well Felndar was at least a foot shorter than the creature; the path of the dagger flew straight over his head.

It bedded itself in the creature's eye. With a keening bellow it collapsed to its knees. The blue light which emanated from the disjointed cracks of its body flickered as if somehow expressing its pain as it attempted to pull the dagger out. The being which Ferebe had ridden past was now running towards them up the beach. Without waiting to assess the situation Ferebe raced back towards the still running Felndar. This time their grips connected and she hauled him up behind her, gritting her teeth against the pain as her injured foot twisted in the stirrup.

Once Felndar was behind her, Ferebe had little thought but to flee. She spurred her horse into a gallop towards the very point of the headland . . .

'Ferebe. Wait . . . look . . .'

She ignored him, whipping the horse into a lather, feeling a tide of nerves threatening to overwhelm her.

'Stop. Stop . . .' She reined in.

'What?' Her voice was sharper than she intended, her nerves jangling. She twisted in the saddle to see where Felndar was pointing.

The creatures were being consumed by their own blue fire. All three had collapsed onto the sand and their bodies were obscured by the blue light. Frowning, Ferebe walked her horse warily back towards them but before she reached the nearest creature, its blue fire pulsed away to nothing. And when the fire was gone, the creatures had vanished.

'Onrir's balls,' she muttered through ragged breath, 'what were those things?' Felndar slid down off the back of her mount and stooped to retrieve his sword which had fallen to the sand as he ran. For a moment he said nothing and when he looked up at Ferebe his face was taut with shock – his eyes grim and guarded.

It does not sit well with him that I have saved his honour again, she realised.

'You'd better ask your father,' he said harshly. 'I'm sure he'll tell you, since you are one of the elite.'

'One of the elite that just saved your arse, you thankless cur,' she fumed.

'I would have managed,' he protested.

'A "thank you" wouldn't go amiss . . .' He took hold of her horse's bridle and began to lead the exhausted creature up the beach.

'Thank you,' he said stiffly. This annoyed her even more intensely.

'I'm sure it's after midnight now, Officer Felndar. You can call me Ma'am.'

He said nothing else all the way back to Kamala Sev.

Chapter Three

Maybe they'll leave her alone now. Just leave her alone. She doesn't need this shit. Effie turns her sound system up loud and moves back to the mirror to finish applying her mascara. Her hand moves in swift, jerky strokes which convey her annoyance as succinctly as if she had punched a wall. *Messing with my brain,* she fumes. *Why can't they just leave it alone? My mother's dead for chrissakes! I think my face is looking thinner . . .*

She peers more closely at her face, sucking in her cheeks although there is little need to do so; Effie is thin to the point of gauntness. Her black shoulder-length hair is lacklustre and unwashed but she fusses with it anyway, holding it back as she considers tying it into a ponytail to go out.

Yiska is wrong, she thinks. *He thinks I'm a junkie . . .* She frowns in frustration as her hand shakes slightly as she applies her lip-liner. Finishing with lurid red lipstick, she blows her reflection a kiss.

'Dazzling, dahling,' she mocks. She doesn't believe it, knows she has three layers of powder and foundation on beneath her eyes. 'Sick but pretty . . .'

The doorbell rings but Effie ignores it at first, still messing around with her hair. When it rings again she frowns towards it as if she already knows who is outside. *Yiska.*

'I don't want to know, Yiska. Get lost.'

'Well, that's nice that is.' The voice confuses her for a moment, it has a soft Irish accent. She peers through the peephole. There's a young blond man standing fidgeting slightly in the hallway – for a moment she's confused, doesn't remember – perhaps he has the wrong flat . . . She looks again. *It's the boy. The boy from the club. Fuck.*

'What is it? I'm just going out,' she says.

'You left something in the taxi, Effie. I'm just returning your bag.'

'Oh.' She opens the door, smiling brightly but knowing her cheeks were burning with embarrassment. 'Hi there,' she says awkwardly.

He strides in, his confidence reminding her of the night in the club more strongly than his face. He was like that, wasn't he? He had the cockiness which came with being young, blond, thin and a trainee solicitor . . . *Oh yeah. I'd forgotten that bit,* she thinks. Her handbag is tucked under her arm and he passes it to her wordlessly. There's only tissues and make-up enough to do a minimal face with – she hasn't even missed it until now. 'Thanks . . . would you like a coffee?' She feels it's only polite to offer but hopes he'll say no.

'No thanks.' He rakes her with an appraising gaze which she does not appreciate. *God, how stoned was I?* 'Are you goin' out again tonight, then?'

'Yeah.'

'Clubbing?'

'Might do. Meeting some friends first,' she lies in case he wants to come with her.

Flashing a blinding smile he says, 'D'you want some "e"?'

She laughs harshly. 'Not from you.' *Christ, what is his name? Not that it matters . . .* 'The last one almost killed me.'

'That wasn't my fault,' he looks genuinely shocked that she should accuse him of something so heinous as supplying dodgy 'e's. 'You *were* mixing it with a lot of alcohol.'

'Well . . .' she has to admit, he has her on that point. It's probably true. 'Possibly. Got any coke?'

'Yeah. Not much, though. There's not much call for it at the moment.'

She laughs at this seemingly innocuous comment and he laughs as well, although his laughter has an impatient edge. He sells her a wrap of cocaine, mentions the club he'll be at that evening – just in case she wants to buy him a drink or anything – and then he turns to go.

He stops at the door. 'My name's Mark by the way . . .'

Great. My dealer's called Mark. Should I care?

'. . . didn't think you'd remember.'

'No,' she admits. 'Mark – did we – did we – you know – have sex?' It's killing her to ask the little jerk but maybe she should go for the morning-after pill if it's not too late.

He chuckles, as if she's said something ridiculous, as if it's beneath him to sleep with some junkie. 'You're joking aren't you? I'd break you in half. Lady, you look like you're dyin'.'

He leaves without further comment and she just stands there in the middle of the floor, staring after him, her expression one of stunned surprise. She won't give him the satisfaction of having made her cry, she thinks – somewhat pointlessly since he's gone – but she feels a familiar constriction of her throat and knows she might retch.

'Food,' she mutters. 'I should eat. I *must* eat.' She sounds as if she's disciplining herself, saying an affirmation and in fact, she is. Eating hurts.

Striding over to the larder cupboard she flings open the door and a tidal wave of junk food falls out: chocolate, biscuits, crisps, mini apple pies, pre-cooked sausages (because she has to have something savoury, her conscience will not allow otherwise) and scotch eggs. She gathers up an armful and then heads back to sit on the futon, thoughts of going out on the back burner for the moment.

But she doesn't eat chaotically, doesn't cram like she knows some other girls do, she takes quiet pride in the fact, in her tiny display of self-control. She lays the food out beside her on the futon as if she were organising a feast. Untidy wrappers irritate her so she discards all foil and cellophane into the bin, except for the Tunnock's Teacakes, she likes the smart silver and red foil wrappers. When all is ready, she surveys the spread for long moments, testing herself. She wants it all. Now. But in the back of her mind, the tiny kernel of dispassionate knowledge is warning her of everything she already knows through experience. Self-disgust is for afters.

She starts to eat, quietly, primly rubbing her fingers together to dislodge the crumbs, turning up the CD player with the remote so as to cover the sound of her chewing; she hates that, that wet, masticating noise.

The pace of her eating increases but she doesn't allow herself to become 'panicked' as she eats – she's done that once before and almost choked herself. She steals tiny glances towards the wrap of speed, she can't take it now, will have to wait until she's purged or it will be wasted.

The doorbell rings again, just as she begins a packet of fig rolls – they're a favourite binge food as they melt down easily making her purging easier. *It must be Yiska this time . . .*

She doesn't like to be disturbed, feels sick and ashamed too soon. It's like being cheated, the whole meal is ruined. She freezes, hardly daring to breathe for some reason, the sound of the CD player is too loud to pretend she's not in. Just as she picks up the remote to turn the music back down, the phone begins to ring.

'Shit, shit . . .' she mutters. 'Yiska, go away!' The doorbell rings again, swiftly followed by someone banging with their fist on the wood.

'Effie, it's Talisker. C'mon, we need to talk to you.'

'Just a minute.' She picks up the phone and cradles it under her chin. 'Hello?' . . . and slides her interrupted feast into the storage box beside the futon, picking the speed out and sticking it in her jeans pocket.

'Effie. It's Uncle Sandro. How are you?'

'Good . . . good, Uncle Sandro,' She squashes the lid down on the box, an apple pie ruptures out from the handle hole as she pushes down. Frantically, she grabs a towel and flings it over the top.

'I'm sorry I couldn't call earlier. How did your meeting with Duncan go?'

'Actually, he's at the door now – just hang on a sec.'

She takes the chain off the door and pulls it open; the lock is burst after Yiska's intervention the other day. Talisker is there with Yiska. He looks marginally better than when she saw him in hospital, but he's still pale, still has that faded angst about his expression.

'Effie, I . . . oh, sorry.'

She waves them in but then turns her back on them as she speaks to Sandro. 'It's just too much, Uncle Sandro. I can't take it all in.'

'Is that Sandro?' Talisker sounds delighted. 'Let me talk to him.'

She makes an irritated shushing gesture. 'About my mother and everything . . . you know.'

There's a slight pause on the other end of the line and then Sandro sighs. 'Listen to me Effie. You can believe him. It's true. All of it.'

'They're called Shards,' General Vezul eyed his dishevelled daughter coolly, she knew he hadn't forgiven her for stalking off during the ceremony but Ferebe was past caring. 'We don't know where they're coming from but this is the first time they've been reported this far south. It was a lucky escape you had, both of you, I hear they're virtually impossible to kill.'

'There was no luck involved,' Ferebe replied, tight-lipped. She and Felndar stood together in the ante-room of her father's quarters. They had said little to one another since the incident on the beach except to disagree whether to wake Ferebe's father – Ferebe had insisted and she had won the argument. 'I don't understand why they died . . . or whatever it was that happened to them.'

'No.' Vezul paused. 'Officer Felndar, you must be exhausted. Dismissed. Permission granted not to report to your superior officer tomorrow,' he glanced at Ferebe, 'until afternoon.'

Felndar saluted the General but as he turned to go, he risked giving Ferebe a contemptuous look. She knew he was silently accusing her of elitism yet again. He had a chip on his shoulder the size of Sutra, it seemed. Holding his gaze she saluted him stiffly. 'Thank you, Officer Felndar. I will see you tomorrow.'

He saluted once more but left without comment.

Once Felndar was gone, Vezul relaxed visibly. He wore a loose robe over his nightshirt and he pulled it tighter around himself. 'It's cold,' he muttered. 'Come in the bedroom, Ferebe – there is a fire burning.' He wandered back through the doorway as he spoke, without waiting for her response.

'But I'll wake mother,' she protested in a whisper.

'Your mother's . . . not here,' her father replied absently, 'She doesn't often sleep here.'

'Oh.' This insight into her parent's marital arrangements made her feel more unsettled than she already was by the night's events.

'Here,' her father had poured her a drink of Dremsi and proffered it towards her. 'It'll warm you through. Sit down.'

She'd never drunk in front of her father before but Ferebe took the silver cup without protest. She was suffering from some delayed reaction, fighting to stop her limbs from shaking and her teeth from chattering. Her twisted ankle was sending hot pains lancing into her calf. However, as she sipped at the sweet spirit, she instantly felt her muscles relax.

'I'm sorry your commission came as such a shock to you, Rebe. But I cannot say I disagree with it. You will make a great officer, just because there have been few females before doesn't mean we cannot break with tradition. Your mother tried to get me to petition the Emperor, said you wanted to marry that little upstart Felndar,' he laughed, 'could you imagine that!'

'No,' she muttered weakly.

'Anyway, I declined. The Emperor sets one's life-course very diligently, Ferebe. He has priests and advisors who do special magics . . . scrying and things . . .' It was clear to Ferebe that her father had no idea how the esoteric ceremonies were conducted but she said nothing. 'It must have been decided for good reason and, once I got used to the idea I realised what an ideal candidate you were . . . Oh, here are your papers.'

She frowned, 'Papers?'

'Your orders. Look, there's a special message here,' he pointed. 'You are to liase with me only.'

'Why? I don't understand.'

'It's the Shards, Ferebe. The Emperor wants us to investigate them. In the last six months almost two hundred have been reported. Usually they kill the first person they see, they appear to be mindless, or of little intelligence. We think the Fine rebels have somehow created them but perhaps are struggling to control them,' he shrugged. 'We just don't know. I'd like you to take a week or so and tour the Fine settlements, see what you can find out. Take half a dozen men with you but do not discuss your findings with any of them.'

'Yes, Father.'

'You must call me General or sir, now,' he chided.

'Yessir.' Ferebe was engulfed by exhaustion. The thought of curling up in her father's big leather chair was quite appealing, so she stood up to go, carefully putting her weight onto her uninjured foot and saluted as smartly as she was able.

Her father nodded in acknowledgement. 'Take Felndar with you.'

'I'd rather not, Fath – sir.'

'That's an order. The lad deserves a chance to see some action – regain some pride.' He smiled briefly.

He's very astute, Ferebe realised. She turned to go.

'Oh, Ferebe . . . how is your hand?'

'My hand?' She glanced down at her palm suddenly remembering she had had her Life-day ceremony. The cut in her palm began to smart once she looked at it but, up until now she had given it no thought at all. She sighed, it had been a long night.

They talked all night. Or rather, Talisker talked and Effie and Yiska mostly just listened; Effie swallowing her incredulity in the absence of her binge-feast. The little gas fire made a background hiss as the traffic noise died away and the streets outside fell quiet. Talisker's voice became a rich, disembodied sound, his story compelling and fantastic. At first, his speech was punctuated by apologies and disclaimers, like 'I'm sorry, I know this is really hard to believe . . .' but after a while he stopped protesting the truth of his tale. He spoke of the other world – Sutra – and his life there, he had had a wife and two children – all dead now in the swift passage of Sutra time. His daughter, Regan, had come across to this world but had been killed by someone called Jahl – who Talisker was notably reluctant to talk about.

It was difficult to know how much Yiska believed. He said little, but watched Talisker closely as he spoke, as if trying to gauge the truth of his story from his body posture and movements. Only once did he interrupt and that was to ask if anyone wanted a drink. As he sat down again with his coffee, his knee knocked against Effie's storage box knocking the lid askew and smearing apple pie filling on his jeans. He glanced down at the contents of the box – his brows arched in surprise – and then looked meaningfully at Effie who held his questioning gaze for only seconds before she looked away, her cheeks burning with embarrassment.

It was about four in the morning when Talisker finished telling his tale. Effie was feeling sick by then – she had eaten quite a lot of food before Talisker and Yiska arrived and had not found an opportunity to purge before it settled in her gut. She'd considered going to the toilet to vomit but was pretty sure they'd hear her. She kept thinking about the fact she was digesting now despite being enthralled by Talisker's story.

'Now, Yiska and Malky think I have to find a way back,' he was saying. 'Something has happened to my body from crossing back and forth. My immune system is breaking down and eventually, if I stay here, I'll die.'

'Does that bother you? You are a hundred and ten after all.'

He looked surprised at her question. 'It's a fair point, Effie, and to be honest, while I was in hospital, no, the thought didn't bother me much. But now, Yiska and Malk reckon I'm needed back in Sutra and I find myself wanting to see it again before I die.'

'Hmm. Excuse me, I just have to go to the loo.' Effie felt disconnected from all this. 'That's nice,' she muttered.

She was halfway across the room when she heard Talisker say; 'I'd like you to come with us, Effie.'

'What?' She laughed, she couldn't help it. Believing that he believed was one thing – *actually* believing was something else. Talisker didn't look offended, just smiled slightly and shook his head as though he had known that would be her response.

'You don't believe me really do you?' He held up his hand to cut off her response. 'Come here, Effie. I've got something for you.'

'What?' she said. She felt like a child being given pocket money by an uncle but she went over and held her hand out all the same. Talisker took something from his pocket and placed it in her hand. *Perhaps it's proof,* she thought, *some kind of treasure.* But no, at least it was very ordinary treasure; a gold St Christopher on a chain. It was a good one, quite heavy, definitely intended for a man. Effie felt a slight rush of disappointment. 'Oh. Thank you . . .'

'Your mother gave it to me, Effie, not long before she died. She didn't believe me either, but she believed *in* me.'

'About Sutra?'

'No, about something else. The murders. She never

71

judged me, even when everyone else had.' Talisker was suddenly emotional, his eyes lost their deadened cast and, although he was smiling slightly at the memory of Shula, he looked saddened. 'She told me that no soul was irredeemable, Effie. That's what she thought.'

'But I can't go. I've got college and . . .'

'Effie's bulimic,' Yiska said quietly. 'She needs to be in her own environment and know there is the security of plenty of food.'

No one had ever said that before. Effie was suddenly breathless as if someone had punched her in the stomach. 'I . . . I . . .' words would not come, nor air. The room seemed to buckle and move as she gasped. *See, see, this is what happens when I eat . . .*

'Calm down,' Yiska was beside her, his arm across her shoulders. 'Listen, just breathe slowly. It's just an anxiety attack. Just breathe.'

She had to listen to him or she was going to die. She just knew it. But she was so angry. *How dare he say that*!

'Here,' he held a paper bag in front of her face. 'Breathe into here and watch the bag.' She did as he told her. 'That's right. Now, slow down, slowly, slowly . . . good.'

It took about five minutes before Effie felt normal again – she was shaken to the core, this had never happened to her before. She shrugged Yiska's hand off her shoulder and rounded on him, tears streaming down her cheeks which were drained of all colour.

'That was your fault, you sanctimonious bastard! Who do you think you are? I don't need your help. Just leave me alone . . .' She stormed off to the bathroom in tears and slammed the door.

The bathroom was always cold; over the last few hours the heat from the little gas fire had built up in the bed-sitting room making it stifling and airless. The chill of the tiled room was calming. Effie didn't bother to switch the light on, it was almost daybreak anyway and a faint grey light filtered in, made green by the slats of the louvre blind. As she went to the sink to splash her face with cold water she realised she was still holding onto the St Christopher; she stared down at the gold disk which seemed to glow with warmth in the muted cool of the room. It had been her mother's – she had precious few of her mother's things – and her mother had given it to Duncan Talisker. She dropped it onto the side of the sink in the little hollow for the soap and continued to stare at it as if hypnotised while she splashed her face. Calmness descended; she could hear the low baritone sound of Talisker and Yiska's voices in the sitting room and, although she couldn't make out what they were saying it was clear they were having a disagreement – probably about her.

There was a cautious knock at the door. 'Effie, I'm really sorry. I shouldn't have said it quite like that . . . I thought you were probably getting treatment already . . .'

'It's all right, Yiska, just leave me alone.'

'No, it's not all right. I didn't mean to disrespect you.'

She gave a quiet laugh at this, it seemed such an American thing to say. 'I'm fine. Really, I'll be out in a minute or two.'

As she patted her face dry Effie heard another,

slightly higher pitched voice joining the conversation and knew it must be Malky as no one had rung the doorbell. She had a moment of clarity as she realised that she already accepted the presence of the ghost without fear or surprise. *Who needs the drugs,* she thought, *life is absurd enough . . .*

She popped a couple of laxatives and went back into the sitting room.

'D'you think she'll want to come though?' Malky was standing with his back to her. 'I mean, ye can see why she thinks you're mad an' that.'

'What's going on?' She switched off the fire and opened the window, a fresh morning breeze wafted in, lifting the shabby net curtain and making it dance and billow like a dawn phantom.

'Oh, hiya, Effie. I was jist saying tae Duncan . . .'

'Malky's been down Mary King's Close.' Talisker said. 'The gateway's gone. Most of the Close was destroyed during the earthquake in 2002. There's no way through to Sutra there. So we're going to New Mexico to see if Yiska's uncle can help.'

'Oh . . .' She struggled to assimilate this new information. It felt as though things were getting out of hand, running away with her. Perhaps this would be her last chance to bail out, to cling to the vestiges of normality that her life offered; college, clubbing, a few pills and food. Even her bingeing and purging gave a regular pattern to her existence, something she could supposedly control. As the thoughts ran through her tired brain, her stomach began to cramp as the laxatives hit her empty system – it was a familiar feeling too.

'We wondered if you want to come, Effie. I'll pay your fare.'

No. It's too much. Too much to believe, too much even to think about. She wanted them to go away. They were all looking at her, unable to disguise their concern. She didn't want their pity though, she didn't . . . Her stomach cramped again. Familiar. Miserable.

'Okay,' she said, feeling a thrill of shock to hear the words issue from her own mouth. 'I'll come.'

She clutched the St Christopher in the warmth of her hand and smiled slightly at their surprised faces.

Chapter Four

The sun beat down mercilessly on the tiny jeep as it jolted and jarred its way across the desert floor. There was nothing for miles, the desert was truly featureless as far as the eye could see; just red dirt and scrub.

The driver didn't care, he was oblivious to the bleak grandeur of his surroundings and the vast blue expanse of the sky.

'Kitchy–kitchy ya ya mama, kitchy-kitchy ya ya meee,' he sang – completely tunelessly, thumping the steering wheel in time with the tinny sound of the radio. He'd turned it up full blast to try and get some bass out of the thing but it was a lost cause. The general cacophony was like an explosion in a spanner factory.

'Voulez vous couchez avec moi? C'est soir . . . voulez . . .' mercifully, the signal died before the song reached its high-pitched crescendo. 'Aw man . . . piece o *shit*,' he cursed, bashing the radio snatch plate with his fist. No signal. It wasn't that there was anything in the way to block the signal either, it was just that there was no point in any channel beaming anything over the huge expanse of emptiness. And if there was one thing Lake 'First-Eagle' McKinnon couldn't stand, it was silence. He stopped the truck, glaring around the desert almost suspiciously; *yeah, plenty of space out here for a man to hear himself think . . . to go fucking mad . . .*

A sudden noise from above could not fail to catch his attention; it was the high, clear sound of an eagle. Despite his mirrored shades he had to shield his eyes as he looked up into the glare of the sun. It was a bald eagle. A good omen, maybe . . .

'What you lookin' at?' he growled. A wide grin split his handsome features. 'Hey. You lookin' at me? You lookin' at me?' He'd always thought his De Niro was pretty good. The eagle however, seemed unimpressed – tilting its vast wings it caught the edge of a thermal and whooshed effortlessly upwards.

Lake turned his attention back to the pressing problem of having no sounds in the jeep. He'd hired it in Vegas but hadn't thought of bringing a selection of his own CDs. 'Oh c'mon,' he muttered staring into the glovebox, 'just one . . .' Nothing there. He was about to give up when the silver glare of a disc caught his attention; it was on the floor of the jeep – probably scratched to ribbons – just sticking out from under the edge of the mat. 'Yes!' he chuckled triumphantly. 'Muzak!' Picking the disc up he gave it a perfunctory wipe with the back of his shirt sleeve and popped it in the player. Music blared out with a suddenness that made him jump. 'Wow, Shania,' he grinned. He took a large slurp of Jim Bean from a brown bagged bottle which was propped up on the passenger seat and gunned the engine again, making his wheels spin and producing a red cloud of dust.

'You don't impress me much,' he sang. 'Yeah . . .'

Away in the distance he at last spied a feature; a mountain. He'd be crossing into the Navajo Nation pretty soon now. Miles ahead he could see the dark clouds of the cold weather front – he'd heard they'd had loads of snow. But then a freezing welcome was kinda what Lake expected. *The Rez,* he thought, *gotta love it* . . . 'Welcome home, buddy-boy . . .'

The desert wasn't what he had expected. It was vibrant, alive with colours; red, orange, silver and green. The landscape slipped by the truck in vast expanses of solitary grandeur, even this late in the year it was warm, although the air was humid with the promise of rain or coldness to come with the nightfall. Talisker had never seen such a big sky before either, in places the blue and white seemed impossibly bold, cartoon-like fluffy clouds scurried across the massive canvas of the heavens. The sun hung low in the sky, blessing the desert with touches of quartz pink warmth and yet Talisker was cold, the air-conditioning was on full blast. He glanced towards Yiska who was driving, dark sunglasses shading his eyes and giving him a cool but expressionless look. Was he always so quiet, Talisker wondered? It seemed the Navajo didn't indulge in much small talk.

'When will we be on the Navajo Reservation?' he asked.

'What are you expecting, a little cluster of wigwams?' Yiska replied, somewhat curtly. 'We've been on the Navajo Nation lands for the last two hours, it covers over seven thousand square miles altogether.'

'Wow . . . that's big.'

'Yeah, bigger than West Virginia, so the guide-books say. We have our own local government, schools, police . . .' he flashed a white grin rather suddenly making Talisker doubt his previous tone. 'Don't be guided by Hollywood, Mr Talisker – it's not all "Dances With Wolves."'

'I'm rather fond of wolves myself,' Talisker stared out into the distance. 'Some of my best friends were wolves. Call me Duncan, Yiska. There's no need to stand on ceremony. What do you think we should do about Malky?' He glanced back to where Effie was asleep on the back seat wrapped in a thick fluffy blanket, her hair blown across her face; she was clutching a wooden box to her chest as if it were a soft teddy bear rather than something sharp-cornered and cold. Malky was in the box. At least they *hoped* Malky's spirit was in the box – Malcolm himself had seemed both sceptical and reluctant to get in.

'It's no gonna work,' he moaned. 'Everyone kens ghosts canny cross water.'

'Oh, *everyone* eh?' Talisker mocked. 'Must be right then.' Malky had relented in the end and then vanished, they could only assume he'd somehow managed to become contained. 'Like a genie in a bottle,' Effie had commented.

To help the process, Yiska had sprinkled the herbs his grandfather had given him for 'binding' into the base of the box, but they wouldn't know for sure that it had worked – or indeed that Malky had cooperated until they tried to call him out again.

'I think we should wait until we've spoken to grand-father. If he can't help you there might be no point in getting Malcolm out. Are you okay, Duncan? You look tired.'

'Yeah. I've taken my meds. I might have a nap if you don't mind.'

'Sure thing. I'm used to driving distances.'

Talisker adjusted his seat back and settled down. 'Yiska?'

'Yes?'

'Are you sure your grandfather will believe me? I mean, it seems strange to me that you and Effie are on side. Why would he?'

'My grandfather is an amazing man, Duncan. A wise man of great humility and humour – you'll like him. Anyway, it was his dreams which took me to you, so all this is his doing. He'll want to see it through. I'm just not sure if he'll know how.' There was a high-pitched noise and Yiska picked up his mobile phone from the dashboard. 'Hello? Yes . . . we're on the one-sixty heading towards . . . why? What's . . .' Yiska stopped the truck rather abruptly at the side of the side of the road and Effie's sleeping figure was jolted forward in her seat.

'Wha . . . what's going on? Are we there?' she asked.

Yiska ignored her. He had begun to speak in mixture of English and an unrecognisable language, which Talisker guessed was Navajo. Without comment to either Talisker or Effie, he opened the door of the truck letting in a blast of relatively warm air and, leaping down off the high sill, began to stride a little way up and down the road, talking excitedly. It was the most animated Talisker had yet seen him and something in Yiska's tone made him uneasy.

'I don't know, Effie,' he said. 'But I'm not sure I like the look of it.'

Effie rubbed her eyes which were watering in the glare. Already the air in the truck was becoming still and stale, as Yiska had switched off the engine. 'Wish he'd hurry up,' she muttered.

After a few minutes Yiska came back. It was difficult to read his expression because of his sunglasses but his mouth was set in a grim line. 'Is something wrong, Yiska?' Talisker asked.

'Yeah. Change of plan. We're going to meet Grandfather at my Aunt Millie's hogan. Something weird is happening on the rez.'

Despite the heat, Talisker felt a chill run down the back of his neck. 'Weird?'

'Hmm.' Yiska would not be drawn further. 'Grandfather will tell us about it when we arrive.'

'Is it far?'

'About an hour that way.' He pointed out into the desert and spun the truck around. There didn't appear to be any road where he was pointing but as he left the highway it became clear that wide dirt tracks criss-crossed the scrubland unnoticed until you were actually travelling them. 'We'll be lucky to make it before dusk.'

'They are dying in their sleep.' Grandfather Rodney's voice hung in the night air, the desert was so still nothing stirred them away. 'People are afraid to sleep.'

'How many, *Sicheii?*'

'Around twelve, I think. Mostly elders.'

'Twelve!'

Rodney sipped his lukewarm coffee but his eyes were fixed on Talisker, his gaze faintly accusing somehow, it was the same look he had been giving him since they arrived.

Aunt Millie's hogan was a large hexagonal-shaped building made of cleverly crossed logs and roofed with turf and mud. A single, short chimney stuck out of the middle of the roof and, inside, a small fire burned in a brazier in the centre of the floor space. Yiska described his aunt's dwelling as a 'female' hogan although Talisker wasn't sure what he meant by this. However, Aunt Millie didn't actually live there; a modern prefab bungalow stood some way behind it in the shade of some small trees set in an almost impossibly lush desert garden. Yiska explained that the hogan was special and used by his extended family for ceremonies – sings or curing. His Grandfather and his father had built it. Aunt Millie ushered them in and took great care showing them where they must sit around the perimeter wall. Talisker she sat opposite the doorway, Yiska to the left and Effie to the right. She was a delightful woman who seemed to speak little English, although she fussed around effectively enough like aunties the world over. She appeared concerned at how thin Effie was and spoke to Yiska about it.

'She is asking me if you have been ill,' he explained politely. 'She says you are too thin.'

'Oh,' Effie managed a smile even though the journey had exhausted her. 'No. Tell her I'm fine . . . thank you.'

Yiska said something to Aunt Millie who looked faintly surprised and sucked air through her teeth in expressive disapproval. When she brought coffee for everyone she presented Effie with a mug of strange-smelling liquid.

'What is it?' Effie frowned.

'One of Aunt Millie's herbal teas,' Yiska smiled. 'It's a traditional ancient recipe. You'd best drink it or she'll be offended.'

Effie tipped the cup up and gulped the tisane down; it was bitter and made her mouth tingle after she had swallowed it. She didn't see Yiska winking at his Aunt.

Once she had finished Aunt Millie took the cup from her. 'Very good,' she said approvingly. 'It will make you stronger.'

'But I thought you couldn't speak . . .'

Aunt Millie giggled, covering her mouth with her hand as she did so in a strangely girlish gesture.

Yiska looked amused. 'Aunty's just foolin' with you.'

Grandfather Rodney arrived in a long-base pick-up truck, its cheerful yellow paint obscured by the red dust of the desert. When the introductions had been made he sat next to Talisker, opposite the doorway, and Talisker realised he had been put in a prominent position which inferred some importance on his part. Aunt Millie lit a couple of gas burners as it grew darker outside and brought Rodney a cup of coffee, then she left them to their discussion.

Once Rodney had delivered the news of what he called the 'sleeping deaths' he turned to Talisker as if looking for an answer. 'Can you help us in some way, Mr Talisker? Michael has told me some of your story. I didn't believe it,' he said bluntly.

'Has something changed your mind?'

'Yes. Some have awoken from the dreams and they all describe the same thing. A moving darkness, shaped like the sun – they feel themselves drawn towards it as if it will swallow them up but they wake before they are consumed by it. I'm guessing those who did not wake were pulled in . . .'

'Grandfather, since most of the deaths are elders, isn't it possible there's some virus killing them?' Yiska asked.

Rodney shook his head. 'No, they're all in the morgue at Shiprock. Died of heart failure, all of them. Not just Dinéh either, a couple of Hopi and some Zuni pueblo dwellers – I don't know which tribe, I just overheard it while I was at the morgue.'

'Why were you at the morgue, *Sicheii*?'

'One of my friends . . . I will tell you outside the hogan . . .'

'I'm sorry.'

'Anyway, Mr Talisker. Those who have survived the dream all place the apparition in the same place – the Mummy Cave in Canyon De Chelly.'

'Wow,' Effie could not contain her excitement. 'I've always wanted to go there!'

'It's not easy at this time of year, most roads will be closed. There's flash floods, ice and snow. No easy way down, either.'

'But we can do it, right?' Talisker asked.

'Yes.' Rodney said the word with slow deliberation, his doubts showing clearly in his eyes as he glanced at Effie. 'But it's not easy,' he repeated.

Effie was trying to sleep but, despite her exhaustion, sleep would not come. She was in the house with Aunt Millie who would be leaving early to make the journey to the canyon with one of her friends. Yiska, Rodney and Talisker were sleeping in the hogan with sleeping bags covered over with thick sheepskin. They'd talked for ages about the journey to the bottom of the canyon and had only stopped when Effie dozed off, her head lolling until, with a shock of realisation she jerked awake again. It was too late, though; they had seen her. 'I'm sorry,' she mumbled.

'It's all right, Effie,' Yiska said. He walked her up to the house, which in the darkness, looked for all the world like a fairy-tale cottage. In the cold night air the scent of Aunt Millie's garden was like crisp perfume that mingled with the smell of mesquite and wood-smoke rising from the chimney.

'How are you feeling Effie?' Yiska asked. He had wrapped a warming blanket around her shoulders and kept his arm there. Effie, not normally a tactile person, found she didn't mind this comfort.

'I'm okay, just tired.'

'Good. It was good to see you eat something at dinner. You haven't . . .'

'No. I don't always purge,' she felt irritation rise at his concern. No one had ever known, ever talked to her directly about it before and it still made her uneasy. 'I'm not stupid, you know.'

'No, I know that,' he said.

The familiar sound of a television had greeted them at the front door, some advert with a manically happy jingle blared out from the living room. Yiska knocked quietly and then went in, climbing over the bags Millie had packed for her journey. Aunt Millie was happily

ensconced on the settee with a large bag of crisps – or
rather, chips, Effie reminded herself – but she sprang up
smiling when they came in. She made Effie a glorious
cup of hot chocolate and showed her to the bedroom,
chiding Yiska for keeping the poor girl up so late.

That had been around two hours ago. The blare of the
television had stopped just after Yiska left and there
was little sound to be heard except the occasional
flapping of the window blind as it caught a breeze and
tapped against the frame. Effie turned over again trying
to get comfortable but only succeeded in wrapping her
nightshirt tighter around her torso. She sighed and sat
up knowing that when she got like this there was little
point in just lying for ages with her eyes shut; her mind
would not be still.

Her gaze picked out the regular shape of Malky's box
on the dresser at the other side of the room. Without
much thought she went over, picked it up and carried it
back to the bed. Once back under her covers she opened
the box.

'Malky,' she whispered. 'Malky, are you there?' There
was no response, just the cool smell of the cedar wood
and the herbs Yiska had sprinkled in the base. Effie was
disappointed – maybe they had completely failed and
Malky would be unable to materialise in America, or
maybe he would only come for Talisker . . . that seemed
likely, he was like Talisker's guardian angel or something. She closed the lid of the box with a quiet snap
and reached over to put it on the bedside table. The
voice came from the other side of the bed.

'Are ye no goin' tae talk tae me then?'

She turned back. Malky was standing there,

disconcertingly transparent against the lurid fabric of the blinds. 'Malk . . .' she whispered. 'Keep your voice down. It's good to see you . . .'

Malky glanced around the room. 'So, are we in the Americas then? Disnae look much different . . . smells funny . . .'

Effie pointed to the ceiling where bunches of dried herbs were hanging. 'Millie makes her own wool and dyes it . . .'

'Are you all right Effie? You look kinda worried or something? Did ye just call me here for a wee chat?'

Effie bunched her knees up beneath the covers and rested her chin on them giving an exasperated sigh. 'I don't know, Malky . . . when Talisker asked me to come I was really excited. I felt as if he wanted me along, as if it was important to him for my sake – not just some nostalgia about my mother – but now I think he thinks he made a rash decision.'

'What makes you say that? I ken he likes you.'

'Yeah, but . . . They both keep looking at me as if they think I need looking after. I wish Yiska had never told Talisker about my eating.'

'There's nothing wrong with them wanting to look out for you, though,' Malky said. 'That's what friends do.'

'But can't you see, Malk. They think I'm going to hold them back. They're planning a big, dangerous trip into the bottom of the Canyon De Chelly in winter conditions – they're probably discussing me right now, wondering if I'm strong enough . . .'

Malky sat down on the end of her bed; at least, that's how it appeared. The Highlander's contact with physical objects seemed to happen on a fairly arbitrary basis. 'And *are* ye strong enough, Effie? You've got tae be honest with yersel first.'

Effie felt a flare of irritation at Malky's doubt. 'Yes,' she replied without thinking. 'Well at least, I think so . . . They don't really know me yet. What can I do, Malk? How can I prove to them that I'm not some pathetic little girl – Shula's orphan?'

In the quiet dark of the room Malky could just make out the soft gold outline of the St Christopher which Effie had been wearing constantly since Talisker gave it to her. 'There's no shame in bein' Shula's orphan lass.'

'I know, I know, but . . .'

'If you ask me, eating yer meals might be a start – and no puking them up again.'

'It doesn't mean I'm weak, Malk. It doesn't make me a victim.'

Malky's mild features twisted into an expression of genuine puzzlement. 'Does it no? What does it mean then?'

'It – it's just a problem I have to deal with. I can control it.'

'But Effie, doll, no eatin' makes ye physically weak. There's nae gettin' away from that. And that's the very thing *could* make ye a liability. Duncan and Yiska – they're no judgin' ye – but it's only common sense tae think mebbe you couldn'ae walk for ten miles or something carrying yer gear.'

'Talisker's been in hospital, you know,' Effie replied. 'He might not be very strong either . . .'

'True,' Malky nodded. 'But Duncan, ye see . . .' his voice acquired a strangely nostalgic tone, 'he's special.

If'n he needs to, he'll pull some energy from some-where.'

'You're very proud of him, aren't you, Malcolm?'

'Mebbe. S'pose . . .'

Talisker had said little to Effie for much of the journey and he'd certainly not shown the same level of animation that he had on the night when he told her and Yiska about Sutra. It was hard to equate the quiet, taciturn man with the image that Malky seemed to have of him.

'He's quite hard to get to know,' she ventured.

'Aye. He is that. But don't let that stop ye tryin', lass.' Malky smiled. 'You'd better get some sleep now. You must be tired if we've really travelled roond the world.'

Effie slid down under the covers like an obedient child. 'Malky, will you stay till I'm asleep?' she whispered. She didn't really know why she asked him, she simply found his presence calming.

'Aye. I'll just sit here by the bed,' he muttered. 'Rest me bones.'

Effie laughed softly at the idea but, as she drifted off to sleep the irony of the fact she had asked the ghost to remain in her room so soon after declaring her independence was not lost on her. Still, she didn't regret asking, after all, if you *knew* the ghost was there, how bad could it be? Her sleep was unhaunted.

It took them two days to reach the end of the interstate highway where it was closed for the winter; they were the worst of Effie's life. The weather conditions had deteriorated and the way north sometimes seemed to involve actually travelling south for fifty miles – roads were obscured by flash floods as the rainwater swept unchecked across the open spaces of the desert. In some areas you could see the weather coming for miles and Yiska would attempt to outrace it, speaking to Rodney via a short-wave radio and spinning the jeep around, but other times the thunderheads and rain clouds appeared as if from nowhere, cresting the flat tops of the mesas with such suddenness it was as if they'd been hiding; waiting to spring out on the unsuspecting travellers. It grew colder and colder, and Effie grew sicker and sicker but she dared say nothing – knew she would get no sympathy because there had been an 'incident'.

It was the morning they were leaving aunt Millie's. Effie had slept well and woke with new resolve to be useful. Someone had knocked on her door to waken her – she wasn't sure who – when she went through to the tiny kitchen there was no one there so she made herself an instant coffee, bemoaning the chicory which she didn't like. Her thoughts were occupied with the coming venture and she hummed tunelessly, and stared down at her knuckles which still had red crusty sores caused by her vomiting. The sight of the sores made her in equal measure pleased and ashamed; pleased because they were healing over as she hadn't stuck her fingers down her throat for four days, but ashamed because they were there in the first place – sick badges of honour in the battle for her sanity. The idea formed from nowhere that she would get rid of her laxatives while she felt so positive. She didn't stop to analyse the thought but marched back through to the room and grabbed her 'kit' – Effie was fastidiously organised about her condition, in fact her obsessiveness was a classic symptom.

Inside the blue vanity bag were: laxatives, heavy duty brown paper bags, non-acidic mouthwash – because her teeth were already showing signs of damage – Ipecac syrup to induce severe vomiting; she had only taken it once and it was violent stuff. It had almost killed her, the hospital staff had been only grudgingly sympathetic, but then the skull and crossbones on the bottle should have been warning enough. Some people – bulimics – took the syrup often but she hoped she'd never get that bad. There was cortisone cream for her knuckles and a mirror also, a flat, plain square of glass for checking her teeth.

Effie took almost everything from the bag and decided to begin with tipping the Ipecac syrup down the sink – in part she couldn't believe she had ever been so low as to buy it, but then, she couldn't believe people were so bloody low as to sell it when they knew what it was for. She struggled with the lid for a few moments and then patted her jeans pockets looking for keys or something to prise the lid off. As she felt her left pocket she groaned aloud and reaching in, took out the wrap of cocaine which had been in there totally forgotten until now.

She was tempted; she couldn't pretend otherwise even though she was the world expert at denial. In the slight breeze from the noisy aircon unit, the little white bag of dust danced and trembled slightly. As if to bring her resolve into the light, Effie spoke to it.

'Well, you're going down the sink first, pal.' She

pulled the flimsy wrap apart too eagerly and the fine powder spilled out, catching the breeze, coating her stuff in a minuscule film but landing primarily . . . on the mirror.

And it just *would* be that moment Yiska walks in. Effie compounds his impression further as she fights against a sneeze – seems she's accidentally inhaled some of the stuff anyway. She rubs her nose.

He freezes, the easy, morning smile of greeting melts off his face like so much candle-wax to be replaced by . . . nothing much; a hardening of expression that's almost impossible to read. Where perhaps she could have understood disappointment, shock or anger there was just something else. It was as if, in that instant, Effie became a stranger to him all over again.

'It's not . . . what you think,' she mutters, aware of how useless that sounds. Still, he says nothing, just nods coldly and walks back out into the living room. Effie curses, and begins to fling things back into the case. 'No really,' she calls, her voice shaking. 'Yiska, wait up, listen . . .' But he doesn't want to wait up or listen, he is closed to her, his friendship, his care, withdrawn with what seemed frightening finality.

Over the next few days, Effie had given up trying to reach him. As her apologies and explanations continued to fall on stony ground she became increasingly angry at his inflexibility but also, if she was honest with herself, she understood his position better. Even beer was forbidden on The Navajo Nation lands; in common with other Native American tribes the Navajo had outlawed alcohol and drugs so even incoming tourists were not allowed to bring it in for their own consumption. Yiska had warned Talisker and Effie about this so the very idea that Effie had brought cocaine onto the 'Rez' was deeply offensive to him – it meant that she had deliberately flouted the law and cared little for their friendship.

Still, she tried her hardest to explain, and when her efforts failed she took the opportunity to speak to Talisker when they stopped at the Lucky Eight Motel on the first night. Yiska and Rodney had already gone to bed but Effie and Talisker both found it difficult to sleep. Effie heard Talisker's door click open and then a few moments later, the faint sound of a match being struck as he lit a cigarette. She put her heavy coat and hat on over her nightshirt and went out to join him.

Talisker was leaning against the high sides of the jeep which was still faintly warm so Effie did as well, unconsciously mirroring his posture. Talisker was over a foot taller than she, as was Yiska, perhaps that was why she so often felt like a child in their company, so she was strangely thrilled when he said nothing at first, just wordlessly handed her the cigarette. It was like smoking behind the bike-sheds; an act of inclusion. She took a deep drag, enjoying the warmth of the smoke as much as the taste. 'Talisker, will you speak to Yiska for me,' she found herself unexpectedly emotional about it, his silent accusation was weighing more heavily on her than she had realised. 'Please. It was a mistake. I don't know what he's told you but it wasn't what he thought.' Talisker stared at her face for a few moments as if the truth of the matter might be discernable from her eyes.

'He told me he found you snorting coke in his Aunt

Millie's kitchen. It's difficult to see how he could be mistaken about something like that.'

'Yeah. I – I know. But actually I was getting rid of it all. I mean, why else would I do it in the kitchen? I was just about to pour stuff down the sink . . . the Ipecac syrup and stuff . . .'

He frowned, obviously not sure what Ipecac syrup was. 'But Effie, even if that's true, you smuggled cocaine through US customs. Have you *any idea* what could have happened to us? I'm an ex-con. They would've thrown away the key. You put all of us at risk.'

'I know – I'm sorry. I don't know how many times I have to say "sorry" to Yiska. It's like he doesn't want to know me now – like he's given up on me already.'

Talisker nodded into the darkness blowing a huge plume of smoke into the cold air. 'He's lost faith in you, Effie. You can't blame him for that. He told me about the state you were in when he first found you as well.'

Effie gazed assiduously at the gritty sand of the road and began to trace little patterns into it with her boot. 'Yeah, well . . .'

'You've got to admit, there's a pattern emerging so far as he's concerned. He came to find me – he didn't sign up to save your soul.'

'Who said I want my soul to be saved?' she frowned. 'I never asked him.'

Talisker gave a small laugh. 'Yeah, well, when some people care about you, they can't help themselves. Your mother was a bit like that, Effie.'

'You think he cares about me?' she squirmed but her injured vanity would not allow the question to pass.

'As a friend. From what I can tell he's a very sincere

person. It's a fine quality but liable to misinterpretation – at least, in this world – Sutra should suit Yiska quite well.'

'But not me, right? You don't want to take a bad seed into the place.'

'What gave you that idea?'

'I know it's what you're thinking,' she tilted her chin up defiantly, blowing smoke from her turn of the cigarette. 'I've seen you two in a huddle with Rodney. Don't blame you, really.' To her surprise Talisker seemed amused by this, he laughed again, not ironically this time, right out into the night air. 'What's so funny?' she scowled.

'I'm not gonna lie to you, Effie, you're right. We're still deciding whether you're fit enough – or trustworthy enough – to go . . .'

'So, what's so bloody funny?' she repeated, her ire rising.

'You just reminded me of someone when you did that, that's all. She was wilful, bloody-minded and stubborn as well.' His smile faded, 'Got us into all sorts of trouble . . .'

She stubbed the cigarette into the sand, crushing it with the toe of her boot, 'And did you give up on her?' she said acidly. She didn't wait for his response but stalked back towards her room. Talisker watched her go, his expression one of sadness. Had he given up on Regan, he wondered? Not till the last, but then she was his daughter.

'Didn't mean I didn't love her,' he called after Effie's retreating figure, 'Some people just . . .' her door clicked shut and the metallic noise of the bolt being drawn shot across the space. 'Some people just don't make it easy,' he muttered.

As they travelled further north-east it was notable that there was no one around. Winter was enveloping the desert; although the sun shone with flint-sharp light in the mornings it failed to warm the frozen ground. The wind-chill made it worse, any time spent out of the jeep was a bright agony of stinging faces and hands. By the time they reached Chinle, the snow clouds were gathering . . .

Chapter Five

He had been tracking the beast for over two hours now. Dusk was enveloping the forest and the coolness of the evening air gently ushered away the faint warmth of the day. Birdsong filled the lush green silence as the forest creatures settled down to roost, soon it would give way to the restful quiet of the night, interrupted only by those nocturnal beasts whose rightful home it was.

The creature Raco was tracking did not belong here, not only that, it seemed to have little sense of where *here* was. It lumbered through bushes and brambles alike suffering no apparent injury and for the first while Raco suspected it had little purpose or direction in mind. However, once they crested a ridge about twenty miles south-west of Ruannoch Were, Raco's quarry increased its pace, and its path became less erratic. Raco fervently hoped it wasn't heading home to a whole pack of the creatures – he wasn't quite sure if he could manage to kill this one.

It had been a week since a child of the Fine had been killed and his friends – all around ten years old – had come screaming back over the causeway into the keep, blood-spattered and hysterical. They led Raco and a group of watchmen back to the clearing but would not go closer than a certain distance away from the body. Raco couldn't blame them; the boy had been torn apart, his limbs removed from his torso in a way that

97

reminded Raco of picking the legs off a spider when he was a boy. As he sent up a prayer to the Goddess he hoped the victim had been already dead by the time the creature had mutilated his body.

'It could have been a bear,' Harra suggested. He was the senior watchman, a veteran of the Battle for Or Coille and the failed uprising of five years ago – both he and Raco were dispossessed from Durghanti, now living in the crannog city to the east. It took a lot to rattle Harra's composure but even he looked pale at the sight of the young boy's suffering.

'I don't think so Harra, look,' Raco pointed at the tree nearest him. 'Have you ever known a bear bash its victim's head in on a tree trunk before?' Blood and bone fragments were smeared down the front of the tree and it was sickeningly obvious that the unresisting body had been swung against it with huge force.

'Could be,' Harra argued, unwilling to give up his first theory. 'None o' the lads are strong enough, for sure.' He glanced back at the huddle of sniffling boys, 'We'll have to get them to tell us better when they've calmed down a bit,' he sighed.

'Is he dead?' A high tremulous voice carried across the clearing. It seemed ridiculous that anyone should ask such a thing but the youngest boy – Raco thought he was called Cam – was only seven. The others were holding him back.

'Don't look, Cammie. Don't look,' they urged.

Raco walked back over to the group purposely putting himself in Cam's line of vision. 'Yes, I'm afraid so, Cam . . .' He looked at the older boys. 'When you've all been home and let your mothers know you're all right, I'll come and see you so you can tell me exactly what happened.'

They all began talking at once. Excited fragments about some demonic beast which they had accidentally disturbed . . . something about blue lights . . . Raco held up his hands for quiet.

'Not now,' he shouted. 'Tell me later. Go home.'

'Sir,' Cam tugged on the edge of his buckskin robe. 'I don't want to go back through the trees, sir . . .' he shot a fearful glance behind him.

'It's all right, Cam,' Raco did his best to smile reassuringly, although the thought of the carnage behind him was doing things to the greasy chicken he'd had for lunch. His stomach was in danger of rebelling. He beckoned over two of the watchmen and instructed them to see the boys home – he was sure the older boys were glad Cam had spoken up as they did not want to make the walk back alone either but, as their bravado re-asserted itself, would have been reluctant to say so.

'D'you believe them?' he asked Harra when they'd gone.

'Dunno,' Harra grunted. 'If'n it ain't true, it had to be one o' the big lads – or two even, if they held onto his hands an' feet . . . But I'm thinkin' I'd rather it *was* a monster.'

Raco nodded. 'Me too,' he said.

It was true, of course, he knew that now. Another death had followed with similar eyewitness accounts from older, more credible witnesses. The watchmen had been patrolling the shoreline for the last few days to ensure nothing got into the city. Raco had taken his small band of Sidhe trackers out, but to no avail; it was as if the demon beast simply disappeared between the attacks, which made it all the more fearsome to the children and youth of Ruannoch Were. When Raco had sighted the strange creature on his third trip out he had impulsively followed it into the forest, unwilling to lose sight of it. After the first five miles or so he wished he'd reported back for reinforcements as instructed by Harra, but his stubbornness would not allow him to break off pursuit and so he had arrived here; ten miles from any assistance, where no one would hear if the beast decided to shred him apart the way it had its other victims.

In the gloom of early evening, the strange blue glow that emanated from his quarry made tracking relatively easy but Raco was tiring. Now more than ever, he wished he could transform into his bear form as his fathers and forefathers had been able to do.

In fact Raco had only ever transformed once, before the sickness had robbed the Sidhe warriors of their ability, it had been almost six years ago. He remembered the day, the very hour of that first transformation the sheer joy and power. The *knowing* he was *Kellid* – a bear of the Sidhe. And, as quickly as the embrace of his totem animal gave his life meaning, it was gone. He knew only that *Kellid*'s spirit was lost to him as were all other Sidhe's totems; unreachable, perhaps forever. This sudden death of the Sidhe's magical ability had plunged the scattered tribes into deep mourning. There was no cure and no apparent explanation, but many speculated that the Gods were displeased at their disunity and ultimately the Sidhe would die out. Raco was scornful of this idea, unable even to countenance it, but he had to admit – if only to himself – that it could come to pass in relatively few generations as the Sidhe bloodline was absorbed by the Fine. Now this curse had struck the few purebloods still able to transform, it seemed a final, bitter blow to their nation.

Still, he considered, this moment was its own – as his father had often counselled – and he must make do with the weapons the Gods had seen fit to charge him with. He still carried a battleaxe which Harra had given him. It was so heavy his arm was beginning to go numb but he wasn't about to put the thing down. His only other weapon was a long dagger but he didn't want to reach close enough quarters to use it. He would have to act soon, he knew – either give up and report back to Harra (who would be completely unimpressed by his failure to get help and call him a stubborn bastard) or attack before he got too tired to have any chance. Despite the cold, sweat was forming on his brow and upper lip.

He didn't know how it happened. One second the thought was there, flitting through his mind and the next, he acted on it.

'Ho there, beast,' he yelled. He regretted his impulse immediately the words echoed through the forest, if he could have taken them back or swallowed them up he would have, but it was too late. The lumbering creature stopped, turned around and, seemingly with equal lack of deliberation, it charged back towards Raco, bellowing as it came.

Raco's mouth went completely dry, his throat constricted and his heart began to hammer so hard in his chest it seemed he would die before his assailant reached him. If his legs would have moved he might have run away but his limbs were leaden, rooted to the spot. Bending into a slight crouch he drew back his axe as the creature cleared the trees and he had his first clear impression of its face.

'Sweet Goddess!' he yelped.

There was no time to wield his weapon before the creature was upon him. It was fast, much faster than he'd expected – its charge flung him backwards as if a ram had struck him in the chest and he would have fallen except for the tree behind him. He heard a flat, sickening sound as his head hit the trunk and his vision blurred instantly. Panic seized him as he realised he'd dropped his axe and he screamed in fear and frustration at his own stupidity.

Blue light surrounded Raco as the beast's freezing hand clamped around his throat and he was yanked forward in its grip like a rag doll. Somewhere in the tiny space of his mind that was still calm, the sickening realisation formed that the beast was preparing to smack him backwards into the tree and dash his brains, killing as it had before.

Except it didn't happen. Suddenly the constricting grip pulled back from his neck and the beast itself was pulled backward with inexplicable speed and force. For a moment Raco was confused and dizzy; he fell forward onto his knees as his trembling legs gave way but he kept watching the beast, its blue light pulsing in a strange frenzy as it lost its footing and was dragged backwards through the brambles.

'What . . . ?' Raco scrambled forward on his hands and

knees ignoring the nettles which brushed his arms. As he heard the snicker of a horse on the other side of the bushes and excited voices he realised what had happened; someone had roped the beast around its chest and dragged it backward from horseback. He remained crouching in the undergrowth and peered cautiously out at his rescuers whose whole attention was on the beast.

He had been saved by a company of Shoreth riders. There were six altogether, three of whom had ropes around the legs and chest of their captive who was squirming and struggling in the wet grass. As the blue light pulsed and flickered in a strangely appropriate display of distress, the Shoreth were hard pushed to control the flight instinct of their horses, who seemed to think the reflections on their legs and flanks were a danger to them. Just as Raco's breathing was beginning to calm down, there was a collective gasp from the soldiers as their captive disappeared. The blue lights grew brighter, more intense until the creature was obscured from view, as they died away it was clear the creature had simply vanished leaving nothing behind but a faint, disquieting smell. The riders were left holding limp, empty nooses.

'It's g-gone Ma'am,' one of the soldiers said.

'I can see that,' as the leader of the band removed her ornate silver headgear, very definitely feminine ash blonde hair spilled out. Raco was surprised, he'd never seen or heard of a woman Shoreth Rider before, and certainly not one in command. 'Where's the man he was attacking? Look in the undergrowth – use your swords.'

She turned her horse to face where Raco was hidden and he dared not look directly at her for fear of catching her gaze. 'You may as well come out,' she said calmly as her men began hacking at the bushes. 'You have my word you will not be harmed . . .' If her statement was meant to be reassuring, her clipped, officious tones did little to help.

'Perhaps he's unable to come out,' her second-in-command offered. 'Perhaps it killed him.' She said nothing in response, simply scowled.

Raco had little option, he glanced behind to see if there was a clear escape but one of the soldiers had dismounted his horse and was hacking his way towards the bush which concealed Raco, his sword catching the dusk light as he swung it to and fro in great arcs like a scythe.

'I'm here, I'm here . . .' Raco stumbled out of hiding, his arms raised in conciliatory surrender. Although the Shoreth and the Fine were no longer at war, relations between them could never be described as friendly – it seemed to Raco that if they could leave a Fine (or a Sidhe, they didn't make any distinction) dead in the forest they'd have little hesitation. He stared up at the woman commander, suddenly aware of his sweat, cuts and stings. Tears were flowing unchecked down his grimy face so it would be impossible to appear nonchalant – he didn't even try any bravado.

'My name is Ferebe Vezul,' the officer said, leaning forward in her saddle. She spoke to him as if he were a child or a simpleton. 'What do you know of the creature? Are you its creator, by chance? You do not look like a mage . . .'

'V-Vezul?' He knew that name, had fought against his soldiers at Durghanti.

She nodded, noting his recognition. 'You fought against my father perhaps?'

'Perhaps,' he agreed. 'I was tracking the creature hoping to kill it. It's killed two people on the shores at Ruannoch Were. And by the way, this is Fine territory.'

Ferebe ignored his comment but cast a scathing glance over his wounds and bruised throat. 'Hmm, seems you were defending yourself rather poorly.'

Raco bristled at this; imperious though she seemed, this Ferebe could be no more than twenty, too young to have fought in any major campaign, an unseasoned officer. 'It had the advantage of surprise, Ferebe Vezul.'

'How so?'

'Because it had my father's face and he died five years ago at Durghanti.'

Three hours later, Raco was wishing he'd kept this germ of information to himself. The Shoreth Riders had bound him hand and foot and then ignored him as they began setting up camp for the night. The light was fading and a soft rain had begun to fall as they pitched their tents, which seemed to Raco to be made of woefully thin fabric. He stifled a smirk as the night breeze caught the sides of the tent and billowed it out of the Rider's hands. Still, he reflected, it was done with a great deal less cursing than the Fine would have done in similar circumstances, the men were disciplined, each working as part of the team. Four of the Riders worked under the gaze of Ferebe Vezul's second-in-command. A couple of times Raco noted the man –

Felndar, they called him – stealing looks at Ferebe which seemed largely resentful. Ferebe sat alone near the horses reading some papers and seldom looked up as the encampment took shape.

There were only two tents; a long, low one for the Riders and, a surprisingly large and grand one for Ferebe. Raco reflected that they must have been travelling for a week or more as the silver crest embroidered onto the door-flap was dull and dirty looking. Once the tents were up, the Riders set a fire and began to cook; soon the tantalisingly familiar smell of rabbit stew or soup hung in the night air. To Raco's dismay, they didn't offer him anything.

'We're not at war, you know,' he grumbled, 'I don't think much of Shoreth hospitality . . . and you *are* in Fine territory.'

Felndar looked up from his bowl, a thin trickle of meat juices running down his chin. 'Shut up,' he scowled.

'He's right, Felndar,' Ferebe said mildly. 'After you have eaten, untie his hands and give him some food.' She did not look over from her engrossing papers and so missed the contemptuous glare Felndar gave her in return for this instruction.

The stew was going cold by the time Felndar ungraciously consented to give him any but Raco was too hungry to care; he grabbed the bowl without thanks and began to shovel the food into his mouth with the metal spoon he had been given without pausing to look up.

'It's true, the Fine are animals,' Felndar noted to his companions in a tone of feigned amusement. 'See, they eat like pigs.' His men laughed somewhat dutifully and Raco looked up, scowling through a curtain of sweaty black hair.

'I am a Sidhe warrior, you ignorant upstart. We are a free people. At least the Fine build their own cities, they're not a nation of cuckoos. That's what they call you Shoreth — a stinkin' useless bird with only one bloody song . . .'

Felndar looked momentarily startled by this — obviously he had not known — but rather than argue his point he turned back around and kicked Raco in the side. It hurt like blazes but Raco forced himself to remain upright and eat another spoonful of stew. He caught Felndar's slightly confused expression as he wondered why his kick apparently had no effect on his prisoner. Rather than dwell on it for too long though, he pulled his foot back for another go.

'Felndar,' Ferebe's voice issued commandingly from her tent. 'Bring the prisoner here. I want to talk to him.'

Raco was yanked immediately to his feet, causing him to drop his bowl. He winced slightly as the sudden movement wrenched the area of his side where the kick had landed, he knew it would bruise badly but hoped there was no real damage inside.

'You heard, let's go,' Felndar muttered.

'So what's it like, taking orders from a girl?' Raco enquired brightly. Felndar did not reply but cut the straps from around his ankles and shoved him forward. Raco stumbled on numbed feet but managed to pause before going in to Ferebe's tent and push his dishevelled hair from his face; it wasn't vanity exactly but he was less than happy about Felndar's assertion that the Fine were animals and tried to look tidy. As he hurriedly straightened his robe and trews, Felndar grabbed hold of his arm and pushed him inside.

The tent had only been up for an hour and already it was warm. Raco glanced wonderingly around, perhaps he had been wrong about the fabric. Ferebe was sitting on a low wooden stool, her long legs stretched out in front of her. She had removed her riding boots and her helm revealing her silver hair, which was short like a young boy's; there could be little doubting her femininity however, soft tendrils curled in onto her cheeks framing a face that was at once both delicate and strong, its sharp features bleached further and softened by the light of the lanterns which hung around the tent. Raco wondered fleetingly whether her men found her attractive, she was so unlike the robust, fulsome women of the Fine or Sidhe, so thin and wiry looking . . .

'Sit down, *Yekt*,' she commanded, gesturing to another of the stools. 'Felndar, you may leave us.'

'But Ferebe, you may need me,' Felndar protested. She shot him an annoyed look and he saluted smartly and rather unexpectedly. 'I'll be just outside,' he said with great deliberation, glancing at Raco. Raco grinned widely, enjoying Felndar's discomfort.

'My name is Raco,' he said to Ferebe. 'I don't answer to *Yekt*.' He knew it was a derogatory term although he had no idea what it meant.

Ferebe gave a small, insincere smile which told Raco she couldn't care less if he was offended. 'So, Raco,' she pronounced his name with a heavy accent and sounded the 'R' – *Rrr-ako*. 'Tell me about the Shards.'

This completely threw him, 'Shards?' he frowned.

'Do you mean those creatures? You know more than me, the Shoreth must have made them. *We* don't have a name for them,' he ended triumphantly as if this must prove his point.

She leaned in towards him and gave him a chilling smile, her breath warm and honey scented on his face. 'Listen, *Yekt*, we can just sit here amicably, maybe even have a glass of warmed wine, and you can tell me what you know. Or I can let Cerez do his work on you and get the answers. He's an Inquisitor.'

Raco could tell she was bluffing although he had to admire her gall. He had seen Shoreth Inquisitors before; a group of them riding the trail North where Durghanti and Ruannoch Were regions met. He'd watched them pass from within the cover of the trees and it was as close as he would want to get. It wasn't just their severe clothes that marked them out as Inquisitors; to a man, they had scarred faces and hands – *as if they practised on themselves,* he remembered thinking – and they had an ageless quality about them. They rode their horses as if their thoughts were totally detached from their surroundings, as if the wind on their face meant nothing.

'Your threat might be more frightening if I hadn't just eaten his rabbit bone stew,' Raco observed mildly. Ferebe did not react to his taunt in any way – and why should she he thought? – even if her man was not an Inquisitor, he was sure they could devise some creative way to cause him pain. The Shoreth were renowned for their cold-bloodedness; only a couple of years earlier it had not been unusual to stumble across random crucifixions in the forest. He sighed. 'Do what you will, Ferebe Vezul. I can only tell you what I know and that is very little. It will gain the Shoreth no advantage if they truly do not know the source of the beasts.'

Ferebe continued to meet his gaze for a few moments longer as she sized up the likelihood that he was lying to her. Finally, she nodded her assent rather sharply. 'But you have told us something, warrior, which must be significant. The creature had the face of your dead father. How can that be possible?'

'I have no idea. Certainly the Fine nor the Sidhe have no such foul magics.' Although he fought to keep the tone of accusation from his voice, Ferebe still detected it. Her expression hardened slightly and she was about to make a reply, which was surely caustic, when there was a strangled scream from outside. Sounds of panicked horses and men erupted in the quiet of the forest. Ferebe leapt up, sprinting for the doorway and grabbing her sword without stopping to pull her boots back on. 'Felndar!' she yelled. 'Felndar, what's going on?'

'Ferebe Vezul!' Raco shouted, 'Wait!' Raco knew trouble when he heard it and she was about to leave him behind with no weapon. He ran from the tent behind her casting around desperately for something to defend himself. The scene which greeted him was carnage.

Two Shards had lumbered into the encampment; both carried crude weapons fashioned from tree trunks. A shock ran through Raco as he recognised a flash of dirty mangled plaid which clung to the torso of the Shard nearest him. The creature was clutching his first unfortunate victim by the hair and dragging him across the ground, as he screamed and thrashed his legs had kicked into the campfire and his limbs were now ablaze as he continued to shriek in increasing agony and panic. The Shard seemed oblivious to the plight of his victim, as though it considered him already dealt with, it moved with a strange purposefulness across the clearing toward Ferebe who was yelling orders to her men.

The other Shard was being held at bay by two soldiers who had cleverly managed to stay outside the swing of its massive club – one of the men was jabbing at it with a burning torch which he had pulled from the ground. The screams and, increasingly, the smell of the burning man permeated everything. Mercifully, there was no time in which to grasp the full horror of his death throes, Raco was still frantically looking for a weapon as Ferebe and Felndar moved forward to engage their target.

He glimpsed another Shoreth rider – mounted for some reason – at the edge of the clearing, his eyes round with horror, crippled by fear and indecision. 'You there! Yes, you,' Raco yelled. 'Throw me a weapon. Anything, man . . .' For long seconds the man looked right through Raco, his face a slack mask, unable to assimilate what he was seeing. Then he shook himself and reached out for a long sword from the weapon stack just by him.

'No!' Ferebe yelled. 'Don't arm the prisoner!'

'For mercy's sake, Ferebe Vezul . . .' It was too late anyway, the hesitant rider, once galvanised into action, moved quickly and threw the sheathed blade to Raco who caught the sword and lunged forward to help assail the Shard.

Raco had the sensibilities of *Kellid.* He could no longer transform but vestiges of his totem remained; in battle this meant his hearing and vision became clearer, sharper. Sound became alive, jagged fragments jumbled into a sense image of red and ultraviolet. So, as he joined Ferebe and Felndar, he was still aware of what was happening off to his right in the shadows of the trees. Another being was coming but he knew before he even saw it that it was not a Shard – no lumbering brute this – it moved fast, its footsteps making light, slick contact with the loam of the forest floor. As it came within range of Raco's beleaguered senses a stagnant purple stain spread across the clearing towards him. In the same instant a choking cry came from the soldier on the horse.

Raco glanced sideways, such a fast glimpse that it was over before his brain had time to rationalise what he saw. The source of the sound and the colour was there, standing next to the rider – not fighting, it held no weapon – it appeared almost as though he had reached out to pat the horse. He was *skinless.*

'Felndar!' Ferebe's yell immediately demanded Raco's attention. Felndar had strayed within range of the Shard's reach and, dropping the dying victim it already carried, it reached out and grabbed another. To his immense credit Felndar did not scream or even struggle much, instead as the creature pulled him towards its mangled face his arm arced out fast and plunged a dagger into the Shard's eyes.

It made a curious keening sound and as it staggered back towards the fire, dropping its weapon to flail uselessly at its eyes. But it did not drop Felndar who was still gripped tightly around the neck, his breathing beginning to rasp from his throat. Raco and Ferebe rushed forward to press the advantage, Ferebe hacking at the Shard's legs and Raco kicking it in the ribs. It had the desired result, unbalancing the beast, but just the instant before it toppled backwards into the scattered campfire, it reached across and crushed Felndar's skull like so much eggshell. It was mercifully fast, there was no time for him to cry out and in the same moment, the burning man also died. The Shard toppled back in a slow, almost graceful, fall and, as it did so, the battle scene was plunged into a strange quiet. There was a long 'whummmp' sound, sparks sprayed outwards from the fire as the body landed. Felndar's limp corpse rolled away as the Shard's grip flew open. Ferebe ran towards his body although she must have known what she would find . . .

. . . and it was still there. In the silence and shadow. The skinless man. Raco turned his attention to the mounted soldier who was unnaturally still. There was no sound from the other side of the clearing and Raco was sure that was bad news but he walked back towards the treeline where the rider sat.

He could hear Ferebe crying softly behind him, a wet snuffling which she was fighting to contain. *Kellid*'s senses were still with him and the dark sound and movement of the wind in the trees appeared as a soft, vermilion flicker. There . . . to the left . . . a movement. Fast, light, almost like the trees. Raco broke into a run but didn't go far. He knew the skinless man had simply vanished within the forest canopy – only the trees were alive as far as he, and *Kellid,* could see.

'Why didn't you ride it down?' he said as he returned to the rider. 'You could have saved Fel . . . oh. Ferebe, come and look at this. Ferebe!'

Both rider and horse were dead. It looked as if they just didn't know it yet. Their skins were dried up like tanned leather reminding Raco of the strange burials he had seen further north where the bodies were laid in peat. Their attitude and pose was as in life, the rider sitting forward in his saddle, his mouth agape to shout something, perhaps a warning to Felndar which never came. Raco touched the horse's flank, it was freezing cold as if the blood had literally turned to stone in the creature's veins. He glanced away to call Ferebe again, she was crouched on the ground beside Felndar, her face obscured by the veil of her white hair. 'Ferebe . . .'

When he looked back the rider was moving. Only slowly, an agonised, incredulous movement as the head swivelled on the man's neck to look at Raco; the movement accompanied by a sound like the twisting of a dry rope.

Raco opened his mouth to say something to the rider but for the life of him could think of nothing to say. The man's expression was abject as he tried to move his lower jaw to speak but before he could even try, his horse collapsed beneath him. The whole thing shattered as one: horse, rider, weapons, all gone shattered into a heap of dry flakes which quickly dulled to a uniform black colour. Raco shuddered, a wave of nausea washing over him – there had been a moment of *knowing* for the luckless rider – a moment of supreme horror and helplessness he could only imagine.

He staggered back towards Ferebe desperately trying to ignore the hot saliva which filled his mouth as a prelude to vomit. It was no good; just before he spoke to her he had to turn aside and puke the undigested remains of his rabbit stew into the grass.

'Ah . . . yuk,' he spluttered. 'Eeee-yuk. How is everybody?'

There was no response from Ferebe so he walked towards the fire. The Shards had gone – disintegrated into the blue lights once again to whichever hell they came from – but the broken corpses of five Shoreth Riders littered the forest. Raco and Ferebe were the only ones left alive.

It took a couple of hours to dispose of the bodies. It was pitch dark and freezing cold, a low mist drifted across the ground and was only dissipated by the remains of the campfire. Still, Ferebe insisted on certain things which seemed strange to Raco: the graves must all point their feet east towards the homelands of the Shoreth, the men must be stripped naked, as their Goddess cared nothing for earthly tokens, their eyes she covered with a thin strip of fabric which she ripped from the tent. Most disconcertingly, she wanted to crucify Felndar's corpse but Raco put his foot down.

'He died valiantly, isn't that enough? Doesn't he deserve to rest peacefully?'

She scowled. 'How can I expect you to understand, *Yekt*. It is not an insult – it is a great honour, he should be raised above the battleground so the Goddess may see him first.'

'So you mean it's a *compliment*?'

'If you will. We respect those who die in battle, leaders of men . . . why do you find that strange?'

Raco's mind reeled, why indeed? It seemed quite reasonable when considered in such a way. 'Ah . . . but they're not always dead first, are they?'

She smiled thinly. 'No. But dead or dying – the difference is only a matter of time from one moment to the next.' She pointed at the still smouldering corpse of the first rider killed by the Shards. 'For some who die in battle that moment goes unnoted, does it not?'

Raco nodded glumly in response and walked over to the body, the man's legs were little but charred sticks mercifully obscured by the encroaching mist. As he crouched down to examine the warrior Raco held his sleeve against his nose and mouth to obscure the smell. This unbalanced him slightly so when the 'corpse' jerked its arm up he fell backwards into the grass with a yell. Ferebe came running over and knelt beside the stricken soldier.

'Rest easy, rest easy,' she murmured. In the darkness it wasn't clear to either of them whether the man was in fact still alive or if the fire had twisted his corpse so much that the muscles were twitching. Whichever it was, the arm dropped again immediately and the soldier was still for good.

'Well,' Raco muttered darkly, 'As you said, Ferebe Vezul, from moment to moment . . .' He began to push himself up when his hand caught on something hard in the grass. 'Ouch . . . what?'

He picked the object up. It was cold and quite heavy – metallic – in his hand and he tilted it towards the fire which they had hurriedly rekindled with the tent lamps. In the orange glow of the flames the links of a heavy chain glinted richly, attached to which was an amulet the size and shape of a thrush's egg. 'How much do you pay your officers, Ferebe?'

'What? What's that?' She came over and stared down at the metal egg; it was covered with dazzlingly crafted filigree which was wrought in silver which encased what Raco assumed to be the solid golden body of the egg. 'Let me see,' Ferebe snapped. She held her hand out commandingly.

Raco cradled his find to his chest. 'No . . . no, I found it. I think I want to keep it.'

She shrugged, and turned away back towards her fallen comrade. Raco was taken off guard by her easy assent and totally unprepared for the roundhouse kick which sent him crashing back into the grass. Ferebe smiled down at him, her booted foot grinding into his chest. 'Let me see,' she repeated.

Cursing, and telling himself that he had only been bested by a woman because she had cheated, he handed her the amulet which she snatched from him before she let him up. 'Really, I would like to . . .'

She silenced him with an imperious wave of her hand. '*Yekt*,' she snapped. 'This is important . . .'

'I told you my name . . .'

'Look.' She touched some concealed mechanism on the bottom of the egg and there was a tiny 'click' as the front of the filigree opened out, reminding Raco of a beetle's wing-casing. Snuggled inside the hollow of the egg something was glowing, bright fingers of light sparkled in the night air, red, blue, yellow and green.

'Salkit's tits,' Raco whispered. 'What is it, Ferebe?'

Ferebe's expression was one of consternation. 'It must be a very precious thing *Yekt* . . .' Raco decided to let that one go by for the sake of brevity. 'Magics are not common amongst my people and this has to be magical in origin. Have you ever seen its like?'

Raco shook his head and then jerked his thumb towards the unfortunate warrior. 'So, how did our friend here come by it?'

'I don't think he did. Look here.'

Caught within the links of the chain were small but unmistakeable fragments, coarse hair and equally coarse fabric. 'Looks like . . .' Raco rolled the cloth between his fingers, straightening it flat. 'It is, it's plaid wool. The Shard was wearing this?'

Ferebe nodded glumly, her mind already racing to the conclusion Raco was about to draw. 'The Shards are somehow Shoreth in origin. I don't understand . . . why would they send me to . . .'

She was quick, and Raco had to admit that once he'd finished feeling such a stupid fool for letting his guard down in her company again. One moment, he was simply looking at the fabric, his mind idly pondering the conundrum they had been presented with – the next moment, there was a flash of silver as a dagger was pressed to his throat.

'What! What are you doing, Ferebe?'

She pressed the blade in slightly just beneath his larynx, thankfully angling it slightly to avoid actually slitting his throat. 'Sit down, *Yekt.*'

'What?'

'Sit down.' She shoved him back but held on to the

front of his jerkin so he didn't actually fall. Once he was on the ground again she walked around so she was behind his back. 'Lie down,' she commanded. 'On your belly.'

'So this is it? You're going to kill me?' Raco was too incredulous to be angry. 'After I fought beside you? It's true then, the Shoreth are vicious kill . . . ouch.' She had shoved her heel into his back right between his shoulder blades, then she kicked his legs wide apart – Raco knew this was to make it more difficult for him to get up quickly. 'Ah, the Shoreth mating ritual . . .' he joked.

'I'm not going to kill you, *Yekt*.' She sounded uneasy.

'I told you my . . .'

Pain and then darkness . . . She knocked him out.

'Sorry. I knew you'd struggle.' Raco woke up and groaned loudly as his first instinct to touch the lump on the back of his head was denied him due to his hands being tightly bound behind his back.

'Sorry? You're sorry? You could have killed me.'

'I know. It was a gamble – I've never deliberately knocked anyone out before . . .'

Raco looked around him, blinking to try and clear the black spots which swam in his vision. It was morning but it was so grey as to make little difference to the level of light. The mist had not cleared and seemed to add a somehow appropriate blanket to the row of five shallow graves in the clearing. Ferebe had marked each with a large stone and some branches cut from a nearby rowan. The fifth grave was smaller, about half the length of the others and Raco guessed it held the strange leathery remains of the soldier and horse who had perished so mysteriously.

'I don't understand, Ferebe Vezul. Does honour count for nothing amongst your people? I fought beside you – perhaps the first time a Sidhe and Shoreth have fought side-by-side – and this is how you repay me? Are you going to leave me here bound like this?'

Ferebe was busy readying her horse to ride. She yanked its girth tightly and glanced back towards Raco frowning. 'I have no intention of leaving you here, *yekt*. We're going to Durghanti to tell the Emperor what we've discovered.'

'*Durghanti?* I can't go back there – not like this!' he tried to indicate his bound hands.

'Listen Raco. I'm not in the best of moods – I've just buried five of my men – one of them my future husband. There's no way I'm leaving you alone to go back to Ruannoch Were and tell them the Shards are coming from the Shoreth . . .'

'I hadn't even thought about it,' he complained.

'. . . so the choices are; either come with me back to Durghanti as my prisoner, or, I'll kill you now.'

Raco sighed. 'All right, since you put it that way . . . but you'll have to help me onto my horse.'

Chapter Six

They had arrived at Chinle at last, were actually staying in a good hotel, planning to set out for the Canyon De Chelly in the morning. 'Get some sleep,' Talisker had cautioned. 'If it happens quickly and we manage to go through to Sutra tomorrow your body won't know what's hit it – it's a bit like extreme jet lag.'

'World lag, huh?' Effie said. Talisker had laughed at this but Yiska had still not cracked a smile – at least not in her direction – since Aunt Millie's.

'Yeah, I guess you could call it world lag.' Talisker became pensive, paused with his hand outstretched on the door of the room he was sharing with Yiska. 'Maybe that's what's wrong with me . . . You know, some mornings I wake up and every-dammed-thing hurts. *Everything.* D'you think it's just because I'm old?'

A chambermaid was working down the hall pushing a trolley loaded with the debris from peoples rooms. She had obviously overheard Talisker's remark. 'Honey, you don't *know* old . . .' she tutted as she passed.

'Night then,' Effie said. She smiled at Talisker but Yiska, still, would not meet her gaze. Without switching on the light in her room she made straight for the bathroom, scooping up the blue kitbag on the way.

It was cold the next morning. The whole area had had about four inches of snow, which was not unusual for

February. When Effie arrived at the jeep, Rodney, Yiska and Talisker were looking at a map of the canyon. At first, none of them looked up as she walked over but then Talisker stopped to slurp coffee from the steaming mug he held.

'Morning, Effie . . . are you okay?'

Yiska looked up too then. 'Effie, you look terrible,' he frowned.

'Like you give a shit,' she snarled. Actually, she'd spent the night puking her guts up – not in her usual deliberate fashion but uncontrollably – she felt incredibly weak and was pretty sure she was running a fever but she wasn't going to tell them that. She got in the back of the jeep and slammed the door. Talisker and Yiska exchanged glances but said nothing.

It was cosy in the jeep, if a little airless; Effie could smell Talisker's coffee mingled with the warm leather from the saddlebags which Rodney had thrown into the back. She closed her eyes but the colours of the snowbound desert and sharp winter sunlight conspired to make her see the red inside her eyelids. The sun on her face felt good and she drifted back into sleep.

'Effie . . . Wake up, Effie. We're here.' Talisker was smiling down at her – he'd obviously forgiven or forgotten her earlier outburst. Also there was something different about him, he seemed animated and happy. Perhaps Yiska had given him something for his pain or maybe it was the prospect of going back to Sutra.

'Here?'

'Canyon De Chelly. We can't drive any further so one of Rodney's other grandsons has lent us some horses. Come and look. C'mon, you're missing it.'

Moaning to herself she got out of the jeep, immediately aware that her legs were shaking. Despite her discomfort and the increasing pain just beneath her ribs, Effie was transfixed by her surroundings. For the first time in a long time, her introspection was shattered.

The Canyon was beautiful, amazing. From where they stood they could look over into the red distance to the east where the flat-topped plateau ended abruptly in dizzying sandstone cliffs – it was as if someone had taken a giant cookie cutter and stamped the canyon into the ground – the colours of the place were so vivid, so bright, no photograph could hope to convey them. In the foreground a spectacular narrow pillar of rock towered impossibly high from the base of the canyon, its peak white with a fresh blanket of snow.

'That's Defiance Plateau,' Yiska's voice came from behind her but she didn't turn around, 'over there, the mesa, and that is Spider Rock, this is a sacred place to the Navajo. Here . . .' he wrapped a blanket around her shoulders as he had that night at Aunt Millie's, it was a small gesture but she sensed it meant some kind of truce between them. 'You should have worn a hat.'

'Oh, it's in the jeep. Why's it called Spider Rock? It doesn't look like a spider.' She squinted at it to see if the outline resembled any arachnid she'd ever seen.

'We Navajo believe that Spider Woman lives at the top. She is a great deity, she came from the time of creation when the Dinéh emerged from the First World into this – the Fourth. She taught the ancestors how to weave on a loom . . .'

'That doesn't sound very important,' she turned around to face him.

He looked surprised at her comment and, perhaps, disappointed. Effie mentally berated herself, just as she was making progress! 'But it is, Effie, it is very important. To us.'

'I'm sorry, Yiska.' She wasn't sure what she was apologising for so she didn't qualify her comment but let the 'sorry' stand for everything. 'How are we going to get down?'

Yiska nodded back towards where Talisker and Rodney were standing. They were talking to a young couple who seemed to be leading a whole herd of horses. 'There's a trail down . . .'

Effie's eyes widened in amazement,' but I can't ride a horse Yiska! I've never ridden in my life.' She was feeling sick again, the pain in her side wouldn't let up.

'Then today is a good day to learn, Effie. Look how beautiful it is down there. Listen to the quiet.' He sounded so calm about it, for a second she believed him.

'But – but . . .'

'But you're afraid.'

'No. Okay, well, maybe just a bit nervous.' Trying to conceal her pain from Yiska, Effie reached inside her jacket and clutched at her side. To her alarm her ribs were radiating intense heat. She couldn't tell him – she had taken the Ipecac syrup last night – he would say her illness was self-inflicted (as she knew it was) and he would go back to ignoring her. He would withdraw his good opinion of her once more as if it were a choice chocolate he could tease her with.

'Come on, we'll find you an old nag,' Yiska smiled. It was like the sun coming out.

'Please, Ferebe Vezul . . .'

'Will you just shut up, *Yekt*!'

'Don't you understand? Durghanti is my home city – the place of my birth – the home I was exiled from. We sing songs about it, we tell stories about it . . . My tribe of Sidhe are affiliated to the Fine who lived there . . . Don't make me go back in chains.'

She didn't even turn around. 'You're breaking my heart, Raco. I never did get all that Fine/ Sidhe stuff.'

'What do you mean?'

'Well, I can't tell the difference.'

'You can't tell I'm Sidhe? Incredible! The Shoreth haven't made much effort to understand the locals, have they? Look, we'll be able to see Durghanti soon, can't you just . . .'

Ferebe reined in her horse and turned around. She looked tired, exhausted. Worse still, it appeared she had been crying although she'd given no sign of it to Raco. After holding herself together all night, engaging in combat, burying her men, breaking camp, not to mention taking him prisoner, she had finally found time for silent tears when none would observe her. It was raining, and cold droplets fell from the front of her hood as if to obscure her tears – her fair skin was a strange, almost translucent colour in the wet and tendrils of her hair were plastered to her forehead and cheeks. Only her eyes betrayed her, she had rubbed them so the skin was a pearly pink.

'What part of "no" don't you understand?'

Being a general's daughter must have been tough, Raco observed.

It was late afternoon by the time they reached Durghanti. Although it was not far distant if travelling in a straight line, Ferebe and Raco had to backtrack to cross the bridge over Cerne's Gorge. Nothing expressed the differences in the Fine and Shoreth cultures more that the bridge, *Aon Crann*; it was a massive structure, shored up by a middle island of rock, an outcrop which divided the centre of the canyon. No one of the Fine remembered who had first built the bridge – there were no *Seanachaidhs* any more that Raco knew of to carry the oral tradition of the Fine – only that the clans of Ruannoch Were and Durghanti were bound to keep it in order. It was wooden, made out of what appeared to be one gigantic tree – hence its name – but this was patently impossible, Cerne's Gorge was almost a mile wide and the width of the bridge was such that carts and horses could cross it three or four abreast. Raco had spent some time as a youngster trying to dig his knife into the bridge but what seemed to be wood, in fact, had the texture of stone. He had concluded then that somehow the bridge was artfully carved to give its organic appearance although that did not explain the fact that, each spring, green shoots peeped out from amongst its craggy, gargantuan body. The Fine revered *Aon Crann* and repaired it diligently as best they could with clay and wood where necessary – the Shoreth however, having coolly assented to the usefulness of the bridge, encased their end in a lattice of steel and posted a sentry box at the mid-point.

Raco was looking forward to seeing *Aon Crann* because just over the other side was Durghanti and he had not laid eyes on the city for five years. He would not go back after the battle as he knew others had; slinking through the trees to gaze upon their lost home with heavy hearts. It grieved him more than he could say to be going back there a prisoner, hands bound and bladder bursting. Ferebe would not undo his wrists even to allow him to relieve himself; she was afraid, and rightly so. The conclusion she had reached far more quickly than Raco was correct – if freed he would rush back to Ruannoch Were and alert the city that the Shoreth were creating monsters, probably building an army of the mindless beasts to overrun Ruannoch Were. The fact that the obscene creations were mindless, and killed anyone in their path, was perhaps the only thing that could buy the Fine time as they were perfected. But the Fine would not prepare if not alerted to the danger . . .

Raco's reverie was interrupted as Ferebe spurred her horse into a faster pace; she was leading his mare who followed the stallion's every move anyway. 'Are you awake, *Yekt?*' she called back. 'The bridge and Durghanti are just over that rise.'

'I don't need you to tell me that, Ferebe Vezul,' he scowled.

Durghanti was not like the other cities of Sutra. Not fortified like Soulis Mor or Ruannoch Were, it was built into the hillside with Cerne's Gorge on its eastern flank, while to the west the hills fell away steeply over an inhospitable landscape for twenty miles before

127

reaching the ocean. The city needed no defences other than those nature had provided and so the buildings were more ornate than functional, built of the local red clay. The central bailey was less a castle and more a grand civic building, long fluted columns forming an elegant, impressive avenue into the central courtyard, statues lining the streets. Artisans from all over Sutra had chosen Durghanti as their home; silversmiths, sculptors, poets. Durghanti was as much the spiritual homeland of the Fine as Soulis Mor was its martial base. The native Fine had been horse-traders and skilled riders – some said the loss of the city to the Shoreth had broken the fighting spirit of the Fine in the same way as gelding a Durghanti stallion.

Ferebe and Raco stopped at the sentry box halfway across *Aon Crann*. The rain had become heavier and they made a bedraggled pair, their horses steaming and white with lather. The sentry looked less than impressed. 'Greetings. State your business.'

'Ferebe Vezul . . . yes, daughter of General Vezul . . . I bring urgent news for the Emperor.'

The sentry saluted. 'Very well, Ma'am, I will tell General Zarrus that you are here.'

'No,' Ferebe's voice was sharp, impatient. 'I will speak only to the Emperor. Do you understand?' The sentry studied her face for a moment as though he was about to question her authority – Raco, whose horse had drawn alongside the stallion, glanced at her also – but her gaze and stony self-assurance never wavered.

'Very well, Ma'am. Please proceed to the main quadrangle. I will signal your arrival to the tower and someone will meet you.'

She nodded but said nothing else, just continued across the bridge. 'The Emperor!' Raco hissed incredulously. 'We're going to see the Emperor! What's he like?'

'I've no idea. I've never seen him before either. Don't speak to me directly when we're in there . . .'

'You know, you . . . the Shoreth, have no right to hold me. We're not at war.'

'Wake up, Raco. It's only a matter of time.'

The Shoreth Emperor was an impressive man, even Raco had to admit that. He had granted Ferebe's request for a private audience although he kept them waiting for over an hour.

'Why did you insist on seeing him alone, Ferebe?' Raco asked. He was feeling a lot better having been allowed to wash and use the privy before their appointment. He was also unbound. It seemed the Shoreth were unsure of how to treat him – further evidence, he pointed out to Ferebe, that they were nervous of provoking an incident with the Fine – and they had put him in an adjoining room to Ferebe's. However, his room had guards posted outside whereas hers did not. From simple curiosity Raco had gently tugged on the door between them, it had been locked on the other side.

She fidgeted and fingered the locket, which she was wearing around her neck, although concealed within her clothes. 'There's something wrong,' she frowned. 'Something . . .'

Finally, rather than being called in as they had both anticipated, a large, sumptuously clad man entered the antechamber and strode past them. 'Well, come on then

Ferebe Vezul,' he said as he pushed open the door. His voice was rich and genial and he didn't look back at them as he spoke. 'Bring your friend.'

The Emperor – Tebron – seemed impatient with formality. 'Yes, yes,' he waved dismissively as Ferebe went down on one knee and bowed her torso forward, arms outstretched. Raco did nothing but conceal a smirk, the Shoreth were not prone to obeisance in the company of the Fine and it seemed their formalised bow was designed to be uncomfortable. Ferebe wavered slightly. The Emperor poured drinks, three – much to Raco's delight – 'Get up, Lieutenant Vezul. I understand you have recently seen combat – in truth I can still smell the death on you.'

Ferebe stood up, frowning. 'I have had a wash, sir,' she said in confusion.

'I was speaking metaphorically,' the Emperor replied with a smile. He handed her a drink. 'Please sit down and be at ease.' He walked over to Raco and stood almost nose-to-nose with the Sidhe, regarding his face closely. 'Hmm, bear clan if I'm not mistaken.'

'Yes, yes sir . . .' Raco risked a pointed look at Ferebe as the Emperor turned his back. 'Originally from Durghanti, sir.'

'Ah. Well, sit down also – what's your name?'

'Raco.'

'You can both tell me what happened.'

Ferebe did most of the talking. Raco sipped his drink with immense enjoyment, his attention switching between the surprisingly austere decor of the room and the Emperor's expression, which grew more serious as

Ferebe talked. He didn't seem *surprised* though, Raco
decided. It was clear the Emperor already knew something of the Shards and the other creatures. He nodded
grimly when Ferebe spoke of how the mounted warrior
was killed. 'We have called them Flays, skinned men.
And they *are* men, it appears – or once were – Fine and
Sidhe. What say you, Raco?'

'We know nothing of their origin, sir. They have
killed many Fine and Sidhe. We have no such magics.'

'Aye . . .' Tebron assented. 'That is my opinion also.
But they must be coming from somewhere.' He had the
pale eyes of the Shoreth and they looked grave as he
considered the options.

'Sir, we found this. We think one of the Shards was
wearing it – perhaps had taken it from its creator . . .'
she took the necklace from around her neck and gave it
to Tebron who blanched visibly. He did not open it or
examine it closely, it was clear he knew exactly what it
was and, probably, who it belonged to. 'Very . . . very
few people may possess these,' he muttered. 'Very few.'

There was a moment's silence as the Emperor
collected his thoughts.

'I am sorry, sir,' Ferebe said. 'It appears we have
brought you bad news.'

'Worse than you know, Ferebe Vezul. I have had
word that yesterday afternoon the barracks at Kamala
Sev were attacked by around fifty Shards and Flays.
Young warriors training for my own guard were killed.
The monsters reached the compound and killed some
of the *Sanah*.'

Ferebe's eyes widened in alarm. 'Storm? Is Storm all
right?'

'Yes, although *Sanah* Tasc gave his life to hold back the Flay until help arrived. Eventually the barracks were gutted by fire and that either destroyed them, or they vanished as you describe.'

Ferebe was visibly shaken.

'Who's Storm?' Raco frowned.

They ignored his question. 'And my father?'

'He is well . . .' the Emperor looked saddened and weary. 'And now, the evidence would seem to suggest that one of our own is planning these attacks. A traitor in our midst.' He stared down at the necklace and clenched his long, white fingers more tightly around it as if he could throttle its owner through such an action.

'He knows,' Raco thought. *'He knows who it is . . .'*

'I must speak with Zarrus and review the situation,' Tebron sighed. 'Ferebe Vezul, try and get some sleep. Report back here in the morning. I suspect there is nothing to be done that need concern you. You will want to get home to Kamala Sev. Raco, perhaps you can be our ambassador, unofficially of course, and assure our neighbours we are dealing with the matter.'

The very idea of being an ambassador for the Shoreth – officially or otherwise – was an affront to Raco but he could see that Tebron was tired and in for a long night, so he held his peace and simply smiled non-committally. 'So I am free to go?'

'Indeed. Lieutenant Vezul's actions were perfectly wise and correct, of course, but it would appear events have overtaken us.'

*

Once they left the audience chamber, Raco could not resist a jibe. 'So, you went to all that trouble to truss me up and the big chief says I can go home . . .'

Ferebe didn't respond.

'So who's Storm? Is it your favourite horse? Hmm?'

Still she didn't respond. Her expression was grim and set. Finally, they reached the door to their rooms and she turned on him. 'I'm glad it's all so laughable to you, Raco. Friends of mine have been killed, my teacher *Sanah* is dead. Still, you can go home in the morning and the Fine can relax in the knowledge that this is a plague the Shoreth have visited on themselves. Goodnight.' She went into her room and slammed the door – Raco half expected to hear dramatic sobbing from within but Ferebe was made of sterner stuff. He shrugged awkwardly at the guards by his own door at the same time berating himself for being a stupid, insensitive fool. 'Women, eh?'

Once inside his room he stood by the through door listening but could hear nothing from Ferebe's side. He knocked quietly. 'I'm sorry, Ferebe Vezul . . .' there was no reply so he went to bed feeling less than pleased with himself. The bed was cold and uncomfortable but he was exhausted and drifted into sleep without extinguishing the lantern.

He woke suddenly, immediately aware that a sound had woken him. It was an instinctive movement to sit bolt upright and reach for his sword; except his sword was not there and he bashed his head on the ornate wooden carving of the bedhead. 'Oww!'

There was the small, unmistakeable sound of suppressed laughter, which escaped as something of a snort. Ferebe Vezul stood at the side of his bed clutching a heavy blanket around her.

'Don't get any ideas, *Yekt*. I couldn't sleep, that's all.' She smiled as she said this, still amused by his awakening. 'Thought you might like some company.' She didn't wait for him to accept or decline her invitation but climbed onto the bed to sit at the other end. Her pale, delicate feet protruded from the end of the quilted blanket, reminding Raco of the rag-bodied dolls with clay feet and hands which the Fine children played with. Although he did not for a moment consider himself attracted to Ferebe Vezul, Raco had the inexplicable desire to take hold of her feet, to feel if they were cold and to warm them . . . he checked himself.

'I don't think it's a good idea that you're in my room, Ferebe,' he said.

'Oh rubbish. No one will know . . . Just relax will you . . . oh.' She coloured suddenly, and not unattractively.

'What?'

'Oh . . .'

'What?'

'You don't think I came in to seduce you do you?'

'*No.*'

'You *do*, don't you? You're not my type, you know,' she mocked. 'I don't see men outside my species.'

'Ha! How d'you explain Felndar then? A pig if ever there was one.'

Her smile faded and she looked instantly chastened. Raco was struggling with this other version of Ferebe Vezul, this one who could be hurt by mere words – he fleetingly missed the Ferebe who had knocked him out and captured him. 'I'm sorry . . . look . . .' he began fumbling beneath the coverlet. 'Raco!' she was shocked and her hand flew to cover her mouth in salacious, very girlish glee.

'No! No, look. Look,' he insisted. He tilted to one side and showed her the mass of black and purple bruising which covered his ribs.

'By the Goddess,' she breathed, 'did that happen in the battle with the Shards?'

'No,' he said, his tone one of righteous indignation. 'It happened before. This is how Felndar treated prisoners.'

'Oh. I didn't know him very well. It's just that we were supposed to be betrothed – at least I thought we were before I was drafted. So did everyone else. He didn't like me, anyway,' she looked slightly petulant about this, 'didn't like the fact I was drafted into an immediate officer position – even though I could ride better and fight better than he could. Still, there's no point speaking ill of the dead.'

'No,' Raco thought perhaps he should steer the conversation onto more cheerful ground. 'So tell me about your horse – Storm – he must be pretty special if you asked after him before your father.'

She laughed, 'Storm's not a horse! He's a mammoth. He's *the* White Mammoth.'

'Wow.' Raco was impressed. He'd heard about the Shoreth mammoths but he'd never seen one – they had not used them in the battle for Durghanti and he had heard that they were all stabled – if that was the correct word – at Kamala Sev as the slightly warmer weather there was better for them. None of the Fine had seen the mammoths for quite a few years and it was believed their numbers were in decline. 'A white mammoth eh? That's pretty special.'

'Yes,' she yawned. 'His birth was foretold by our Priestesses. He and I have a special connection – I saw him on the night he was born. Would you like to see him? Just come to Kamala Sev sometime and ask for me . . .' They both knew that was never likely to happen but for the moment they let the idea that Raco could just drop by to Kamala Sev stand. Raco had slid back under the covers from his sitting position and Ferebe was also lying down. It was still raining outside and both listened silently to the sound of the deluge spattering against the wooden shutters and trickling down through the grooves of the old stone building.

'Are you going to sleep, Ferebe?' Raco asked wearily. She didn't answer and so he assumed she had already drifted off. He glanced again at her feet, which seemed almost to glow in the low light of the room. Giving in to his impulse, he reached out and gently but firmly took hold of them – they were cold as marble – and began to stroke them. There was nothing overtly sexual in the caress; it was simply an expression of warm exhaustion. Ferebe's breathing was slowing as she fell asleep and she did not react at first. Then, just as Raco was beginning to black out himself, he heard her sleepy voice.

'Raco, I'm sorry I called you *Yekt*.'

True to his word, Yiska had selected the oldest, calmest horse for Effie who had mounted up with great trepidation, feeling renewed self-consciousness as she watched the others who all appeared to be experienced riders. She wondered how Talisker had learned to ride so well in Edinburgh until she reminded herself he had spent years in Sutra. Perhaps, if he really was deluded, he'd never ridden before like her but he believed he was a great rider – whichever it was it seemed to work for him and he looked happy and comfortable in the saddle.

Comfort was not something Effie was currently *au fait* with. Despite the bright frozen cold she was sweating profusely; the sweat was immediately chilled and made prickly on her skin by the wind. She felt sick, which, strangely enough was quite unusual for Effie – apart from the unfortunate episode when she and Yiska had first met, Effie rarely *felt* sick. Self-infliction was different; she told herself it was control. Now, she had lost that control by setting something in motion in her body by drinking the Ipecac – something that she increasingly feared might be liver failure.

Around her the awesome beauty of the Canyon De Chelly became a red blur as moment by moment she slipped into a world of delirium and pain. Yiska had been right, it was quiet in the canyon, only the gentle sound of the horses and the occasional sharp, high call of an eagle or buzzard broke the silence. Or so she thought at first. After a while she realised there were sounds, tiny scuttling or dry rattling as rodents or snakes cleared the way for the riders. The horse's breathing was calming and Effie felt herself joining in, breathing in long unison – after a few minutes she was sure she could hear another sound. She couldn't identify it at first; a steady mellow pulsation that seemed to emanate from no one source but travel with her and the other riders. When she realised that what she could hear was a heartbeat, she was unable to decide whether or not it was her own or the horses – perhaps even the other riders. This thought, this realisation that she had enhanced awareness, frightened her somehow and she gave a nervous laugh, which was louder than she intended and echoed around the canyon.

'Effie, are you all right?' Yiska called back without looking.

'Fine,' she lied.

They reached the floor of the canyon before she collapsed. Her last thought was *'sorry . . .'* as she pitched dramatically off her horse and landed in the white sand although she couldn't have said who she thought she was apologising to.

'Oh Christ!' Talisker who was riding just ahead of her, leapt off the back of his horse. 'Yiska, Rodney, wait up!' They gathered around her crumpled body, Yiska began checking her pulse and looking at her pupils. He said nothing but his face was strained, almost frightened looking.

'Why didn't she say something?' Talisker fumed uselessly. 'I knew she didn't look well but . . . what's wrong with her, Yiska?'

Yiska looked up into the unforgiving glare of the sun. 'She's dying, Talisker.'

Effie knows none of this. She is somewhere else, somewhere *other* . . . It's jumbled at first, she's galloping on a horse, then in a boat, then she flies, arms out-stretched like the Angel of the North, buzzing and spinning in dizzying freefall. The pain is still there, but it is contained in its own, separate place that may or may not be part of her. The pain is yellow. Bright yellow . . . but *she* is blue and green, she is music and momentum. She will dance forever . . .

Up ahead, there's cessation. She can see the dark. It's frightening – her music can't go there . . .

'Effie.' There's someone beside her. They're still flying, moving like bird/fish in a sky/sea. The other says nothing. With a flare of light it draws ahead, twisting and weaving inviting Effie to follow. There's no thought connected with Effie's flight but somewhere, deep in her brain she knows she doesn't want to pursue the lights – it's going *there* . . .

So she tries to protest. 'No!' But there's no being, no physical entity to vocalise her shout. Colours flash in the stream like belligerent fireworks. 'No!'

Maybe they're here. Maybe her friends are around her – she just can't see them – Talisker, Yiska, maybe Malky . . . 'Help meeee!'

But she's lost. Swept away towards oblivion. When the pain stops, Effie will stop too.

Chapter Seven

It seems he is affecting me. The imp. In unexpected ways. For example, he doesn't like me writing this journal, it threatens him somehow. It has been some time since he . . . joined me and, for the most part, physically, I have fared well. But mentally, it's different.

I think about the fact he's there; inside me. Although I have thought about it rationally, he cannot be in the same repulsive form. It is not possible. Surely not.

Ah, he's trying to stop me. My hands are cramping . . . for a moment there, I lost the sense of the words. They seemed to dance meaninglessly across the page as though taunting me. I wonder fleetingly, why he is so threatened but then, I remember, words have power – words imprisoned him and words, my words to be precise, set him free.

So I must be brief. But I will record what I have done so far and what I . . . we plan to do. It might be treason and genocide but he has convinced me the rewards will be mine.

Oh, but before I go on I must digress briefly. My appearance is changing and people have begun to notice. My hair has turned from its faded gold blond to jet black and my skin has acquired a slightly sallow appearance. Whilst these changes do not worry me in themselves and none of my captains or lieutenants would dare to question me, it grieves me to think that they might assume they are simply vanity. I ask him about them (I can do this by merely thinking) and the 'answer' comes from within my own mind, drifting like a disembodied song.

'Unimportant. Maybe I looked like that . . . cannot remember.' He still speaks to me in the language of the Fine but his 'voice' – as I hear it – has changed some-what, grown stronger and less rasping.

Anyway, he woke me somehow. It was two nights after the end of the failed Durghanti uprising. 'I have something to show you,' he told me. I thought that this might necessitate me walking through the palace so I got up to put my robes on. 'No, no,' he whispered impatiently, 'just close your eyes.'

I did as he bid me and, immediately, an image formed in my mind; it was a dark foreboding place whose cavernous ceilings reached so high above that birds or bats flitted noiselessly amongst the rafters. It was cold, chill winds blew from nowhere and although I peered into the far distance I was unable to see any means of entrance.

But the thought occurred within moments that it was no mere image I was seeing. I reached out and touched the nearest stone column; it was cold and solid to the touch as I expected. I was here . . . wherever here might be.

'Where is this place?' I said aloud.

'Elsewhere . . .' he attempted to be casual but I could discern from his tone that the place was somehow of his creation. 'Do not whisper, Zarrus. It is yours. Speak loud.'

I did not see that this mattered but I said nothing, he was obviously proud of his creation.

'Look behind you.'

I turned around; a gasp escaped me and I stumbled back in my shock and surprise until my back made contact with the stone of the column.

Rows and rows of stone slabs, neat lines which stretched away into the darkness in regimented grimness. On each slab was a dead body. I walked towards the nearest one feeling my legs tremble like some virgin warrior in his first combat. He was a Fine warrior, killed by an axe or sword blow to the chest – and the next, another warrior whose head was all but decapitated, held on by a ropey piece of sinew . . . and the next, and the next. There are Sidhe amongst the fallen and a few Shoreth. I knew within moments of seeing the first corpse who these unfortunates were; the Lost. The fallen of the Durghanti uprising.

Inside my head I felt him – I did not wish to know what was going on in there but my impression was that he was capering mindlessly as he had on the night we met. I felt nauseated – not by the corpses, I had seen many before and death did not move me – but by him. His laughter was unbearably loud.

'Behold,' he said. 'Your army awaits.'

He taught me much. He taught me the depths of mine own iniquity. He taught me the pleasure to be had in exerting power over the souls of the dead. It took me some practice, and my early samples we set 'free' at random in the forests for the fun of it. I watched them through scrying. They came to be called 'Shards' by both the Fine and the Shoreth but those early creatures were not strong enough to survive for longer than a few hours. As I perfected my craft, working with the corpses, whittling their fat, rejoining or remaking limbs which I plundered from other bodies, the magics grew stronger . . .

Wait, wait . . . let me tell it . . .

But all power must have a source. And to continue my making I needed raw, magical energy. This I took from the Sidhe with no resistance. It wasn't as if they consciously gave up their transformation magics but rather that we took them unchallenged. This surprised me somewhat – it was as if they didn't know what they had. With the Sidhe power we forged a link to the deepest reaches of the void – a well, into which we cast the discarded souls of the dead to replace them with hellish spirits whose burning desire to find form made them extremely suitable to reanimate the empty corpses . . .

. . . but it does not matter if they know. This book will only be read in the event of my demise. I will tell you later. Sometimes it seems as if he sleeps. I want to tell you about the prayers . . .

'Raco! Wake up!' There was a cold 'whummph' sound as something was thrown on top of Raco's sleeping figure, something heavy like a riding cloak.

'Wha . . . ?'

'Move it! Now!' It was Ferebe's voice. Not the younger, softer Ferebe of the night before, but the I'm-in-charge Ferebe who Raco respected. Raco opened his eyes.

It was only just dawn, a weak light spread questing fingers through the crack in the shutters and the room was cold. Ferebe was standing at the end of the bed, fully clothed in the silver and black of a Shoreth Rider. Her face was a picture of consternation. 'Get dressed, quickly!'

Her tone was so urgent that Raco obeyed without hesitation; he was mostly dressed anyway, the room had been so cold the night before. He slipped on his buckskin boots as he spoke. 'What's going on?'

'I've just been down to the kitchens and . . . oh no!' There was the solid sound of running feet coming up the corridor. 'Hide!'

'What for?'

'Just do it!' she commanded.

Without much inspiration Raco ducked down under the cover on the far side of the bed. There wasn't much space beneath the bed but, once the covers were bundled over him he squeezed himself under. His hiding place wouldn't bear much inspection but he hoped there wouldn't be any. He heard Ferebe run out into the hall. 'I've searched his room. He's not there . . . You there, check the privies at the end of the hall. Has anyone been to the kitchens? He must have passed through that way. You. Go and alert the stable master . . .'

'There was a chorus of 'Yes Ma'ams' plus a 'Yessir!' from one of the guards who couldn't come to terms with the idea of a female superior. The footsteps dispersed and there was a long moment of silence before Ferebe came back into the room, closing the door with a soft click. 'Raco? Come on . . .'

Cursing under his breath Raco managed to slide out of his cramped position. 'I'm not going anywhere until you tell me what's happening, Ferebe.'

'Fair enough, let them kill you,' she scowled.

'Why?'

'It's the Emperor. He's dead. Assassinated in the night. You were the only Fine in the centre of the city.'

'What?' Raco was horrified and saddened. Against all expectations, he'd liked the Shoreth Emperor. 'I'm the prime suspect?'

'Yes, let's go.' She walked across to the window and cautiously pushed back the shutters, looking around before beckoning him forward. It was an easy escape route; beneath the level of the window an ornate portico stuck out a few feet. It would be an easy matter to drop down off the side. Ferebe had thought of everything even under such pressure, two horses were tethered nearby – even better, by chance, the guards could only exit on the other side of the building, making their route longer if Raco's escape was detected. Raco hesitated.

'Come on,' Ferebe urged.

'Wait a minute,' he frowned. 'I didn't kill the Emperor. I was asleep, here, all night . . . with you. Ferebe, why are you doing this? You could provide me with an alibi.'

She wouldn't meet his gaze. 'I – I can't. Look there's no time to discuss this . . .'

'You mean you *won't*.' He folded his arms, refusing to budge.

'Please, Raco. I would be dishonoured.'

'But nothing happened.'

'They don't know that.'

'So, for the sake of a minor indiscretion, I will be branded an assassin?'

'It will not be considered minor. I will be flogged. Please . . . please go.'

The sound of commotion from somewhere behind them urged Raco to action. 'All right, Ferebe Vezul, but you must come too.'

She nodded sharply. 'You will need my help anyway to get over the bridge. I can distract the sentry.' Raco was already climbing through the window trying to find his footing on the sloping tiles above the portico which were slippery with the rain. 'You will owe me a big favour, Ferebe . . . owww!' He slid gracelessly down the tiles, his already bruised ribcage taking a fresh battering. Ferebe followed without comment, eventually landing lightly on the ground beside him.

They almost made it to the bridge without detection, the horses were fresh and fast and Ferebe's quick thinking had gained them precious minutes. However, just as *Aon Crann* hove into view there was a shout from behind them.

'She is aiding the assassin's escape! After them!' Ferebe cursed in response to this and they both pressed their horses into a full gallop.

Raco risked a glance back, it was difficult to make out much as he was thrown around by the motion of his horse, but it appeared only three or four of the palace guards were following them at first. At the forefront though was a different looking rider, the way he sat his horse instantly recognisable to Raco; an Inquisitor. It was the Inquisitor who had shouted. A bell was ringing from the city and more riders were streaming through the gates. Some were only just appraised of the situation, calling to each other – 'The Emperor is dead! The Fine have assassinated the Emperor!'

Raco urged his horse forward, it was breathing hard, a rasping sound catching in its throat. 'Come on, horse, don't fail me,' he muttered through gritted teeth. Ferebe was ahead of him and she managed to catch the sentry unawares. He had just stepped out from the guard post the see what the commotion was about as she galloped past, kicking out with a booted foot which landed square in his chest. Raco heard her screech as she exhorted her horse forward. Raco passed the unfortunate sentry as he was picking himself off the ground but didn't draw a weapon on him – the man was winded and no threat.

The Inquisitor rider was gaining, Raco could hear the harsh snorting and breathing of his mount. The other riders were much further behind. Raco decided to make a stand at the end of *Aon Crann* if his pursuer maintained the distance between them. They were on the Fine portion of the bridge now.

There was a cry from behind him which he first took to be a curse – perhaps the Inquisitor's horse had stumbled – but then, a green flash zipped over him and exploded just above Ferebe's head in a blaze of green light. The sound, which ricocheted up and down the river valley was enough to spook both horses and Raco fought for control as his mount reared, whinnying in sharp terror.

As he pulled his reins around to contain the horse's fright by leading it in a circle, the Inquisitor was within fifty feet of him. He cursed, 'Come on horse, come on . . .' He knew it was useless to let the sound of panic enter his voice but it was difficult – almost impossible – to do otherwise. The Inquisitor was grinning nastily as he knew he could close in for the kill.

'*Yekt*,' he taunted. 'taste the Emperor's justice.' In the instant he spoke Raco had a flash of insight; this man *knew* he had not killed the Emperor. But the feeling was fleeting, gone before he could acknowledge it. A scream issued from behind him as Ferebe was thrown from her mount. Raco drew his sword, but to his surprise, the Inquisitor stopped his horse a few feet away and then turned and trotted off the bridge.

'Coward!' Raco yelled, not without some satisfaction. 'Come on then!'

'Raco!' He ignored Ferebe's shout at first as he waited for the Inquisitor to turn back and charge into the fray. It was the rider's smug expression which alerted him to the fact Ferebe was in big trouble.

Aon Crann was alive; the green flare had been some unexpected magic by the Inquisitor bringing dark, unnatural life to its timbers. The sound of wood splintering rent the air as huge green tendrils spewed forth from inside the bridge. All Raco's boyhood questions were answered; *Aon Crann was* one tree, had always been alive. But now, no longer constrained by whatever ancient magics had commanded it to be a bridge, the spirit of *Aon Crann* was angry. Ferebe was already entangled by tentacles, one from either side of the bridge had wrapped around her legs, anchoring her while another snaked out to wrap around her neck. She lashed about her with her sword but there were simply too many – smaller, thinner tendrils came from cracks which rent the ground of the tree beneath her feet.

Raco ran forward unhesitatingly and chopped away at the bonds around her neck first and then her legs. It seemed he had precious moments before the bridge became aware of his presence. The green snake-like tendrils were sinewy and hard to break, each one took a few blows. Raco noticed from the corner of his eye that dismembered shoots writhed for a moment before relenting to become vegetable matter once more, some pieces even crawled away like fat repugnant caterpillars.

Even as he freed Ferebe, *Aon Crann* made Raco captive; there was a strange, high-pitched sound as the tentacles unwound, as if the bridge were screaming. Ferebe turned to help him the instant she was freed but Raco could see the hopelessness of it. 'Run, Ferebe Vezul!' he yelled.

She hesitated for a moment and the bridge sent questing shoots slithering along the ground towards her. With a snarl she hacked the ends of them but began to do as Raco had said and retreated across the bridge.

The branches were thick and corpulent with unnatural life. Soon, Raco could see nothing but *Aon Crann*; his whole vision obscured by a cage of new branches. He could feel the organic manacles around his waist and neck begin to tighten and, dropping his blade in order to tear helplessly at his neck, Raco knew he was doomed. He cried aloud to the Goddess Salkit to save him, or at the very least accept his soul.

And, for a moment, it seemed his prayer was heard. Raco became *Kellid*. As the power of *Kellid* surged through his body, Raco's yell became a bellow and then a growl. He ripped the fronds away as though they were made of paper and, sensing the change in its victim, *Aon Crann* began to withdraw. But Raco's transformation was being made on borrowed magics and as the contact was lost those areas of his body which were clear of branches became Raco once more – so that he was at once both Raco and *Kellid*, a state of being that was dangerous and unnatural. And once the bridge sensed Raco as a man again, it attacked with renewed speed and venom.

In one moment Raco's neck and head transformed from bear to man, back to bear once more. *Kellid* fought Raco's mind as well as his wracked body for control. *Kellid*'s instincts were ever to stand and fight but, in the frenzy of twisting and bellowing, Raco managed to form a coherent thought: 'Run!' If he could run, once the branches loosed him, he would become Raco again and he would stand a small chance of survival if he could outdistance the limbs of *Aon Crann*.

As soon as *Kellid* ripped away the bonds around his hips and thighs Raco began to move forward with as much speed as he could muster. Bears could be deadly fast creatures when they chose but *Kellid*'s legs were undergoing the change back to Raco's own and that slowed him. Raco ignored the burning pain the clash of magics was causing, his only thought to move forward, to run, to survive. He sensed the disappointment of *Kellid* but knew his totem would allow Raco control, it was ever thus between the Sidhe and their cohorts, and so he pressed ahead, becoming less *Kellid* and more Raco – faster but more vulnerable.

He could see the end of *Aon Crann* and he was almost all Raco now. Pain wracked up and down his body, his legs were flashes of flame – Ferebe was there, he saw her react as he burst through the writhing screen of branches. Just as he began to entertain thoughts of safety, he heard Ferebe scream a warning as a thick snake of malevolent vine whipped towards him from the entryway of the bridge. There was no way past, only one escape. Without pause, Raco turned and leapt from the side of the bridge to the river, half a league below. As he fell, the searing agony left him for blissful seconds before he hit the water.

It was mid-afternoon by the time she found him. There were few tracks down into Cerne's Gorge and Ferebe was being followed. Twice she had seen searching patrols; once of Palace Guards and once Shoreth Riders. The former were easy to avoid, they blundered about the undergrowth as if mounted on mammoths, their searching half-hearted, but the latter were silent, more focussed and disciplined. After Raco's heart-stopping leap from *Aon Crann* the bridge had fallen silent and inactive once more. Ferebe had not stopped to see but she imagined the search parties had waited a while before crossing – this had allowed her an unknown length of time to get ahead.

She travelled on foot, since her horse had skittered off in panic during the fight at the bridge, but it didn't matter, the terrain was easier on foot. At first she had followed the trail, but after about an hour she left the path and tried a more direct descent through the trees. The sides of the gorge were steep but the trees and undergrowth impeded her progress so that, rather than gain unwanted momentum, she slithered down a bit at a time, crashing to a partially controlled halt by another tree further down. Occasionally, where the ground was really muddy from the overnight rain, she lost her footing completely and tumbled helplessly for twenty or thirty yards. She didn't cry out as instinct demanded but cursed silently the worst oaths she knew. There was no opportunity to cover her tracks but the brambles and ivy which blanketed the slopes did her a favour and sprung back after she passed. A good tracker could follow her easily, but only if he noted where she'd left the trail – and she had taken great care at that point.

By the time she neared the base of the gorge, Ferebe was covered in cuts and stings. Her pale skin was especially sensitive to plant pollens and spores and the side of her face was hugely bloated where a bramble had snagged her and caused a nasty reaction. The sleeves of her jerkin were virtually shredded and green plant stains streaked her arms where she'd grabbed on to ivy creepers. Still, she congratulated herself on having made good time as she dabbed at her bleeding nose.

The river was wide here, a rushing torrent after the rain, the grey granite pebbles of its banks blackened in the wet. Ferebe followed the current downstream fervently hoping Raco had not been washed to the opposite shore. She was sure he would be dead but felt she should check. If she was honest with herself, the idea of his death dismayed her but she refused to acknowledge this feeling too directly. She ignored the pain in her chest, the physical manifestation of her fear and so, when she saw his body – a crumpled mess of sodden buckskin entangled with detritus from the river – she was appalled when a thin wail of sorrow escaped her.

'Raco!' She broke into a run but stopped short near his body afraid to touch it for some reason. His long black hair was spread outwards like a birds' wing, obscuring his face; she had not noticed, or rather, not acknowledged before, that he had many tiny brown and white feathers plaited into it. He was lying awkwardly on his front with his left arm trapped beneath him and his hips twisted to one side – she could imagine he was sleeping . . .

'Raco,' she breathed. 'I'm so sorry.' Kneeling down beside him she pushed the hair away from his face and tried to straighten his body. It was cold but still pliant. She reached to untangle his feet from the mass of weed and twigs which had become anchored there. Ferebe did not weep easily but she told herself delayed reaction was setting in as she felt the warm sting of tears on her face.

'Ferebe Vezul . . .'

She started. 'Raco? Raco? Did you speak?'

'No, you imagined it . . .' His voice was weak and pain-addled but he was alive.

'Thank the gods. It's a miracle.'

He groaned aloud as he tried to sit up. 'If it was a miracle, it wouldn't bloody hurt so much. Did you see that bastard?'

'What?' Ferebe was confused for a moment, still amazed that Raco had survived.

'On the bridge. The one who brought *Aon Crann* to

life – he was dressed like an Inquisitor . . . what's wrong? Oh . . .'

Ferebe was staring in a mixture of fascination and horror at Raco's left arm. From the shoulder down it was the arm of Raco's transformed self – the bear, *Kellid.* 'Does – does it hurt?' she whispered.

'No.' Raco flexed the arm and wriggled the fingers which were now brown, curved claws. 'It feels . . . funny. Doesn't hurt though. I'd guess that it's how *Kellid* kept me alive – left me his strength as I dived off the bridge.'

Ferebe was not sure about the machinations of the Sidhe and their totem animals. She had heard about it but never seen such a thing. 'Does that mean he – *Kellid* – wherever he goes when he's not with you, does that mean he has your arm?'

'Possibly. I'm not sure,' Raco admitted.

Ferebe reached out and touched the dank fur, beneath the pelt were huge muscles, twice the thickness of Raco's other arm. When she withdrew her hand she instinctively sniffed at her fingers; the scent of bear was not unpleasant, just a warm musk.

Raco grinned at her as he stood up, testing his legs and wincing with pain – she noted the way he pushed with his bear's arm already favouring its strength. 'Seems I'll have to groom it!'

She laughed at the idea.

'So what now?' Raco asked.

'I can't go back,' Ferebe shrugged. 'They think I'm in league with you and . . .'

' . . . and they think the Fine infiltrated Durghanti to assassinate the Emperor. What a mess,' Raco groaned.

'Much as it grieves me to say this, I think we should warn Ruannoch Were.'

'Warn?'

'You don't think the Shoreth will take the murder of their Emperor lying down do you? Someone will be made to pay and my guess is, it will be Ruannoch Were.'

There was much debate about Effie. Yiska and Rodney argued for a while in low voices – it made little difference to Talisker as they were speaking predominantly in Navajo, although a few words like 'hospital' and 'Chinle' were obvious.

Talisker sat on the ground with Effie cradled against him, wrapped in a warming blanket like some giant baby. He studied her face closely, remembering how he had mistaken her for Shula when he first saw her in the hospital; she was very like her mother physically but, emotionally Effie was a minefield all her own. He couldn't believe he'd let Shula's daughter feel so alone that she abused herself to the point of death. Talisker knew all about self-loathing, he was a past master, and yet he hadn't even thought to enquire how she was over the past couple of years. Apart from letting her the apartment via Sandro, he'd had no contact with Effie. She wasn't his responsibility and yet no one could tell him he hadn't let her down. Beneath the thin skin of her eyelids a shadow moved as her eyes tracked back and forth.

'She's dreaming, Yiska. Is that good?' He didn't look up or wait for Yiska's response. 'Effie . . . I know where you are. I've been there . . . it's a dark place but . . .' He looked up at Yiska and Rodney who were observing him with a kind of stoic sympathy. 'Yiska, can we make camp here?'

'Sure, but it might be better to take her back to Chinle to the hospital. In fact, I'm sure they have a 'copter. Maybe we . . .'

Rodney interrupted him. 'You know there's little time, Michael.'

'And so there's equally little time to send for a *ndilniihii.*' Yiska snapped.

'A what?'

'*Sicheii* wants to send for a hand-trembler to diagnose her,' he shrugged. 'It would make little difference, if we went the traditional route – we know what's wrong, and there's no singer in the area as far as I know.' Yiska took out his two-way radio and frowned down at it. 'Maybe I can raise help . . .' He fiddled with the buttons but there, directly beneath the canyon walls, the reception was poor; static and the occasional disjointed sound that might have been a voice were all that could be heard.

Talisker's mind was so taken aback at this strange fusion of culture and technology that, for a moment, he forgot what he had been going to suggest. 'I have an idea,' he said. 'If we can make camp and make her comfortable . . .'

Yiska nodded. 'I suspect she's taken something nasty that's upset her liver and her kidneys. If we could flush her system with water it *might* help – too late to pump her stomach, I'm afraid.'

'But she'd have to be conscious to get fluids into her unless you've got saline in your bag.'

'No, even if I did, we couldn't rig up an IV. What's your idea?'

Talisker nodded towards the small cedar box that had fallen from Effie's bag when she toppled from her horse. 'I think we should send someone to get her.'

Effie's drifting. The music is gone, there's just stagnation and silence. The yellow is still there somewhere – like an unseen sky – not unconsciousness exactly, but rather a different consciousness. She's still afraid and she hums to herself, a tuneless little hum which sounds like a child's voice carrying out across the vast emptiness. Her thoughts are disjointed fragments of emotion rather than expression but she feels sure that the other light she saw had been her mother. So much she could have said had she only been able and her mother not trying to guide her to oblivion. *Gee, thanks ma* . . .

'Effie.' It's Malky. He's just suddenly there, beside her. She's not 'flying' any more like she was. She looks down. She is standing on a black featureless ground, surrounded by black, featureless . . . well, nothing. But at least she can see her own body, arms, legs, feet.

'Hiya, Malky. You look . . . nice.' So he does – why would he be a ghost here? If here is where he can be *real* . . . 'Am I dead?'

'Naw hen. But no a kick in the arse off it either.'

'Oh. I took some stupid medicine.'

'Aye.'

'They'll never let me come with them now.'

'Eh?'

'To Sutra. They'll never let me now.'

'Ah don't think they've thought about it yet,' Malky said tactfully.

'Yeah well . . . it's true, I'm a liability.'

'Mebbe so but I think they'd prefer you to be a live liability.'

'There's nothing I can do.' She was walking now, quite purposefully although she had no idea where she was going. Malky didn't follow her, he was giving her a disapproving look. 'But that's no true Effie. It's all about taking control . . .'

She stopped. 'Malky, what kind of psychobabble shite is that? Trust me, I've heard it all before. I've been in therapy for three years.'

'Well, I'd ask for my money back . . .'

'Why aren't you walking with me?'

'I dinnae want tae get stuck here and I will if I follow ye – I've got stuff tae do. And so have you. It's different now – you've got folk that care about you. Talisker and Yiska are in a right state.' Malky was having to raise his voice now, as he was further away.

'Really?' She called back. She had to admit, that pleased her somewhat.

'Effie? Goan' come back eh? Please . . .' His voice dwindled into the distance and she wondered who was more upset, Talisker or Yiska. She knew what she hoped and was ashamed of herself for being so needy. *Not an attractive quality, Euphemia,* she chided herself.

'Look. If I get stuck here, ah'm bloody well goin' tae bug you fer ever an' ever.' Malky appeared again. It wasn't that he'd walked or run to catch up, rather he'd vanished – maybe gone back to his box? – and reappeared.

'For ever and ever, eh? That's a bloody long time to look at your ugly mug Malky.'

He grinned. 'So you'll come then?'

Chapter Eight

Although Talisker hadn't thought about it directly he'd been making the assumption they would be practically alone in the canyon. So he was surprised when he saw lights tracking down the rim and others further along the canyon floor west, towards Chinle. When he pointed them out to Yiska he didn't seem worried.

'The canyon is populated by shepherds and farmers, Duncan. The soil here is fertile, the rainwater carries nutrients from Defiance Plateau. Where we are heading along Canyon Del Muerto, there's not many folk.' He nodded towards the lights. 'I think they're coming to find the gateway too, though – they just don't know it yet. *Sicheii* says his friend told him many are heading for the place they saw in their dreams.'

'Many – how many?' Talisker felt something akin to panic although he couldn't fathom why.

Yiska shrugged. 'Hundred maybe . . .'

'Oh no. We'll have to send them away again, Yiska. They could be in danger if we get the gateway open – I've seen it before, things can come through . . .'

'We are not in charge, Talisker. If people want to come, who are we to stop them?' Yiska seemed unfased. 'How is she?' he nodded towards Effie.

'I don't know. Malk said he'd try to help but he was pretty pessimistic about it.' Talisker had called Malky and spoken to him out of sight of the little encampment

160

they'd made. Rodney had looked curious when he'd wandered off with the little box but he'd said nothing. It was a relief to Talisker to know Malky was around but he didn't feel ready to show him off to anyone else.

That was the problem really, he thought as he watched the wavering lights; it was like showing your unique and personal neurosis to complete strangers. Talisker was under no illusions about Malky's existence – he knew it to be true – but, like Sutra, like all of the things that had happened to him over the last hundred or so years, it was deeply personal. The only other person who could understand was Sandro and for the first time (but he was sure it wouldn't be the last) Talisker wished he'd just called him and asked him to come along. He sighed, pride was a terrible thing and his worse than most.

'I guess we'll know soon,' he muttered to Yiska.

Lake glanced back at the wide-eyed silent children who were following him down the trail. It's good to have fans, he thought, self-mockingly. There were five of them, all aged about under ten – except perhaps the biggest who may have been a teenager – and they had appeared over the rim of the trail a few minutes earlier. They hadn't tried to strike up any conversation but the smallest girl kept giggling every now and then which was beginning to irritate him. Lake wasn't big on children, to be honest they unnerved him and he knew it was because they wouldn't swallow any BS. And BS was something he *was* pretty big on.

He stopped suddenly in his tracks and heard their feet scuffing in the dirt as they tried to stop in time to maintain their 'safe' distance. Turning slowly from his hips he lowered his sunglasses down his nose and waggled his eyebrows at them in his best Magnum P.I. impersonation. This prompted a ripple of giggling and even a shriek of laughter from the girls.

'Hey, any of you kids fast runners? I mean *real* fast?'

They glanced at one another nervously before the oldest boy spoke up. 'We're all real fast mister.'

'Oh good. That's good . . .' The boy frowned, awaiting Lake's response but Lake paused with great deliberation. 'Y'see, I reckon the snow's gonna start soon and down there,' he nodded his head towards the base of the trail, 'my ma has got some stew with my name on it. But she don't know I'm coming – it's a surprise.' He put his pack on the ground and opened the top; the youngest children craned their necks forward to peer in, curiosity getting the better of them. 'Hmm, I know it's here somewhere . . . aha,' with a triumphant flourish Lake pulled a bag of fun-sized Hersheys from the pack. This drew a small, satisfying chorus of 'oooohs'. 'Like to split this among you?'

'Yeaaah,' salacious anticipation dropped from every mouth.

'Well, you kids just whiz on ahead and tell my ma I'm comin'. So she don't eat all the stew see . . .'

The kids raced past him on the trail and then came to an abrupt halt as they all had the same thought simultaneously. 'Mister? Who's your mother?' the eldest boy asked.

'Renee Yazzie – d'you know her?'

'Yeah. Didn't know she had any sons, though . . .'

Yeah. That'll be right.

'My name's Lake McKinnon.'

'Lake McKinnon?' The boy thought about this for a few seconds as if the name might mean something to him and he was trying to remember where he'd heard it.

'I'm an actor,' Lake prompted.

'Oh, okay . . .' The boy shrugged and the group turned to race off down the trail without any further comment.

Lake felt stupidly deflated by this exchange – nothing, not a flicker of recognition. Seemed his mother wasn't exactly shouting his name from the mountain-tops – in fact it seemed she wasn't mentioning him *at all*. He sighed, adjusted his Ray-Bans and dusted the first sprinkling of snow from his crocodile boots by rubbing each one on the back of his legs. It had only been four years, for chrissakes.

The snow was beginning to lie by the time he reached the bottom of the trail. Large confetti-like flakes were coming down fast enough to have dusted the vehicles and tents with a white coating which loaned an unearned cleanliness to some of the rust-bucket cars. It was only the beginning, he had heard on the radio – before it lost its signal – that a cold front of snowstorms was about to dump feet and inches of the stuff all over the area. He didn't understand why there was a pow-wow here and now. He'd been told by his cousin who sent the email that they were going to perform the Enemy Way ceremony as well, although he was sure she must have been mistaken.

For a moment, Lake had the eerie feeling that he was alone in the encampment – the snow had been enough to send most people scurrying indoors to tend to their fires or put more layers of clothing on. A dog was barking somewhere in the distance, the noise like a disconsolate echo, then he heard the low beating sound coming from the mouth of the Mummy Cave. It drifted outwards as if buffeted by the snow; the steady heartbeat of a drum and the mingling of voices which always made the hair stand up on the back of his neck. It was true then, a Singer was in attendance and something extremely unusual was going on . . .

As he glanced in the direction of the cave he saw someone standing in the middle of the path; arms folded tightly across her chest beneath a heavy blanket, her expression a curious mixture of disbelief and annoyance.

'Ma!' Lake dropped his pack and ran forward, grabbing Renee into a warm bear-hug, mainly to shut out the image of her stern, un-amused face. She was wearing what he always used to think of as her 'turtle' expression – that sharp tightness of her upper lip which pulled her normally gentle features into something quite intimidating. At least, it had intimidated him as a child; now, Lake pretended to be oblivious to her displeasure, sure he could win her round. 'Let's go in ma. I don't think this snow's gonna let up . . .' He began to steer her back towards her tent.

'Lake?' she said, bristling with indignation. 'What kinda name is *that*?'

'It's my acting name, ma.'

'So being named after a saint's not good enough for you?'

'Course it is. It was just . . . there was someone else

with the same name and that's not allowed in Hollywood. It's the rules – actors' union . . .'

She sniffed derisively, 'And does the actors' union also have a rule that you're not supposed to write your mother for a year at a time – not supposed to let her know you're alive?'

'It's . . . been difficult, ma. I was filming in the Caribbean.'

She stared at him hard for a moment and, even behind the shelter of his mirrored glasses he could hardly meet her gaze. *Did she know he'd been in rehab? How could she know?* For a moment, he weakened, considered telling her the truth, but then he smiled broadly. 'It's just been hard, ma. I've been so busy and all . . .'

They ducked inside an orange tent which looked like an army surplus medical tent. Millie Talloak was sitting just inside drinking coffee and staring out at the snow with a foreboding expression. 'David,' she said quietly. 'How good to see you.' She said it with a tiny inflection, the veiled implication that she knew he wasn't using that name anymore but she'd be damned if she – his oldest aunt – was going to use some *Hollywood* name.

'How long are you staying son?' his mother asked. 'Have you heard what's been happening?'

Long enough to ask you for a loan, mother. A big loan to get some bad people off my case. Long enough to break your heart all over again . . .

'I'm not sure. Yeah, I heard. Seems pretty unbelievable, though.'

Mille gulped the last of her coffee and stared

dejectedly out towards the Mummy Cave. 'Believe it, David,' she said.

'And so, we were exiled from our homeland after the civil war because we look different from the other Shoreth and they came to believe that the Gods had marked us out. My father says we are not conquerors by choice but by necessity,' Ferebe said. She kept her voice low and stared out towards the river as she spoke; sure she had heard footsteps. It was dusk already and she and Raco had taken shelter in a cave someway up the rock face in one of the steeper, more rugged parts of the gorge. Her instinct was to keep moving, as she knew how single minded the Shoreth Riders were, but they had to stop, Raco was in trouble. She glanced back at him as she realised he had not replied. 'Are you listening to me?'

'Yes,' he mumbled, 'fascinating . . .' He was burning up with fever, a combination of shock and river-water had conspired against him and he could no longer keep going. They had little choice but to find somewhere to hide; although they could not see the rim of the gorge from down here Ferebe could hear the bells ringing out from Durghanti and she knew the woodland of Cerne's Gorge would be teeming with her fellow Shoreth just as soon as they could get Riders down the trail in an organised fashion.

If *Kellid* had saved him as Raco thought, it seemed his totem had deserted him now – when the strength and speed of the animal would have been extremely useful. 'Tell me something,' she urged. 'Tell me about the Sidhe, and why they are so different from the Fine . . .'

she glanced at his bear's limb as she spoke. It seemed the Sidhe were rather more different than the Shoreth appreciated – at least as far as she knew.

'We were exiles too once,' he said. 'Bet you didn't know we had so much in common . . .' he laughed but then broke into a spasm of coughing. 'We came from another world called Lys or Lysmair.'

'Another *world*?' she frowned. 'No, that can't be possible.'

'It was then. The Gods did it . . .' his voice was weakening and Ferebe was pretty sure he was going to pass out into fevered delirium, if he wasn't delirious already. His assertion of another world was unsettling in the quiet darkness.

'Why would the Gods . . .?' she paused, realising that her question implied belief in the Fine and Sidhe Gods and she was still coming to terms with believing in her own. She shook her head in puzzlement.

'It was kind of an accident,' she could only just hear his voice above the sound of the river. '. . . side-effect of a big spell . . .'

Ferebe threw another stick on the fire. She didn't think she'd gathered enough and they were going to get pretty cold over the course of the night. The cave was damp, water trickling through cracks in the rocks leaving streaks of lime on the walls, the tiny sound of the leeching water made the hair on the back of Ferebe's neck prickle, an accompaniment to her nerves. Still, there was a dry ledge near the back of the cave and she'd made Raco lie there giving him her heavy riding cloak to wrap himself in while she attempted to dry off his clothes. She knew the fire was risky and would become even more so as it grew darker but she hoped any tracking Shoreth would be thinking about making camp themselves. As luck would have it, the smoke from the fire, rather than carrying out of the mouth of the cave, was sucked upwards through unseen fissures in the roof – this might be of some benefit, but Ferebe knew that the smell of the woodsmoke was pervasive and would drift downriver in the direction of the wind.

The firelight flared as the weak flames took hold of the fresh piece of wood making the cave momentarily bright. Ferebe glanced towards Raco vaguely planning to ask more about the Sidhe's fables and Gods; 'Shit . . .' she muttered.

Raco had transformed into *Kellid* as unconsciousness claimed him. She had no idea whether this was something voluntary on Raco's part or whether *Kellid* somehow knew when his host was in trouble as Raco had hinted earlier. All she knew was that she was now sharing a cave with a giant bear. It must have been eight or nine spans tall and it wasn't unconscious as Raco had been – it lay there calmly for the moment, its dark black eyes glinting in the firelight.

Ferebe froze, her trembling hand still outstretched to pick up another stick, her mind racing. Did *Kellid* know she was a friend, she wondered? Just how much of Raco was still there? '*Kellid*,' she said solemnly, feeling stupidly self-conscious, 'welcome.'

The bear of course, said nothing but it blinked and then yawned; its great jaws showing an expanse of sparkling white teeth. Ferebe relaxed, but only slightly, and decided not to make any sudden movements. It made sense after all that *Kellid* had come, Raco needed his strength, possibly would not survive the night without it. She reached over slowly, her gaze fixed on *Kellid*, and pulled her riding cloak back towards her over the floor of the cave – the bear made no move so she wrapped it back around herself, grateful for the extra layer. She drifted into a light doze still sitting bolt upright.

Effie is walking now. Since she spoke to Malky she's struck out on her own. She had kind of agreed she would go back and Malky disappeared again straight away but then, she'd realised she didn't know how. So she's still in trouble. It seemed having the intention to go back isn't enough but she's mystified as to what is the right thing to do – she vaguely considers clicking her Nikes together and chanting, 'There's no place like home, there's no place like home . . .' but since home isn't exactly where she wants to go either she elects to just keep moving.

She isn't simply unconscious, Effie decides. Arriving here she was pretty sure she was dying – so that means this is that place Talisker told them about. The place where people went when they died before they got to heaven or hell, wherever it was they were destined for . . . the void, he'd called it . . .

Well, give the man a medal for his powers of description, she thinks, looking around rather pointlessly. There's nothing here. Every now and then she hears a sound, murmuring voices, quiet laughter, that makes her think other people are making a journey through this place but she instinctively knows their paths will never cross. The mind-blowing realisation that the void, by definition, is an infinite space, makes her stop in her tracks and stand for a moment listlessly running her fingers through her hair. If the void is infinite, she reasons, standing still or walking would make no difference . . . she's battling with this conundrum when she sees something. A movement up ahead, pretty hard to miss around here . . .

'Hello?' she calls out. For some reason, 'hello' sounds pretty inadequate, her voice young and girlish. She begins to run to catch up if that's possible. As she draws closer she can make out the details of her quarry. It's a man, she can tell that much from behind – and he's not running, just walking with a long ambling stride. He's wearing strange clothes; a tunic and trousers made out of soft buckskin and he has long black hair.

A Native American, she thinks, *like Yiska.* 'Hello?'

He stops and turns around, a puzzled expression on his face. Effie stifles a gasp of surprise; the young man has the arm of a bear! She wonders briefly if she's in the kind of dream-state where this might be a metaphor for something, although it's difficult to imagine what . . .

'Greetings,' the man says. Effie smiles weakly in response. 'Are you a guardian of this place? I do not usually come here when *Kellid* takes control . . . at least, I don't think it's usual . . .'

'Uh-huh . . .' she has no idea what he's talking about. Apart from the hairy-arm thing, he's quite attractive. Not as good-looking as Yiska, but then perhaps slightly less uptight. 'No, I am a stranger here myself,' she says. It reminds her of some lame exchange at a nightclub and she giggles slightly nervously.

'Who are you?'

'My name is Effie – Euphemia Morgan. I think I'm here cos I nearly died,' she says matter-of-factly. 'I . . . um . . . can't seem to find the exit.'

He nods his understanding of her predicament. 'My name is Raco, I am from the Bear clan Sídhe, exile of Durghanti.'

'Did you have an accident?' she frowns towards his arm.

'I suppose you could call it that.' He begins to walk again and she walks with him, her feet moving at a double pace to keep up with his long stride.

'Why are we walking?'

'Do you always ask so many questions Effie – Euphemia Morgan?'

'No. Just call me Effie.' A sudden inspiration strikes her from nowhere. 'You're from Sutra aren't you?' She breaks into a wide grin – it seems she has somehow beaten Talisker, Yiska and Malky to the punch. 'Too cool,' she enthuses.

He looks mildly irritated by her. 'Where else would I be from?'

'Ha! Just wait till I tell Talisker I've met someone from his precious Sutra!' she crows. She knows it's childish and possibly, if she doesn't make it back, completely irrelevant.

Raco stops. 'Talisker? Tal-ees-ker? The Worldwalker?'

She's impressed. 'You *know* him?'

'Know him? No. That would be impossible. Our legends speak of him. He saved our nation once – and the Fine of course. But that was nearly two hundred years ago . . . If he's still alive, the Gods must have granted him a very long life as a reward I suppose.'

'Nah, nothing like that. Look, you can ask him yourself and he'll explain it to you. We're . . . um . . . coming to visit.'

'He's returning?' Raco looks ecstatically pleased about this – *yet another fan of Duncan's*, Effie thinks, somewhat sourly – 'The Fine have always said he would return if ever they are in trouble or danger.'

'Kinda like King Arthur huh?'

'Who?'

'Never mind. What about Malky? He must be a great hero as well. Don't the legends mention Talisker's companions?'

'The *Seanachaidh*, Alessandro Chaplin and also Talisker's shadow – they say that when in battle, his shadow becomes another warrior and slays separately . . . it has no name of course, just his shadow.'

She laughs. 'Shucks, Malky will be pleased . . . So, look, do you know how I can get out of here?'

He shakes his head, 'This place is not only a place; it is a time also. The Fine call it the "time-between". My guess is that we remain here until we are no longer displaced from our time.'

'But Malky said that walking is bad. That the void becomes used to us – it's dangerous . . .'

Raco stops walking, 'I must go,' he says. He looks around as if sensing something and, sure enough, a breeze starts up from nowhere; Effie can smell woodsmoke and a dank, stony smell. 'I will tell them, Euphemia Morgan,' he begins to fade before her eyes. 'That the Worldwalker is coming . . .' For a moment, as Raco's figure dissolves, Effie imagines his outline completely takes the shape of a bear – which is strange because the bear figure is much bigger and taller than Raco himself – but the impression only lasts a second, so fast that she's not sure she saw it at all. 'Yeah, right,' she mutters. 'Right, I'll just . . . hang here.'

Effie is left alone again in the vastness of the void.

'It's called the Enemy Way ceremony – but white folks call it the War Dance or Squaw Dance,' Rodney explained. 'In fact, it is not usually done in the winter and was never done to prepare for war. An enemy is often unseen – ghosts which come to us in times of trauma or even, as now, in our dreams.'

Talisker was aghast. There must have been three hundred people camping before the Mummy Cave, the atmosphere was noticeably tense but the people were not silent. They stood a respectful distance from the cave in little groups and chatted quietly. Some even sat watching from jeeps and a couple of battered looking cars that had somehow made it down into the canyon but, predominantly the people had come on foot or horseback.

It had taken all day to get into the northern arm of the canyon – Canyon Del Muerto – and they had back-tracked parallel to Route Seven. Yiska had explained that although there was another trail down near the Mummy Cave overlook, it had been blocked that morning by a rockslide. He still carried the two-way radio that he'd been using and, as they cleared the rim of the canyon the signal improved. Over the course of the day, talked to quite a few people who informed him about the weather conditions. One man – who seemed to be another cousin – told him about the Enemy Way

Ceremony taking place at the Mummy Cave; apparently the singer who had come to perform the ceremony was greatly respected and very expensive. However, because the ghostly enemy was attacking the tribes indiscriminately many families had pitched in to pay. The sing was already in its third day and would end at dusk.

No one paid them much attention when they first arrived; everyone was absorbed in the Enemy Way Ceremony. Talisker was relieved about this and Yiska's remark that 'we are not in charge of this,' made more sense to him; here was a community dealing with the problem as they saw it. *Chindi*, bad ghosts, were attacking their people and they were completely correct in their assessment of the situation. Talisker was however the only person who perhaps appreciated that the visiting *Chindi* might just be the tip of the iceberg.

He held Effie close against him across his saddle; she was swathed in blankets and he couldn't be sure, but he thought her temperature may have dropped in the last hour, her fever broken at last. This could only be a good sign but he noted, as he pushed the blanket and her hair aside to look at her face, that she was still deathly pale.

'Talisker, here, give her to me.' Yiska was reaching out to take Effie from him so he could dismount his horse. Talisker felt a strange reluctance to let her go but then passed her down to Yiska and Rodney. To his surprise, Aunt Millie had appeared from the fringes of the crowd along with a couple of friends; they immediately started fussing over Effie, Aunt Millie having a few sharp words with Yiska. Talisker suppressed a wry smile – it seemed I-told-you-so was the same in any language. Millie had arrived only that morning before the trail became impassable but already, her encampment had an air of an organised establishment.

A young man peered out from beneath the tent-flap to see what all the commotion was about. He wore mirrored sunglasses, had bronzed skin which looked almost unnaturally tanned and had possibly the glossiest jet black hair Talisker had ever seen. He grinned broadly when he saw Yiska.

'Mike! Hey, Mikey!'

'Dave? Jeez, is that you?' Yiska looked genuinely surprised although Talisker thought he detected a slight reticence in his tone. Rodney looked at Renee and raised a questioning eyebrow but said nothing.

'Hi, *Sicheii*,' the young man – Dave – seemed oblivious or uncaring of the slight tension of those around him. He strode from the tent grinning broadly, pumped Yiska's hand whilst slapping him on the back. 'Good to see you, Mikey,' he beamed. 'How's life amongst the sick these days?'

Yiska grinned back although his smile was notably absent from his eyes. 'Hell, you should know right? Living in L.A.'

'Yeah, right,' Dave laughed. 'By the way, I've changed my name to Lake – Lake "First Eagle" McKinnon.'

'Well, it's very . . . Hollywood, Lake.'

'Yup, that's the idea.'

They might have talked more but Aunt Millie interrupted them with a torrent of scolding, obviously eager to get Effie out of the cold. Her friend joined in and Yiska and Lake were respectfully silent.

'Aunt Millie's friend, Renee Yazzie, said we can put Effie in her tent tonight. Lake's gonna have to bunk somewhere else. The ladies are all gonna be there anyway so they can keep an eye on her,' Yiska explained. 'I think she's going to be fine now, Talisker. She gave me a scare back there, though.'

Talisker dismounted and began walking with the small group towards one of the jeeps which had an orange utility tent pitched beside it. They received some curious stares along the way as they supported Effie's prostrate form between them. 'Why isn't she waking up, Yiska?' he frowned.

'She will. In her own time. Renee reckons she was poisoned and I have to agree with her. But knowing Effie we must conclude it was her own doing.'

'Poor kid.' Renee said. Talisker nodded his response. It seemed Renee must be knowledgeable as Millie, Rodney and Yiska all paid attention to her pronouncements, perhaps she was a hand-trembler as Yiska had mentioned.

The tent was large, allowing enough space for four or five people if necessary. Once they had settled Effie on a comfortable sleeping bag Millie and Renee directed to Talisker and Yiska towards a blue van on the other side of the space in front of the cave which – incredibly it seemed to Talisker – was serving food.

It was almost dusk, the shadows of the outcrops of the canyon walls making long pools of cold darkness. Here and there a stubborn lozenge of snow clung to the rocks like patches of skin although Canyon Del Muerto had not received as much snowfall as the wider arms of the canyon. The sound of the singers echoed and ricocheted away into the darkness and seemed as much a natural part of the landscape as the sound of the river that meandered a bright ribbon-like path across the floor of the canyon. The constant sound was punctuated every minute or so by a discordant yell which was part of the sing.

'Yiska, how did all these cars get down here? I thought there was no roads.'

'At this time of year getting in and out by road's pretty hard. Most of these folk farm in the canyon so the vehicles live here,' Yiska explained. 'Are you hungry?'

Talisker hadn't thought about eating for a long time but now realised he was starving. For a few cents they purchased a large tin cup of mutton stew each and a flat piece of bread, which Yiska referred to as 'fry bread'. He watched the crowd as he ate, although he was unable to see the singer from where they sat; the rhythmic swaying of the circle of people spread outwards so that even those not involved with the ceremony swayed in time. Behind them, the gas jets of the blue food van hissed in the cold air and the comforting smell of the stew and soup pervaded the scene, mingling with the ever-present tang of the piñon-juniper trees. It was all so not what Talisker had expected – and the blending of the modern Navajo culture seemed strange to him until he realised he was comparing it to similar Sidhe ceremonies – but he was impressed by the pragmatic faith of the Dinéh and the fact that they knew how to have a good time. The gathering was obviously a chance for relatives and friends to meet, a serious ceremony with an attached social event.

As he finished his stew, which was delicious,

mopping it up with the bread, a large dog detached itself from the shadows of the food van and came over to sit solemnly in front of Talisker waiting for some food. It was a mangy-looking creature with shaggy red-brown fur and amber eyes; it seemed possible that its mother had had a liaison with a wolf or a coyote. It did not whine or whimper to scrounge some food but simply sat there quietly fixing Talisker with a sanguine gaze. 'Hi boy,' Talisker muttered, 'you hungry?' He was about to offer the dog the last of his bread when Rodney stopped him.

'You must not feed the dog while the sing is happening. It will be ruined.'

'You mean, they'd have to stop?'

Rodney nodded. 'The Dog could be a Trickster or . . . or worse.'

'Don't think I'd be very popular either after all their hard work,' Talisker mused. 'Sorry, dog. Come and see me later, eh?'

His gaze tracked back to Renee Yazzie's orange tent; Renee, Millie and a couple of younger women were sitting out on camping chairs chatting and carding some wool. Their expressions were grave however and he imagined they might be talking about someone – a relative, perhaps – who had been killed by the *chindi* in their dreams. He nodded towards them. 'What's the story with Dave/Lake? I get the impression not many are pleased to see him.'

'He's a waste of space,' Yiska scowled.

'That's harsh.'

'Yeah well, I've bailed him out more times than I remember. Paid for his rehab, repaid his gambling debts. He hasn't been home for years and Renee worries about him but she doesn't know the truth. I told him not to come home.'

'Maybe he missed her – missed the Navajo Nation,' Talisker frowned. 'It's hard to be away from home for so long.'

'Nah, he has no feelings for the Rez. He left at fifteen . . .' as Yiska spoke, Talisker had the distinct impression that choosing whether to stay and live and work on the Navajo Nation or leave in search of work was a huge decision for the young people. He glanced at Rodney and noted the baleful, judgemental quality of his stare. Lake, it seemed had turned his back on his family and then proceeded to make big, big mistakes. His family, his people did not forgive such behaviour in a hurry. 'He will be back to ask Renee for money, probably her life savings . . .'

Talisker decided to change the subject, feeling slightly sorry for the unfortunate Lake. 'The ladies look sad,' he remarked. 'Maybe they have lost someone.'

Rodney nodded. 'They have – I know at least two of them have lost elders of their family but they will not speak of it, Talisker – not here where the *chindi* might be listening, or in their hogan. Young Shannon has had to move out of her family's hogan as her uncle died in his dreams there.'

'Can they go back after the funeral?'

'No. They will never go back. The hogan will be deserted, left just as it was. We make a special doorway for the trapped *chindi* to leave.'

This seemed eminently sensible to Talisker so he said nothing.

'When can we go in and check for the gateway, *Sicheii*?' Yiska asked.

'I think we will wait for dawn.'

Talisker awoke before dawn. It was cold and cramped in the cab of the jeep even with the swathes of blankets Rodney had given him. It had snowed further overnight, giving the campground a deserted air although everyone was simply sleeping in the tents, shelters and cars. The snow would make it difficult for people to get out of the canyon even those with four wheel drive. There were few people moving around and a dog barking over the other side of the camp area had woken him; the sound carried through the crisp air, in gauche challenge to the night.

Talisker groaned and began to stretch his long legs and waggle his feet to get the circulation going. Rubbing the frosted window of the cab he stared out. *Today could be the day he went back to Sutra . . .*

Just as he thought this, a jackrabbit scurried into his line of vision, he'd never seen one up close before and it struck him as more hare than rabbit-like. It stopped within a few feet of the cab, sitting bolt upright, its long whiskers twitching, beaded with snow which glinted in the first, faint light. Talisker had always loved the regalness of hares: there was something special and wise which marked them out from their cousins the lowly rabbit. He grinned in delight, his breath frosting up the window again just as the dog barked once more and the jackrabbit darted for cover. Not that he believed in omens, but this had to be a good one.

'Talisker.' He jumped as someone tapped on the

window behind him. It was Yiska and Rodney who had spent the night in one of the shelters nearer the cave, visiting with relatives.

'Morning, you two,' he smiled as he opened the window. The pair reminded him of oversized boy scouts kitted up for a camping expedition; Yiska had an impressive looking rucksack on his back which had previously been riding in the flatbed of the jeep. Rodney also had something less bulky slung around his back which Talisker couldn't make out as it was wrapped in a large chamois cloth.

'We should start now,' Rodney said without pre-amble. 'The singer has gone so no one will mind if we enter the cave.'

'What, no breakfast?'

'. . . but they might ask questions.' Rodney finished patiently. Talisker chided himself for interrupting; the Dinéh set great store by listening – *completely* listening that was – until a speaker had finished. Because of this, Talisker had noted, in their conversations with one another there were very few of the habitual sounds of agreement or encouragement which naturally litter western speech.

They crossed the space before the Mummy Cave in silence. Talisker couldn't help but feel furtive about it as they moved amongst the sleeping tents. In the early light the cliff-face above the gash of the cave loomed like a giant frown, a blast of heavy air blew towards them smelling of cold rock and picking up and whirling the loose powder of the snow. Talisker paused before they went in.

'You all right, Talisker?'

'Yeah. I'm just thinking I should have said goodbye to Effie . . .'

'She'll be fine. Millie and Renee will look after her until we get back.'

'I know. It's just that she . . . she should be here.'

Rodney nodded agreement. 'But there is little time. Each night the dreaming die.'

Talisker shrugged. 'Who knows . . . might not work anyway.'

They walked into the darkness. Talisker expected it to be as freezing as the outside if not colder but in fact, the rocks had still maintained a vague taint of heat from the day before. Towards the front of the space were the jagged outlines of low rock walls which had once been buildings; to the left the low remains of a circular structure.

'That was a Kiva,' Yiska explained in a low voice.

'Did the Navajo live in the caves once?'

'No, these were made by the Anasazi. An ancient tribe that vanished.'

'What do you mean vanished?'

'No one knows why they died out. They are just gone. But in their time they were great builders and artisans.'

Talisker walked into the circle of the Kiva. 'What's this, Yiska?' There was a fine dusting of powder on the floor and Talisker crouched down to look.

'Whoa! Don't step on that. It must be where the singer made a sand-painting. At the end of the ceremony, last night, the sand was all swept away and dispersed back into the winds.'

'Well they didn't make a very good job of sweeping up,' Talisker remarked dryly.

Yiska frowned at the floor. 'It's true,' he observed. 'It should have been finished better.' He glanced towards the blackness of the back of the cave and then back out to the brightness of the canyon outside. From in here, the snow-scattered scene was almost impossibly bright. 'Maybe something spooked them and they were in a hurry to leave,' he muttered. 'Maybe they saw the *chindi* . . .'

'Speaking of *chindi* . . .' Talisker unwrapped the cedar box he was carrying and began to walk to the back of the cave.

'What's he doing?' Rodney frowned. 'The ghosts have been sent away.'

'*Sicheii*,' Yiska took his uncle by the arm and walked into the back of the cave also. 'I don't want you to panic . . .'

Rodney gave him an austere, slightly contemptuous look. 'Why would I?'

'Malky. Malky. Are you there? You can come out.' Talisker had laid the box on the floor and opened it. Malky appeared, his indistinct form wavering in the grey light.

'Hiya, Duncan. Did Effie make it back?'

'Yeah. We think so . . .'

Rodney was speechless. He gasped for air, he covered his mouth with his hand as if afraid some curse would escape him. 'It's okay, *Sicheii*,' Yiska reassured him, 'Malky is a friend – Talisker's friend.'

'Malcolm McLeod,' Malky smiled toothily towards Rodney. 'Ah'm actually Duncan's great-great-great-something grandfaither. Kin ye see the resemblance?'

To his great credit, Rodney recovered from the shock far more quickly than Talisker had at first meeting his ancestor. He nodded to Malky. 'I am Rodney Talloak from Black Mesa Arizona, of the Black Streaked Wood People, born for Those Who Walk. You may call me Hosteen.'

Malky looked impressed by this and, as ever, behaved solemnly as the occasion demanded. 'Well, Hosteen, are you coming to Sutra to help us lay the spirits to rest?'

'No, I will stay here and watch by the gateway. Mebbe Effie will watch with me . . .'

'Huh, you want to be careful about that – the last person who watched one o' these things ended up stuck fer two hundred years!'

'Malky,' Talisker frowned and shook his head in warning not to worry Rodney.

'Er . . .' Malky cast around to change the subject. 'So, Effie's no coming then? She'll be gutted. She'll be right annoyed, Duncan – she telt me when I saw her in the void . . .'

'Talisker – I have a small gift for you,' Rodney interrupted, quickly realizing that Malcolm was prone to chatter. 'I heard you mention that you wished you had a sword . . .'

'That's right, Hosteen – I couldn't chance bringing mine through customs.'

'Here,' Rodney gave him the bundle he had carried across his back, his matter somewhat awkward. Talisker unwrapped the chamois; there was a bundle of grey fabric inside and wrapped within that, a sword.

He gave a low whistle. 'It's fantastic. Where did you get this?'

'My family had it from the time of the Civil War – it was a Confederate cavalry officer's. I'm not sure if it was ever used in action or if it was just for show, but it looks solid enough.'

'You've sharpened the blade,' Talisker murmured admiringly. 'And . . .' he shook out the grey garment, '. . . is this real too?'

'Yes. Try it on.'

Talisker did so. The jacket was a bit large on him, the Confederate soldier must have been a broad shouldered man, but he liked the feel of the silver-grey serge instantly. There was a bullet hole surrounded by a powder burn on the left shoulder, Talisker found himself hoping the officer had survived. The sword buckled neatly around his waist and sat just on his hip.

'Wow. But – I *really* appreciate it Rodney . . . Hosteen . . . but shouldn't you give it to Yiska?'

Rodney didn't exactly laugh but his tone was amused. 'A scalpel is more Yiska's thing. He might do himself more damage with one of those.'

Yiska smiled, obviously not offended by this. 'It's true.'

'So you're goin' through tae Sutra with no weapon,' Malky fretted. 'That's a worry . . . assuming we can get through, of course.'

'Oh, we can get through.' Talisker had begun to walk into the back of the cave and the others followed.

Up ahead was blackness. Not just shadow, not just the absence of light. The blackness had texture like a stagnant pool. The walls of the cave vanished into it in such a way that Talisker formed the idea the gateway had *eaten up* the reality of the cave. A cold breeze which smelt like nothing guttered out towards them.

'Stay here, Rodney,' Talisker cautioned. 'Don't come any nearer.'

'Is it always like this, Talisker?' Yiska licked his lips nervously. 'I mean when you've been before?'

Talisker laughed humourlessly. 'No, I'm usually dying when I cross over. No one has ever conjured a gate from the other side of the void before.' *Or from within the void,* he thought. 'Yiska, I'll understand if you don't want to come.'

'No, Talisker. The message came to the Dinéh, there must be a reason – I will be proud to represent them.'

'Okay. Here. Take my hand.'

'Is it really . . .'

'Unless you want to get trapped in the void. Goodbye, Rodney.'

'Goodbye, *Sicheii.*'

'Let's go.'

It is the same but different. The same, because how could the void ever be anything other? But different in that Talisker is moving through it, willingly, alive and unscathed. He feels Yiska's hand but does not look at him. He knows his friend is frightened; understands his fear completely, but Talisker has walked this path before . . . once through water and once through fire. Coming from Earth to Sutra is never easy. Not that there is actually any path. But that doesn't worry him, he has come to believe that walking through the void is an entirely individual journey. If he just moves ahead he will arrive.

'Duncan, wait up,' Malky's voice echoes from somewhere behind him. He lets go of Yiska's hand once he has heard it knowing that the Highlander will watch out for him.

Is this it then, he thinks? No challenge . . . no flames, no water . . . as he thinks this the realisation hits him. There's no air.

He stops breathing instantly, holds his breath although he knows he will be unable to hold it for long. Had he been warned, he would have taken a great big lungful but he was breathing easily, lightly when they entered the void.

He hears a sound beside him, a hot rasping, and knows that Yiska is struggling to breathe also. But he is breathing, with difficulty. Perhaps there is some small amount of air after all. Cautiously, Talisker inhales. It tastes like smoke, like ashes, like hot carbon but perhaps he can survive on it till the other side.

There's someone ahead. He grips his new sword tightly, part of him still celebrating the magnificent gift. Glancing down he sees the purity of its steel glinting in a light that comes from nowhere; grimly he acknowledges that the blade must have killed. He just knows.

It's a man. It is impossible to identify his origin because he's naked. But his hair is long and his body wiry and muscled like a clansman – Talisker is sure he is a Fine. As he draws near he expects some reaction, some message from the warrior but there is nothing. The man stumbles around blindly, his hands are bound together. All over his body is a criss-cross lattice of deep cuts and gouges as though some surgeon has started but not finished his work.

'Ho there,' Talisker stops the man, taking him by the shoulders but when he looks into his eyes, only the void is reflected there; a bitter darkness. The man's jaw hangs slackly as if he had died in a thousand agonies. When Talisker releases his grip the distressed soul falls down.

Yiska is instantly there. Tears are streaming down his face as he breathes the noxious air but he stops to help – thinks that he can. He kneels beside the prostrate form, his long hair shadowing his face into the darkness so that Talisker can only see the blood red of his shirt. 'I don't think I want to go there,' he says surveying the devastated body. His choked voice sounds flat and lifeless in the airless space. 'I don't think . . .'

Talisker reaches out and touches his shoulder. 'Come on, Yiska, there's nothing you can do. We have to keep moving.'

He hears a sound then, a warm, soft shuffling like . . . like . . .

'Talisker!' Malky yells.

Talisker looks up. 'Ohmigod,' he whispers.

They are coming. Hundreds, maybe thousands of them. Dead warriors, weeping silent tears, bleeding lifeless blood, filling the void with pain.

Chapter Nine

'This is all your fault, *yekt*,' Ferebe snarled.

Raco said nothing. Far more pressing than the fact that he had plummeted once more in Ferebe's alarmingly fickle affections was the four Shoreth Riders who were now circling them.

Their leader was the one from the bridge, the Inquisitor. Raco remembered his weasely smile and the arrogance with which he sat his horse. The Shoreth were good at arrogance. If he were honest with himself, Raco knew he would have been ashamed to tell his father the ease with which the Riders had trapped them, were his father still alive rather than . . . that thing. He and Ferebe had been behaving as if they were on an afternoon jaunt rather than trying to evade capture. Raco still weak and too tired to care and Ferebe . . . well, she had been preoccupied with something, the Goddess knew what. Perhaps the fact that she was now considered a traitor and probably a slut by her countrymen was distracting her. Whichever it was neither of them noticed the pursuit until it was too late. The Shoreth Riders efficiently managed to herd them into the freezing water of the river where they now stood, up to their knees and back to back, their swords drawn.

'Well, if it isn't Ferebe Vezul,' the lead rider sneered. 'Tut-tut, what's daddy going to make of this? That is, when I take him your head!' He rode closer, closing the circle more tightly around them but still well outside the reach of a sword.

'Come and try then, Horza, I'll take your balls first – if Zarrus hasn't had them removed already.'

'That's right, calm the situation,' Raco groaned. He leant further forward to try and balance his sword better; although the bear's arm might be useful in close combat it was heavier than his other arm and made him feel unbalanced.

Horza grinned mirthlessly and, in preparation for the attack Raco acted instinctively, tossing his blade from hand to hand . . . except it wasn't a hand. His brown-black claws still felt slightly alien to him and he was too slow. He dropped his blade in the river and, as he bent down to scramble for it he heard the peals of laughter and derision coming from the Riders. He coloured, angrier with himself than anything; as he plunged his hand in the water to retrieve the blade, an idea, born of desperation, came to him.

He let out a yell and began splashing the water wildly, scooping up great waves with his arms and then kicking with his feet. The afternoon sun caught the arc of the water, flashing through like myriad diamonds. The rider who had begun towards him was caught unawares as his horse panicked slightly and began sidestepping and snorting.

'Ya! Ya!' Raco yelled kicking and waving his arms. The horse, instinctively decided to flee but as its rider tried to urge it forward it reared instead, unseating the man and throwing him cursing into the river. Raco turned his attention to the other horse, hoping to repeat his luck but the job was already done for him as the panic spread to the other geldings.

Ferebe was also trying to unsettle the horses and succeeded with one but Horza was too quick and pulled back. Still, the odds were slightly better as the three unseated riders drew their weapons and Horza hesitated on the bank, his mare skitting and snorting.

'Not too shabby, *Yekt,*' Ferebe grinned.

'If you're trying to endear yourself to me, try using my name,' Raco growled.

'Let's just say I might forgive you for being such an idiot in the first place . . . Come on!' she screeched at the advancing Shoreth who was ploughing through the water. Raco grinned, admiring her bravado.

It wasn't a question of whether they would win the sword fight or not; Ferebe was the best swordswoman Raco had ever seen and two of the Shoreth took her on while Raco was left with the third who, luckily for him, appeared nervous – perhaps the sight of Raco's bear arm was enough to do the job. But still, nature was the great leveller and as they clashed, Raco stumbled on a jagged rock beneath the waterline. As he reeled and fought to keep from falling over his opponent pressed his unexpected advantage, yelling and rushing forward as well as he was able. Just as Raco was righting himself, the youth was upon him and with more instinct than thought he lashed out with his bear arm.

There was a scream as the youth fell backwards into the water, blood pouring from the gash where his neck was sliced open. For an instant, Raco glared at his own arm in horror realising that *Kellid*'s spirit was somehow still in there. The bear would show no mercy when attacked; hesitation was weakness in a battle situation.

'Sorry.' Raco dispatched the youth with a merciful sword thrust to the heart. He meant it – the Sidhe were great warriors but killing was never construed as glorious – fleetingly, he thought of the lad's mother and family and he touched the flat of his blade to his face in brief silent salute.

He had turned towards Ferebe, who had killed one of the Riders already and was engaged in a heated flurry of blows with the other. As he waded towards the struggling pair he heard a sound; it was like an angry insect. Raco had no time to wonder what it was however. It was a whiplash. His arms were pinned to his side and the snare of the whip was pulled tight around him, he heard Horza's nasty laugh just before he was tugged over and he fell helplessly into the river, his legs having lost most of their feeling in the freezing water, flailing helplessly. Horza reeled him in, dragging him backwards towards the bank, his back and legs bumping and bashing against the rocks of the riverbed.

'Ferebe!' He submerged and then came to the surface again, choking and spluttering, the inexorable tug of the whip bringing him closer to Horza who would no doubt kill him.

But Horza had no intention of making a kill, much as it would have delighted him. As soon as Raco was within reach of his mount, he allowed him to push himself up by his elbows and find his feet. Then, as Raco stood there shaking, sucking air like a landed fish, Horza walked his steed forward and, grabbing him by his hair, stuck a dagger to his throat.

'Drop your blade, Ferebe Vezul.' His voice cut across the river with the same sting as his whip. 'Do it now!'

Ferebe looked over, her gaze flickered across Raco, assessing the situation. 'Kill him then,' she said. 'He's only a *Yekt*.'

'Ferebe!' Raco couldn't believe she would betray him like this.

There was silence for long seconds as Horza considered his next move. What may have happened next became an irrelevance because a miracle occurred.

He wants to run. He really wants to break into a run. But something tells him that his blind panic will be to no avail. His breathing is harsh and hot as they close in around him, pressing against him, bumping and nudging, so that their dead blood is covering his clothes in a black stain. He can smell the blood. He can smell decay and perhaps, if indeed it is possible, he can smell something else; despair.

He can hear weeping, choked sobs, and realises it is Yiska who is walking close beside him. How unbearable for a healer! The dead are unaccusing, stumbling aimlessly as the first warrior they saw but there are so many . . . so many . . . Their deaths have been violent but that is the least of it. Their white corpses have been disturbed, mutilated. Fine and Sidhe – he notes the long hair and the taller, thinner stature of the Sidhe – but they are all blinded, mad and horribly, horribly, silent. There is only the soft shuffling sound of their feet.

'Talisker . . .' Yiska says nothing else, just his name, but it is sufficient to convey his rising panic and fear. Some of the lost souls reach out spasmodically and

grab at hair and clothes. Talisker glances aside and sees Yiska, his face a mask of fright and confusion, he is smeared with blood, his face and hair slick and wet.

'Soon,' Talisker says.

'Steady, lad,' Malky soothes. Death holds no fear for Malcolm McLeod but there is an edge of puzzlement and anger to his voice.

'I can't – I can't . . .' There is a sudden surge of movement as Yiska's panic takes hold. He tries to run ahead but the dead block his way. He pushes and barges, puts his arm up before his face to blot out the sight of their hopelessness and fights his way forward. His breath comes in ragged sighs or sobs and it seems he is speaking in Navajo, crying out to his ancestors for protection.

'Wait! Yiska, wait!'

It's no use. He is lost from sight within a few moments. The crowd press in behind him so there is no path to follow. 'Oh naw,' Malky groans. 'Rodney's goin' tae kill us if he's lost.'

Talisker says nothing, just presses ahead; at last the crowd thins out. It seems they are moving through the void together like a lost herd of animals and Talisker, Yiska and Malky's presence in the void has made little difference to them, they have simply streamed around like the sea around a pebble. Up ahead there is a wall of fire. At least Talisker knows this is the right way. He holds his jacket up to shield his face and brandishes his sword ahead of his body, firelight dancing cleanly along its edge.

'C'mon, Malk, whatever's in Sutra'll be no problem after that . . .'

*

There was a sound like . . . well, a rushing sound. Raco's first thought was that somehow the river had been dammed further up and then broken through, but the sound was instantly followed by a flash of intense light which exploded outwards from some unseen central point. A huge disk of light hung suspended just over the river, only feet away from where both Ferebe and her aggressor stood, gawping in disbelief.

'By the Goddess,' Raco breathed.

A figure appears in the circle. It is a man – a Sidhe possibly – running, running fast as if his life depends on it. Suddenly, the man ruptures forth from the light, which for an instant makes a tracery of brightness across his figure as if reluctant to release him. As he does so, his sound comes with him, he is yelling something in some strange language which neither Raco nor the Shoreth recognise. He is covered in blood, each watcher instinctively recognises it as such although it is old, stagnant blood that has turned into blackness. As soon as his feet make contact with the water and the rocks of the riverbed, the man stumbles forward to his knees, so that the water is up to his chest, and begins vomiting into the river.

No one moves or reacts – before they have time to do anything, two more figures appear. Raco thinks they are Fine clansmen – the shorter of the two is certainly dressed in a garb similar to the Fine – but the other, the taller one, is wearing heavy blue trousers and a grey jacket, his red hair is long past his shoulders and he is wielding a sword which still crackles and dances with the light of the portal.

Both of the men are similarly smeared with blood and are running also, but appear less disorientated than the first – they exit the portal and splash into the river as if somehow unsurprised by their surroundings. Raco fleetingly wonders if they have been pursuing the first man but as the smaller clansman starts forward, his bearing is one of concern rather than attack.

No one moves: Ferebe and her opponent stand in frozen postures although both have lowered their weapons, Horza presses his dagger against Raco's throat once more but says nothing for long moments as he fights to regain command of the situation.

'What witchery is this?' he demands. His tone sounds less than confident but he has not dropped his guard and still holds the dagger firm.

The taller man observes the scene calmly then tips the point of his blade up towards Horza. 'Let him go,' he says. 'There is no implied threat; his tone is pleasant, almost casual – so much so that Horza is worried. There's five of us now and only two of you,' he nods toward Ferebe and her opponent, 'whichever one is your lackey.'

Horza sneers towards Yiska who is still coughing and spluttering into the river. 'I'd say four. And if I kill this one . . .'

He tried to move unexpectedly but Raco felt the tell-tale tension in the bunching of his leg muscles; all Horza needed to do was draw the blade across his throat but the action of leaning over unbalanced him. Raco managed to reach up and tug hard on Horza's wrist. With an outraged cry Horza tumbled gracelessly from his mount and, as he released his grip on the whip, the coils around Raco's torso were immediately loosed. Raco leaped on top of his prostrate figure and pinned him to the ground; gripping him by the neck with *Kellid*'s claws.

'By the Goddess, I should kill you now . . .'

But Horza was not finished; his wiry frame was unexpectedly strong and built for speed. He flipped Raco off him so they tussled on the grass for a few moments before Horza was on top – kneeling across Raco's chest and pinning his arms down – Raco distantly had to admit he was a smart opponent. 'Let's just finish this, shall we?' Horza grabbed his dagger from the grass and had raised his arm to strike when the weapon was knocked from his hand and a cold length of alien steel was against his throat.

'I think not.' The stranger said.

'Don't kill him,' Raco was reluctant to save Horza's skin but realised it was necessary. 'We need him to deliver a message.'

They sat Horza and his last remaining Rider on their horses but bound their hands to the pommel of their saddles. Ferebe assured them that Shoreth Riders were good enough to steer with only the pressure of their knees, although Raco wasn't too sure about this; Horza looked pretty steady but the other Rider was already sliding a little as they rode off up the slope. However he was past caring whether they reached Durghanti to deliver their denial or spent the night in a patch of brambles. Ferebe busied herself burying the dead Shoreth as she had before with her own men.

'Must you bury everybody?' Raco complained unhappily. He was sitting on the bank examining his minor cuts and bruises, but he was already developing a horrible headache from where he'd bashed his head against a stone during his brief tussle with Horza.

'Why didn't you transform?' The strangers had all come ashore. The clansman was helping Ferebe but the other two were trying to wash the worst of stale blood off their clothes. 'You're bear clan Sidhe right? You could have taken him any time.'

Raco stared at the red-haired stranger through narrowed eyes – he must have been away for a long time. 'Duncan Talisker?'

Talisker was speechless. 'How . . . ?'

'Where is Effie Morgan? She told me you were coming.'

Yiska surreptitiously stared at his hand to see if he had stopped shaking – although he was sure he could put it down to having been doused in the river if anyone noticed. He felt miserable and said nothing as Talisker and Malky both behaved . . . well, normally. He hadn't been prepared; okay, they'd said a journey through the void was dangerous but not in the sense that it could drive a person insane. How could he ever have *hozro* again when he wanted to take his brain out and scrub it with some good carbolic soap? Every time he so much as blinked, he saw them; the dead, the white walking flesh devoid of soul or reason. They'd touched him with their stark fingers, they'd moved against and beside him, they'd . . .

'Yiska? You all right?' He looked up at Malky's

198

concerned face. And that was the other thing; Malky was different here – like a real person, only still dead-looking. Details that could simply be overlooked while he was in his rather more transparent form now screamed for attention. Things like the scars and cuts that had presumably killed him originally or, the fact his skin was as white and dead looking as . . . them.

'Duncan, ah think Yiska might be no well,' Malky frowned when Yiska didn't respond. It seemed as if the Highlander was talking from a great distance away and Talisker strode over and peered down to where he sat.

'You'll be fine, Yiska,' he said. 'I'm sorry, I know that was difficult to bear, but it's over now. It's over . . .'

'Mind Sandro wiz the same when he got here,' Malky observed.

Talisker nodded. 'But that crossing was easy compared to this one, Malk, and Yiska's not used to . . . supernatural things.'

Malky laughed,but not unkindly. 'So it'll be a baptism o' fire then!'

'Yeah. Do you want some other clothes? Looks like you've reverted to . . .'

'Look!' Malky pointed back out over the river again. Once they had been spat out of the void, the portal had disappeared or become dormant again; now the light was back.

'What the hell?'

'Effie mebbe?'

But nothing appeared for long moments; the watchers on the bank fidgeted and gripped their swords tighter. Yiska stared helplessly at the ring of light starkly afraid that *they* were going to follow through the gateway.

'There's nothing . . .'

'Wait, look!'

Neither a man nor a *chindi*. It walked on four legs, its head down, its gait loping like a coyote . . . 'Bloody hell! It's the dug!' Malky chuckled. 'I canny believe it – Duncan, he must've followed ye!'

Talisker chuckled too. *How could he laugh so soon?* Yiska wondered. *Was he impervious to suffering?*

'Come here dug,' Malky called. The dog seemed confused by the fact it was suddenly in the river up to its neck but as soon as it heard Malky's voice it gamely paddled over and loped up the bank towards them. 'Good dug,' Malky enthused, 'good . . . aw, gerroff!' The dog had begun to shake itself dry and seemed to have brought most of the river out in its coat. Once it had shaken though it calmly looked at them all with it's solemn brown eyes and then padded over and sat down beside Yiska on the bank, giving a little whine of greeting.

Yiska flinched. 'Keep it away from me,' he said, the ragged edges of hysteria still making his voice uneven. 'It could be a Skinwalker.' He shuffled along the bank away from the creature and eyed the dog with suspicion; it met his appraisal with calm amber eyes.

'Aw, dinnae say that – look, he likes ye,' Malky beamed. The dog licked Yiska's hand and arm with its warm, rough tongue.

'Yeah.'

'Well, seems you should name him Yiska since he likes you so much.'

Yiska looked confused. 'I – I thought he already had a name?'

'Huh?

'Doug. I thought Malky had named him Doug. What? What's so funny?'

Talisker was laughing. It was the first time Yiska had seen him really laugh, right out and it had a hysterical edge to it. A release of tension, which had been building for a long, long time. He laughed so much tears trickled down his bloodied face and he struggled for breath. 'Doug! Doug! Oh, that's funny . . .'

Malky, the only other person in a position to appreciate the joke, pulled a wry face at first. 'It's no *that* funny,' he muttered, but then he chuckled too. 'Dug – aye I can see how ye'd . . .'

'Fine, so we've named the dog,' Ferebe cut in, 'we should move. There's bound to be more riders on the way.'

They walked five miles along the riverbank before Ferebe thought it safe to stop. The cliffs of the gorge were higher here, the river deeper and wider. They found a bolthole quite by accident, the cliff face dictated they must climb and there was a pathway of sorts, a narrow trail probably used by goats and the Durghanti wild horses. After rising steeply above the level of the river the path divided into two; one branch carrying straight on, the other leading steeply up onto a flat mini plateau. They checked around a bit and Raco found an entrance to a cave. It was quite large and mercifully dry after the depredations of soaked clothes.

'Should be easy to defend as long as we post watch,' Raco observed.

They made camp in relative quiet, each caught up in their own thoughts. Yiska said very little, his eyes still had the guarded look of someone who has suffered a great fright. He sat on a rock and slowly began to examine the contents of his backpack to see if things could be dried out. Dog sat next to him and licked the back of his hand every time it came within reach. After a few minutes Yiska stroked Dog's head and tickled him under the chin, which was gratefully and solemnly received.

'It's true isn't it?' Raco marvelled when he sat down having got the fire going. 'You are Tal-ees-ker, aren't you?'

Talisker nodded. 'How did you see Effie, Raco?'

Raco outlined his brief sojourn in the void and his meeting with Effie. 'Sounds like oor Effie,' Malky nodded. 'Was she goin' back when you saw her?'

'I think so. She said she couldn't find the . . . "exit?"'

'Hopefully she will have by now,' Talisker said.

'So, you must be the *Seanachaidh*?' Raco said to Malky. 'You don't look like it says in the legends.'

'Naw, that's Sandro – Alessandro Chaplin – he didn'ae come wi' us this time.'

'Oh.' Raco looked slightly disappointed.

'Ah'm Malcolm McLeod.'

'Oh.'

'Well don't the legends tell o' me?'

'Well no.'

'Tsk.' Malky was mock-offended. 'I don't know why I bother.'

'I'm sorry Malcolm – Malky. It's just that there are no *Seanachaidhs* any more . . .'

'No *Seanachaidhs*! But they were well important tae the Fine!'

'We've been gone for a long time . . .'

'One hundred and eighty years, Tal-ees-ker.'

'Yes. Tell us about Sutra.'

'There is no *hozro* here,' Yiska said suddenly.

'What?' Everyone turned to look at Yiska but he sat silently stroking Dog, looking for all the world as if he had never spoken. When they turned back to the fire Malky shrugged at Talisker and they carried on talking.

They talked for a long time. Raco knew little about Soulis Mor and whether the Thane there was a descendant of Tristan and Grace. He'd never been to the city, he had been born in Durghanti twenty-five years earlier and exiled to Ruannoch Were when he was seven – he still thought of Durghanti as his home city, though – at least the city with which his tribe of Sidhe were affiliated. He had fought beside his father during the failed uprising five years earlier. It was clear that Raco was uneasy talking about it in front of Ferebe least she think he was picking an argument but, diplomatic as he was she still scowled at him when he described the Shoreth invasion.

'So the Shoreth now possess Kamala Sev *and* Durghanti,' he explained. 'There has been a peace of sorts these past few years but only because the Shoreth have contented themselves with two cities thus far.'

Ferebe laughed bitterly. 'True enough, *yekt*. The Warrior Path dictates that we conquer and move on, assimilating territory. But not all Shoreth want it to be that way . . .' she checked herself; obviously fearing she had said too much.

'What do you mean, Ferebe Vezul?'

'Nothing. It's just – remember I told you about Storm?'

'The white mammoth?'

'Yes. They say – that is, our legends say – that when the White Mammoth is born, the Shoreth have reached their homeland . . .'

'So, ye can stop movin' and conquering folk?' Malky said. 'So it's just been born then? What's a mammoth?'

'No. It – she – was born eighteen years ago, just before the taking of Durghanti. The generals, including my father, persuaded the Emperor to keep her birth secret in case the knowledge disturbed those preparing for the campaign against Durghanti. Storm has been a captive all her life.'

'But why didn't they tell everyone after the battle?'

She shrugged. 'Politics, I'd guess. I don't really know, but I do know the Warrior Path is everything to many of the Shoreth. Stopping . . . settling down is unthinkable to some. Horza's General, Zarrus, typifies the Warrior Path and his men adore him . . .'

'How do you know about the mammoth – Storm?' Talisker asked.

'Because I was there the night she was born,' Ferebe smiled almost shyly. 'She is very beautiful. And clever, she . . .' She stopped.

'What's wrong?' Raco asked.

'The attack on Kamala Sev – what if they were aiming to kill Storm?'

'Seems a lot of trouble to go to. Anyway, the attack was by those things – Shards and Flays – they're completely mindless as far as anyone can tell.'

'Someone must know where they're coming from . . .'

'I can tell you where they've been,' Talisker said

quietly. 'They've been through the void – the Time Between – I think we saw the spirits of their victims there.' He glanced at Yiska. 'It's probably the worst thing I've ever seen. And I've seen some pretty bad things in my time.'

They fell silent. Each one busying themselves preparing for the night ahead. The cave may have been dry but there was no way they were going to get it particularly warm. Raco had first watch and he stationed himself a little further back down the trail, just before the widening of the plateau. He wasn't surprised when Ferebe came to speak to him in private.

'Do you trust them, *yekt*?' she frowned. 'Because I'm not sure.'

'Ferebe Vezul,' Raco muttered tiredly, 'you saw them magically appear from the sky. How much convincing do you need?'

'I'm sorry. I have a naturally suspicious nature. Raco, thank you.'

'For what? You wouldn't be in this mess without me.'

She nodded gravely. 'I know. But it has been my honour to fight beside you. I do not say that lightly. Perhaps we have proved that Shoreth and Fine are not inherently opposed.'

He peered towards he in the darkness. 'Sounds like "goodbye" Ferebe Vezul.'

She shrugged, 'No, no . . . I am just tired. I really must get some sleep. And I hate goodbyes.'

Raco was hardly surprised when they awoke at dawn to find Ferebe was gone.

*

Effie was furious. She had woken up and had breakfast that Aunt Millie and Renee had kindly made her. She felt weak but better than she could have imagined. It was a bit like a bad hangover; her hands shook slightly and she was still clammy from where the sweat had dried on her skin. Sipping the big mug of sweet herbal tea she stared around the tent – it was certainly different than the hogan, looked like something the army would pitch at the site of a disaster. Still, it was warm inside, if a trifle damp from condensation.

'Where's Yiska and Duncan?' she asked Aunt Millie. Millie had frowned at her worriedly when she said this and left the tent – presumably to get them.

When Millie returned however, it was only Rodney who came with her. He was wrapped up, muffled against the snow, only his eyes showing above a big orange scarf that covered his nose and mouth; but his eyes were enough to show Effie the old man was worried.

'Where are they?' she demanded.

Rodney pushed his scarf away from his face. 'Effie . . .'

'Oh no. It worked, didn't it? They've gone haven't they? They've gone without me?'

'They were too worried about your health, Miss Morgan,' Rodney explained as if she were a child.

And Effie, to her shame, reacted just like a child. She threw a complete tantrum – spat the dummy, threw a benny. She screeched and threw her tea against the side of the tent where it made a not-very-satisfying thud; she kicked her legs and thumped her fists on her thighs. 'No, no, no!' Finally, bunching her knees up she buried her face in the sleeping bag and sobbed pathetically, rocking back and forwards.

'Effie.' Aunt Mille addressed her quietly. 'That's no way to behave.'

She raised her tear-stained face and looked at Millie through fever-lank hair. 'You don't understand Aunt Millie. They wanted me to go. Asked me to come with them, and then I do something bloody . . . bloody stupid. And now they've gone without me. They must hate me now – think I'm pathetic. I am bloody pathetic.'

Millie nodded sympathetically, although Effie wasn't sure that she actually knew where her nephew and Talisker had gone. 'Taking that medicine was a stupid thing to do.' She said it without hint of accusation, just plain speaking. 'But we all do stupid things sometimes, Effie.'

Effie wiped her face with the back of her sleeve; Millie's words were cold comfort but somehow they helped her more than if she had lied to her and said trivial, banal things. 'You're right, Aunt Millie. And you know what the most stupid thing I've done is? Coming in the first damned place! I guess I wanted to be a part of it because Talisker knew my mother,' she played with her St Christopher as she spoke. 'Well, that's it for me. They couldn't wait for me and I'm bloody well not waiting for them. I'm going back to Chinle and then, home.'

'You'll have to wait, Effie. Canyon de Chelly is snowed in. All the people from the Ceremony are still here. We're having an unexpected pow-wow.'

Effie sniffed, feeling calmer. 'Is that a real thing, then?'

'It's like a party and a campout. There's usually properly organised stuff like a rodeo – but this is just to pass the time until the thaw in a few days. Here, I'll get you some more tea.'

As Millie lifted the flap of the tent to go out, Effie saw the blinding white flash of the snow-bound canyon. She wanted to go home now, she thought. Once she was up and could pack, she would sneak away and go home because she should never have come in the first place.

We all do stupid things – but some people just keep doing them.

Chapter Ten

He is sleeping. Or doing whatever it is he does when I do not hear him for hours. It is late, well past midnight but I have woken again deliberately to write in this journal. I want to record something very strange which happened yesterday, something which disturbed me greatly as it indicated the strength of his hold now over my physical form.

We were in the Council Chamber and I had managed to arrange that all of the new Emperor Tulann's loyal entourage follow him into the forest of Or Coille in a pathetic – and pointless – attempt to lay siege to Ruannoch Were. Those who were to remain in the city were my loyal warriors, servants to keep the city running for our benefit, and those few Councillors who could easily be made to see the wisdom of switching their allegiances.

I was pleased with the morning's work and so I can assure you I was in excellent spirits. As I walked from the chamber, I caught sight of myself in the ornate mirror just by the door. Someone was talking to me, Jate Sorrinsklaz I believe, one of Tulann's less ardent admirers, talking about provisions for the army; but I became distracted by my own reflection and could only hear his voice droning on in the background in ceaseless monotone.

Walking up to the mirror, I studied my features –

handsome in a way, I supposed, delicately boned with a high forehead – but not me. It wasn't myself staring back at me and that feeling is almost too disconcerting to describe. I noticed that there appeared to be something like a bluish bruise running along the line of one cheek but I could not account for any injury.

'Do you think I've changed, Jate? What are people saying about me?'

The young man stopped in confusion. 'Well . . . I . . .'

'Oh come now, people must have noticed?' I said. I had managed to effectively conceal the darkness of my new hair by shaving it close to my head – but the rest was not so easy.

'Y-yes. We thought perhaps you are tired, or unwell.'

I was listening to his reply, somewhat distantly, imagining I could spread a plausible cover story, when, the thing happened.

It was only a white feather, I have no idea where it came from; it floated down from the ceiling so perhaps a bird had gotten into the rafters. I saw it first as a reflection at the top right of my vision. Drifting, dancing a leisurely trail. My own instincts would be to ignore such trivialities but instead, I – I realised later of course that it was him, able to take over whenever he chose – reached out my hand and caught the feather. Staring down at its delicate shape in my palm, I felt a deep, overwhelming sadness. Already I had inadvertently crushed its softer downy bracts. Its white vulnerability was unbearable. I began to cry. Right there, in front of Jate and those few others who had not left the Council Chamber. At first, gentle, sorrowful tears but then, a great racking sob escaped me.

'Sir? Sir? Are you ill?' Jate looked alarmed, as well he might. I staggered back slightly and someone pressed me back into a seat. Trying desperately to stop from making a further exhibition of myself I held onto my ribs as if seeking to hold the unwanted emotions in by force. But I could not stop the tears nor the devastating sadness.

Someone pressed a glass of water into my hand and I gulped it down mainly in order to prevent any further sound. My mind was screaming; Stop it! Stop. Calm down.

Eventually he – and I – did calm down of course but I gather I cried openly in front of at least ten people for a good five minutes. Gossip which could prove gold dust to any of my Commanders seeking to depose me.

I kept the feather. I looked at it in my room late that night. He was sullen and unresponsive when I asked him why a mere feather could provoke such an emotional outpouring. I made him look at it as if it were a punishment – these are still my eyes after all.

'Beautiful day,' the stranger commented.

'Oh . . . yes,' Nancy smiled shyly. He was tall and handsome although possibly a bit old for her – still, she'd be prepared to make an exception. 'Here's your change, sir. Have a nice day.'

'Thanks. Is this the quickest road into the canyon?'

'Canyon De Chelly? You won't get down there for a few days,' she glanced out at the four wheel drive pick-up – still very clean, obviously a hire car – 'even with one of those. Snow's too thick; the roads get pretty treacherous. Route Seven's definitely closed. Best wait till the thaw,' she smiled brightly. 'There's a couple of real nice inns in Chinle and they say a nice warm wind is on the way . . .'

'Really.' He smiled a disarming white smile, almost wolfish, and pulled his shades down his nose slightly so he could peer over the top of them. 'Guess I'll have to walk down.'

'Wow, you're keen,' she laughed. 'You have to have a Navajo guide and I'm pretty sure they won't be taking anyone down. Tell you what, here's my uncle's number, give him a call – he's a park certified guide – he'll let you know what the chances are.'

'Thank you . . .' he read her badge, 'Nancy Begay. I'll sure do that.'

'Are you in a hurry to get there?' she asked.

'Yup. I've got to meet my god-daughter there.'

Nancy shook her head. 'No, she won't be in the canyon,' she said. 'I'll bet she's holed up in a hotel in Chinle. You'll see . . .'

'Well, I kinda hope you're right.' He scooped the mixture of candy and junk food he'd just purchased into his arms and made for the door where he stopped to fumble awkwardly with the handle. Jerking the door back, he wedged it open with his foot. A blast of light snow and freezing air gusted into the gas station shop.

'Good luck.'

'Thanks. *Ciao, bella.*'

They had decided to head north, but getting out of Cerne's Gorge was the first problem. Raco knew of the few paths on the north-west spur of the canyon where Ruannoch Were territory ended but their evasion of the Shoreth Riders had taken them into the larger area of the canyon that ran one hundred lush green miles West to East across the belly of Sutra. This was Raco's Sidhe clan's ancestral territory but he was not familiar with it.

'My father told me my clan used to take messages and trade for Durghanti and Kamala Sev,' he commented bitterly. 'No Fine ever knew the canyon so well as my people. Now look at me – I can't even find the way back up.'

'Dinny blame yersel, Raco,' Malky assured him. 'You're no responsible for what's happened to your clan.'

'Malky's right,' Yiska commented. 'You cannot take it all upon yourself, Raco.'

Yiska was feeling slightly better, the walking helped; the canyon was beautiful and quite different from Canyon De Chelly. The scenery was less arid, occasional waterfalls tumbled in spectacular freezing spray from the plateaux above. The rocks were mainly black basalt or granite, which made outcrops like huge, jagged splinters impervious to weathering unlike the soft Arizona sandstone. Also, as he walked, Dog walked beside him so that if he stretched out his fingers he made contact with the warm, coarse fur of his mangy neck. Yiska knew animals could sense pain and shock and thought perhaps Dog would change his allegiance once he detected Yiska was recovered but for now he was grateful for the small comfort of the contact.

Still, there was something badly wrong with this place. It felt strangely empty. Just as he thought this, Talisker asked him what *hozro* meant. And then he knew what was wrong.

'It means a kind of harmony. Living in harmony with

the spirits of the world and your own spirit. Walking in beauty, we call it.'

Talisker nodded. 'You say Sutra has none?'

'It's just a feeling, Talisker. I can't describe it – a kinda emptiness.' He fell silent again and watched Raco who was walking ahead of him. Yiska was struck by the similarity of Raco's features to some Native Americans; Talisker had told him that the bear clan Sidhe were the most similar to the Fine – the Lynx and Eagle clans less so as their totems evidently exerted a stronger influence on their genes. It seemed reasonable to assume that Rodney had seen them in his dreams because of some ancestral or spiritual link but, when he asked, Raco had no idea who might have called out to them.

'All of our magic is gone,' he said glumly. 'Even the Council of Tema is powerless – fading to a rumour, their heads stuck in the past.' His tone was slightly sarcastic but mostly saddened.

'Mebbe Yiska should tell them what's happening to his people,' Malky remarked. 'Could be a connection.'

Tulann III stared about him, his eyes wide with fury. He was the emperor now dammit, so everyone had to do as he said. So why did it seem that already, his father's lackeys were still treating him as a child?

'I am telling you,' he repeated, despising his own thin, unbroken voice, 'my father will be avenged. And quickly. I see no reason to give the Fine time to prepare their defences. We will attack Ruannoch Were in three days' time.'

'Majesty,' Zarrus smiled from the other side of the table. 'You are correct – so astute, your father would be proud – delay will give them time to prepare . . . ah, to a point.'

From most people this would come across as sycophantic toadying, but Tulann was prepared to accept the word of Zarrus – he was a proper soldier after all, had seen action and crucified many. Tulann's father – vapid old fool that he was – spoke highly of Zarrus and he was popular with the other generals as well as the rank and file. Women wanted to bed him and men wanted to be him – Tulann regarded Zarrus thoughtfully, there was something different about the General but he couldn't quite put his finger on it. He had shaved his hair close into his head which made it look surprisingly dark, he was off colour too, dark circles under his eyes made him look older.

'Are you well, General Zarrus?' Tulann frowned.

'Indeed sir, thank you for your concern. I am afraid the loss of your beloved father has taken us all rather hard.'

There were murmurs of assent from around the table and Tulann nodded and then yawned expressively watching the reactions of the others around the council table. They looked nervous and so they should – if they had their finger on the pulse of Durghanti gossip they would know that Tulann was widely known as 'The Poisoner Prince'. It amused him immensely to note how many full wine goblets there still were on the table.

The word 'siege' cut across his thoughts. 'A siege situation . . .' Zarrus had said.

'No, no, no, Zarrus. We *attack* Ruannoch Were. What part of that don't you understand? A siege is not acceptable.'

'It would not be by choice, sir,' Zarrus replied. 'Ruannoch Were is brilliantly defended – it is unreachable except by water – there is one causeway across the lake. We can cut it off and starve them out but they may have enough food for six months – even longer . . .'

Tulann III had never actually been to Ruannoch Were and had no idea the city might prove so difficult. 'How in hell's name did the *yekts* have the skill to build something like that?' he mused. 'Everyone knows they're stupid.'

Zarrus opened his mouth to say something but then obviously thought better of it; he cleared his throat and glanced towards Councillor Almasey for some input or support.

'Actually, sir,' Almasey intervened, 'I believe the Fine did not build Ruannoch Were or Soulis Mor in the north. At some stage in their history they must have been like us . . .'

'They have *never* been like us . . .' Tulann cut in acidly.

'I – I meant . . . warrior conquerors, sir . . .'

'I know what you meant, Almasey. So, this is what we do . . . we go to Ruannoch Were and sort it out when we get there. Perhaps we can shoot fire-arrows at it or something, or . . .' he waved rather vaguely. 'Who is their Thane, Zarrus?'

'Thane Sigrid, sir. He's quite elderly – older than your father.'

'Good. If we lure him out under a pretext of a council of war we can hold him hostage.' Tulann smiled. 'Three days then. Have the men ready.'

'Yes sir.'

Tulann III stood up and left the chamber and the Councillors and Generals stood up and bowed. When the door closed they waited until Tulann's footsteps receded down the passageway before speaking. Then, they all spoke at once.

'This is sheer madness,' Almasey complained. 'It will become a siege whether he wants it or no.'

'Yes,' Zarrus glanced meaningfully at the door and grinned slyly. 'But you cannot blame the young Emperor for wishing to avenge his father's murder. And he has some good ideas already about breaking the siege . . . should it develop as such.'

Almasey's eyes widened as he realised Zarrus was hinting that Tulann was still outside. 'Oh indeed.'

'Zarrus, General Zarrus . . .' Helene, the only woman Shoreth General tapped him on the shoulder. 'Look.'

They had thought Counsellor Tavi was asleep; but he had not survived the meeting. He sat slumped forward in his chair, chin on chest, as though having the kind of snooze one easily fell into in long council meetings.

Zarrus said nothing; it seemed that Tulann III might be more trouble than he had anticipated. Outside the door Tulann laughed silently, Tavi's death was nothing to do with him, the old man had simply had a heart attack or something. Still, he would not work too hard to disavow his Councillors of the conclusion they had immediately leapt to. It suited his purposes for them to be afraid. He gestured his page to walk quietly back along the corridor and meet him halfway.

*

'Is it true, Rebe? Can it be true?' Her father looked strangely vulnerable sitting propped up on his pillows, the silver-grey of the moonlight bleaching out his features even further. The lines of his face that Ferebe secretly treasured and respected – so wise, so powerful – now just made the General look old.

'Who told you?' She stood behind the door; still crouching in the shadow although her mind would not countenance the fact he might call out and betray her. Vezul slept with a sword by his bed, as did many warriors, and Ferebe saw his gaze flicker across it, but he did not reach for the blade.

'They sent message birds from Durghanti. They say you helped a *yekt* assassinate Emperor Tebron.'

'They are animals, Ferebe. Why would you defend them?'

'I would not defend them if I thought they were guilty but it's simply not true. I – I was with him all night.' Once the damning words were spoken she expected an explosion of rage from her father but none came; he waited for her explanation, which was to his credit, but he was unable to keep the shock from registering on his face. 'We were only talking, I swear . . .'

'It matters little – there is an order for your arrest, I am sure a liaison with a *yekt* is the least of your problems.'

She nodded. He was right; it seemed an irrelevance compared to the small matter of regicide. 'Don't – you won't tell mother will you?'

'So, if it wasn't you, then who?'

'We suspect it to be . . .' she quailed; this wasn't going to be easy.

'Spit it out, girl.'

'We're pretty sure . . . it's Zarrus. General Zarrus.'

'No! It's not possible.'

'It is, Father. He is the only one who was there when we spoke to the Emperor and . . .'

'You spoke to Emperor?'

'The night he died, yes. We took him proof that the Shards and Flays are Shoreth in origin. I know, it pains me too, Father, but it doesn't stop the truth. Nothing can. The Emperor recognised the amulet which Raco and I found near the body of one killed by a Flay.'

'But, why would Zarrus be involved in such a thing. He had the Emperor's respect, command of the Imperial Army – what would he have to gain?'

There was a sound outside; perhaps Vezul's squire had heard something. They both paused as the footsteps stopped at Vezul's door. Whoever it was stood silently, listening for a few moments. Vezul obligingly snored gently.

'I must go,' Ferebe whispered when the listener had gone. 'I am a traitor. They cannot find me here. Listen, Father, think about what I've said. Zarrus is dangerous – I don't exactly know why.'

'Where will you go, Rebe?'

'I'm not sure. I'll go and see Storm first. Is she well?'

'Unsettled after the attack last week, but seeing you will cheer her,' he chuckled quietly, 'if a mammoth can be cheered . . .'

'I will come home when this is all settled, I promise. Tell mother . . . tell her I am no murderer.'

'She knows, Ferebe.'

'Goodbye Father.'

'Gods protect you.'

Vezul lay and stared into the shadow for a long time after she had gone. Sleep came only with the dawn.

And so that left her here; sharing a bed with Storm. Warm enough, a bit smelly – but Ferebe was used to the smell. It was five days since she'd left Raco and the others in Cerne's Gorge, six nights since the death of Emperor Tebron. Ferebe stared at the hay sticking between her toes and sighed, 'Wonder what Raco's up to, eh?'

Storm snored softly, her great flanks heaving as though being pumped by giant bellows. She certainly seemed pleased to have Ferebe back although – the Emperor had neglected to mention – one of the other mammoths had been killed by a Flay and this, and the death of the *Sanah*, had unsettled the whole herd. Storm had been enraged and frightened by the incident and this was making her dangerous to the other *Sanah* so, she had been clamped with a manacle around her front leg to a huge iron stake in the ground. Ferebe thought this was stupid – Storm could easily pull it out with a bit of effort. But so far, she had cooperated. From here she could see the stars through the vast netting the Shoreth had slung over the top of the quarry that housed the mammoths; Ferebe leaned in the curve of Storm's back leg enjoying the warmth and idly plaiting a handful of hair as she had done since she was a little girl.

It was a subtle change in the herd that alerted her – Ferebe had been around the creatures since she was a little girl and when they became restless the signs were there to see for those who knew. Storm woke up, and although she didn't stand her ears began to judder and fidget. After a minute she began to pick up pieces of hay with her trunk and fling them over her back.

'Easy, girl,' Ferebe soothed. Other mammoths that were free to roam around the vast space of the quarry also woke up for no apparent reason. They fidgeted increasingly nervously and made subdued trumpeting sounds to one another. In the semi-darkness lit only by the stars and a few lanterns Ferebe could just make out the looming shapes moving around as if they were checking on one another. Storm's mother – an elderly cow named Maple – came over and ran her trunk down the side of Storm's head as if consoling her.

That's exactly what they are doing, Ferebe thought. *They can sense it; a predator is coming.*

They were over the top of the canyon when they saw the first of the creatures. It had taken two days to find the south-eastern rill where there were still steps and a wooden pulley – long rotted and broken – which had been used for lifting horses to the top rather then take them to the other paths out which were all miles behind them. The stairs were usable but not particularly safe. It was raining; a dull, obfuscating grey, which hung suspended in the air. The steps were slimy and covered in lichen, some were already rotted through and others disintegrated when any weight was placed on them. Fortunately, they were angled just sharply enough so that losing one step did not mean a fast trip to the canyon floor. There were few handholds left but there were natural features to cling onto, rocks, creepers and tree roots.

Still, it was hard work. The drizzle soon soaked everyone through to the skin and, mingled with perspiration, made a clammy, sticky sweat. Raco, who was third in line behind Malky and Talisker, said little – he was preoccupied by the strength of his *Kellid* bear arm, still fascinated to find it was his. Just when he thought he was becoming accustomed to it, he would find it strange all over again. He watched himself reaching out, gripping at tree roots, flexing the brown talons and grasping onto handholds which would have eluded his human fingers. It renewed his respect for *Kellid* and his sadness that he would never commune with the great bear again.

Yiska was bringing up the rear. He was a fit person with great stamina and he was accustomed to rock-climbing and traversing but he had an extra burden – Dog. The beginnings of the steps were too steep and Dog had scrabbled gamely before falling back and whining piteously. Yiska had frowned back at him for a moment; the Navajos' relationship with dogs was pragmatic and for the most part unsentimental. They were working animals in the main, used to herd the sheep or guard outbuildings – many wandered off and became semi-feral on the Rez which is where Dog had followed them from. He probably had fleas and all sorts of . . .

'You'll need tae pick him up.' Malky had stopped and everyone else had to stop behind him.

'He'll manage.'

'Naw, the stairs are too steep.'

'He'll unbalance me, I've got my backpack on.'

'I'll take that. Here, pass it forwards.'

So Malky carried Yiska's Timberland backpack –

which he seemed inordinately thrilled about – and Yiska grudgingly picked up Dog.

'Ah yuck, he stinks!' It seemed Dog's frame was mostly skin and bone but he had long skinny legs, which stuck out at all angles when Yiska picked him up. Everyone laughed at his undignified position but Dog didn't seem to mind and licked Yiska's face gratefully.

That had been an hour ago. The humour of the situation had swiftly been lost on Yiska – Dog was bloody heavy. Luckily, there were a few landings where the stairs changed direction and Yiska stopped and put Dog on the ground where he shook the wetness from his coat back on to Yiska.

When they reached the head of the steps, Yiska heard Malky curse, and then Raco, but was too preoccupied to give it much thought. He lugged Dog up the last few steps and then practically threw him down onto the grass. Then he looked around him.

He hadn't stopped to question what the season was in Sutra but if he'd had to guess he would have said fall. In fact, the relative fecundity of Cerne's Gorge had given them a false impression. It was winter, at least a winter of sorts. No cleansing snow had fallen, the plateau was dry and blasted by a scorching ice. An odd stillness muffled the air, sound cut short by the grey haze, which up here hung in suspension like mist. They were on the fringes of a forest stretched away as far as Yiska could see but the stark, denuded trees were dry scorched just like the ground.

But it was worse than that; Yiska's impression that the *hozro* of Sutra was gone – that the spirits of the trees, the rocks and the water were offended or had fled – was confirmed here. Everyone felt it. Talisker crouched on the ground and wordlessly touched the grass, which broke beneath his hands into pale brown splinters.

'What is it?' Malky breathed. 'Kin you feel it anall Yiska? It's like as if something has stabbed the land in its heart.'

'Yes.'

'Where are we, Raco?' Talisker asked.

'We should be about seventy leagues south-east of Ruannoch Were. This is the southern fringes of Or Coille – do you know it?'

'Not this particular part, no.'

'Well, I'm going to head to Ruannoch Were to warn them. Are you coming?'

'No, it will be too late by the time we get there on foot – if the Shoreth are going to attack it takes little time from Durghanti.'

'Reckon it'll be a siege onnyways,' Malky said.

Dog growled, his hackles standing up in a ridge that extended right down his back. 'Get down,' Yiska whispered.

They crouched behind the now-derelict wall that had once housed the winch used for the horse platform. 'Be quiet, Dog,' Yiska cautioned. Surprisingly Dog did as he was told. For long moments there was nothing to see, no breeze stirred the branches of the frozen forest; it was completely still.

Then, the air was rent by sharp cracking and snapping as something crashed through the forest oblivious to anything in its path. Except it wasn't just one; within moments the expanse of Or Coille was teaming with corrupt life. There must have been a hundred Shards and perhaps fifty Flays. They didn't speak as they ran but the rough sound of the Shards' ragged breathing, which came as grunts and groans, made bizarre concert with the sound of their destruction of Or Coille. The Flays moved effortlessly by comparison, their bare feet making light, brief contact with the soil, the red and purple of their skinned bodies mercifully dulled by the mist. The whole crowd was moving fast, running with a silent purpose although there was no obvious leader.

Yiska hardly dared breathe least he attract attention from the horde. 'Look,' Raco nudged him and whispered so quietly he was not quite sure he had spoken, 'over there.'

The creatures were running right to left across Yiska's field of vision and at first he couldn't see what Raco was pointing at. He could see so many of the nightmarish creatures he wished he could scrub his eyeballs out, but then he saw what Raco meant.

A different kind of nightmare; beings that resembled moving shadow. Their shapes were shifting, moving as if composed of . . . flies, insects . . . as if they were a moving swarm rather than a solid figure. Yiska felt his stomach turn over.

Talisker and Malky exchanged a worried glance. 'Aw naw, Duncan,' Malky groaned.

'What are they?'

Talisker spat to clear the nasty taste in his mouth. 'Corrannyeid' he said.

*

Ferebe stood on top of the watchtower staring out into the starlit darkness. She knew there was a risk that she might be seen, especially from the little cluster of buildings where the *Sanah* slept – but something was really upsetting the herd. A light had come on in one of the huts and she was pretty sure someone would be coming to check to see what all the noise was below.

The wooden ladder extended out of the hole of the old quarry where the mammoths were housed and was then enclosed by a makeshift wooden and leather tower. It had been built for the purpose of sending messages into Kamala Sev by means of covering and uncovering lantern lights. The quarry was over a league from the outskirts of the city which had watchtowers of its own but in fact, they were rarely used – the *Sanah* lived and worked in the quarry, rarely going into the city unless for provisions or herbs for their beloved charges.

The stars were bright tonight and a soft breeze carried from the north, stirring her hair and clothes. She thought about Raco and wondered if he'd made it back to Ruannoch Were before the Shoreth attack – little good it would have done him. If the city was under attack he could hardly break his way in, nor could the strangers.

There was a movement. Up ahead, to the north. She stared, willing her eyesight to pierce the gloom. No. Perhaps she had imagined it, maybe it was a sheep or a . . . No, there it was again. And there! Something was coming. A whole host of something coming to Kamala Sev from the north-east.

'By the Gods . . .' Ferebe was galvanized into action and climbed back down into the quarry floor. She was just about to go to Storm and take off her manacles when the door opened and *Sanah* Velmer stood there, still in his nightclothes.

'Velmer – quick! I think the city is going to be attacked!'

'Ferebe Vezul? What are you doing here? You'll be arrested – they say you . . .' He stopped speaking as Ferebe drew her blade and held it before her.

'Listen. Listen to me, Velmer. I did not kill the Emperor. Neither did the Fine. There is treachery afoot which we have no time to discuss now. An army is coming to attack the city.' She pointed back up the tower, 'I've just seen it, Velmer. It's true. They're coming from the east, Go and look if you don't believe me.'

Behind where she stood the herd had gathered together into a tight group, the bulls on the outside, the three calves protected in the middle. Velmer had worked with the herd for many years and he'd never observed such behaviour before. 'I believe you Ferebe – we must warn the city. If they are coming from the east as you say they will hit the residential area before they reach the fortress. They will be slaughtered in their beds.'

'Take Breeze – she is the only female with no calf, and she's fast. Ride to the western gate. Quickly!'

'Yes, yes . . .' Velmer rushed over to Breeze and began to soothe her by feeding her hay – Ferebe was fleetingly worried that she would be unwilling to leave the security of the herd but Breeze knew Velmer well and trusted the old man. 'What will you do, Ferebe?' As he spoke, more *Sanah* piled into the quarry aware of the disturbance. They stopped short when they saw Ferebe. 'You must do as she says,' Velmer shouted from Breeze's back. 'The city is in danger!'

'Mount up everyone!' she glanced fearfully at the bulls but hoped their relationships with their handlers would ensure cooperation. 'There is a force coming from the east – we'll take the herd across the beach and around the front of Kamala Sev to alert the residents – but we must move fast! Let's go!'

For a frightening moment the *Sanah* just stood and stared at her. 'You heard her!' Velmer yelled – he was already on his way out the great doors.

And so the herd of thirty mammoths ran along the beach led by Ferebe Vezul on Storm. Outside the *Sanah*, no one in Kamala Sev had ever seen the white mammoth before but that seemed to matter little now. Storm was ecstatic at being outside and Ferebe struggled to control her when she saw the ocean for the first time, but the bulls were running just behind her and Storm was one with the herd. Ferebe had never before experienced the herd in full charge – the sound was awesome, a pounding, thundering rhythm echoed by the crashing of the surf. She yelled in exaltation and Storm brayed a response.

As they rounded the headland they could see the western edge of Kamala Sev off to their left. Lights were on and alarm bells beginning to clang, shattering the sleep of the city's denizens. But the most vulnerable, the worker Shoreth, artisans, teachers, cooks, builders, architects, engineers, all lived on the eastern side, unarmed and unprotected for the most part. Ferebe prayed she would reach them in time to rouse them from their beds and prepare a defence. Her mind raced ahead – very few would have seen the Shards and Flays before – probably none would know to stay outwith the reach of the Flays, whose single touch meant death.

Screams from the far edges of the city alerted her to the fact their rescue might be too late for some. As they charged up the main street, the first wave of creatures had crashed into the city like a hellish tsunami. It was bedlam; people were running from their houses – women clutching their children, panicked into fleeing where hiding in a cellar would have served them better. The Shards were already killing indiscriminately, picking up people and breaking them like twigs. As the mammoths came into the end of the broad avenue the hysterical residents had little time to wonder at Storm. Ferebe heard the *Sanah* behind her calling to one another – they were nervous and their mounts picked up their fear. One of the bulls – Tornnak – trumpeted a loud attack call designed to frighten any aggressor and began to charge; his Sanah was helpless to do anything but hang on as Tornnak trampled a Shard underfoot. A little girl stood next in his path, staring wildly at the massive beast; as if she could read Ferebe's mind, Storm barged into the side of Tornnak sending him off course, then she gently plucked up the terrified child and deposited her on her broad back behind Ferebe.

'Yes! Pick them up,' Ferebe screamed. 'Pick up the children!'

Some of the *Sanah* heard her and began to launch into the chaos, reaching down themselves and grabbing children upwards – Ferebe saw one tiny baby boy plucked from its mother's arms just as a Shard grabbed the woman from behind – she was mindless with fear but Ferebe imagined she caught a flicker of relief in her expression as she saw her baby rescued just as she died.

The Shards were attacking the mammoths with clubs and spears; the strangely indignant squealing of the great beasts in pain broke Ferebe's heart as much as anything, but the sound served as a rallying cry. The mammoths were precious to the Shoreth and the realization that the fabled White Mammoth was *here* on the battleground gave the beleaguered citizens heart. They fought back with any weapons they could find; pokers, boiling water from their night heaters, rakes, hoes, anything with which they could hit the Shards at length.

And then the Flays walked on to the field. 'No! Don't touch them! Don't let them touch you!' Ferebe shouted. But her voice was swallowed up by the bedlam. She repeated her instruction to the nearest *Sanah* who signaled that they had heard and pressed further into the crowd, shouting the message at the tops of the voices. It was too late for many, of course, the Flays were chillingly fast; in fact, Ferebe was unsure whether they were running from place to place or disappearing and reappearing – it was a silent, flickering motion which the eye could not follow. They left a trail of instant mummified corpses in their wake.

The buildings were ablaze now; a lurid orange against the first grey light of the morning. Ferebe gathered four children and a young woman on to the back of Storm but realized there was room for no more. She was frantically wondering what to do next when she saw a young man with a spade trying to protect his family from two Shards. She slid down off Storm's back and ran to his aid.

'Here,' she shouted. 'Put them up on Storm . . .' The man backed away, guiding his two children towards the mammoth as Ferebe stepped in to take his place.

She was in luck, one of the Shards was picked off from behind as the children's mother staved its head in with an iron bar – the other, she managed to dispatch in mere moments. She was used to the beasts now, knew the mindless way they fought, they were immensely strong but slow, lumbering and directionless. They were hard to kill but she had found their weakness – at the base of the throat in the hollow of the clavicle bone there was still soft tissue.

The children on the back of Storm were squealing with terror and as she turned back, she realised why; a Flay had killed the young father and was, without pause, reaching out to touch Storm. 'No! Storm!' she yelled.

But it was no use. She was only a few yards away but all the Flay had to do was reach out and touch Storm. Amazingly Storm seemed fascinated by the creature and reached out towards it with her trunk. Ferebe ran towards the strange tableaux her gaze fixed on the patch of space where they would make fatal contact. She tripped and fell headlong with a curse but looked up as soon as she was on the ground.

It was too late. The Flay had touched Storm. 'Oh no,' she groaned. But nothing happened. The Flay, unaware that it had no effect, moved on in its flickering leprous mission – Storm simply turned towards Ferebe as if awaiting further instruction.

Ferebe was jubilant, she crowed with delight as she picked herself off the ground. 'Storm, you clever, clever girl . . .' although the fact that Storm was impervious to the Flay's touch was entirely involuntary.

Her jubilation was short-lived however; once she had remounted (which was a bit of a squeeze now with eight passengers) she had a birds-eye view of the devastation. The residential district was destroyed. Pitched battles were still taking place but the Flays were the silent killers, walking into a battle grouping and leaving it decimated. She noted with sick horror that they were indiscriminate and killed the Shards carelessly. Two mammoths were down, their ungainly corpses like islands in the chaos around which the battle streamed. Behind her, the main citadel was burning also, the stench of burning gripping her already constricted throat. Ahead the dawn light illuminated a grim truth; the hillside to the east was swarming with the demons.

'Ferebe . . .' She turned around, soundless tears tracking through the mire of her cheeks. Her father was there with around a hundred Shoreth warriors. His expression was bleak but he had ordered his men to form a barrier and they were already dragging wagons between the burning buildings to form a wall of sorts. They shouted to the civilians to help or get behind their makeshift line – those on the wrong side would be doomed once they became entrenched.

It was a noble effort but Ferebe and her father exchanged a look that said everything – it would not be enough. There were simply too many. Kamala Sev would fall; it was just a matter of time.

'Take the women and children,' Vezul instructed.

'Round them up. Use your precious mammoths and head for Durghanti – the Emperor must protect you.'

'Father, I . . .'

'Do it, Lieutenant Vezul.'

'Yes sir.'

She looked back only once and he was watching her; she saluted him with her blade. It was all she could do to say goodbye.

Chapter Eleven

Horza groaned as freezing salt water was flung onto his back, burning his newly flogged skin as if it were hot needles. Failure cost when Zarrus was your leader – he had known that when he returned to Durghanti – but Horza understood the General's iron regime, respected it, discipline was a harsh mistress after all.

He shook his head to clear the water from his hair and ears. Determined not to show weakness he pushed himself away from the oak post and, willing his legs not to shake, reached for his jacket. His hands shook as he fumbled in the pocket for the silver *derz* to pay the lashman.

'Here,' he flipped the coin to the waiting acolyte who caught it deftly, 'choke on it why don't you.' The man grinned, obviously uncaring about Horza's insult as long as he got paid. As he turned to leave Horza shouted after him, 'I must see Zarrus! Tell the general I must see him!'

He had no idea whether or not the lashman had heard him or had any intention of delivering his message so he sat down and began to wash his face, wiping away the blood where he'd bitten his lip to stop from crying out. The door was open. He knew he was free to leave and take up his position once more, but he was in no hurry. The army had departed for Ruannoch Were but he knew that was the least of it.

His reverie was interrupted by the sound of a slow, sardonic handclap. 'Bravo Horza.' Zarrus had come in and was standing behind him, admiring the lash pattern on his back as if it were a particularly fine work of art. 'That's what I like about flogging – a particularly liberating punishment, is it not? You may have flogged yourself with birch branches had I not done it for you. Now you are cleansed – forgiven. You wanted to see me? I received your message as soon as you arrived back in Durghanti, but I have been unavoidably detained dealing with our illustrious new leader.'

And that was it – what made Zarrus quite so chilling. Horza imagined him receiving his message and airily waving his hand; 'Have him flogged' – just to fill in the time because he was busy.

'Sir, I have seen something miraculous . . .'

'Ah well, miraculous is of great interest to me, Horza. Go on.'

'A gateway . . .' he groped for the right words. 'A fracture in reality. When I was fighting with Ferebe Vezul and her ally. It –it was the only reason they overpowered me. This fracture opened up, there was a bright white light, and people came through . . .'

'Really Horza, it seems a lame excuse.'

'It's true, sir, I swear.'

'How many people?'

'Three. All men – one looked like a Sidhe. I can take you there if you like. I have memorised the location.' Zarrus looked fascinated, in fact his face acquired a dreamy, distant expression. 'Sir?'

'A Sidhe you say?'

'Yes sir. But I think . . . I think they were coming from another world. Does that sound ridiculous?'

'No, Horza, it sounds miraculous as you said. Unbelievable.' Zarrus studied Horza's expression closely. 'Have you been praying, Horza? Praying every hour as I command?'

'Yes Zarrus . . . Lord.'

'So, your soul will know no regret.' Without warning Zarrus reached out and grabbed Horza's face, his fingers spread across his forehead, his thumb and little finger digging into his temples. Horza, so brave, so calm when being flogged for his master, acted instinctively, throwing his hands outward to knock Zarrus' grip away. Light exploded in his skull, pain coursed through the centre of his body sloughing outwards through his arms and legs.

Zarrus saw his mind, pillaged his memory; fortunately for Horza this took mere moments. As Zarrus released him his legs gave way and he crumpled to the floor, his resolve and dignity useless. 'Well done Horza, you spoke truly. I sense it is the way to another world . . .' Ignoring Horza's body was creased into a foetal position at his feet Zarrus stepped over him, his thoughts elsewhere. 'If they are Sidhe, I can use them, I *need* them.' He turned back as though it was an afterthought and only then seemed to register what he had done to his acolyte. Horza was attempting to pick himself off the floor but so far, had only managed to sit up. Zarrus crouched beside him, a frighteningly genial smile lighting up his austere face.

'Do you believe in synchronicity my friend?'

In fact, Horza's blasted brain could not remember

what synchronicity was. 'Erm . . . yes Lord,' he flinched, waiting for a new attack but Zarrus seemed pleased by this answer.

'Yes, I need more believers. Kamala Sev will provide little succour – it will be a symbolic victory only, especially with the death of the White Mammoth. Shoreth make weak, useless Shards. Horza, stand up.'

'Yes, sir . . .'

'Do you trust us?'

'Us?'

'Me. Do you trust me?'

'With my life, sir.'

Zarrus stepped forward and placed his hands on Horza's shoulders – Horza stared in puzzlement into the eyes of his master. He was different, he'd changed, his face had grown darker and perhaps more delicate looking – his eyes, once bright, speedwell blue were now so dark brown as to be effectively black. How could that be?

'What about your soul?' Zarrus did not wait for his commander's answer. There was a strange *wet* sound. 'Keep looking at me, Horza,' Zarrus cautioned. But drawn by the unidentifiable noise, Horza glanced down. He screamed.

It was an impression, that was all, a fleeting glimpse of something. But that was horror enough; a brown-black thing was moving between them – leaping – from inside Zarrus' chest, into Horza's unsuspecting body. It was wet and scaly, its stick-like limbs pointed, almost like an insect.

Horza pulled himself from Zarrus' grasp yelling in terror. But it was to late to stop it, the creature had vanished inside him. Doubling up, Horza retched dryly, all physical pain forgotten. But then, as he straightened up, planning to round on Zarrus he felt the first surge of power course through his body. It was in his mind, looking out through his eyes but in return, it told him *everything*. Horza looked at Zarrus with renewed respect – he would be a *God*.

Zarrus grinned sardonically, sensing that his acolyte's share of the power would be enough to keep him happy for a time – knowing that his knowledge made him dangerous and ultimately sealed his doom. 'You must take a force through to that world, Horza. There will be a harvest.'

It was raining again. It had been raining for the past three days, a strangely dismal rain which seemed to leech the very life from the landscape. The ground in the skeletal forest was so hardened by the frost that the water simply sat on the surface and pooled in any depressions. Walking was a bleak trudge punctuated by stops to eat what scant game they could find in the death throes of Or Coille. They ate drowned rabbit that they cooked over ailing, smoky campfires, which they had to constantly tend to keep going. Yiska had brought a lighter in his backpack and Talisker, after initial mixed feelings about the first piece of plastic to enter Sutra, was glad of it when the fire needed to be relit many times.

Twice more they saw the hordes of beasts running through the forest with chilling purpose. It was difficult to know where they were coming from as each time they appeared from a different direction – it seemed as if some giant hand had just put them in the forest, their feet already running as they hit the ground. The creatures were easy to avoid, behaving as they did with the apparent single thought of a swarm of insects.

As they moved further north, Or Coille improved somewhat and resumed the appearance of a more natural winter forest; birdsong filtered plaintively from the treetops – a sound that they had not known they were missing but was now like a sweet blessing.

They knew they were level with the back of Ruannoch Were when they saw patrols of Shoreth in the distance marking the edges of the lake upon which the ancient city was built. It was harder to escape their detection than that of the Shards and also, Raco reminded them there would be lookouts on the battlements. They tried to stay within the curves of the landscape and they made a cheerless camp with no fire.

'It's no good,' Raco announced, 'I cannot just go past.'

'D'you have family in there, lad? Seems the siege has started,' Malky said.

Raco shook his head. 'Well, no immediate family. It's not that, though, we of the bear clan Sidhe are now affiliated with Ruannoch Were because we have lost our cities to the Shoreth, we are its guardians now – and now the Shoreth have followed us there like some blight . . .'

'What about the lynx clan, Raco?' Talisker asked. 'I thought they used to be Ruannoch Were's guardians?'

'There are few of the lynx clan left, Talisker; likewise the clan of the wolf is greatly diminished. Only eagle and bear remain strong,' he glanced at his arm as he spoke. 'Well, I mean still have many families – the tribes are scattered and impotent.'

'I'm sorry, Raco. I had great friends in both lynx and wolf clans, as did Sandro.'

'There are still a few, you must speak to the Council when you near Soulis Mor. I am not going north,' he said. 'I must find my way in to Ruannoch Were. If I tell Thane Sigrid about the murder of the Emperor perhaps we can broker a peace.'

'Raco, without you to speak for us the Council will probably not grant us a hearing.'

'Aye, we need you, laddie,' Malky urged.

'The Shoreth are a warlike race,' Yiska pointed out. 'They assimilate and move on. If the new Emperor wants a siege I can't see much changing his mind.'

Raco thought about Ferebe. 'Until I knew Ferebe Vezul I would have agreed with you Yiska, but she showed me they're not all cold-blooded.'

'Knowing the face of your enemy is a dangerous thing, their lives, their hopes, their children – knowing these things can cripple a warrior on the Enemy Way.'

Raco nodded glum agreement.

'I'll tell you what,' Talisker said. 'If I can get you into the city for a couple of days – will you come to Soulis Mor after that?'

'There's no way in,' Raco argued. 'If we go around the front we will be captured – and I don't think I'll survive very long if the Shoreth get their hands on me. There's no causeway across the back and even if we could find a coracle, the shore's . . .'

'There's a tunnel. I know there is.'

*

Effie was stuck, physically and metaphorically. She'd harangued Renee Yazzie until the women had reluctantly agreed to loan her a pick-up truck. 'It's not safe, Effie,' Renee cautioned. 'If it were safe there would not still be over two hundred people camping in the canyon. Most of these folks have jobs and reasons to be elsewhere y'know.'

Yeah, well . . . Not as good a reason as Effie – or so she told herself in the midst of her stubborn fury. No one cared that she was here; her friends had deserted her at the first possible opportunity, left her amongst strangers who kept looking at her in a kind of puzzled and sympathetic way that she found increasingly infuriating. Millie and Renee had been kind and hospitable but it was obvious to Effie they thought she was some strange, deranged Scotswoman who should not be left alone with any sharp implements. When Renee had finally agreed to loan her the truck to drive back to Chinle it was with the unspoken impression that she was happy to wash her hands of the troublesome girl.

And she'd made it halfway up the hill before the truck had become grounded in a massive pothole that had been obscured by snow. It was infuriating – she could still see the campsite at the mouth of the Mummy Cave behind and below her. Thankfully, she was sure they couldn't see her as the access road was cut into a high rill of rock. Okay, maybe, just maybe, Renee Yazzie had been right, but that didn't mean Effie was about to walk back down to the campsite and eat humble pie. She had some food with her, Renee had insisted she pack some provisions and a flask of coffee, and she still had Hershey bars in her rucksack. Her vague plan was to wait until the morning – she had managed to convince herself that the air was warmer here and the snow about to thaw.

She was standing by the truck nibbling the edges of her flatbread wrap when she first noticed something wrong in the canyon below – something very wrong.

'Jeez,' she muttered, 'What the hell's that?' Grabbing a pair of binoculars Renee had left on the dashboard she squinted down into the canyon. As she fussed about with the focus, the first screams reached her, drifting up like disembodied phantoms.

Something was erupting from the mouth of the cave; a blast of darkness so stark against the landscape it reminded Effie of a film from which the emulsion was burnt, leaving a gaping hole in the reality of the scene. There was a low rumbling sound as the plume of black spewed out under immense pressure. She could see people running away, scattering outwards towards the river. Once the black plume vanished it was replaced by its opposite; white light. And from within the whiteness came people – a few on horseback but about thirty or so on foot. They stopped within a short distance of the cave – probably getting their bearings – and Effie noticed a few of the Dinéh were turning back to look, their curiosity getting the better of them.

'Keep running,' she muttered. She scanned across the river basin and saw Aunt Millie and Renee Yazzie crouching behind a large boulder – there was no sign of Rodney though. Pulling the focus of the bins to the foreground she gasped aloud and then cursed.

'Aw Christ. What the f . . .'

It could only be the vanguard of an army. To the front of the group was a cluster of ten soldiers or warriors of some kind – they wore black clothes and fancy-looking light body armour. They had helmets that reminded Effie of traditional 'knights-in-armour' type of headgear, but they didn't cover their faces. They all looked similar, fair-skinned, pale brows and probably – it was hard to tell from this distance – blue eyes. Where their hair showed beneath the edges of their helmets it was varying degrees of blond.

It wasn't the warriors who had drawn her gasp of fear and dismay though – vicious looking as they were – but their foot soldiers.

She examined the Shards for long moments – frowning at the blue light they radiated, trying to make sense of what she was seeing – until she realised her hands were shaking. Just as she was about to take the binoculars away from her horrified gaze, she saw a Flay. Her stomach flipped over and she groaned quietly.

'Man, that's disgusting,' she said aloud.

'Guess I'd better have a look then,' someone said behind her. A man's hands reached out and took the bins away. She turned; barely daring to believe the speaker was whom she thought.

'Uncle Sandro! Oh God! Thank God you're here!' She flung her arms around his neck almost choking his windpipe in her enthusiasm.

Sandro looked amused by her greeting at first – unaware of the scene below he literally assumed Effie was just happy to see him. 'Where's Duncan?' he said as he put the binoculars to his face. Then, 'Holy shit!' As he spoke, he instinctively pulled Effie back into the shadow of the canyon wall. 'What the hell's going on, Effie?'

'You tell me,' she said. 'They said the gateway to Sutra is down there in the Mummy Cave.'

Before he could reply a gunshot rang out as one of the Navajo fired a rifle at the strange army. The ricochet echoed around the canyon dying away like a distant rumble of thunder but, with a blue flash, the bullet was deflected a few feet away from the Rider it had been aimed at. It seemed the invaders were protected by strong magics.

'Looks like Duncan left it open,' Sandro groaned.

Lake was arguing with Rodney when the trouble started. He'd been messing around with some of the teenage lads – showing them his karate moves, making 'doosh, doosh,' noises as he'd thrown punches and performed some impressive kicks.

'This is the move Jackie Chan taught me,' he said as he spun, flicking an empty plastic bottle off the top of the rim of the flatbed truck with his foot. They were impressed, he could tell, but they said nothing – a tough crowd – he was less than impressed with himself, truth be known. He was a black belt, he wasn't just making it up for the kids but he'd let his skills lapse in the last year, become flabby. He could feel himself getting winded and decided to take a break before continuing with the display. 'I've just gotta talk to my uncle over here . . . be back in a minute,' he grinned. One of the younger lads clapped with surprising enthusiasm so Lake pretended to turn up his collar, gave his best Elvis sneer and said; '*Thankyooverymuch . . .*'

'Is it ever really you "Lake?"' Rodney asked sombrely as he walked towards him.

'I was just mucking about, *Sicheii*,' Lake frowned. 'The kids are bored.'

'Have you asked your mother yet?' Rodney assiduously dusted the snow off a large rock and leant against it.

'What?'

'For the money. It's all you ever come back for.'

Lake flushed angrily. 'Maybe I just wanted to see her – Michael told me she had been ill. Where is Michael anyway?'

Rodney shrugged. 'How much d'you need?'

There was a slight pause as Lake decided on whether continued denial was the best tactic. He glanced around him slightly furtively, 'Ten thousand dollars,' he mumbled.

Rodney started to laugh; it wasn't particularly cruel laughter, just genuine disbelief that Lake could be so naïve as to assume his mother had that kind of money – ultimately though, it was at Lake's expense and Lake was not amused.

'You think it's funny do you, old man,' his face lost its normally genial expression, something like bitterness etched in the hard lines around his mouth. 'I owe people who aren't gonna ask me nicely for their money back – plus interest.'

'And whose fault's that, Lake? What did you spend it on this time? Gambling? Cocaine?' Rodney turned away but Lake grabbed him by the shoulder – more roughly than he intended.

'Has it ever occurred to you that I might come back here more often if you all weren't so fuc . . .'

The repercussions of grabbing *Sicheii* and then swearing at him would never be known however – it was that moment the explosion of darkness boomed out from the Mummy Cave.

'What the hell's that?' Lake glanced at Rodney's face as he spoke and was surprised and frightened to see a look of blank resignation there. When he looked back, the white light had come and people were beginning to run away, some screaming in panic.

As they were standing behind the level of the cave entrance, slightly concealed by an outcrop of rock Lake and Rodney saw the riders appear from behind. A wail of fright escaped one of the boys – there were four of them who had been waiting for Lake's next demonstration – one was the boy Lake had given the Hersheys to so that he could split them with his friends, he'd noticed his pockets were stuffed with the candy.

'Shhh,' Lake ushered Rodney and the boys back into the lea of the outcrop. 'Stay here . . .' Then he crept forward again to peer out over the edge just as the first gunshot sounded. 'Jeeez,' Lake whispered. 'They – they must be aliens or something.'

Despite his warning, Rodney had come back to stand next to him. 'Michael didn't mention those,' he frowned.

'*Sicheii*, get down!' Lake hissed; the old man was standing fully upright, not making any effort at concealment. Too late, one of the Shoreth warriors turned his horse towards the wall of the canyon and saw them straight away. He cantered towards them drawing a sword, three Shards following behind. Lake assessed the situation quickly and turned to the boys. 'They're not very fast – run!'

They scattered in all directions, which served to confuse the rider and the Shards. Two were caught immediately and struggled uselessly with the Shards, but the other two were faster.

'Hey, over here! Over here! Come on then!' Lake yelled. He leapt out from the rill of the outcrop grabbing the pole he had been intending to use for his demonstration. The Shard which was unoccupied lumbered towards him and was subjected to a flurry of blows – they were not strong enough to affect the creature, though, and it kept on coming.

Lake fought a defensive battle but was satisfied when another of the Shards was distracted enough to loose its grip of its writhing captive who kicked out strongly and then ran away into the snow. There was only Lake and Hershey boy left now . . .

Lake noticed the rider spurring his horse towards him; he kicked out hard, hitting the Shard in the chest area and toppling its bulky frame, then he grabbed his pole with both hands and, bracing himself for the impact, he used it as a lance. The tip of the pole hit the rider in the ribs, unseating him from his horse. He went down heavily, cursing in some strange language. Lake, winded and frightened out of his mind danced back and forth on his tiptoes shaking his lance in the air. 'Yeah!' he grinned, 'Yeah! How'd like them apples huh!' His exaltation was short-lived however as the Shard he'd knocked over and forgotten about walked up behind him and, grabbing the pole from his fist, snapped it one-handed as if it were a mere twig. There was no time to react; the creature gripped him by the neck and began to shove him forward. He saw the boy being propelled also towards a central point where the warriors and the beasts were corralling their prisoners like cattle. As he passed the winded rider who was still sitting on the floor, Lake spat at him with gusto. 'I'll be back,' he said.

It was surprisingly easy to remember where the tunnel extended from Ruannoch Were; getting there and getting in was a whole different thing. Because it was only about five hundred yards past the edges of the loch it brought the travellers perilously close to the Shoreth patrols. Fortunately, the patrols were few and far between as the back of the loch was obviously not deemed a priority.

A few of the Fine had tried to escape across the water in the tiny fishing coracles which plied their trade on the loch and took people back and forth by boat from the eastern shoreline so that travellers didn't have to go around to access the causeway. The escapees however, had been killed – put to the sword; their bodies left where they died, snared in the bushes in casual disregard for their souls. Raco, who now understood more of the Shoreth death rituals, was doubly furious. Men and women – and two small children – had been slaughtered as casually as butchered cattle. None were crucified, signifying the Shoreth thought them of little consequence. Talisker said nothing, just squeezed Raco's shoulder in a comforting gesture. Yiska – never having seen battle or killing before – was horrified in a completely different sense.

'They were murdered,' he said. 'This is not a battlefield.' He reached out and closed the eyes of a dead woman who was staring vacantly back across the loch to her home.

'Come on. We've got to keep moving, Yiska. I reckon we've got three minutes till the next patrol arrives.'

'Yeah, okay.'

The warriors came into the shelter and pulled forward some of the prisoners to take them away. Hershey boy was amongst them – he was older than Lake first realised when they met on the trail, perhaps as old as fifteen. He put up a good fight when caught and had a black eye to prove it. As he passed by Lake he smiled briefly but then tilted his head proudly and stared straight ahead – he still had his pockets crammed full of chocolate although he'd obviously eaten a couple. Something about his child-like love of sweets was in such stark contrast to his bravado and Lake felt a surge of panic. He wanted to make the grand gesture and offer himself instead but reaction had set in and he was quaking inside, fighting to keep from vomiting and showing himself up. He'd found his mother with Millie and they were both okay; just shaken as he was.

'What do you think they want?' Millie whispered. 'I think they'll be going to question them, to get information about this world.' The consensus of opinion seemed to be that the strange visitors were aliens, that their magic was in fact a technology far in advance of planet Earth's.

Inside the shelter people were huddled in little groups talking in low whispers, they were shocked and frightened but not panicking yet. Everyone was standing as the ground was wet with snow which their

249

continued trampling had turned to grey slush. Lake was worried about Rodney who was standing in the corner and chanting quietly, almost under his breath, it was an unnerving sound. His eyes were closed and his expression serene.

'What is he singing?' Lake asked his mother.

'It is part of the Ghost Way,' she replied. 'Rodney believes the skinless men and the blue-light people must be *Chindi*.' She shook her head. 'He has seen his death many weeks ago in dreams. He believes he will not survive this.'

Lake tutted impatiently and lit a cigarette with shaking hands. Pulling in a huge draw of smoke he exhaled towards his uncle who ignored the resultant pollution and continued his song. 'None of us might survive this,' he muttered, glancing through the transparent wall of their strange prison towards the prisoners who'd been taken for questioning.

'But he says, help is coming,' Renee replied.

'I'm frightened, Uncle Sandro.'

'I know, Effie. But sometimes we have to do things in spite of our fears. We could run away, but what would that do for them?' Sandro nodded down into the Canyon Del Muerto where a pall of silence had fallen with the fresh snow. In the last hour things had become much, much worse. The invading warriors had murdered around eight people.

To begin with, the Shards had been sent out to scour the canyon basin for those who had had the sense to flee; but they had not killed their prey immediately – something which alerted Sandro to the fact they had some purpose in mind for their victims – bringing them back instead to where the warriors had set up a base outside the Mummy Cave. Once there they were corralled within an area netted off by some web-like fabric, which had a tell-tale signature of blue light.

'It's got some magical energy,' Sandro explained to Effie. 'I don't think they could get out of there without killing themselves.'

The Navajo quickly noticed this as well and began to fight back more strongly once caught by their pursuers but the Shards were immensely strong and their resistance only served to gain them injuries – broken limbs and bloody noses – which were heartbreaking to watch.

It was when Aunt Millie and Renee Yazzie were caught both together that things escalated into a more desperate state. Someone got in one of the pick-ups and drove it desperately toward the main group of warriors still mounted on the horses. The vehicle's path was erratic, its tyres skidding and wheel-spinning in the snow, its brakes squealing as if it were alive. Something about the desperation and recklessness of the attempt was heartening to see, but ultimately doomed.

'Oh no,' Sandro murmured. As the pick-up reached the perimeter of the Shoreth's lines it crashed – suddenly and inexplicably – into some invisible barrier. The whole front of the hood staved in as surely as if it had hit the wall of the canyon. Both doors flew open as the two young men inside leapt out obviously fearing the truck would explode. From their vantage point above Sandro and Effie could clearly see they were injured – the passenger more so than the driver, his right leg was bloodied and mangled but he tried his best to run, his instinct to escape strong.

But there was nowhere to run to. They were rounded up with little effort by the Shards and brought before the leader of the warriors along with a few other young men who had fought particularly strongly. Their pride was strong and they had to be forced to their knees – it seemed the Shoreth leader was speaking to them, walking his horse calmly up and down the ragged line.

'I don't like the look of this.' Sandro instinctively tried to push Effie back but she seemed compelled to look; horrified fascination and disbelief making her unable to look away.

But she didn't *know* what was going to happen. Nothing in her small, provincial reality could have prepared her – Sandro sensed it.

And Lake sensed it. With a suddenness that gripped his stomach with freezing fingers. 'No!' he screamed.

The youths were killed. From above it seemed almost strangely choreographed; the horses wheeled aside and the other monsters walked through the gap. They reached out and touched each of the young men on the tops of their heads. Only one strangled scream issued forth from the poor unfortunate soul whose luckless honour it was to be last. He had perhaps a minute in which to realise what was about to happen to him.

Lake was screeching hysterically. 'It's Hershey boy. He's just a kid. Just a kid. And I was gonna go . . . I was . . .'

Everyone else was silent for long agonising moments. As the boy fell forward, something scattered from the pocket of his coat – chocolate wrappers, their colours vivid in the swirling whiteness; they caught the breeze and fluttered away as if hopelessly lost.

As they began to pitch forward into the snow, Sandro became aware of Effie's panicked breathing. A low gasping which turned into a sick groan. As she dragged in a deep breath Sandro clamped his hand over her mouth and dragged her back away from the rim.

'Effie. Effie, look at me. Look at me . . .' She stared into his face, her eyes huge with panic and fear. Slowly he took his hand away, ready to clamp it back on should she unexpectedly cry out.

'They k-killed them . . .'

'I know. I'm sorry, I should have got you out of the way. Are you all right?'

'N-no.' Her teeth had started chattering and she suddenly felt the coldness of the afternoon very keenly. 'No.'

'At least it was quick for them,' Sandro said.

She frowned, unable to understand for a moment how her beloved, genial uncle could be so calm in the face of what they had just witnessed. 'How can you say that? They're dead! They're fucking dead!' Her voice was borderline hysterical and a dry sob escaped her.

'I know.' Uncle Sandro didn't seem offended; it was then she consciously realised that there was no denying the truth any more – that *everything* was true about Sutra – and, given that fact, Alessandro Chaplin had seen battle many times – had seen men slain, probably far more dramatically. Perhaps had killed in battle himself. He seemed to know what she was thinking. As he wrapped a blanket around her shoulders and guided her towards the Jeep he said, 'It never gets any easier, Effie. Never.'

They sat in the relative warmth of the cab and drank the last of the coffee. It was getting darker now, although still only late afternoon. Another storm was coming, much worse than the previous one; the sky turned a featureless grey-white and large snowflakes began to drift down.

'I think we're stuck here till the morning,' Effie said miserably. 'Maybe then we can go and get help.'

Sandro shook his head, 'No.'

'But we can't just leave them there!'

'If it's happening in the canyon, it's contained,' Sandro argued. 'Anyway, who's going to believe us?'

'All these people will be missing.'

'But most of them live in the Canyon, Effie.'

'So what are we going to do?' As she spoke Effie realised her voice sounded somewhat pathetic but it was difficult to sound otherwise – her stomach was cramping from the coffee and she had a strong urge to eat – no, to cram – which she realised was wholly inappropriate. She was in touch with her own condition enough to dimly recognise that her urge sprang from a twisted desire to exert some control over the situation. *Nice one, Effie. The world's gone mad and you want food.*

Sandro sighed. 'Much as it pains me to say it, we're gonna have to go and get Talisker or someone from Sutra. I've no idea what we're dealing with; they make the Scoor look positively cute.'

'The what?'

'Nothing. Look, we have to go down there and get through the gateway.'

'But we can't!' There was no disguising her fear so she didn't even try. 'They're right outside the cave!'

'Maybe we can get by them at night – maybe they'll just post sentries. We've got to try, Effie.'

'I'm frightened, Uncle Sandro.'

They were all frightened now. There was no further discussion of the enemy's motivations. There was no anything – the silence of exhaustion had fallen in the shelter because continual fear was exhausting. Rodney still chanted and Lake was smoking his seventh cigarette. Behind his mirrored sunglasses his eyes were red with tears.

Nightfall brought the worst of the storm. They were the worst weather conditions the Canyon De Chelly had experienced for ten years but to Sandro and Effie it was a boon. Visibility was around ten feet and Sandro reckoned that anyone on sentry duty would be concentrating on keeping warm.

'We don't know that,' Effie moaned. 'Those things probably don't feel the cold . . . or they feel cold all the time.' She called the Flays 'Skinners' and the Shards, 'Blues' because of their light. Sandro watched the encampment until about one in the morning; Effie had dozed off in the jeep by then, the adrenalin of fear having taken its inevitable toll. She really, really wanted to eat but they had finished all the provisions now. It was getting colder in the cab, they couldn't run the engine for fear of being heard so Effie was muffled in the heavy blankets Renee had stored in the jeep. Effie felt a pang of conscience when she thought of Aunt Millie and Renee Yazzie – she had been a complete cow to them and all they had done was try to help her. Still, maybe she could make amends in a big way if she and Sandro managed to get help.

There was a quiet click as Sandro opened the door of the jeep. 'Effie,' he said, his voice low and urgent, 'it's time to go.'

She climbed out of the jeep, wincing at the cold wind. Sandro pulled her blanket tight around her in an abstracted hug. 'You okay?'

'Yeah . . . no . . . I don't know.'

'Now listen. If we get split up, keep going. Find Duncan, or maybe . . .'

'What?'

'Someone called Morias. No, don't worry, just aim to find Duncan.'

'We'll find him together, Uncle Sandro,' she frowned.

'Yeah, I know. Oh, by the way, your Aunt Bea asked me to give you this.' He rummaged in his pocket and pulled out a small box that he gave to her. When she opened it, she smiled. It was a St Christopher; smaller than the one her mother had given to Talisker, made for a woman. 'It was blessed by the Pope.' Sandro explained.

'Oh.' She didn't know what to say so she showed him the one she already wore. 'My mother gave it to Talisker,' she explained. 'He thought I'd like it.'

Sandro nodded. 'I never thought he'd part with that,' he said. 'It was so important to him.'

'Tell you what, I'll wear them both on the same chain,' she replied. 'But I'll have to do it when my hands aren't shaking.'

He laughed quietly and gave her a quick hug. 'C'mon then.'

It went well at first. They reached the canyon floor unobserved – the snow both impeding and covering their progress. The world became a frozen blur as Effie peered out through the gap between her scarf, which was covering her nose and mouth, and the hood of her parka. She kept her eyes fixed on Sandro's back and walked in his footsteps, he moved with deliberate slowness least their movement attract any attention. A few times she stumbled into him as he stopped to check their path was clear.

Just before the cave was the corral where the Navajo were being held. It was pretty full; people huddled together for warmth as it had only one tarp thrown over a corner to afford any protection from the elements. Effie wondered if the invaders had erected the shelter, as it seemed a strangely uncharacteristic kindness. She could hear the sound of soft, muffled sobbing coming from within and her heart went out to the captives. Her chest constricted and she felt tears – initially warm but frozen by the time they were absorbed by her scarf. Without stopping to consider what she was doing, she deviated from the tracks and shuffled through the snow up to the back of the shelter.

'Hello?' she whispered. 'Hello? Don't speak. It's me, Effie Morgan. Millie and Renee know me. I'm going to get help.' There was no response as she had instructed and she had a sudden doubt that anyone had heard her. 'Cough or something if you heard . . .'

She almost cried out as she felt someone grab her arm but when she looked up it was only Sandro. 'Come on Effie,' he whispered. 'We can't stop.'

She nodded and turned to follow him. Just as she glanced back at the shelter she heard a cough. It had a deliberateness to it that made her smile. Perhaps she had already repaid Millie and Renee in part if she had given them a small gift of hope.

When they reached the mouth of the cave the sudden cessation of the storm was startling. The wind whistled across the front opening, sending dart sharp flurries of flakes that appeared like a white curtain from within the black darkness. For a moment Effie was disorientated but then Sandro gripped her arm again and gestured towards the back. He sprinted forward and Effie, not understanding his sudden urgency, paused before she followed him. The pause possibly saved her life as two 'Blues' lumbered out of the shadow at the side of the cave to pursue Sandro.

'Sandro, look out,' she yelled, all stealth forgotten. Seeing them up close for the first time made the creatures even more horrific than when seen through a lens.

'Catch him.' A dry voice issued from the shadows and the speaker strode forward into the light. It was the one they had seen earlier, walking his horse up and down the row of captives just before his servants killed them. It was easy to believe the whole scene in the cave was stark monotone when one looked into his face; the snow-light somehow reflecting an undeserved purity. Effie had run a few steps after Sandro but she stopped feet away from the stranger, spellbound by the very alien quality of him. She stared at his face and he held her gaze with hypnotic contempt.

There was a yell from the back of the cave as the Blues captured Sandro. They came back towards Effie and their commander holding their struggling victim between them. As the warrior glanced towards them his hold on Effie was broken. She backed away a few imperceptible steps and let them come past her. The dumb beasts paid her little attention, only able to focus on one command at a time. Three other Shoreth warriors stepped up beside their leader drawing swords which flashed cold in the pale light of the cave. Effie lost a precious couple of seconds – for some reason she was unable to face the fact the warriors would attack her.

'Effie! Run!'

But not on my own, Uncle Sandro . . .

She had no choice. She whirled around and sprinted for the back of the cave. If the gateway was gone, she was as good as dead. Perhaps her flight would be a short, glorious defiance as the short journey of the doomed truck had been earlier that day; perhaps there were more warriors at the back of the cave that would cut her down from the shadows. Perhaps. All she could do was run. Run for her life.

Chapter Twelve

They found the tunnel entrance not far from the bodies, although they did not recognise it as such at first. The structure had collapsed around the hole where the big wooden doors had long since rotted away. Fortunately, it was well concealed behind a natural mound which was covered in trees and low, scrubby brambles. From the shoreline it would be difficult to detect and as long as they were quiet they could escape the notice of the patrols. Keeping quiet was difficult; the rotted wood fell apart as they moved it sending cascades of loam and rocks into the entrance. Talisker posted Malky as a sentry and he lay flat on the top of the mound so he could signal them to be quiet when necessary.

Dog seemed to sense their purpose and began to dig away earth and rubble with his strong front legs. Raco was also an asset; his bear's arm was tremendously strong and he lifted planks and rocks effortlessly, his technique fascinating to watch.

It took two hours and it was dark by the time they cleared enough room to scramble through into the space beyond. There was no way of telling whether the tunnel still extended under the lake, or if the whole thing had collapsed, without squeezing through to look. Once they were in, Raco covered the gap behind them with some smaller rocks and branches so they could light torches to see their way.

The tunnel was vast. Talisker had never been through it himself, only heard about it from Sandro when he told him the story of the two sisters – Kyra and Ulla. Kyra had been bewitched by Corvus in her dreams and had opened the doors of the tunnel to let the invading army into Ruannoch Were. Women and children who had been using the tunnel as an escape route had been slaughtered and Ulla – who much later became Thane – had killed her sister in a rage.

Cold echoes of dripping water carried in the chill air and the smell of stagnation and wet decay filled the space. The tunnel walls had allowed the loch to trickle through one teardrop at a time but over the last hundred or so years it was enough to form a still brackish river along the floor.

'D'you think it's safe?' Malky whispered. His voice carried off into the distance, a strangely sibilant ricochet that struck against the ancient granite.

'Guess we'll soon find out,' Yiska said. 'Why are we whispering?'

'Dunno, it's just kinda . . . spooky.'

The very idea of Malcolm finding something 'spooky' tickled Yiska and he laughed aloud and immediately had to observe that Malky was right, as the sound of his laughter became a haunting banshee.

'What's that?' Malky frowned. 'I thought I heard something.' Dog growled.

'It's just rats, Malk. Stop being so twitchy,' Talisker said handing him one of the torches. 'Here, you bring up the rear. Let's go.'

They walked in silence rather than have the discomfiture of their echoing voices. Dog padded

ahead, his paws making a soft splashing sound in the
water; his hackles were up, forming a complete ridge
down his back. Every few minutes he would growl at a
scurrying rat but he didn't bark. The place was
oppressive, the silence pressing in around them.

They had been walking for a while when they found
the first skeletons. The bleached white of the bones
shone hauntingly bright in the yellow fire of the brand
Talisker carried. 'Seems the tunnel has had some use,'
he observed. It was clear the bones had been laid to rest
down here; each was set within a niche in the wall.
They were the nobility of Ruannoch Were – each held a
sword or shield and some wore beautiful bronze
armour, which could only be decorative.

'Look, Duncan.' Malky had gone ahead while Talisker
examined one of the first burials. He waded over to
where Malky was standing; this was a slightly different
burial. No ceremonial garb here, just a simple circlet
crown and a large brooch which had held together a
plaid cloak some of which remained intact, beneath the
cloak was a simple brown dress which had been
painstakingly patched and repaired many times.

'Lady Ulla,' Talisker whispered.

'Aye.'

'Did you know her, Talisker?' Raco asked.

'Yes. She was a great lady. She helped Sandro learn
the genealogy of the clans,' he laughed, but it was a
small, dismal sound. 'She had quite a sense of
humour . . . she had a lot of pain in her life.'

There was a long silence. Talisker touched the hem of
the brown dress disconsolately, rubbing the fabric
between his fingers, his gaze distant and unreachable.

Yiska shot a questioning glance at Malky who shrugged and shook his head.

'Are you all right, Duncan?'

'Dust and bones Malky. All gone, everyone. I'm back in Sutra and I have no meaning here any more.'

'That's not true, Talisker. They called out to you,' Yiska said. He reached out and patted Talisker's shoulder. 'They need you.'

Talisker fixed Yiska with an impenetrable gaze. 'Actually, they didn't, Yiska – they called out to you. The Sidhe are in as much trouble as the Fine.'

Malcolm tutted loudly, 'Aww, I hate it when yer like this. Whur's Sandro when ye need him?'

Effie keeps running. She will not stop. She knows this is the void because she has been there before in less physical form but she doesn't care. She feels no awe of the place, no fear of its other occupants – because she's only ever met Raco – she feels nothing but grief. Tears slough from her cheeks as she moves through the darkness; Uncle Sandro will be dead by now . . .

Of course it is possible they will put him in the cage they had created along with the other captives – and Effie embraces that thought like an old friend – but then, they had been pursuing her with drawn swords. They kill with little compunction, she has seen it. God, yes, she can still see it – those bodies pitching forward into the snow – the images repeat through her brain like a particularly nasty song which has become so stuck in her consciousness she will wake up singing it.

But she cannot run at such a pace for long. She hobbles to a sudden halt as the calf muscles of her left leg spasm into an agonising cramp. She has been so cold the blood supply to her leg is sluggish and weak.

'Arrrgh.' She rubs the leg vigorously, wallowing in her own sheer misery. It's ironic that Talisker thinks of Sutra as some bloody wonderful place – she hasn't even reached there yet and all she's seen is blood and destruction. And how in the hell is she going to tell him what happened to Uncle Sandro? They're kinda weird about each other – she sensed they'd had some big falling out when Talisker came back from Sutra that last time – but they are like family. They might not have spoken for years but it didn't mean they didn't care. Now she would have to tell him that Uncle Sandro was quite probably dead. 'Quite probably dead.' The phrase reverberates in her brain like a bad Scooby-Doo moment.

She lurches forward again; her calf is tender from the cramp but she's sure now she hasn't pulled a hamstring or anything. 'Quite probably dead,' she repeats aloud. The sound is flattened, has nothing to echo against and is swallowed up by the immensity of the distance. It seems she's stopped crying and this surprises her at first – she's hungry, in pain, and has just seen her favourite uncle captured or slain – how much worse could it be?

As if in unspoken answer to her question she detects a movement up ahead. 'Stupid cow,' she berates herself. 'What kind of cretinous thought was that?' She stops, her eyes piercing the darkness, until she sees the white flash again. They are the same dead souls which Talisker, Yiska and Malky had encountered – it is difficult to judge, but perhaps as many as three hundred – but to Effie, they are a completely new horror.

'Oh my God,' she whispers. Her hand moves involuntarily to the gold St Christopher, the one that Talisker gave her. Effie is not a religious person – a lapsed Catholic as her foster parents had been – but she knows St Christopher is supposed to protect travellers on their journey. She glances down at the bright moon of gold. 'Come on, do your stuff, dammit!'

They are near enough for Effie to make out far more detail than she could ever want to see; she hears a strangled sound escape from her own throat, a sob, perhaps, or a prelude to vomit. Perhaps the most frightening thing is their silence and the soft movement of their bare white feet, the slapping and rustling of the dead skin, as they move inexorably closer.

'No, no, no,' Effie shakes her head in useless denial. As the crowd comes closer she becomes aware of the randomness of their movement. It seems they cannot see her, are simply moving, drifting through the void on a perpetual dark, endless journey.

She can feel herself trembling but Effie finds enough resolve to run once more, ignoring the pull of her calf muscle she breaks into a sprint heading west, to the left of the crowd. There is no question of stopping to see if they follow her but she thinks that they will not. She has a sick, constricted feeling in her throat but she blesses the blackness of the void in her mind, thinks that perhaps, just sometimes the black is preferable to what will be etched in her brain forever.

Up ahead there's fire. She doesn't question it. Talisker told her: through an element . . . fire or water. A choked laugh springs unbidden from her throat. She had been hoping for water – she is a strong swimmer.

265

'It's gonna hurt,' she says. And it does. But not in the way she expected. It's not like burning, well, not what she thought burning would feel like. It hurts. She watches the skin of her hands, which she has outstretched before her, crisp and slough away . . . wonders what she looks like . . . hears the distant warm drumming of her own labouring heart . . . wishes Uncle Sandro was here . . . keeps running . . . wishes her mother was . . . it should be her mother . . . She screams as panic seizes her . . . and she is screaming when she arrives.

'Are you *sure* they're under siege?' Malky frowned towards the end of the tunnel from where the faint but unmistakable sound of a party issued.

Raco smiled, 'It's just typical of the old coot – Thane Sigrid I mean. He's probably doing it deliberately hoping the noise will carry out to the Shoreth.'

'Defiance eh? Hope it can last,' Talisker said.

'I'm sure he knows what he's doing,' Raco replied somewhat defensively. 'Ruannoch Were was built to withstand a siege situation – it's only been actually attacked once.' He stopped himself, realising that both Talisker and Malky had been in the city on that occasion.

'Oh aye, the black dugs. Nasty beggars,' Malky commented.

The tunnel ended in what at first appeared to be a brick wall but in fact, was a wattle and daub screen – it seemed no Thane had been buried in the crypt for quite some time, and as the place had fallen into disuse the entrance had been covered over in an effort to keep out the cold and dank smell.

Yiska tapped on the panel. 'I guess we can just break through – it's pretty thin. There's a small axe in my backpack, Malk.'

'Oh aye, I used it fer the fire.'

It only took a few minutes – once the panel was pierced through the plaster-like coating of wattle and daub broke away in large sheets. However, as they worked to tear away the larger sections to allow a passageway through they became aware of something worrying. All sound from the other side had stopped. They could sense the tension as everyone on the other side fixed their gaze on the panel.

Talisker and Malky walked through first, Yiska and Raco behind them. The stunned silence hung uneasily in the smoky air. The kitchens were full of servants, cooks and warriors. Whole sides of beef and pork were being readied to be taken up to the banquet, the smell was intoxicating. The few warriors sat around a rough wooden table drinking beer and playing dice. The oldest looking one sitting at the end of the table, stood up frowning towards them. At the corner of his vision Talisker noted the slight, small motion of hands creeping towards weapons. Belatedly he realised that their appearance, covered in the grey-white dust from the screen, was probably akin to what the superstitious Fine would consider ghosts to look like – and they had emerged from the crypt of the Thanes.

'Who are you?' The warrior demanded.

Raco pushed his way forward. 'Harra, it's me. Raco.' He began brushing the dust from his face as he spoke. The stony expressions of the crowd did not soften and

Talisker began to feel the first tell-tale prickle of the hair on his neck as his body began to anticipate a fight situation. He was surprised at himself when he realised he welcomed the feeling.

Harra sat back down in his chair. 'Raco's dead. Ghosts?' he said. Someone near to Malky reached out and ran his finger across Malky's arm. 'I don't think so, Harra. Just some rather dusty people.'

There was a ripple of laughter amongst the crowd but Talisker did not relax. He bowed, slightly unsure of Harra's position in the Fine. 'You know Raco then. My name is Duncan . . . McGriegor. This is Malky McLeod and Yiska Talloak.' Malky shot Talisker a questioning glance in regard to his pseudonym but said nothing.

'And what business have you here in Ruannoch Were? Most folk would be tunnelling *out* of the city at this time.'

Talisker nodded towards Raco. 'Our paths crossed in Or Coille – Raco here was escaping a Shoreth patrol.'

People had begun to notice Raco's arm and there was a low muttering amongst the crowd. Near to Harra stood two tall, elegant looking Sidhe, Talisker guessed one to be Bear clan but the other . . . he wasn't sure, possibly wolf.

'What happened to you Raco? Did you transform?' One of them asked.

Raco grinned. 'Yes. Yes I did. I was *Kellid*. He came to me when I was in danger.' This led to more muttering from the crowd.

'And what danger were you in?' Harra asked. 'Was it when you were tracking the creature?'

'No, I was attacked by *Aon Crann*. It was brought to life by a Shoreth sorcerer.'

'*Aon Crann*? You were attacked by the bridge?' Harra frowned, obviously perplexed. 'By the Goddess Raco, you were ever in trouble.' He stood up. 'Come with me. I think the Thane will be interested in your story.'

'Harra, I'm really, really hungry,' Raco began. He was silenced with a sharp look from the older warrior.

'You can eat when Sigrid says so.'

The travellers followed Harra and a small group of the warriors away from the kitchens. Talisker was still tense – they were not exactly under arrest but they were surrounded by the Fine and the Sidhe who had spoken to Raco. The Thane would decide what was to be done with them and that could mean anything depending on the whim of the man. Ruannoch Were had changed little, he observed; he had always had a great affection for the place where he and Una had first become lovers. It was less imposing than its cousin, Soulis Mor in the north, more robust, but warm and welcoming. There was more ornate decor than he recalled but perhaps that was Thane Sigrid's taste.

Just before they entered the council chamber, someone called out. 'Raco? Raco? Is it really you?' A tall red-haired girl ran over to them and gave Raco a warm hug. Raco looked somewhat abashed, not least because the girl was heavily pregnant, but he seemed pleased to see her.

'Freya. Told you I'd come back once I slaughtered the beast.' He grinned.

'What happened to your arm?'

'Freya. Curb your curiosity,' Harra said mildly. 'Raco is just about to give his account to your father if you'd like to come in.'

269

'Ohhh, thanks, Harra,' Freya replied somewhat salaciously, linking her arm with Raco's normal one. Talisker and Yiska, who were walking next to each other, exchanged a wondering glance. Raco had specifically said he had no immediate family within the city but he and Freya seemed pretty close – perhaps he was even the father of her baby.

They entered Sigrid's main chamber, which was dominated by a huge oak table; there was no fire in the grate and the room was notably cold after the banqueting hall. The heads of stags and boars decorated the walls, their tusks and antlers casting disconcerting looming shapes in the light from the lanterns, hurriedly lit by the Thane's attendants.

Thane Sigrid entered from another doorway at the same time. He was an imposing man dressed in dark blue robes with trousers beneath. His hair was steely grey but, although he moved somewhat slowly, his gaze as he appraised the group of dusty interlopers was sharp and calculating. 'Get some fire going in here,' Sigrid frowned. 'I am an old man, dammit. Get some logs from the fire in the hall or it'll take all night to get going . . . oh, and bring us some warmed cider.' He sat down at the head of the table and gestured the travellers to be seated.

He didn't waste any time. 'So, Raco . . . Harra reported you missing over a week ago. I know, because Freya mentioned you to me,' he sniffed somewhat disdainfully. 'What happened?'

'Well, I killed the beast,' Raco lied glibly, 'but then I was caught by a Shoreth patrol who were also hunting the creature.'

'How so? Were you in Durghanti lands?'

'No sir, they had strayed into Ruannoch Were territory without being aware of their trespass.' Raco decided to stick to a version of the truth, which was as undramatic as possible. He talked about meeting the Shoreth emperor with Ferebe, explaining about Ferebe's reasoning connected with the amulet. When he came to the part about the emperor's murder, Sigrid was aghast. 'So this is why they are at our gates! They think we assassinated their emperor? Cerne's balls!'

'I'm . . . I'm sorry my Thane,' Raco muttered.

'Well it's not your fault . . . unless you're telling me you did kill him?'

'No, sir. Actually, I quite liked him.'

Sigrid nodded. 'I met him after the Durghanti uprising to discuss terms for our surrender. He seemed an honourable enough man.'

The drinks were brought as Raco continued his tale. As he neared the part about meeting Talisker, Yiska and Malky, he glanced towards Talisker while taking a gulp of his drink. Talisker widened his eyes in warning and gave the tiniest shake of his head.

'Well, that's when our luck changed and T . . . Duncan, Malky and Yiska happened upon us,' he said as vaguely as possible.

'And what was your business in the Gorge?' Sigrid asked mildly.

'We were, ah, coming to Ruannoch Were . . . from Soulis Mor. We were trying to evade Shoreth Riders – there are many patrols around – ended up in Cerne's Gorge.'

Sigrid nodded, they are massing on the shoreline of

Ruannoch Were. To be honest, I don't understand their thinking. We can survive a siege situation for a long time and it looks to me as though they have committed almost the entire Shoreth army to the endeavour.'

'Sir, perhaps the new Emperor – Tulann – is just looking to prove himself,' Raco suggested.

'Yes, perhaps,' Sigrid agreed, 'but something about it makes me uneasy. And if that is his thought, he will go home with his tail between his legs.'

'Aye,' Raco sipped the warmed cider they had been brought, his hands wrapped around the leather tankard for warmth. Talisker noted the frankness and ease with which Sigrid discussed matters; as far as he knew Raco had little stature within Ruannoch Were but Sigrid was willing to hear him – it said a lot for the old Thane.

'And then there are the other beasts abroad in the forest – too many to count now, pointless to track them. You say the Shoreth are responsible for their creation, Raco?'

'Well, we think so – and Ferebe Vezul was extremely unwilling to think such a thing – but the emperor was unaware of it.'

'So someone in the Shoreth court is playing a game all their own . . .' Sigrid would have continued but Freya let out a loud groan and doubled over in her chair clutching her belly. 'Daughter? What . . .'

'Ahhh, father, it hurts.' Freya rocked back and forward.

'The baby? Surely it's too soon?' Raco spoke without thinking.

'Dammed right it's too soon!' Freya cursed.

'Raco.' Sigrid had stood up to come to his daughter's

aid – although all this seemed to involve was patting her uselessly on the shoulder. With surprising speed he reached out and grabbed Raco's shirt. 'If I find out this bastard babe is your get, and you have denied her, I'll kill you myself.'

Raco looked rattled, he obviously had a lot of respect for the old man. 'I swear, the babe is not mine, sir. But if it were, I would be proud.'

Sigrid seemed satisfied with this answer and let go, pushing Raco back slightly and grunting some response. Freya yelled again.

'How far on are you, Lady Freya?' Yiska was kneeling by her chair and was holding Freya's wrist, taking her pulse as inconspicuously as possible.

'Ahhh . . . who the hell are you? Let go of me.' The Thane's daughter was in no mood to cooperate. Sigrid frowned towards Yiska.

'Sir, please let Yiska aid her. He is a healer,' Raco explained.

Sigrid seemed about to object and perhaps demand Yiska's credentials when Freya groaned once more. He paled visibly. 'Very well. Raco and Yiska, you may escort Lady Freya to her chambers.' Yiska glanced at Talisker, uncertain about being separated in the unfamiliar city.

'We'll come and find you later,' Raco said helpfully.

'They'll be in the barracks,' Sigrid said.

Raco and Yiska left, supporting Freya between them. Sigrid watched them go fretfully. 'She's in good hands Sir,' Malky said. 'Yiska is a great healer.'

Sigrid gulped down the last dregs of his cider. 'I hope so, Malcolm, she is to be Thane one day – bastard or no.'

'What'll happen to the baby, if you dinnae mind me asking.'

'It will be found a good home.'

Talisker and Malky exchanged glances; half an hour spent in the company of Freya was enough to tell them she would probably have other ideas on the matter. 'Now, I don't know about you, but I'm hungry,' Sigrid smiled wanly, obviously worried about his daughter. 'And there's a banquet on the battlements.'

'On the battlements?' Talisker said, unable to hide his surprise. 'It's pretty cold out there.'

'Aye. But the drinks are hot and the music is loud. We can't let the Shoreth bastards think they can break our spirits now, can we?'

Perhaps it was because she was running with no thought at all as to the direction; perhaps it was the panic and the flames; or perhaps, she would reflect later, it was just that nothing in Effie's life was ever fated to be simple. Whichever was true, Effie did not exit the void in Cerne's Gorge as Talisker, Malky and Yiska had done, but instead was spat out with some force, just beside one of the minor pathways which fed into the main road towards Ruannoch Were. This meant nothing to Effie; she was still screaming. There was a single split second of time in which she was still in the void, still *of* the void – the flames licked around her frame so that she appeared to be composed of a hysterical, agonising light. Her mouth was open but at first the sound of her scream was strangely absent, and light issued forth instead. Then, as the realities aligned, the sound kicked in, a high-pitched keening which sent the woodland birds wheeling into the sky in cacophonous fright.

It didn't take long for Effie to note the change in her surroundings and although part of her mind realised the fires of the void were a transient mirage, when she spied a large puddle of water she reacted instinctively, pitching forward into it, collapsing first to her knees and then fully into the loamy water. She was sure she would probably steam and hiss like smelted iron but no such thing occurred. In fact the pool was more mud than anything and she sat up again hurriedly staring aghast at her clothes and her brown arms.

'Fuck,' she said.

Then she heard the laughter; a man's voice, a rich sonorous tone but unmistakably young. She grimaced for a second – she must have looked pretty stupid kneeling in a puddle of mud – and looked around. Her smile froze as she saw the source of the laughter; she didn't know the term 'Shoreth' yet, but she recognised the youth as from the same race currently engaged in small-scale genocide of the Navajo. He was on horseback and met her gaze from dark eyes, currently filled with laughter at a stranger's misfortune.

'You know there's a fish which wallows around in the mud at the edge of pools,' he said. 'A mud-skipper, I think it's called . . . didn't know they were that big.'

'Yeah well, I'd rather be a mud-skipper than a . . . a murdering . . . murderer.' she ended lamely.

He frowned at this, apparently having no idea what she was talking about – which was a good thing, she decided – and dismounted his horse. A stab of alarm ran through her at the idea he was about to come towards her, the silent film played through her mind again, the bodies, the young men, dying in the snow.

'Stay back!' The words came out more shrill than she had intended.

He seemed bemused by this – and her hostility. 'Or?'

He was right of course, she had no weapon and anyway, the strange people seemed impervious to things like guns. Before she gave it a thought Effie scooped a large handful of mud and hurled it towards the man. It landed on the light silver chain mail of his chest, spattering outwards onto his face and into his silver hair. His eyes widened in pure disbelief. 'You . . . you . . .' he was speechless.

Effie grinned recklessly; *she* couldn't get any muddier. She slung another mud ball towards her would-be assailant who spluttered in outrage. 'I'll have you hung for this, mud-skipper,' he blustered. Then, completely unexpectedly, he returned her fire, scooping mud from a brackish pool at the base of a tree. His aim was good too, catching Effie on her shoulder, but it mattered little to her, since she resembled a pig wallowing in its sty. She found herself laughing both at the absurdity of the situation and the expression of complete incredulity on the man's face. Also, she had realised he seemed to be on his own without any accompanying monsters so she figured she had a pretty good chance of survival.

As she turned her attention briefly away to gather more wet mud and in those few seconds he ran up behind her and rammed a fistful of mud and leaf mould into her hair. She could hear him laughing – a strangely rusty sound. Squealing indignantly Effie grabbed the youth about his knees and yanked him over. He toppled with a satisfying yelp and she pressed her advantage by pinning him down and rubbing more mud into his face. Then she sat back, winded and laughing.

The youth picked pieces of grass and dead leaves from his silver hair in an exaggerated fashion, as if fastidiously cleaning just a few specks of dust. He was still grinning and Effie felt herself relax slightly. But just as she did so, she saw his face change as he saw something behind her.

'No! Stop!' He yelled.

Effie smirked. She wasn't that easily fooled – she'd look behind her and he'd plaster more . . .

'My Lord.'

She stiffened as she heard the voice behind her. Turning her head slowly lest they think she was making any move to a weapon, she glanced back. There were three more of *them,* on horseback. The one nearest to her held a sword within inches of her head.

'What's your name, mud-skipper?' The youth stood up again and continued to brush himself off even though it was clearly a lost cause.

'Effie Morgan. What's yours?' she said defiantly.

'Tulann. Emperor Tulann the Third.'

'Ah.'

Lady Freya's rooms were spacious and elegant – at least, they probably were for about an hour each week when the maids had been in and cleaned them. It seemed Lady Freya was not given to worrying about her interior decor – her clothes lay scattered around and hung from every curlicue of the gothic looking bed, a red cloak even hung rakishly from the chandelier, but mercifully the candles were not lit. The floors in the castle were strewn with rushes and meadowsweet – something which Yiska recognised, as some Navajo also strewed herbs on the earthen floors of their hogans. Something less familiar to him, though, were the cats; there were at least five of them in the rooms, mangy looking things with bitten ears and matted fur. The warm musky scent, intensified by the heat of the fire which was banked up to heat the rooms, immediately made his eyes water as he was allergic to the creatures. Dog had followed them without being invited and he sniffed amicably at a large tabby which fluffed itself out to twice its size in response to Dog's questing nose.

Freya had calmed somewhat by the time they arrived in her chambers, walking unaided. She had even chatted and joked with Raco as they came up the stairs.

'Lady Freya.' Yiska sneezed. 'Would you mind if . . .' he sneezed again.

She laughed. 'Oh dear. Raco, would you mind shooing them out?'

Raco obliged as she made herself comfortable on the bed, propping herself up with huge, overstuffed pillows – to Yiska, everything in the room was pervaded with the smell of cats, even the bedding, so when Freya thumped the feather bolsters he imagined he could smell the feline musk even more strongly.

'So, we're not a cat person, Yiska?' Freya smiled. 'I have to say, I don't completely trust dog people.' He must have looked mystified at first, thinking Freya was referring to yet another tribe of Sidhe, but she nodded towards Dog as she spoke. 'My father maintains that most folk are either dog people or cat people and I'm inclined to agree with him.'

Raco had sat himself – rather presumptuously Yiska thought – on the end of Freya's bed. 'And what about those who are neither?' he asked.

'Oh, you wouldn't want to bother with those,' she smiled. Her smiled was cut short though as another pain lanced across her belly. 'Ahhh! It's happening again,' she panted. 'It's too early, I know it.'

'May I examine you, Lady Freya?' Yiska asked. 'I have a lot of experience with birthing.'

'Really?' she frowned. 'I thought only women could be midwives.'

This threw him off guard somewhat. 'Ah, yes . . .'

'Yiska's mother was a midwife for the Sidhe,' Raco lied. 'When he was training to be a healer he learned many of her skills.'

'I suppose it's all right if you say so, Raco . . .'

Yiska examined Freya's belly and it didn't take him long to ascertain she was not in labour – the head was nowhere near engaged and although she appeared to be having mild contractions he was sure they were merely her body's practice for the coming event.

After an hour or so, when they had settled her for the night, Yiska and Raco took their leave; Yiska promising to look in on Lady Freya first thing in the morning. As they left the warmth of the rooms and descended the cold stairs, Raco stopped Yiska, clapping his bear hand onto the other man's shoulder.

'I know what you're thinking, Yiska, but you're wrong.'

'No, you don't know,' Raco frowned.

'You probably think I'm the father but . . .'

Yiska held his hand up to stop Raco's denial. 'Really, it's none of my business.'

'The child,' Raco glanced up and down the stairwell to check for servants, 'the child is my brother's – Jevedran's. He was killed four months ago in an accident.'

'Oh, I'm sorry, Raco.'

'He never knew about the baby – she was waiting for the right time to tell him and it never arrived. I feel I have some duty towards Freya but it has drawn her father's suspicion to me.'

'Can't Freya just tell him?'

Raco shook his head. 'There was no love lost between my brother and Thane Sigrid.' They carried on to the bottom of the stairwell in silence. 'So what were you thinking, Yiska?'

'Nothing.'

'Oh, come on.'

Yiska sighed and pulled Raco back into the shadows of the lintel. 'I am sorry Raco. I was thinking that the baby might not survive.'

'What!'

'There's something . . . something very strange about it.'

Three days had passed since Effie's arrival. She consoled herself about the fact she had not alerted anyone about the plight of the Navajo because she knew about the difference of the passage of time between Sutra and the 'real' world. Only a couple of hours had probably passed in Arizona – still, a persistent voice in her mind kept telling her that a few hours was all the Shoreth needed to murder all their captives. She fretted, but there was nothing she could do for the moment.

Being Tulann's new 'best buddy' had its advantages; the food was great and she had been allocated a rather posh tent in the Shoreth encampment just behind Tulann's. However, the young emperor was something of a high maintenance friend, he wanted Effie to attend all his meetings and go riding with him through the forest. It didn't take her long to realise that Tulann liked her because she spoke her mind – to the point of argument if necessary. No one else around him treated him that way, in fact, if Effie had to guess, she'd say they were afraid of him, which seemed ridiculous. In the meetings with his commanders, which were tedious in the extreme, people never contradicted him and rarely even met his gaze. Effie couldn't figure it out at first; it seemed to her they had created a monster by their own behaviour.

It wasn't until the evening of the second day as she returned to her tent that someone saw fit to warn her. It was dark and the lights of the massive encampment gave the forest a soft, almost enchanted glow. Small campfires were dotted around and the Shoreth army were at their ease, talking in low voices, polishing their boots and silver armour. Although they were drinking, there was no sign of dissent or rowdiness – it seemed to Effie that the Shoreth were a rather dispassionate people who didn't know much about letting their hair down.

'Lady Morgan?' Someone grabbed her wrist and she

started. The man was wearing a dark riding cloak and the shadow of the hood concealed most of his face but she thought she recognised the voice as one she had listened to drone on earlier in the day. 'I'm sorry. I didn't mean to frighten you.'

'What is it?' she sighed. 'Does Tulann want me?'

'No. I wanted to warn you – about Tulann.'

She frowned. 'What about him? I can take care of myself.'

'I've seen him do this before. He gets a new friend and spends hours in their company. We are all expected to treat the friend as if they are as important as the Emperor himself.'

Effie bristled; 'I haven't asked for any special treatment – is that what this is about, petty jealousy?' She understood Tulann's behaviour, he was obsessive and she knew the pitfalls of that only too well. 'Look, if you would all stop treating him like, like you do – if you would all speak your mind . . .'

'We would not survive.'

'What?' She felt a hot shiver run up the back of her neck into her scalp. 'What do you mean?'

The man peered around furtively and then took her arm and began walking back to her tent with her. 'Tulann may well make a great leader for the Shoreth one day – he is seeking to prove himself with this folly. But he has the emotional maturity of a child and a particularly spoilt child at that.' They were in her tent now and the man lowered his hood – it was Almasey. 'When he tires of his friends, and he ultimately does because he spends so much time with them, they vanish, they disappear.'

'Where? Oh.'

'He is named "The Poisoner Prince", Lady Morgan.'

Effie was horrified. 'No. It can't be . . . He's not an evil person.' She remembered the arrogance of his laughter when they had met in the mud pool. 'Is he?'

Almasey sat down heavily on the ornate lacquered chair Tulann had sent to Effie's quarters. The old man looked tired, he kneaded his brow to relieve the tension and ran his fingers through his sparse white hair. 'No, I do not believe he is evil. Not truly. But there are some who would disagree with me. Tulann has not been taught to value people.'

'Are you sure? Are you saying he . . .'

'Poisons them. Yes, we think so.' Almasey stood up to go. 'I don't know you, Lady Morgan but you seem like a kind and forthright young woman. I thought it only fair that you know what you're dealing with. Please be on your guard.'

'Th-thank-you, I think.'

Almasey smiled and gave a small bow before departing into the night. Effie stared around her beautifully decorated tent with a new awareness. 'Great, just great,' she muttered. 'Yay, me and my taste in men.' She began undressing, pulling off the ornately crafted leather boots which Tulann had given her and the warm, fur lined cloak which Tulann . . . She sighed and buried her head in her hands; it just couldn't be true – could it? Okay, he was a spoilt brat but she *liked* him. He was witty and clever, he made her laugh – although now she thought about it, some of his jokes were on the cruel side and directed at his unfortunate underlings. Effie understood him, she could see that something inside Tulann was twisted, she could hear it in his laugh and see it in his eyes. But he had risen above it – he had conquered his loneliness and fear – hadn't he?

She liked him. And so, she resolved to confront him about it.

They were leaving for Soulis Mor in the morning. Talisker felt excited at the prospect of seeing the fortress city again – always assuming they could still leave Ruannoch Were the way they came in. There seemed little point in staying on; the siege had not even entered what could be described as an 'active' phase yet. Emperor Tulann seemed happy to simply camp out before the city and so far had done nothing to attempt entry or even crossed the causeway. Talisker was sure this would change, but it seemed unlikely the Shoreth would gain the city any time soon.

He had brought his drink up onto the battlements and stood looking out across the water, his thoughts unexpectedly emotional. He remembered standing here before, many years earlier when Sandro had brought him a drink of warmed mead – God, he'd been plastered! They were still bitter enemies then and Sandro had had the balls to tell him to watch his back in the coming battle; he grinned into his drink.

'Must be good stuff.' He turned to see Yiska standing at the turn of the stairs, Dog, as ever, at his ankle. The Navajo was wrapped in his own thick blanket against the night breeze – he looked tired and somewhat strained.

'How's Lady Freya today?' Talisker asked. Yiska had been checking on Freya each morning.

'She's well. I don't think her baby will be arriving until next month – but then you can never tell with first ones – they come in their own time.'

'Where's Malk?'

'I think he and Raco have gone to the tavern,' Yiska smiled. 'Wenching, I think Malky called it?'

Talisker laughed quietly. 'He's kidding, right?' It would take a rather myopic wench to consider Malky a good catch – not to mention the fact that his flesh was cold to the touch.

'Hope so.'

They stood in companionable silence for a few minutes and Yiska was just about to say something when they heard the sound for the first time.

It was like wire; a long length of wire which had been cracked like a whiplash, slicing the air with a high-pitched tautness which rippled outwards across the night sky.

'There,' Yiska pointed in the direction of the sound which repeated itself in an uncanny crackling rhythm. His remark was purely rhetorical; you could hardly fail to see. The night sky was lit with blossoms of colour like some strangely smudged firework display – they exploded outwards at the same time as the sound and hung in the air for long moments.

Yiska frowned. 'Is it a natural phenomena?'

'You mean like the northern lights? I don't think so. I imagine it's mystical in origin and means deep bloody trouble,' Talisker moaned.

'Where . . . ?'

Talisker looked sourly out across the lake; excited noises could be heard from the Shoreth encampment and more lanterns were being lit. Seemed they had no idea what was going on, either.

'It's coming from Durghanti,' he said.

Chapter Thirteen

'Tulann, I need to ask you something.' Effie thought Tulann looked pale. It was obvious he had not slept, his normally meticulous appearance was dishevelled; his hair sticking up at all angles like some silver sea urchin.

'Did you see it? Last night? It was amazing.'

'Eh?' she frowned. 'Nope, I didn't see anything, Tulann.' Her gaze wandered to his breakfast tray – no one had come to her tent this morning so she had suspected something was up. 'What happened?'

'There was a strange sound and lights in the sky – colourful lights, booming out with the sound.'

Fireworks? Effie thought, *Do they have fireworks here*?

'We think it was coming from Durghanti but we're not sure. I've sent some Riders to investigate, although it will take a few days before we get any response. Are you hungry? Please, have some breakfast – I can't eat a thing.'

It was hard to see why he was so agitated, there was little he could do until he knew what the phenomenon was. Perhaps the Shoreth were superstitious, she thought, maybe they would think it was an omen.

Almasey came into the tent with a woman Effie had not met before; she was dressed in military garb and she raked Effie up and down with a withering look which made it plain what she thought Effie was to the emperor. 'Well, sir,' Almasey beamed, 'it seems the Gods are with us. Today must be the day.'

'Indeed, Almasey. I am sending a rider to the gates to demand a meeting with Thane Sigrid this very afternoon.'

'Sir,' The woman warrior bowed her head as she spoke. 'It seems quite likely that the Fine may not feel particularly threatened yet.'

'How can they not feel threatened, Helene? I am camped on the doorstep of their city with eight thousand men,' Tulann blustered.

'Yes, but we haven't devised a way into the city yet, sir. They can hold out for months.' Her gaze flickered uneasily to Almasey, looking for his support. 'We could be in an impasse situation for a long time.'

'Helene', Tulann walked up to the women and stood nose to nose with her, staring fixedly into her eyes. Effie watched closely, Helene tried her hardest to hold Tulann's gaze but the muscles of her jaw twitched and ticked nervously – she *was* afraid of Tulann. 'Do you think I am entirely stupid?'

'N-no, sir – of course not. I am sure you have a plan which I am not privy to, s-sir.'

'Indeed.' There was silence for long moments as Tulann released Helene from his gaze and slunk back to his chair like some predatory big cat. He sat down and beamed at his two advisors. 'Indeed I have.' But if they were expecting an explanation there was none forthcoming. 'How is the weather, Almasey?'

'Dismal, sir. The men are cold and morale is already low. We suspect the rain will turn to snow soon . . . sir?'

'Yes, Almasey?'

But Almasey's nerve deserted him. He glanced over to Effie as if remembering her challenge to speak his mind. 'Nothing, sir. With your permission I will put them to work, increase drill – perhaps build a few more structures if we are to be here for a prolonged time.'

Tulann failed to take the bait. 'As you will, Almasey. Get them moving.'

'Sir.' The two left as uninformed as when they had arrived. Effie sighed in exasperation.

'Tell me, Lady Morgan . . .'

'Well, you know what he was going to say don't you? Wouldn't it be better to have this siege in the spring? The forest will be a mire if this rain keeps up . . .' Effie tailed off as a wicked, slightly frightening grin spread across Tulann's face. 'You do have a plan, don't you?'

'Oh yes. It's extremely simple.'

She could not contain herself. 'Well? What is it? Christ, you are so irritating sometimes!'

He laughed. 'All right. Since you asked so nicely. When they come for the meeting, I'm going to kidnap the Thane.'

'Oh. What will be your terms for his return?'

'They must pay allegiance to the Shoreth,' he shrugged. 'Don't really want their stinking city.'

'So you'll let Sigrid continue to rule if the Fine pay you . . . like taxes or something?'

'Oh no.' Tulann pulled out a silver dagger and stared pensively at the cold light dancing along the blade. 'Oh no . . . an example must be made. I plan to kill the old coot.'

*

As it turned out, the meeting didn't happen until the next day. Tulann took the news that Thane Sigrid was 'unavailable' with uncharacteristic calm, something which Effie was already coming to recognise as a sign of trouble.

'Very well,' he flashed the thinnest of smiles at the messenger, 'Tomorrow at dusk – I will make a neutral meeting point just by the causeway. Tell Sigrid not to keep me waiting.'

Effie was initially relieved, she knew she was literally in the wrong camp and hoped that Talisker and the others were inside the city. Maybe she could persuade Tulann to let her go into Ruannoch Were, but she hadn't yet thought of a way she could make that seem like a good idea. Also, although she was well treated, Effie had begun to feel like a prisoner in the encampment. She contemplated taking a horse and riding off under cover of darkness but she knew it would be pointless as she had no idea where to go.

There was one positive side effect of her enforced stay – she had been with Tulann for five days now and she had not vomited or taken the last of her laxatives which she had stuck in her pocket when preparing for the trip with Uncle Sandro. It wasn't that she didn't want to purge, but there was no privacy to be found and toilet arrangements in Sutra took some getting used to. So, she was forced to stabilise, and if she was completely honest with herself she was glad – already she felt stronger, her hands were healing and the acid sting in the back of her throat had gone. For the first time in two years Effie acknowledged that her food tasted better without the reflux acids which built up in her throat.

As she prepared to ride out with Tulann to his confab with Thane Sigrid she brushed her hair in a silver mirror and congratulated herself on the fact she had some colour in her cheeks.

'Are you ready, Lady Morgan?' Tulann's impatient voice drifted into her tent, cutting across her thoughts.

'Yes. I'm coming.' Adjusting the light silver vest he had kitted her out with and self-consciously pulling the riding cloak around her she wandered out of the tent. Tulann was there waiting along with Almasey, Helene and other officers Effie didn't know. The group consisted of about twenty people. Effie had a strong sense of foreboding about the coming meeting – she knew it was basically a trap and yet she still refused to believe that Tulann would kill the old Thane as he had said. 'Look Tulann, you don't need me,' she began.

'Let's go,' Tulann commanded, somewhat sourly.

She mounted up without further protest, sensing his tension could make him unpredictable. It was raining again, a steady grey drizzle and yet the sun was attempting to shine through, backlighting the droplets so it appeared as though a translucent yellow rain was falling. The light came from the direction of the besieged city, throwing long shadows behind the riders. They rode in silence at first; Effie could feel nerves buzzing in the pit of her stomach, her hands trembled as she held onto the reins. The white flag of truce which Almasey carried before the riders snapped and whipped in the breeze, its sound reminding Effie of hollow laughter.

As they cleared the edges of the campsite and neared the shores of the loch, Effie gasped in dismay, unable to stifle her reaction although aware that no one else in the group reacted at all. Five crucifixions were spread along the path, they were all Shoreth and two of the victims still apparently alive, groaning in low bestial sounds as the last of their breath escaped their agonizing collapsing lungs.

'Tulann,' she breathed, her eyes filling with tears. 'What did they do to deserve this? Dear God.' She did not look at Tulann as she spoke, unable to pull her horrified gaze away.

'Deserters,' she heard him say behind her. 'It is a common punishment. Normally, crucifixion is how we honour our enemies after battle – but for these, it is a way of showing the Gods their shame. Do not look if it upsets you so much.'

She rounded on him. 'Is that what you do? Look away? Do you even know these men's names or why they are here? Is this your justice, Tulann the Third? It's – it's crap . . . okay . . .' she would have liked to spur her horse away into the forest but in fact, she was having trouble controlling it as it sensed her fright. She heard one of the others gasp at her impertinence but she didn't care. She had been wrong about Tulann; he was heartless and spineless to the core.

He took hold of the reins of her mare making soothing noises – whether directed at her or the beast she wasn't sure. Bringing his mount so close to hers that their legs touched he looked closely into her eyes. 'Lady Morgan – Effie. Listen to me. I did not order these executions, they are a matter of routine in a standing army. I know – I know it's harsh but such is a martial life. The officers are still acting on strictures laid down by my father.'

'So do something,' she hissed, her fury making her careless of his anger. 'Show you are your own man, Tulann.' Behind them, a pall of fear and amazement hung over the assembled officers and Riders. No one spoke, only the breathing of the horses and the jingling of the bridles cut the silence.

Tulann reached out and wiped a tear from her face with his thumb – Effie felt a faint chill of shock run through her. It was the first time she realised that Tulann might want her as more than a friend – and she recoiled slightly from his touch. A flicker of dismay passed over his face and he gave a curt nod then turned his horse to face the Riders.

'You – cut them down. From now on, deserters are to be flogged and then demoted to servile duty.' He nodded as if congratulating himself. 'This,' he gestured to the suffering victims, 'is a waste of resources. Lady Morgan is quite correct.' There was a flurry of activity as two of the escort rode over to order the men taken down. 'Now,' Tulann said to Effie, 'can we proceed?'

She nodded, not trusting herself to speak for a moment, the party moved back into formation and carried on towards the end of Ruannoch Were causeway. 'Tulann,' Effie said quietly. 'Thank you . . .'

He did not reply or even acknowledge that she had spoken but she was sure that he had heard.

The gates opened at dusk as agreed and Thane Sigrid rode forth with only three riders beside him. He walked his horse slowly along the causeway as if enjoying the last of the evening sun despite the drizzle. Tulann watched impassively.

'He is trusting you,' Effie whispered.

As they drew closer she realised that the rider beside Sigrid was someone she could not fail to recognise; she had last seen him when struggling for a return to life. 'Raco,' she muttered.

'Do you know them?'

'Only the rider beside Thane Sigrid. His name is Raco . . .'

'Raco! That's the *yekt* who murdered my father!'

'What?'

Tulann drew his dagger and Effie's gaze was drawn towards the white, skeletal-like quality of his knuckles, which were slick with the rain. 'Wait, Tulann,' she whispered. 'Maybe Sigrid is delivering him to you.'

He grunted an unwilling response but sheathed the dagger again before the approaching riders noticed the weapon.

'Greetings, Tulann,' Thane Sigrid called as he came nearer. 'It is a fine day for a parley, is it not?'

'Not really,' Tulann scowled.

There was a gasp from Raco as he realised just who was sitting next to the Emperor. 'Effie Morgan! How did you get here?' He seemed thrilled to see her, almost forgetting for a moment the purpose of their meeting.

'Found the exit,' Effie muttered unhappily. She wanted to shout at them – *Run! Turn around! It's a trap for Gods sake!* But she could not, favourite or not she would be struck down in an instant.

As soon as Sigrid and his escort were within a stone's throw of where they stood, Tulann turned his horse

294

around and began to leave the scene. Effie was supposed to follow him but she stood as if rooted to the spot.

'What's this, Tulann?' Sigrid thundered as Shoreth riders pressed in around the group with long silver lances lowered. 'They told me it would be a trap but I said no – your father was a man of honour – such a pity that his son is a craven schemer.'

Tulann stopped his horse and turned around. 'Drop your weapons,' he commanded.

'We have no weapons. We are men of honour and we agreed to talk. Do not judge us by your own standards.'

'If you want to know about craven cowards – ask your escort there. He was the one who murdered my father in his bed. How is *that* for honour?' Tulann replied, full of righteous indignation. 'Bind them,' he commanded. 'I will speak to them later. That one can answer to an Inquisitor.'

Thane Sigrid and his party had no defence and offered little resistance as their horses were led away by Shoreth Riders. Raco gave Effie a penetrating look as he came past her. 'I'm – I'm sorry, Raco,' she said quietly. 'I'll see what I can do.'

He said nothing, just held his head high and stared proudly ahead but his silence was eloquent enough.

After everyone had gone Effie still stood at the edge of the loch listening to the gentle sounds of the water. It was getting darker now and she was cold but she could not bring herself to go and spend any time with Tulann. As she stared towards Ruannoch Were deep in thought, blazing arrows were fired from the battlements, streaking high into the grey-blue of the sky, their orange plumes trailing after them like mini comets. The Fine knew the shoreline was out of range of their bows but Effie understood their desire for expression of anger at the double-dealing of the Shoreth; *We knew,* the lights seemed to say. *We warned him you had no honour.*

Sighing heavily she turned her mount around and headed back into the encampment.

'But you can't be serious,' Effie fumed. 'You cannot just kill the Thane. Matters will simply escalate . . . he's an old man, Tulann, for chrissakes.'

Tulann regarded her closely over his wine goblet. 'Fascinating,' he muttered.

'What?'

'Well, when you become impassioned about something, you turn redder. It's a pretty good indicator of your feelings. Mind you, when you laugh, you turn redder, when you cry . . .' he waved his hand airily to indicate his point. His eyes narrowed, 'You are not drinking your wine, Lady Morgan.'

Is this it? Has he tired of me already? Shit, I thought I was more entertaining than that.

'Tulann, I need to ask you something. Don't get mad . . . angry, I mean.'

'Ask.' She noted his long fingers tapping an irritable tattoo on the table in front of him.

'It's just that I've heard some things about you that . . . well' – she decided to go for broke – 'I don't like. And if you want to continue to be my friend, I'd appreciate some honesty.'

'Really. What have you heard?'

'That you are . . .' she squirmed, 'the Poisoner Prince.

That you kill people if they upset you – or even bore you.'

Years of practice on his part made sure that it was difficult to read Tulann's expression. In fact, he was impressed – no one had ever said his somewhat dubious nickname aloud to his face before. 'Worried you're next?' he asked quietly.

'No,' she lied. She tipped up her goblet and gulped down the mulled wine as if it were a drinking competition. In her hurry, some of the wine spilled over onto her cheeks and so when she banged the emptied goblet back onto the table, she wiped the back of her arm across her face, scowling at Tulann as she did so. It was a stupid, reckless thing to do – and it was possible she might not live to regret it. Tulann laughed at her gesture.

'I'm impressed,' he smiled wickedly. 'How do you feel right now?'

Her eyes widened in alarm.

'Joking. Look, Effie, here's what happened. It started as a prank – a rather tragic prank. I kind of accidentally poisoned my tutor. He was annoying me, as tutors do I suppose. I only intended to give the old sod an upset stomach but I must have got the proportions mixed up – he died. When my father found out, he was furious. He sent my best friend away to live at Kamala Sev as a punishment.'

'Just one? Just one incident?' She wasn't sure she believed him.

'Well, over the years I've managed to claim responsibility for a few others – they all died of natural causes but the rumours were easy to spread.'

'*You* spread them? I don't understand.'

'Fear, Effie. I instil fear in people. It's a trait I developed in order to survive. Do you know what my chances were of becoming Emperor? Remote. I'm a young man and behind my back are older, more experienced people who would just love to step into the Emperor's shoes – for the good of the Shoreth, of course.'

She was stunned. 'I don't think I want to come to court,' she muttered. They sat in silence for a moment, Effie staring into the bottom of her goblet trying to decide whether she did actually feel okay.

'You're the only person I've ever told,' Tulann said thoughtfully. He smiled again, his wicked smile – 'Course, if you tell anyone I'll have to kill you.'

'Can I go and see the prisoners?'

'Why would you want to do that? You'll just upset yourself again when they're killed.'

'I know Raco's cousin,' she lied glibly. It seemed an innocuous enough statement; Tulann assumed she was a Fine. 'He might want to give his last message or something.'

'I don't see why I owe him any deference when he murdered my father.'

She sighed. 'Look, I'm looking for some friends and I think he knows where they are.' She felt her stomach cramp unexpectedly, it was the first time in days. Faint tinges of panic began to rise in the back of her mind. How well did she really know Tulann after all? He could be simply lying to her. He might get his kicks from watching her die, talking to her while the minutes ticked away.

'Oh. Sounds important. Tell you what – I'll make a deal with you. Sleep with me and I'll let you see the prisoners. Who knows, I might even spare one of them.'

Effie stared at him, feeling the colour rising in her cheeks. 'That's not very funny, Tulann,' she said stiffly.

'Are you feeling all right, Effie?' he leaned in towards her and she just couldn't tell whether there was a trace of salaciousness about his expression. She could feel sweat trickling down between her shoulder-blades.

'No, look, I've – I've got to go, Tulann.' She didn't wait for his formal dismissal or anything, just launched herself from her chair and out into the crispness of the night air.

Once outside in the coolness of the perpetual drizzle Effie calmed down slightly. Perhaps she'd simply drunk the wine too fast. Tulann must think she was a complete fool – he had confided in her, after all, and she had repaid him by acting in a stupid, ridiculous manner. His casual invitation to sleep with him dismayed her slightly; it seemed Tulann was struggling with the idea of having a female friend and confidant – it was outwith his experience. She did want to trust him – she did. And so she told herself as she stuck her fingers down her throat and vomited in the bushes that her purging was no indication of how she judged him. Merely force of habit.

Yiska is dreaming. Not the vague, transient dreams which normally flit through his sleep. Oh no. This one is different. Technicolor, surround-sound . . . the works. He's standing looking upwards at a waterfall – at least, he thinks it's a waterfall. He can't see the origin of the water but it's thundering down with such force the air is singing with the sound. Droplets of mist are suspended in the air making hundreds of tiny rainbows or fragmented beads of swirling colour. Yiska is standing in the water up to his ankles and his feet are accordingly freezing. He's wearing the Ghost Dance shirt that Uncle Rodney gave him and the glass beads glimmer in the water-light so that he feels that should someone look at him they would see only the beautiful water.

He realises he's singing; he doesn't know many of the Dinéh songs but a few fragments of the hogan blessing ceremonial came to mind unbidden . . .

It will be a hogan of crystal water
It will be a hogan dusted with pollen
It will be a hogan of life long happiness
It will be a hogan with beauty above it
It will be a hogan with beauty all around it.

At the same moment he is wondering why he thinks this, he turns and sees the red-brown adobe plaster of a hogan just by the water's edge. He walks towards it entranced – it's beautifully built, its door facing east so that the rising sun may count its occupants amongst the living each day.

'Hello,' he calls rather self-consciously. It's funny but the sound of the water is no quieter here either inside the hogan or out. He knows he's dreaming but he can smell the earth inside the coolness of the place – it radiates tranquillity and he would like to stop here but he does not. He turns back to the waterfall.

Just as his feet feel the freezing embrace of the water

once more, a movement catches his attention, high up amongst the crisp flash of the water.

'What?' he says.

It is a person, he is sure of it. Someone is plunging over the waterfall, encased in spume like some giant silvered fish. Yiska holds his breath as he watches the leap, although his rational mind says a fast descent like that could kill someone – suffocate, drown – not to mention being smashed to death on the rocks at the bottom. But his irrational mind watches in fearless admiration. It is a dream, after all.

When she – it immediately seems obvious that it is a woman – reaches the base of the falls there is no tragic crashing and tumbling; in fact, she reaches out her hands as if slowing the descent somehow and lands lightly and happily on a rock.

And she is a Sidhe. Yiska cannot yet differentiate the clans but he thinks perhaps she is a lynx – there is something feline, delicate about her movement and her eyes are large, luminous yellow. Her long grey robes are whipped and battered by the spray of the water.

'Yissska' she says.

'Yes.'

She walks past him, towards the hogan, he can smell the earth, air and water on her skin. She is good.

But something happens, the sky darkens as a storm gathers at the pinnacle of the waterfall. Somehow, for an instant, he loses sight of the marvellous woman. He runs towards the hogan as the rain begins to hammer down – there is a light in there now, perhaps she has made a fire. He finds himself aroused by the vision of her perfection, this unbelievable creature. She is a

*Sidhe, but she knows him – knows the landscape of his
dreams. He groans in his sleep.*

*On reaching the hogan he runs inside, even though
it is dark now. But she's not there! What torment is
this? It suddenly occurs to him that this could be the
dream. The one from which no one wakens. She might
be here, hiding in the gloom of the shadow, waiting,
waiting to . . .*

*There's a sound behind him and he turns swiftly as if
someone has frightened him. 'What the . . . ?'*

*It is Dog. Dog is sitting in the middle of the floor, idly
scratching himself.*

*'D-dog?' He walks forwards and reaches out to touch
the beast on the muzzle and as he does so he sees it –
only for an instant, but it is enough. Dog's eyes flash
with intense, unearthly yellow light.*

It was dawn, five days after the lights in the sky and four
since Tulann had captured Thane Sigrid and Raco. Effie
stood by the shore of Ruannoch Were loch and stared
out at the mist which crept across the water as if the day
deserved some intangible caution. She had taken her
walking boots off so that she could feel the grass
beneath her feet but now the chill of the morning had
gotten into her thin frame and she shuddered as much
from apprehension as cold.

She had done all she could. Everything within reason
but the bottom line was that Tulann wanted his pound
of flesh and in a way, she understood that. It was
'known' that Raco had killed the Emperor – although,
when she had been allowed to see him he had denied it
strongly. 'Tell him,' he'd said through cracked and

bloodied lips, 'I would have come for him too – Shoreth bastard.' Effie had winced inwardly at this, defiance would do Raco no favours with Tulann but then precious little would. Today, first Raco and then Thane Sigrid would be executed by arrow fire – a particularly nasty way to die, she imagined – it would not be quick unless the Shoreth bowmen were skilled and extremely merciful. She had asked Tulann why he had chosen this method. 'Tradition,' he responded. 'History will liken me to my ancestor Tarak the Impaler.' Tulann was greatly concerned with how history might perceive him.

Across the water Effie could just see movement on the battlements of Ruannoch Were, the early light flashed off the metal of weapons or armour. The denizens of Ruannoch Were must have known something was happening today – Tulann had made sure the field of execution was being set up within sight of the city – although Effie wasn't sure if they knew Tulann would have the audacity to kill their Thane within sight of his people.

'Lady Morgan, it is a dismal morning is it not?' Almasey appeared beside her – Effie was beginning to wonder whether Tulann had instructed him to keep an eye on her in case she wondered off.

'More dismal for some if it is to be their last.'

'Indeed. Ah, has Tulann spoken to you about this afternoon's events?'

'No, not really, why?'

'He wants you to be there.'

'Well he can want,' she scowled. 'There's no way I'm staying to watch. It's bloody barbaric.'

Almasey looked dismayed and wrung his hands pathetically. 'But you don't understand, Lady Morgan, he ordered me to make sure you attend.'

'And I'm sorry if this puts you in a difficult position, Almasey,' she said coolly. 'Look, I'll speak to him myself. Where is he?'

'In a meeting with some of the generals.'

'Fine. I'll talk to him after.' She stalked off having to cross the execution ground as she did so, walking within ten feet of the posts to which Raco and Sigrid would be bound. 'It's intolerable,' she said aloud, 'bloody intolerable.' She found herself breaking into a run, her feet skipping lightly over the cold ground.

'Effie, Effie . . .' she stopped as she heard her name called.

Raco had been moved out to the execution ground, presumably so he could watch the preparations for his own demise; he was suspended in a hanging cage – there was not even room for him to sit down. Not for the first time, Effie cursed herself for her naivety, her complete *unpreparedness* for a world in which life could be brutally short. It made her compulsive behaviour seem ridiculous, made her feel like an inadequate fraud.

'Raco,' she tried her best to smile although not sure it was appropriate. However he smiled back as if seeking to reassure her she could come closer. 'How are you? God, that's a stupid question.'

'I'm calm, Effie. I have made my peace with my Gods. Salkit will swoop down from the heavens and take my soul away.'

Biting her lip to stop herself from crying at the sheer

hopelessness of Raco's plight she walked up to the cage and took hold of his huge paw; it was warm and soft and he wrapped the brown-black claws around her hand enjoying the tactile comfort which was all she could give. 'I'm so sorry,' she whispered.

'Talisker said you were a spirited girl,' Raco said. 'I've heard the soldiers talk about the influence you are having on Tulann. Effie, do you think you could persuade him to spare Sigrid? He doesn't deserve this, he's an old man.'

'You don't deserve it either. No one deserves it, except maybe Tulann.'

'Come on, you don't mean that.'

She looked up at his face through teary eyes. 'How can you not hate him?'

'In the last hours of my life I won't waste time in hating anyone,' he said.

'For chrissakes, Raco! Get angry! You deserve it – you have a right to anger – no, bloody fury!' She wanted to break down and sob with complete abandon as she had when she was a child, but Raco's calm acceptance stabbed through her self-pitying funk. 'Talisker? When did you speak to him?'

'We travelled to the city together.'

She glanced back at Ruannoch Were which was now veiled in a cloud of mist so dense it appeared to be floating above the loch. 'He's in the city? Yiska and Malky?' The idea that she could – in some abstract way – pass emotional responsibility for the whole mess over to Talisker or the others made her feel both relieved and ashamed.

'No, they were, but they left a few days ago.'

'Left? How could they leave?' She was unable to disguise her dismay.

'They are looking for the Council of Tema – Talisker thinks it's important.'

'Lady Morgan?' Almasey caught up with her and patted her on the shoulder, 'you shouldn't upset yourself like this. There is little to be done once Tulann makes his mind up. I'm sorry.'

'Don't bloody apologise to me – tell it to him!' she raged, gesturing at Raco. She shrugged off Almasey's hand and continued her escape to her tent. She hoped this time Almasey would have more sense than to follow her.

'Please don't make me go, Tulann,' she begged.

'Everyone is waiting,' he said with what Effie recognised as extreme patience.

'I'll never forgive you for this.'

Tulann's expression was thoughtful as if he had never considered that someone might bear anger towards him which he would actually care about. The idea of Effie's accusation or forgiveness was a new concept to him – she had told him he had much to learn before he became a true friend and it seemed she was right. He could get a new best friend if she was serious but something told him that was not the right response either.

They walked from Effie's tent to a fanfare of trumpets which sent a volley of water birds scooting out over the loch. Effie was embarrassed, she hadn't realised the executions would be, well, quite such an occasion.

The archers stood in a regimented row, the breeze

stirring their hair and whipping the short cloaks they wore. Effie stared hard at their faces trying to read their expressions but it was difficult to tell what they were thinking. Tulann, Effie and the Emperor's other aides sat within an enclosure which was sealed off and decorated by the Emperor's standard; although it appeared grand, within the enclosure the seats were simply hard wooden benches taken from various tents; except for Tulann's, of course, his temporary throne had been moved out from his quarters – must have taken about five men to carry it, Effie thought.

From somewhere a sharp drumbeat started causing Effie's stomach to turn over. She felt sick, her heart seemed about to burst from her chest – just as she was about to spring from her seat, unable to bear the coming slaughter, Raco was marched onto the field, his arms bound behind him. He walked with his head held high, although Effie could sense his trembling and fear – it resonated outwards like an intangible echo.

Just as he reached the post, he stumbled, the warriors who held him either side bore him up again and, without pause began lashing him to the post. Raco's lips were moving, and although she was too far away to hear him Effie imagined perhaps he was talking to the soldiers – they said nothing in return, their eyes fixed and impassive as the archers. Raco caught sight of Effie and somehow had the presence of mind to give her a tiny tight smile, it was like some pale absolution. Effie began to cry soundlessly, allowing freezing tears to flow unchecked down her cheeks into the curve of her neck.

Tulann stood up. 'Raco, you have been found guilty of murdering my father, Emperor Tebron in cold blood,' his reedy little voice carried out over the execution field and Effie's heartsick soul cursed him yet again.

'I have had no trial,' Raco shouted, his voice surprisingly strong and even.

'This is the Emperor's justice,' Tulann pronounced without pause. 'I have spoken.' He nodded towards the archers captain who called out some unintelligible command; the archers nocked their bows and took aim.

'Oh God,' Effie whispered. She was clutching onto her double St Christopher and she pressed them to her brow, closing her eyes as she did so. The last thing she was aware of was Tulann raising his hand in order to give the signal.

There was the longest moment of silence she could ever remember. She was dimly aware of a sound in the background which at first, she took to be coming from the loch – then, as it drew nearer, she realised it was hoofbeats. It was Tulann's curse which alerted her they could be important.

She opened her eyes again – her lashes had stuck together from the tears so what she saw was a Shoreth woman galloping a horse hard along the foreshore, the edges of the picture softened and refracted by the light of her tears.

Effie had no idea who the woman might be but there was something unmistakably heroic about her headlong charge. She raced onto the execution field and reined in her horse halfway between the executioners and their victim, obscuring the archers' aim. Beside her, Effie felt Tulann bristle with rage and righteous indignation, which he was so damned good at. It was clear he knew who the woman was.

'Ferebe Vezul,' he said. 'What folly is this? Have you come to join your accomplice in death? How touching.' He was about to signal guards to capture her but he stopped in mid-gesture when she spoke.

'I am no traitor, my Emperor. Kamala Sev has fallen — Durghanti has been isolated — *Aon Crann* destroyed. I bring you the remnants of your people.'

'What! What are you saying? Who has done this?' Tulann was rightly appalled, all around the Shoreth began to murmur their amazement and disbelief.

'Zarrus. General Zarrus. He has betrayed us all.'

Chapter Fourteen

He's a liar! He lied to me! This is not about me becoming a God. This is not about me at all – it's about him. He's getting stronger, remembering who he was and, as he does so, I am compromised. In the last few days when I have been so busy preparing for the onslaught of the Fine and their allies, sometimes I have suddenly come into consciousness and it's the middle of the day! I mean, he has been moving me, talking, eating, laughing with my commanders . . .

I am afraid. If I am to die, I would rather it be in the coming conflict on the battlefield with a sword in my fist than by this low, cunning assimilation. I look in the mirror and I see him – there can be no doubt that the features, the body I now have become, are what he was when last he was alive . . .

I know his name now. It is . . .

'Oh come on. You wanted this power! You could have thrown me in the flames, remember.'

But what is this madness? You are writing now? I stare down at my hands – I am holding a pen in each of them – He writes with my left and I . . .

'Get over it. Can you blame me for my enthusiasm at having – borrowing – a body. Have you any idea what it is like to spend eons in the darkest reaches of the void, shattered pieces of . . .'

But it has not been eons. Nowhere close. I know who

you are.

'So, you know I have been denied my Godhood.'

I am not sure it was ever yours by right. I have read the history of the Fine. And I'm warning you now – any attempt to take over my body I will meet with extreme measures.

'What do you mean?'

I'll kill myself. See, see the ring on the hand you are writing your childlike scrawl with – it holds a poison that kills so fast – in a heartbeat – that it's likely you will be unable to escape my body in time to avoid being pulled back into the darkness with my Gods accursed soul.

'You wouldn't . . .'

You know me. Look into my heart – you will see I am not afraid to die at my own hand.

'I have Horza now.'

Yes, why don't you go and see what he is doing in the other world? Or are you afraid?

'Afraid?'

You have been there before have you not?

There is no answer so I can assume he has gone. Last time I wrote my journal I was going to tell you about the prayers. You see, whether the final ascent to Godhood is his or mine, it will all be achieved by belief. Blind, ignorant belief it may be, but it is sufficient for our purpose. Each time a new Shard or Flay is created, we implant in them a khetourit, that is the ancient Fine tongue for a prayer; it looks like a tiny bead of jet stone and it is a physical manifestation of a prayer. The Shards or Flays have no choice in the matter but, as they move, the khetourit spins and dances, generating the energy we require.

At some point, it will be enough. I do not know when and he has not told me but I suspect it will be soon. He is strong now – for example, he has just shut down his senses to my body to go and look at Horza's operation. But it gives me little relief, he will know still if there is a problem with his host and he will return. He probably knows that my bluff about the fast acting poison is just that – he could be gone from me in moments. The idea of dragging his soul to hell with me is merely wishful thinking.

Oh . . . before he comes back. His name is Jahl.

'This is the story of how Coyote brought fire to the human beings, as it was told to me by my mother Alice Talloak of the Black Water People.' Yiska smiled into the orange glow of the fire at the memory of his mother telling the tale. She 'spoke with her hands' as uncle Rodney said; as she told the tale her hands would dance and flutter like divine white messengers.

This story happened at the beginnings of the world when Human Beings were new to the plains and deserts of the world and lived in harmony with all creatures . . .

Now Coyote, like the rest of the People, had no need for fire. So he didn't really think about it, until one spring day when he was passing a human village. The women were singing a song of mourning for the babies and the old ones who had died in the winter. Their voices moaned like the west wind, prickling the hairs on Coyote's shaggy neck.

Coyote felt sorry for the men and women. He thought maybe, there was something he could do to help them.

He knew of a mountain-top where the three Fire Beings lived . . .'

''s that like trolls?'

'Shut up, Malk.'

These Beings kept fire for themselves, jealously guarding it for fear that man might somehow acquire it and become as strong as they. Coyote thought that he could do a good turn for man at the expense of the selfish Fire Beings. So he went to the mountain and crept to the top, to watch the way that the Beings guarded their fire. As soon as he came near, the Beings leaped to their feet and gazed around their camp, sensing his presence somehow. Their eyes glinted like bloodstones, and their hands were clawed like the talons of the great black vulture.

But when they saw Coyote – he had gone to the mountain-top on all fours, slinking on his belly – the Fire Beings thought it was only an ordinary coyote hunting among the trees. They sat down again and paid Coyote no more attention.

And so, he watched all day and night as the Fire Beings guarded their fire. He saw how they fed it pine cones and dry branches from the pinon trees. He saw how they stamped furiously on runaway rivulets of flame that sometimes nibbled outwards on edges of dry grass. He saw also how, at night, they took turns to guard the fire.

The Beings were always jealously watchful of their fire except during one part of the day – that was in the earliest morning, when the first winds of dawn arose on the mountains. Then the Being by the fire would hurry, shivering, into the cave calling out to her sister to come and watch over the fire. But the next Being would always be slow to go out for her turn, her head spinning with sleep and the thin dreams of dawn.

Coyote, seeing all this, went down the mountain and spoke to some of his friends amongst the People. He told them of poor, hairless man, fearing the cold and death of winter. And he told them of the Fire Beings, and the warmth and brightness of the flame. They all agreed that man should have fire, and they all promised to help Coyote's undertaking.

Then Coyote sped again to the mountain-top. Again the Fire Beings leaped up when he came close, but again, when they looked closely they saw only a grey coyote among the bushes. So they paid him no more attention. Coyote watched as night fell and two of the Beings went off to the cave to sleep. He watched as they changed over at certain times until at last, the dawn winds rose.

Then the Being on guard called out to her sister to come for her watch. And the sister whose turn it was climbed slow and sleepy from her bed, but before she could come out of the cave, Coyote lunged from the bushes, snatched up a glowing portion of fire, and sprang away down the mountainside.

Screaming, the Fire Beings flew after him. Swiftly though Coyote ran, they caught up with him, and one of them reached out a questing, taloned hand. Her fingers touched only the tip of his tail, but it was enough to turn the hairs white, and coyote tail-tips are white to this day. Coyote shouted, and flung the fire away from him. But the others of the People had gathered at the foot of the mountain in case they were needed.

Squirrel first saw the fire falling, and caught it, putting it on her back and running away through the tree-tops. The fire scorched her back so badly that her tail curled up and back, as squirrels' tails still do today. The Fire Beings then chased Squirrel, who threw the fire to Chipmunk.

Chattering in fear, Chipmunk stood still as if rooted to the spot until the Beings were almost upon her. Then, as she turned to run, one Being clawed at her, tearing down the length of her back and leaving three stripes that are to be seen on chipmunks' backs even today.

Chipmunk threw the fire to Frog, and the Beings turned towards him. One of the Beings grasped his tail, but Frog gave a mighty leap and tore himself free, leaving his tail behind in the Being's hand – which of course, is why frogs have had no tails ever since. As the Beings came after him again, Frog flung the fire on to Wood.

And Wood swallowed it. The Fire Beings gathered round, but they could not get the fire out of Wood. They promised it gifts, sang to it and shouted at it. They twisted it and struck it and tore it with their knives. But Wood did not give up the fire. In the end, defeated, the Beings went back to their mountain-top and left the People alone.

But Coyote knew how to get fire out of Wood. And he went to the village of men and showed them how. He showed them the trick of rubbing two dry sticks together, and the trick of spinning a sharpened stick in a hole made in another piece of wood. And so man was from then on warm and safe through the killing cold of winter.

*

Yiska smiled in faint embarrassment – 'It's just a tale we tell our children,' he said. 'I was reminded of it today when watching Dog. We call coyotes a Trickster – we think of them as pretty clever.'

'Aye but Dug's no a coyote though, is he?'

'I don't know, Malk – I wouldn't be surprised if his mother hadn't had a liaison with a coyote – he's got the colouring and the ears – although he's a bit taller and bigger boned.' Talisker nodded.

'What's a liaison?'

'You know, a coyote could've been his father.'

'Oh aye. Is that possible?'

'Yes,' Yiska said. 'There have been many instances where the Inuits' sled dogs have gone feral and bred with wolves.'

Everyone observed Dog for a few moments and he shifted uncomfortably under their scrutiny and whined in confusion. Malky laughed and ruffled Dog's rough mane. 'Hey, dinnae worry, Dug, we'll no hold it against ye.'

'Here, Yiska,' Talisker threw something across the fire and Yiska deftly caught it. It was a stone. He frowned in puzzlement and looked to Talisker for an explanation.

'Is it saying anything to you?'

'*Saying*?'

'Are you getting . . . I don't know, a feeling from it?'

'No, nothing. Why?'

'Does it have *hozro*?'

'No. What's this about?'

'Oh aye, I see,' Malky grinned, 'Talisker thinks ye

might be like Sandro was – a *Seanachaidh* – only he didn'ae ken he was when he came here, the land chose him – that's right, isn't it, Duncan?'

'Yeah, I think so. He became so attuned to the land that the stories he told were bound up with the rocks and the elements; he told me that he didn't even know the stories before the words tumbled out of his mouth. And words have power here – at least they did then.'

Yiska nodded. 'I see your viewpoint, Talisker – the Navajo Way is also very attuned to the elemental world.'

'It's not a *view*,' Talisker replied. 'That's how it is here, or how it was. It was a fact of life – but now it seems the connection is gone, broken.'

Yiska stared down at the stone in his palm, it was a smooth pink granite but there was nothing to suggest that it might mean anything to him.

'Maybe we need Morias,' Malky sighed. 'It was him that helped Sandro tae see what he was here.'

'I don't think I'm a *Seanachaidh*, Malk. Not like that – if we had known that's what was needed we could've brought Alessandro.'

'Aye.' Malky shot an unmistakably accusing look at Duncan. 'Well, if certain folk weren't so bloody stubborn . . .'

'Let's not talk about Chaplin, Malk.' Talisker shot him a warning look but the Highlander was impervious as ever to subtlety.

'Oh. So it's *Chaplin* now, is it? Seems tae me that's what you called him when you weren'ae friends. What happened, Duncan?'

'Nothing. Well, nothing major. We're still friends

really. He just didn't approve of something I did and I've had enough of Sandro's disapproval for three lifetimes.' He lapsed into a stubborn silence and even Malky could tell he would not be drawn on the subject.

He sighed. 'So, Yiska, tell me some more stories. Mebbe the land is listening, ye never know.'

The Warrior Path was everything. The scars on his hands told him this, the lacerations on his back, the disfigurement of his skin by his eye – simple acts of faith, certainty in a cold, cold world.

Horza was not happy. He kept dreaming about that *thing*. The thing which passed between Zarrus' body and his own. In the darkness of his tent, as the sound of the storms discomforted him further, he imagined the thing; not all squashed up as he thought he had seen it in its brief transition, but stretched out to its full size. It was like a little wizened man, or an insect, maybe both. He tried to convince himself that Zarrus had somehow honoured him by giving him this guardian – but it was difficult to see how. It was true that in the days since the incident Horza had felt stronger, but it seemed that coming to this strange place had affected him – his hair for example, had turned dark black almost overnight and the extreme chill had made his pallor somewhat darker. But Horza was a warrior born – coming through the void with his men had caused him less trepidation than the ensuing, seemingly interminable wait for his orders.

It was bitterly cold here, there seemed to be no break in the storms – overnight, ice had rained down like freezing needles and two of his prisoners had died of the cold. Zarrus would be angry at this wastage he knew, so Horza had instructed his men to reinforce the long shelter which housed the prisoners and they had moved in some of the bedding and chairs found around the encampment. It seemed the unfortunates were trapped here by the weather in the first place and Horza appreciated the serendipity of this. Perhaps, if things had been different, he and his warriors would have found no one and could have just turned around and gone back through, as it was though, he felt trapped, as trapped as the victims.

There were things that vaguely worried him too; lights in the sky, sounds like he had never heard as great looming shadows passed high overhead. How many souls did Zarrus need? Should he just slaughter them all? He didn't know; the idea of the mass slaughter troubled him not at all – he just wanted his orders.

The wind howled around the encampment as if the dead were taunting him, taking hold of the fabric of the tent with their dead fingers and shaking the canvas with malicious glee; the cold was in his very bones. Horza stared moodily into the fire clutching his cloak about him.

'Hooorrrza . . .'

He started – for a moment, imagining the wind had spoken his name.

'Z-Zarrus? Sir? Is that you?'

No answer. As his heartbeat began to return to a normal rhythm he realised the sound was within his own head – that he must have imagined it.

'Horza!' He jumped again and there was a dry chuckle in response to his discomfort.

'W-where are you?'

'Inside your mind. I must say, it's kind of empty in here . . . bit of an echo.'

Horza ignored the insult. 'Is it you, General Zarrus?'

'Well . . . yes and no.'

If it wasn't his General, Horza was prepared to be bold. 'Well, which is it?'

There was a short pause as if the voice were considering its answer. *'Just consider me the go-between . . .'*

'I am waiting for General Zarrus' orders. Has he given them to you? Do you know what he wants?'

'How many prisoners are there?'

'About two hundred. All Sidhe as far as we can tell.'

'Two hundred, eh? That should be enough . . . kill them. Kill them all and send their corpses back to Sutra.'

Time had not softened the jagged shapes of the landscape where an ice-quake had heaved and spilt the dark rocks. But the slow persistence of nature had clothed the angular landforms in green grass and moss; a gentle forgiveness for the impudence of its magical tantrum.

Talisker stared off towards the west where the view levelled off into flat moorland. 'The Council of Tema was ever in the west,' he frowned, shading his eyes against the dying brilliance of the setting sun. 'The Sidhe think it is a significant direction, where their magic comes from.'

'Used tae come from,' Malky corrected.

'Yeah. Come on, the moor's not very difficult terrain – reckon we can be halfway over within an hour.'

'It'll be dark by then,' Malky argued. 'Ah think we should make camp.'

'Yiska?'

'I think Malk's right. If we make camp at least we're gonna be fresh in the morning. We don't know what kind of reception we'll get from the Council.'

They camped where the rockforms gave way to the first undulation of the moorland. There was a soft wind blowing up from the south but the jagged ends of the rocks deflected the wind and it was dry and sheltered – the best camp they had made since coming to Sutra.

Talisker told Yiska about the icestorm which had so marked the landscape and how he had flown on the back of a Sidhe eagle as the land buckled and screamed beneath them.

'The land is peaceful now,' Yiska remarked. 'In fact, I would say there is some little *Hozro* here,' he squinted off into the distance where Soulis Mor was concealed by an evening haze. His expression changed, as if he had had a sudden revelation and he turned wordlessly to look back toward the south. 'Dunno why I didn't know before,' he muttered.

'What is it?'

'It's deliberate. Whatever is draining the spirit from the land is doing it deliberately – using the energy for something else.'

'It'll be that Zarrus,' Malky spat into the heather. 'Reckon he's a lot mair powerful than what they know yet.'

Talisker nodded sourly. 'Let's get some sleep.'

*

Yiska drifted into sleep, his limbs heavy and tired from the days exertion. He didn't want to have the dream again; it disturbed him. He realised that things in Sutra didn't just happen with the apparent randomness they did back home – the dream had to be significant but he felt he didn't want to share it with Talisker and Malky.

As the sound of the waterfall claims his semi-conscious mind once more he embraces the sound of the water. He wants to see her again, wants to speak to her, just to have her attention for moments of his dreaming.

But something is wrong, he knows the moment he sees the falls, the water is dark, torrid, the whole place has changed, become malevolent. It is cold. As he turns back to look at the hogan there is a sound, a sound like the end of the world; a mighty crash which shakes the ground beneath his bare feet. He screams aloud as a wall of water rushes to engulf him and in the instant of his scream he knows he will not see her and he feels cheated but that instant is swallowed by the next, by sheer terror as the water claims him in a freezing, battering, stinging rush. He cannot shout any more as his throat is filled with the water. He has a fleeting thought that it has sentience, that it's trying to kill him with a kind of savage deliberateness, when he hears a voice . . .

'Yiska! Yiska . . .'

He opens his eyes to complete darkness. For a few moments his befuddled mind cannot make sense of what's happening, the panic of the dream still grips him and he yells out once more before he realises the voice is Malky's. There is another sound like ripping as lightning rents the sky leaving monochrome after-shocks on the inside of his eyelids. As this is swiftly followed by a peal of thunder, realisation comes with the storm. His tent has collapsed on him, bowed down with the weight of water from a sudden torrential deluge. Still, as he struggles to free himself he cannot quite shrug off the sickening fright, his movements are spasmodic and the leather skin of his tiny lean-to shelter sticks to him like a wet chamois cocoon – he curses in a long stream of gibberish as he frantically tries to pull it off him.

'Calm down, man,' Malky urges as he helps untangle Yiska from the tent. He has to shout because there's almost no break between the thunder and lightning. The lightning is so bright that everything appears to be happening in the kind of stop-go motion of a black strobe light.

'C'mon.' Once Yiska is free Malky pushes him towards the shelter of the nearest splinter-rock and he rushes under the overhang and stares out at the storm willing his legs to stop trembling.

He's never seen a storm like it and he has seen many in the deserts of Arizona – he knows that this is unnatural, that they should have seen some warning, a shift in the wind or a lesser, precursor rainfall. The lightning comes within seconds, three or four gigantic forks at once dancing and sizzling between the clouds and the earth. Sparks fly out from the point of the impact but the moor is too wet to catch aflame. The rain is so dense it appears to be pelting down in sheets – Yiska can hear the tiny sound of the water trickling through the rock which they stood under.

'Where's Talisker?' he asks.

Malky grins ruefully and points upward. Yiska leaves the relative safety of the overhang to look.

Talisker sat on top of the black rock, oblivious to the danger of the lightning; his plaid and hair were soaked flat to his body and the skin of his legs, hands and face shone with a wet, strangely glowing translucence. He was staring into the western sky, in the direction of the storm, and he held his sword out, its point buried in the moss of the rock in mute defiance to the elements.

'Talisker!' Yiska yelled, but his voice was lost in the cacophony of sound. Malky pulled on his sleeve and he ducked back under the shelter.

'What the hell is he doing? Thanks,' he said as Malky handed him a dry blanket to wrap himself in.

'Dunno,' Malky sniffed. 'Sure he'll tell us if he wants tae.'

'Have you seen Dog?'

'No. Reckon he's hiding somewhere. Canny blame him.' Malky scowled out towards the storm as if he was taking it personally.

'Is it just me, or does it seem weird to you?'

Malky nodded. 'Know what you mean – there wasnae any sign o' a storm when we went tae sleep, no rain, nothing. Feels kinda like . . .'

'Like it's come for us,' Yiska finished.

'Christ, dinny say that!'

The storm raged and blasted the land for three hours. By the time it subsided Malky and Yiska had set up camp in a tiny, but miraculously dry area in the underhang of the rocks. They lit a fire and sat staring into it wrapped in their blankets. There was little point in trying to talk, the storm was so loud; their heads ached with the noise and the strange, zingy smell of frying ozone. Their eyes were streaming with tears of exhaustion from the recurrent shock of the lightning – open or closed it made little difference as the cave appeared to dance with the angular shapes and shadows of the after-glare.

At some stage Yiska must have lapsed into some kind of sleep. He had been thinking about *Sicheii* Rodney and how he would tell him about the storm, and the next thing he knew someone was tapping him lightly on the shoulder. Jerking awake he looked up into the pale glow of an exhausted dawn. Talisker was standing looking down at him; he was soaked, could not have been more soaked had he just emerged from the river, but he was smiling a slightly feverish smile.

'Good morning, Yiska.'

'Talisker.' Yiska blinked into wakefulness – at least his eyes were rested – and stood up stiffly. 'You'd better get out of those wet things, here, I'll get you a blanket. What the hell were you doing up there?'

Talisker appeared thoughtful. 'Communing, I guess you'd say. Looking for answers.' He stripped off his sodden clothes which landed in a wet heavy heap.

'And did you get any?'

'Some. Did you think the storm was coming for us?'

'Yes – Malky thought so, too.'

'It was.' Talisker had wrapped the blanket around him and was now crouching next to the remnants of the fire as closely as he dared. 'I mean, I think we attracted it.'

'Why?'

Talisker reached into the heap of his clothes rummaging around for something. When he drew his hand out of the cloth he was clutching a fist-sized gem – Yiska thought it was an emerald, but he'd never seen anything that size before. In the cool morning light of the little cave it was glowing and sparkling as if it had caught hold of the storm. The light made Talisker's fingers seem thin, almost skeletal. Yiska wondered if the gem was hot, but Talisker showed no sign of discomfort.

'Wow, it's . . . it's amazing.'

Behind where Yiska was standing Malky had woken up and was staring at the gem with an expression akin to incredulity. 'You shouldn'ae hae that, Duncan,' he said. 'How come you've got it?'

'Long story, Malk.'

'What is it?' Yiska asked, feeling two steps behind everyone else. 'I mean, is it important?'

'Oh aye. It's important all right,' Malky glowered. 'It's cawed Braznnair.'

The moorland was sodden with the rain, new streams flowed through springy islands of turf and heather. Weak sunshine had come out and was reflected off the standing water so that it seemed a shining silver latticework overlaid the moor, stretching off into the distance, glinting and glistening until the point it was swallowed up by the horizon.

It made the journey slow and cold; only Yiska had dry feet as he still wore his walking boots from Arizona. Talisker and Malk wore the soft leather ankle boots fashioned by the Fine – they kept the water out for quite some time but, eventually, they soaked through. Dog had reappeared from wherever he had hidden during the storm and he picked his way amongst the waterlogged turf with great deliberation, lifting his long front legs high out of the water like some dressage horse.

They had been walking for about three hours when Malky spotted something on the horizon. 'Look, what d'you think that is?'

Yiska shielded his eyes against the glare coming off the water. There was something quite some distance off – a thick white mist blanketing an area of the moor – and there were lights sparking from within the cloud cover, an occasional flash of green and blue.

Talisker had come up behind them; he seemed quiet and preoccupied after the storm. He frowned into the distance. 'Don't like the look of that,' he muttered. He didn't stop, though, and they carried on towards the area with no further discussion.

They must have been half a mile from the mist when the first screams reached them. The sound was long drawn-out and agonized, as if in specific response to a pain being inflicted. Dog growled, a line of hackles ridging his fur. Malky gripped the pommel of his sword. As soon as the screams ended the moorland returned to silence once more, a silence which now seemed unnatural, heavy with fear.

The mist enveloped them with a fierce suddenness; it seemed to Yiska that tendrils of cold slid down his throat like icy water. He glanced nervously towards Malky who was peering ahead, still gripping his blade.

Another scream, closer this time and definitely female. Talisker cleared his throat as if he was about to say something but seemed to think better of it.

'Stay close,' Malky muttered. There was no reason to speak in hushed tones but instinct took over. They walked on in grim silence; Yiska peered so hard into the white obfuscation of the mist that little dots appeared in his vision and swam across his field of view like disconcerting tadpoles. He blinked rapidly, trying to clear them away – stared down at his feet and the strange colourlessness of the grass. When he looked up again he saw something which broke the monotony of the landscape. 'What d'you think that is?' he breathed. It was a purely rhetorical question and he increased his pace to reach the thing.

It was a tattered blue flag on the end of a long pole which was lurching and buckling in the breeze. There was something else on the end of the pole – a gem like Braznnair – which caught and refracted even the dull light of the mist so that fragmented rainbows spilled out in all directions. It struck Yiska that it could be a way marker. There was a faded silver symbol on the flag against the blue background, it looked sad somehow, and spoke to Yiska of faded glory.

'It's the symbol of the Council of Tema,' Talisker said. 'We must be getting close to their meeting place.'

'Don't they have a permanent building or anything?' Yiska peered into the mist with renewed determination, half-expecting to see some monolithic spires or ornate palace he simply hadn't been able to discern before.

'No, they had a separate island once but . . .'

Talisker's explanation was cut short by more screams – distinctly a male and a female this time.

'There's another one over here,' Malky called. 'Another marker.'

As Yiska and Talisker waked over to the second marker another scream split the silence but, this time the sound had taken form – a bright rush of blue light whooshed towards Talisker's face and, taken by surprise, he just managed to avoid contact by flinging himself aside, landing in the cold damp of the boggy ground. Another scream followed, then another – blue and green flares lighting up the mist with lurid sorrow.

Malky had drawn his sword and was swatting uselessly at the lights but after long seconds they vanished once more – fading into the distance or disappearing – it was difficult to tell where they went.

Talisker picked himself off the ground pulling bits of grass and heather from his clothes. Yiska who was nearest to him, could see that Talisker was uncharacteristically rattled by the disembodied sounds. Something about them had shaken him badly – he drew his sword for no reason other than the reassurance it gave him to hold it and scowled and spat towards the flag.

'Are you all right, Talisker?'

'Yeah, it's just . . . for a moment there I thought . . . never mind.'

Yiska was irked by this reaction; for some reason he felt sure that if he had not been there Talisker would have confided in Malky. It only served to remind him he was still a stranger to Sutra. However, he said nothing about it and all three of them walked silently through the oppressive mist, their eyes straining ahead and their breath shallow and cold.

Twice more the screams assaulted them – the second time the blue light wrapped itself around Talisker's head and shoulders and he staggered helplessly like a burning man before it pulled away, echoing into the distance. He stared after it, his face pale and eyes wide with shock. This time, Yiska did not seek to reassure him, just grimly pressed on. 'There's something there,' he frowned. 'Something ahead. Look.'

At first it was difficult to see what the black outlines were – swathed in mist which was darkening as evening neared, two tall, gaunt shapes facing one another. But, before they even reached them all three men had guessed what they were, they had seen enough Shoreth crucifixions since coming to Sutra.

But these were different, notably so. No warriors, no deserters' corpses adorned the two crosses. To the left was a young woman of about fifteen, she had long dark hair mercifully streaking black, obscuring strands across her agonised features; to the right, a young man, smaller than an average Fine. His head was slumped onto his chest and, because the crucifix had moved forward in the soft mud, his body was pulled forward so that he hung suspended entirely from his broken wrists. Both bodies wore a plain gold circlet on their heads.

'Who are they?' Yiska whispered. Talisker had unaccountably sat down between the two crosses as if he could no longer trust his legs to hold him. Dog slunk beside him and licked his face, whimpering softly.

'It's no who they are, Yiska. It's whea they're supposed tae be.' Malky offered no other explanation but drew his dagger and set about cutting down the body of the young woman. Unfortunately, the ropes he cut away from her arms were slick with the mist and he lost his grip, the body fell to the ground next to Talisker who stared at the girl's face with a mixture of horror and incomprehension. 'The sounds – the screams – I thought they were . . . it was like her voice.' Talisker mumbled.

'What? Whose voice? Look, will someone tell me what's going on?' Yiska frowned. 'Am I missing something here?'

Malky grabbed his elbow and moved him away from the crosses. 'They're like the twin Thanes – Talisker's children,' he said, quietly.

'It's a warning,' Talisker said. His voice was shaken but clear. 'A message. To me.'

'It's not possible,' Yiska replied. 'No one knows we're coming. Why would they want to keep us away from the Council? And who . . .'

Talisker stood up and began to manhandle the unfortunate youth from the cross. He muttered something as he did so and, although Yiska was not close enough to hear, he thought it might have been something like; 'I'm so sorry . . .'

'I don't know, Yiska. There's only one person I would credit such wanton waste of life to – and he's definitely dead. Definitely.'

'Who?'

Talisker laughed, a short sound, stifled by the mist. 'My other son.'

They had to leave the bodies where they lay, the ground was too boggy to attempt any burial, but Talisker took a blanket from his pack and covered them over. As they walked away Malky muttered, 'Just like Regan and Tris,' and shook his head sadly.

'Don't mourn for Regan and Tris, Malk. They've been dead for over a hundred years. We'll never know who those two were and they were killed to make some stupid point.'

'Aye and whoever made it is gonna feel the point of my . . .'

There was a sudden, low rumbling sound and the ground gave way beneath them.

Darkness, and the soft, loamy smell of peat.

'Ahhh.' Yiska sat up rubbing his shin. He knew he was going to ache all over. 'Tell me again why Sutra's such a wonderful place, Talisker.' No answer. 'Talisker?'

There was a groan from over to his right so he stood up rather gingerly in case there was any further to fall. The ground was uneven, the end of the plume of the landslide had brought down heather and bushes – Yiska stumbled across roots which protruded from the freshly turned soil. 'That you, Talisker?' he called.

'Nah, it's me, Malk.'

They managed to find one another and Malky lit a brand from Yiska's pack.

'Wow, it's a big place.'

It seemed they were only in a tiny chamber off a cavernous space, their voices echoed into the distance. 'I think I can see another light ahead,' Yiska said. 'Could be Duncan.'

'Come on.' Malky was limping but he made no

comment about any injury, simply forged ahead. In a way, Yiska thought, he was like Dog, as long as he had his people – in his case Talisker – Malky was happy and focussed in the moment. 'Jeez.'

'What is it, Malk? Oh wow . . . awesome.'

The main cavern appeared to be full of people . . . and animals. The firelight from the torch flickered weakly in the huge space casting black shadows of bears, wolves and eagles – but the suggestion of movement was all there was. The creatures were huge; out of proportion with the people. Yiska felt a thrill of fear and admiration as he stared at an eagle; it could only be a Sidhe eagle – a totem.

But there could be no doubt they were not statues; the occupants of the cave were frozen, or turned to stone. Some were covered in the waxen yellow-white of lime which had dripped through the rocks – it was as if the ground was trying to claim them, assimilate them inch by inch. Yiska stared closely at the face of one man, marvelling at his skin and the lines of his face. Near the middle of the space a woman had been talking – it was obvious she held the floor, she was brandishing a talking stick, and her robes were spinning outwards from her body as if she had whirled round suddenly to emphasise a point of debate.

Before the woman on a rock slab in the middle of the space sat Talisker. He looked somewhat bemused by the occupants of the chamber.

'Looks like we've found the Council of Tema,' he said.

Chapter Fifteen

'There's something you should know.' Talisker's voice echoed darkly through the cavern, there could be little doubt that whatever admission he was about to make weighed heavy on him.

Malky and Yiska were sitting on a rill of limestone nearby – Yiska still marvelling at the frozen figures. Some had broken under the intense burden of the limestone; nearby an eagle had toppled over, its head had shattered when it fell. Deeper into the cave towards the back wall the situation was worse – some of the figures were unidentifiable, coated in the brittle yellow casing; some had toppled against each other and were a confusing tangle of limbs. They had been so much alive, animated until one last, impossible moment.

'What's up, Duncan?' Malky frowned. He had seldom seen his friend look so on edge and listless.

'They could have protected themselves if they'd had Braznnair,' he muttered staring at the floor.

'How long d'you think they've been like this?' Yiska asked.

Talisker shrugged. 'Well, it must have been Zarrus – he had the sense to take them out of the picture before they even knew the danger to the Sidhe. Probably a few years.'

'But the limestone's so far advanced – looks like they've been here for a century.'

'Yeah well . . . I don't know, do I? Maybe the magic speeded it up.' Talisker looked miserable, as if Yiska's question was an accusation.

Malky walked over to where Talisker sat and stared down at him with his arms folded. 'Well . . . ?'

'I stole it. All right. I stole Braznnair from the Sidhe.'

'What!' Malky was righteously appalled. 'Why in the hell wid ye do that, Duncan?'

'Like I said, it's a long story, Malk, and I'm not proud of it.'

Malky narrowed his eyes suspiciously. 'Is this why you and Sandro fell out?'

'Yeah. He was *really* angry – we both said stuff . . .' he shrugged. 'You know how it goes.'

'Aye, you two have made a bloody art oot o' being angry with one another. I suppose it involved a woman?'

'What makes you say that?'

'Tell me I'm wrong.'

Talisker grinned despite himself. 'No, you're not wrong. Anyway, I often thought when I was back in Scotland and I started to get ill, that it was some kind of punishment – you know, from the Gods or something.'

Malky walked over to the young woman who had apparently been commanding the debate at the moment the magic seized them. He tapped on her arm thoughtfully, the sound was like hollow stone or plaster. 'Mebbe this is your chance tae make amends, Duncan. I mean, ye've got Braznnair in yer pocket – mebbe it kin help – you know, break the spell.'

'I'd say it's too late for most of them,' Yiska muttered.

'Malk's right. It's worth a try.' Talisker took the gem

from his pocket. It was still glowing as it had the night before when it captured the energy of the lightning. Talisker's face was bathed in the warm green and to Yiska and Malky he seemed as if the years had fallen away, smoothed out by the life-giving magic of Braznnair.

He carried the gem over to the young woman that Malky stood beside. 'I'm sorry,' he said.

'Ah dinnae think she kin . . .' Malky shut up as Yiska gestured him to silence.

Talisker took Braznnair and held it against the woman's throat; she was immediately suffused with the light which made her look more real and animated and somehow younger − perhaps a teenager − but nothing happened for long moments.

'Nothing's happening.'

'Wait.'

'No, nothing's happening, Malk − I can't feel anything.'

'But . . .'

Talisker gave an exasperated sigh and snatched Braznnair away from the Sidhe woman. He cursed and stalked off to the other side of the cave.

'Well, there's nae reason tae sulk about it,' Malky frowned. He was about to go over and encourage Talisker but Yiska stopped him.

'Just give him a minute, Malk,' he said quietly.

Talisker was still muttering to himself when Yiska finally went to check on him. 'What gives, Duncan? Is it just guilt for stealing the gem?'

'Partly. Sometimes . . .' he glanced over to where

Malky sat, occupying himself by shaving sticks of wood to make kindling. 'Yiska, do you know what it's like to have someone believe in you completely – unquestioningly? Someone who believes that you can do anything you set your mind to?'

Yiska thought about it. 'Well, I guess my father was a bit like that when I was growing up.'

'No, it's not the same. Sometimes I think Malky's like a child – don't get me wrong, I'd trust him with my life – have done on numerous occasions – but he has that complete faith. And like a child he just can't comprehend the idea I might fail. I'm not any kind of hero here any more – I've been gone almost two centuries. I'm not – I'm not *relevant* to Sutra now. He doesn't see that, he's like my own Sancho Panza.'

'You still care about Sutra, don't you?'

'Yeah, I'll always care, but . . .'

'Then maybe you have to make yourself relevant again.'

'What does that mean?'

Yiska shrugged. 'I have no idea.'

They were interrupted by a dismayed yell from Malky. 'Aw no.'

It was Dog. He'd obviously been caught in the landslip as well but no one had thought to look for him, he was so much an independent spirit that the assumption was he could take care of himself. But he had suffered badly, he was covered in mud and one eye had been dashed out by a stone. Worst of all, and probably fatal, it looked as if his back was broken, just before his hips. He lurched towards Malky excruciatingly slowly, whining a low, almost subliminal whine in the back of his throat.

'Aw no,' Malky repeated. Ever sentimental, the idea that Dog had been fatally injured through his loyalty was deeply moving to the Highlander. 'Come here, boy,' he said softly – Talisker noted the glint of his dagger and knew he was about to end Dog's suffering. He and Yiska went over to take their leave of their companion.

'Hey boy,' Talisker said, reaching out to ruffle the rough fur behind Dog's ear. 'What happened, eh?'

'Should've stayed on the Rez,' Yiska muttered. For a moment Talisker was unsure whether he was talking about the dog.

There was a flare of light, so unexpected and so powerful that Talisker was thrown backwards, caught off balance as the light emanated from Braznnair which he still held. Dog was instantly enveloped by tendrils of light which began to spin, describing the outline of the dog in a way which was instantly familiar to Talisker and Malky.

Yiska was horrified. 'I *said* he was a Skinwalker – Rodney warned us – you didn't believe me,' he drew his sword and held it before him ready to strike as Dog transformed.

But the transformation of a Sidhe was ever a beautiful, joyous thing to behold, there was no question that Yiska would not use his weapon as his eyes caught the green fire and his expression became a picture of wonder.

And when it was over, she was there; the woman; the Sidhe from his dreams. She was delicate, willowy, her limbs almost stick thin, but her face held an expression of triumph which quickly transmuted to anger as she marched towards Talisker and slapped him hard across the face.

'Hey! Easy,' Malky cautioned.

'Tal-ees-ker.' She spat the name at him. 'Worldwalker. I name you *thief*! Do you know what you have done?' Talisker's cheek bore the red mark of her tiny hand but he said nothing in reply to her accusation merely nodded.

'Miss . . . I mean, Lady,' Yiska decided to try and instigate some conversation since he had no history with the Sidhe and the woman had appeared in his dream. 'My name is Yiska – you have been trying to make contact . . .'

Her answer surprised him; she walked over and stared deeply into his eyes, he flinched under the yellow cat-gaze but after her long scrutiny he was rewarded with a smile. 'Yes. It *is* you. Lorebringer.'

'We are like orphans,' Tulann frowned as he rode into Ruannoch Were with Effie and his riders. 'Mewling brats that no one wants, we have nowhere to call home.'

It was an uneasy peace. The gates of Ruannoch Were had been thrown open but still the Shoreth army chose to remain on the shore. They did not feel they could barrack in the city they had been besieging only days before – they could not go forward and they certainly could not go back. Even if they had felt welcomed there, ten thousand men was more than the city could take – Tulann and his immediate entourage were different of course; Sigrid was enjoying the young emperor's embarrassment so much he insisted they avail themselves of the best quarters.

It was almost impossible to gauge the old Thane's enmity towards Tulann and Effie found this truly remarkable given that Tulann had been about to fasten Sigrid to a post and have him riddled with arrows. Only occasionally, during the long, interminable days of talks did Effie note that, when Tulann looked away, Sigrid's glance became a glare, an accusation of pure iron.

There were incidents, of course; it was one thing for the Thane and the Emperor to be engaged in discussion but there would never be any love lost between the Fine and the Shoreth. Three days after the talks had begun, twenty drunken Fine galloped across the causeway after dark and set fire to a section of the camp. The Shoreth tents, constructed with a delicate, silky fabric, burned brightly, the fire leaping from one to another until a whole row was ablaze. During the melee as people came running to curb the flames, the Fine drew their swords and attacked those warriors who had had the wit to come armed. By the time order was restored and the unrepentant invaders arrested, four Shoreth and two Fine had been killed in the fighting but five further Shoreth perished in the flames.

Tulann was furious. At first he wanted to have the Fine captives executed but Effie and his councillors managed to persuade him that this would not necessarily endear him to Sigrid. He handed the captives back the next day, a slightly sick, laconic smile fixed on his face. 'Just high spirits,' he remarked to Sigrid. 'No real harm done.' He neglected to mention his murdered men, choosing to gloss over the details for the sake of expedience.

Sigrid smiled in response. 'I am sorry, Tulann. Rest assured they will be punished.'

Punished. Effie thought. *How? Slapped wrists, don't do it again.* She scowled at the departing Fine as they rode back across the causeway. It was all politics and the fact that they had killed in cold blood had to be overlooked for the greater good. As Tulann turned back towards the encampment his expression made it plain he liked the situation even less than she did.

'Barbaric savages,' he snarled to no one in particular. He had the murdered men buried with full honours as if to assuage his guilt at their shabby treatment.

The next night, someone shot fire-arrows into the battlements of Ruannoch Were. It must have been done from a boat on the water but no one was caught or laid claim to the act. It mattered little; only the roof joists of the southern tower caught flame and the fire was quickly extinguished with no casualties. Effie noted the coracles the next day, a bobbing cluster tied up on the shoreline – no attempt had been made to conceal them, there were even arrows left in the bottom of one. Tulann did not bother to instigate an enquiry and Effie was not completely sure he had not ordered the incident himself. But the petty tit-for-tat squabbles were soon insignificant; Zarrus was not content to rest on his laurels.

She was trying to sleep. But for the first time in a week she really, *really* wanted to purge. She knew she was bloated and fat like some great white grub, *knew* that if she were to get up and look at herself in the mirror she would have been repulsed by what she might see. In the corner, the dark bulk of the mirror which she had covered with a blanket stood stiffly accusing.

The food in the camp was good, too good and tonight she had allowed herself to relax, as if she were pretending to be someone else for a few hours – perhaps the Effie Morgan Tulann somehow imagined she was.

Since she'd been in Sutra Effie had only purged three times. Once with the last of her laxatives, then after her confab with Tulann and then, a few days later she'd wandered off into the forest and made herself sick. It had been a noisy, unsatisfying vomit and she had been shocked by how much her stomach hurt and cramped for hours afterwards. It seemed she was out of practice and this made her feel panicked and vulnerable. Tulann had asked her if she was all right but she refused to confide in him and simply sat stony-faced, refusing to eat.

So she was laying with her eyes determinedly shut. The act of opening them would make her unable to ignore her desire; she would get up, she knew. She'd look in the hated mirror and see her own pale gauntness reflected back by some sick magic as though she were the great white worm of her repulsed nightmares. The tequila grub.

She opened her eyes anyway, unable to sleep with the constant white-noise static of her own berating consciousness. Maybe she should go and see Tulann. She knew he'd be awake even at this hour, that despite his cocky demeanour the dispossession of his people had frightened him and, more than his detractors might suspect, he felt keenly responsible. But if she went there, at this hour, she knew he would think she'd reconsidered his request – that she would sleep with him. *And would it be so bad*? Her mind taunted her.

And because it was preferable to thinking of her own bloated form she was thinking of Tulann when she saw the shadow move past the tent. It was so close its outline was thrown into sharp relief against the fabric. Effie heard a stifled hiss of air as an involuntary breath escaped her; her immediate thought was that she was glad she could not see the thing for real. She sat very still, her breathing suddenly unnaturally loud in the warm confines of the tent. The creature outside moved silently and slowly, a blundering, thoughtless movement – only along the edges of the silhouette there was a constant blossoming from within the shapeless bulk so that it appeared to move in some bizarre stop-motion. Effie had never seen anything so suggestively repulsive, but she knew what it was instantly, remembered Talisker's inability to suppress a shudder when speaking of Corrannyeid.

She was aware that she was sitting with the coverlet stuffed up against her mouth, her eyes like saucers, knew she looked like an illustration from a children's story book. She wanted to groan aloud as the Corrannyeid rounded the edge of the tent where the door flap was situated.

No . . . go . . . away . . . But in fact she said nothing, held her breath, felt her bowel turn to water as the creature continued on past her all-too-flimsy shelter. She could see a tiny sliver of realness through the slit in the doorway but only for a second; a brown, blue surface from which she was sure maggots were dropping and hatching.

A shuddering breath fell frozen from her constricted throat but she could not move for a long time. And because she was so still, because she was listening for the creatures return, she knew the awfulness that descended upon the sleeping camp. She heard them. A mere suggestion of sound, entering the sleeping quarters of the warriors whose sleep would soon be turned to hellish nightmare. There were moments, burgeoning pauses filled with mute realisation and terror. She knew they became shadows of their victims, could imagine the horror of waking as the creatures loomed forward to subsume their bodies. In fact, it was difficult to know if she really heard the stifled gasps and strangled screams so intense was the mingling of her imagining and the red noise at the edges of her hearing.

It could not last for ever. Even the most soul-destroying fear could only be sustained by the body's senses for so long. Gradually, she slumped down in the bed, rubbing away cold tears from her cheeks with the back of her sleeve. *They could be coming for her . . .* but as the adrenalin subsided from her system and she felt herself unable to move from the bed she felt that somehow – impossible though it seemed – somehow, she might drift into sleep.

She did hear a stifled scream, she was sure of it, but there was nothing she could do, nothing. Her last thought was of Tulann . . . hoped he was okay . . . liked the little jerk really . . .

I can't be going to sleep . . .

. . . can I?

But when the true, natural nightmares came, they

344

were not of Corrannyeid but of bodies pitching forward into the starkness of the snow.

'Lady Morgan? Effie?' She was hurrying across the camp to check on Tulann. When the clamour of alarm bells had woken her she had known immediately that the night's events had been no dream. It was still early and a pre-dawn mist was drifting off the lake playing against her bare legs when they broke the warm cover of her robe as she strode across the parade ground.

She stopped and turned towards the speaker – it was actually unusual to be spoken to by anyone apart from Tulann, Almasey and Raco. Everyone else treated her with respect because they had to, but primarily with suspicion. It was the woman who had saved Raco and the Thane by bringing news of Zarrus' attacks; she was standing by the edge of the lake observing the mammoths having an early morning bathe in the shallows. The herd had lumbered into the encampment about two hours after the arrival of Ferebe Vezul and the Shoreth warriors had gathered in a great cheering crowd to watch their arrival – they were especially excited by the white one which Ferebe was watching now – on their backs they had carried tired and overwhelmed woman and children from the southern city of Kamala Sev, the few survivors of Zarrus' first major victory.

Effie had seen the creatures from a distance but she found their sheer size frightening – horses were enough for her to cope with – and so she didn't approach but called over.

'Ferebe Vezul, isn't it?' Raco had spoken of the Shoreth warrior only the evening before when Effie had shared some wine with him. He'd been unable to keep the admiration from his voice as he described their flight from Durghanti – an admiration probably unique between a Fine and Shoreth. Now Effie considered Ferebe more closely, it was difficult to equate Raco's account with the diminutive figure before her. She'd been expecting someone more . . . solid-looking.

Ferebe nodded and smiled a tight, somehow unconvincing smile, her silver hair drifting on the cold breeze. 'Come over here,' she gestured.

'I've . . . I've got to check on Tulann.'

Ferebe looked surprised at Effie's genuine concern. 'Oh, *he's* fine,' she sniffed. 'People like him always are.' Effie wasn't sure she liked Ferebe's tone but she said nothing. 'Four hundred,' Ferebe muttered.

'Eh? Four hundred what?'

'Dead. Killed in the night by Corrannyeid. If I had been sleeping by the herd as normal I might have been able to raise the alarm – they can sense things. Very intuitive creatures.'

Effie had been about to volunteer the information that she had seen a Corrannyeid at close quarters but she thought better of it. 'Oh,' she said in a small voice, she couldn't think of anything to say.

Ferebe smiled again, slightly more warmly this time, probably in response to Effie's stricken expression. 'Come on, come over – I'll introduce you to Storm.'

Reluctantly Effie walked over to the shoreline. The smell of the herd seemed to have combined with the mist and floated towards her in a pungent fug. She wondered if Ferebe even noticed it since she spent so much time with the beasts.

'Storm, *hutzah*,' Ferebe commanded. The white mammoth obediently stopped what it was doing and ambled over to its mistress. Next to the diminutive form of Ferebe the creature looked even more massive and Effie, who had come to stand beside her took an involuntary step backwards. 'No, no,' Ferebe said, 'stand your ground. She won't hurt you. Come here, sweetness . . .' Storm reached out her trunk and rummaged around Ferebe's jerkin obviously used to finding treats in her pockets. 'Ooh, you're so impatient,' Ferebe laughed. 'Do you want to pat her, Lady Morgan?'

Effie reached out slightly half-heartedly and patted Storm lightly on her trunk. 'Oh,' she said, 'her fur . . .'

'Soft, isn't it?'

'Yeah, I kinda thought it would be all wiry and coarse.'

'I think it's because she's white – the texture is different – the big bull's hair is like that,' Ferebe nodded toward the rest of the herd. 'Here.' She handed Effie a handful of beechnuts. 'Right, hold your palm flat, that's it, thumb out of the way . . .'

Storm didn't hesitate to take the nuts even though they were offered with obvious trepidation. Ferebe beamed as if the mammoth were some child prodigy. 'See, she likes you.'

Effie laughed. 'Well, that makes two people in Sutra.'

'Oh, come on. Raco has spoken well of you to me. And your friends are here – Talisker, Yiska and Malky.'

'I haven't seen them. They left Ruannoch Were just after I arrived.'

Ferebe nodded. 'You are from the other world also, are you not?'

Such a plain assertion threw Effie off guard. She only had one real confidant here – Tulann – and she certainly had not told him. But she remembered that Ferebe was friends with Raco and had been with him when Talisker and the others arrived. She suddenly felt out of her depth and slightly tearful; she had no one really.

'Are you all right?'

'Yeah,' she sighed. 'Well, no, actually . . . I, oh shit.' She felt a tear escape from beneath her lashes and felt stupid and ashamed in front of Ferebe Vezul who seemed to be such a controlled, strong woman. 'I'm not usually like this.'

Ferebe pulled a wry expression. 'By the Goddess, Effie Morgan, you're in a completely new world. Anyone would feel a bit strange – come and sit down.' She gestured to another *Sanah* who had been helping with the herd and he came and took Storm back into the group. Ferebe and Effie wandered off along the shore into the fringes of the woodland, Ferebe perched on a log and Effie found a low branch on a wide chestnut tree just by her.

'I only came to get them,' she explained. 'I had no intention of staying here, certainly not of becoming Tulann's flavour of the month.' Ferebe frowned, not understanding Effie's expression. 'His favourite, his best friend,' Effie added.

'Ah.' Ferebe nodded. 'From what I hear that's a vulnerable position to be in.'

'He's not like that. I mean, he's not how most people think,' Effie felt disloyal for talking about Tulann behind his back, so was quick to jump to his defence. Ferebe quirked her eyebrows and shrugged.

'Well, I don't know him personally Effie, only what I have heard of him . . . but none of it is good.'

'And very little of it is fact. He will be a good emperor for your people, Ferebe, if they give him a chance.'

'That may be true but there's no denying he's gotten off to a really bad start – leading the army and most of the population of Durghanti into Zarrus' trap. Let's hope he gets the chance to redeem himself.'

'I only came to get help. Zarrus has found the way into my own world and he is killing innocent people there, God knows how many by now. I thought I could just get Talisker to come back and sort it out . . .' Her voice cracked as she remembered Uncle Sandro; 'Zarrus has probably killed someone very dear to Talisker – and me – I need to tell him.'

'Raco told me they've gone north-west looking for the Council of . . .' Ferebe wrinkled her brow, trying to remember the name, 'Tema? It seems unlikely that you'll get the chance to find them until all this is over.'

'Tulann won't let me go, anyway,' Effie muttered.

Ferebe laughed derisively. 'So, are you his bound woman? His prisoner? What?'

'No. He's just, he doesn't really understand about friendship. I think he'd believe that I wouldn't come back.'

'And would you? When you find your way back to your own world?' Ferebe frowned and stared more closely at Effie's face, which was slightly flushed. 'Onrir's balls, you're not in love with the little weasel are you?'

Effie was annoyed. 'Is friendship some strange concept to all you Shoreth? And, I would remind you, that "little weasel" is your Emperor.' She pulled her cloak tightly around herself and stood up to go in righteous indignation. 'Good-day, Ferebe Vezul.'

Ferebe looked more bemused than chastised and she watched Effie begin to stalk off, stumbling slightly across the uneven pebbles of the foreshore. 'Effie,' she called. 'You didn't answer my question.'

Yiska was finding it difficult to concentrate; he thought Melicende was the most beautiful thing – woman – he had ever seen. Alien and strange, it was true, but equally enigmatic. She smelt good, like the warmth of the earth after the rain, he remembered thinking. *She knows the landscape of my dreams.*

'I was waiting,' she said. 'Zarrus has stolen the magics of the Sidhe, that's why he dealt with the Council first.' She glanced at Talisker again, unable to disguise her accusation. 'Without Braznnair, what were we? Just a bunch of old men and a very few acolytes. Powerless. The Sidhe no longer look to us for their laws, their culture, we had become mere figureheads, nostalgic remnants of a way of life that was slowly dissipating as our warriors became more entangled with the Fine, marrying Fine women and turning their backs on the way of the Lynx, Bear, Wolf or Eagle. I cannot blame them; you know, Worldwalker, that we came here first as exiles ourselves and it is ever the way of transient peoples to want to belong. Once the warriors found they could not transform it seemed our way of life would be gone forever within a generation. It is like losing one's spirit, but in an almost physical sense; a dismemberment.'

Yiska nodded, thinking how strange it was that the

problems of the Sidhe should seem so real, so familiar. 'So how did you become entrapped in Dog?' he asked. 'Is that what the Sidhe do – take possession of an animal?'

He knew he'd made a remark that could be taken as an insult by Melicende as soon as he'd spoken – Talisker made a small, embarrassed noise in the back of his throat.

'Is that what your Skinwalkers do?' Melicende asked coolly. 'We Sidhe have a life partner that comes to us from the spiritual plain when we transform – we are intertwined from birth.'

'But Dug's no a Sidhe animal,' Malky frowned.

'No. And he was simply following you because you had been kind to him and given him some food. I was in the void with the other souls – Zarrus killed me to use my body for a Flay.'

'So the lost souls we saw . . .'

She nodded. 'There are thousands by now. They – we – cannot rest, cannot find oblivion or paradise, whichever one believes, because our earthly bodies have been stolen.'

Malky frowned. 'So, like . . . how does Zarrus make yer bodies move an stuff?'

'He uses spirits from the deepest reaches of the void. Hellish, mindless spirits. We are violated by them.'

'Christ.'

'So you hitched a lift with Dog.'

'Zarrus has found other allies in the void,' Talisker said. 'We've seen Corrannyeid since we arrived.'

Melicende looked grave. 'This gets worse,' she muttered.

'What does he want – Zarrus – why is he doing this?'

'We do not know.' Melicende stared round at the frozen forms of the Council as she spoke, instinctively drawing her cloak around her. 'They were debating the danger of the Shoreth when this happened. They had sensed a proliferation of dark magics but had not pinpointed the person responsible – it's a moot point now, of course.'

They were silent for a while and the only sound was the drip-dripping of the limestone water doing its inexorable work.

'What can we do, Melicende?' Yiska asked quietly. 'You must have come to tell us or give us some advice.'

'Do you think so,' she taunted. It was obvious she had not forgotten Yiska's comment about the Sidhe taking possession of hapless animals. 'Perhaps I just saw my chance and took it. He was only a dog, after all.'

Yiska smiled, slightly abashed. 'I'm sorry, Melicende, I did not mean to offend you.'

'I think I know how we may awaken the Council. Now that we have Braznnair.'

'We do not have Braznnair. I have Braznnair,' Talisker replied tersely. Malky frowned at his uncooperative response. 'Duncan . . .'

'Someday I'll tell you, Malk – let's just say this gem is extremely attractive to a certain type of woman.'

'I can assure you, Worldwalker, my concern is for the Sidhe and the Fine, not myself. I am dead already. But if you have concerns, of course you must stay while Yiska and I attempt the awakening.'

'Me? What can I do?' Yiska looked surprised.

'It is a simple thing, Yiska, but you may start a chain

reaction which will help Braznnair do its work. There are no *Seanachaidhs* left in the land, no ordinary magics, no belief of the old Gods by the Fine. This is a place without a soul. Perhaps you have noted this yourself?'

'Aye – Yiska says it has nae Hozro. Is that no right, Yiska?' said Malky.

Yiska nodded. 'Yeah, and it's worse nearer to Zarrus' city.'

'But you have brought us a gift from your world. A gift that you carry in here,' she touched his chest where his heart was. 'You carry the lore of your people, the Navajo, who are linked to the Sidhe through time and across worlds.'

'But . . .' Yiska laughed incredulously, 'I am a Christian and a doctor. I have not followed the Navajo way since I was a teenager, I left the Rez. There are others there who would have been a better choice, who walk in beauty.'

'Yet you have enough, it is strong within you, respect and love for your past and your nation. You and I may direct Braznnair. It will be a borrowing for the Sidhe.' Melicende sat back as though this vague explanation had exhausted her, the animation drained from her face and she appeared suddenly bereft and frightened. 'If you refuse to help me, Yiska, I see no solution to Zarrus' overrunning of Sutra. We are all doomed.'

'Yiska,' Talisker beckoned him over to the other side of the cavern for a confab. Yiska glanced back at Melicende as he stood up. She nodded, 'Go and talk to your friends,' she said wearily.

He walked across the chamber, ducking beneath toppled figures and pointing limbs, glancing at the rapt expressions of the Council. Could they know? he thought. Could they be awaiting his decision?

'There's no reason not to do as she says,' he said as soon as he reached Talisker and Malky. 'It might not work but she's right, there's no alternative. Anything else is giving up.'

Talisker glanced towards where Melicende sat, pointedly ignoring them. 'I'm just not sure I trust her. She might want Braznnair for her own reasons.'

'Like what?'

'Braznnair is a thing of great power, Yiska, it could bring her back to life permanently for example. If she's evil she might want to use it for her own agenda – hell, maybe Zarrus sent her.'

'Oh aye, I hadn'ae thought o' that,' Malky muttered.

'Oh come on. Look, I know you have a history with Braznnair and obviously some reason not to trust women, but don't you think you're letting it cloud your judgement? It must have been difficult for her to . . .'

'. . .hitch a lift? Yeah, and that's a whole can of worms. The Sidhe don't generally borrow other forms.'

'Aye, and that means she killed my dug,' Malky added somewhat sourly.

Talisker sighed. 'But I guess you're both right, Yiska, there's no other way forward.'

Yiska nodded and turned to go and tell Melicende. 'Michael,' Talisker clapped a hand on his shoulder, 'I want you to keep your hands on Braznnair throughout, okay?'

Yiska considered this for a moment. 'I will,' he said

solemnly. 'But Talisker, you did steal it from them in the first place and if the Council awakens . . .' he glanced around at looming shadows of the Council, 'They're gonna want it back.'

Effie was leaving. She closed the door as quietly as she could although the gentle 'snick' of the latch sounded loud in the silent confines of the corridor. She and Tulann's immediate retinue were spending the night in Ruannoch Were once again as guests of Sigrid. The attack on the Shoreth campsite the night before by Zarrus' Corrannyeid made the Thane's invitation seem an offer that was difficult to refuse – it was only right that the Emperor was kept safe.

Hurriedly made plans were afoot; in the morning both the Fine and the Shoreth would ready their combined forces and march towards Durghanti. Because of the destruction of *Aon Crann*, the march would entail a fifty mile detour around the northern spur of Cerne's Gorge, thus it would take over a week to reach the northern edge of Durghanti. They would be expected by Zarrus, giving him time to prepare – but there was little option. All were agreed, Zarrus must be stopped. There was no limit to his ambition and apparently, his capacity to achieve it.

Effie didn't care about most of this, she knew it was selfish, but it seemed to her, within her short experience of Sutra, that both the Shoreth and the Fine were warlike peoples and for all she knew it was always like this. They certainly appeared to think little of killing one another; she could not lose the association of her first encounter with the Shoreth and her heart was still sore when she thought of Uncle Sandro. But perhaps the real bugbear was that Tulann was too busy to spend any time with her. She hadn't thought she would ever miss him, but she did. He was the only one here who had any interest in her – she had seen him earlier in the evening, poring over maps with Thane Sigrid and the generals. For the most part expressions were grim, they knew defeat was likely, but, just for a moment, as Tulann pressed home a point of tactics and the Generals nodded in surprised agreement, she caught sight of something else in his gaze. He was loving this – had been born to it – and for the moment, it precluded all else. Although their friendship was not forgotten, it was definitely on hold.

And that left Effie out in the cold. So she had decided to leave; the plan was to take a horse from the stables and ride north-west in the same direction as Talisker and the others. She knew as plans went it was pretty pathetic but maybe she could break the habit of a lifetime and get lucky – she might be able to ask after them if she passed through a village or something. Typically, she had had the foresight to hoard some food from the banquet into a bag – already the idea of not having access to any food at all (unless she killed something) was gnawing at the back of her mind.

She caught herself tip-toeing down the corridor and almost laughed aloud. No one would care where she was going. As she passed the ornate doorway to Tulann's rooms she almost paused but thought better of it. Within the antechamber there would be sentries and she didn't want anyone to think she was on her way to Tulann's bed.

*

Four corridors and two floors later she was cursing herself. She'd always been the same, no sense of direction, and in her efforts to find the central keep she had somehow managed to end up . . . where?

As she paused to rethink her strategy, she heard a muffled noise. It was horrible, as if someone was being tortured whilst their mouth was stopped with rags. She frowned, surely such a thing could only happen in the dungeon.

'Effie? Effie, over here . . .' It was a woman's voice. She cast around into the gloom of the shadows.

'Ferebe?' She walked towards the sound and was yanked unceremoniously into the doorway of a suite of rooms. 'Ferebe, what's going on?'

'Come in.'

The room was a complete tip. Clothes and junk were everywhere, discarded dishes and stale food congealing in the floor rushes by the bed. There were cats sleeping on top of piles of blankets and the place smelt like a mixture of cat musk and sweat.

But in the centre of the chaos was what immediately commanded Effie's attention; a huge, gothic looking bed and, writhing in apparent agony, a young woman who was indeed stopping her own screams by stuffing the blankets into her mouth.

'Ohmigod. She's in labour! We've got to get help, Ferebe.' Effie whirled towards the door but Ferebe ran ahead of her and slammed it shut. 'What's going on?' Effie frowned.

Ferebe licked her lips nervously. 'Have you – have you ever delivered a baby before?'

'No. We need to get . . .'

'We can't – she doesn't want me to get anyone. I found her an hour ago and managed to get her in here.'

'Why wouldn't she want any help? I don't understand.' There was another stifled sound from the bed, almost a low braying, it was tinged with despair.

'Come and see . . . It's Freya, you realise that right? The Thane's daughter.'

'Oh, triffic . . .'

'Freya? Freya?' Ferebe stroked the young woman's hair from her brow where it was plastered by sweat. 'This is Effie Morgan. She's a friend.'

Freya's eyes were dull, glazed with the pain, but she glanced towards Effie and pulled the blanket she had been biting down on from her mouth. 'I know who she is,' she said without inflection. It seemed she was about to say something else about Effie – probably that she was Tulann's spy – but another pain seized her and her face contorted in slack-jawed agony.

'Christ, don't you guys have *any* drugs?' Effie was horrified at Freya's suffering.

Ferebe motioned her to the middle of the bed and pulled back the thin cotton sheet, which was already drenched in blood, as if she were reorganising the bed for Freya's comfort. Her eyes flickered down to where the baby should have been showing by now and Effie followed her gaze. She gasped; what she saw there amongst the blood and mess of labour was enough for her to realise why Freya wanted no attendants at the birth. Only the baby's head was showing – it had 'crowned', she thought – but it was enough to show that this baby was not normal.

*

Ferebe seemed to lose some of her resolve and, for a moment, Effie too was completely at a loss. 'We have to do something,' she muttered. She noted that although Freya had obviously had a strong contraction, the baby had not moved at all.

'What? What can we do?'

'Right, listen, Ferebe. We need something for her pain – she's exhausted and she can't push the baby out.'

'But I don't . . .'

'Get Raco. He'll know where you can get drugs. Get back here as quickly as you can.'

'Can't you go?'

Effie laughed humourlessly. 'I was lost when you found me. Go, go.'

It wasn't until the last sound of Ferebe's running footsteps died away in the corridor that Effie realised what she'd done; she was alone and it seemed likely that she would have to deliver this baby.

'Effie Morgan,' Freya's voice was weak. 'I know what my baby is. Once I have delivered I have to leave the city. My father must not . . . Arrrgh.'

'Listen, Freya. Don't think about that. Focus, think about getting through this. Ferebe Vezul has gone to get something for your pain.' She picked up a discarded dress and wiped Freya's sweat with it. 'Do you have more blankets?'

Freya pointed and Effie managed to find some clean laundry. 'Let's make you comfortable if we can,' she muttered.

*

By the time Ferebe returned with Raco, it was all over. Freya was propped up on her pillows, her face that particular pallor of new mothers, painted by exhaustion and fear. Her bedding was clean and the baby wrapped in a warm blanket.

'Effie! You're a miracle worker,' Ferebe said. 'You must have done this before.'

'Nope, I just winged it,' Effie grinned.

'Raco,' Freya said querulously. 'Come and see your nephew.' Ferebe and Effie exchanged glances.

'Raco . . .' Ferebe grabbed his shoulder, hoping to give him some warning but he ignored her and went over to Freya, kissing her gently on her forehead.

'Be strong,' she said. 'The Sidhe have been given a sign.' He frowned, not understanding her comment. Freya unwrapped her baby and lay him across her knees.

It was beautiful, there was no denying that. The flickering of the sconces caught the dark merriment of its eyes as it kicked and gurgled quite happily. The sounds it made were less recognisable as a baby's cry than as a deep throaty lowing but this was hardly surprising, because Freya's baby was a tiny bear cub.

Chapter Sixteen

It couldn't have been more miserable. It had been raining for three days, and, last night snow had mingled with the rain making the forest a torture of slush and mud. The encampment on the rim of Cerne's Gorge was the most drab, grey place in the whole world – it didn't take a genius to realise the morale of the combined force was pathetically low before a single blow of the battle had been struck.

To make matters worse – much worse – the troops were being constantly harried by Zarrus' monsters; Shards and Flays roamed the forests picking off small groups of men three or four at a time, but they could never exert the kind of terror over the minds of the soldiers that the Corrannyeid did. Although difficult to kill, both Shards and Flays had been seen to be defeated but the Corrannyeid came at night, silent despite their bulk, a children's nightmare made real. Effie had noted how many of the soldiers – both Fine and Shoreth – had red-rimmed eyes and haunted expressions through lack of sleep.

Not that she was sleeping much herself. She was doing her best to boost Tulann's morale, entailing many hours spent with him after his sessions with Sigrid which left him in a black depression – because Thane Sigrid, having lost his daughter, appeared to be losing his grip on reality. He spoke in whispers almost constantly, as if afraid the Corrannyeid could hear him, his steely gaze had become unfocussed and aged, flickering constantly around the corners of the room.

Effie felt terrible when she saw Sigrid – she longed to tell him what had happened and that Freya had gone of her own volition, fearing the birth of her bear-cub baby would be seen as the worst possible omen for the departing troops. Raco had gone with her, they were unsure of their destination – possibly they would make for Soulis Mor where Freya had an aunt but, as the days of travelling through the cursed, monster haunted forest continued, Effie feared the couple might not have made it very far. Raco would protect Freya and her child with his life, Effie knew, but unfortunately his life might be exactly what was required.

But Sigrid had decided his daughter had been spirited away, taken from Ruannoch Were not by Corrannyeid, but by the Gods. They had taken her so that she might be spared the coming darkness. Sigrid had convinced himself already that the efforts of the allies were futile, that Sutra would ultimately be overrun by Zarrus' demonic army.

They had stopped on the rim of the Gorge so that Tulann and Sigrid might finalise plans for the attack – at least, that was the official line. In actuality Tulann was desperately trying to hold the fragile alliance together. Sigrid had talked of surrender – perhaps Zarrus would be merciful, he reasoned. Tulann, who knew Zarrus personally knew the Warrior General considered mercy to be weakness.

'Where do you think the Shards and Flays are coming

from, Sigrid? They were people once. Raco told me he fought a Shard which had the face of his dead father. I didn't believe him then, but I do now. Is that what you want for your people? What about the pride of the Fine?'

The rain battered down on the roof of the tent, trickling and gurgling into the drainage ditch. 'Raco . . .' Sigrid repeated sonorously. His gaze became less fixed and he stared distantly into the flames of the brazier. Tulann sighed and shrugged hopelessly towards Effie.

Once Sigrid and the generals had gone, splashing away through the morass of the camp, Tulann wordlessly poured Effie a glass of wine, his expression was grim.

'Tulann. It'll be all right. Sigrid has good councillors around him – they'll make sure he does the right thing.'

'Will they?' he replied darkly. 'Effie, has it occurred to you that most of the Fine think we Shoreth *deserve* this? That we brought it on ourselves? Zarrus must have been a viper in the nest for years but no one saw it – or maybe they did and chose to ignore it. What about my father? He was supposed to be so bloody wise, how come he never found out? Too trusting, that's why.'

'From what Raco told me, when your father realised what was happening he was murdered.'

'Yes.' He sipped his wine. 'You know I keep looking across the Gorge – we can *see* Durghanti from here but we'll have to make a fifty league detour around the spur of the Gorge to press the attack – Zarrus will know we are coming for days ahead, not to mention exactly where we'll be coming from.'

Huh, if this rain keeps up we'll be able to float across,'

Effie said flippantly. She stared gloomily into the fire just as Sigrid had done.

'You all right, Eff?'

'Yeah, I . . . I keep dreaming. When I sleep, that is.'

'What about?'

How could she tell him – the bodies, one second so alive, so defiant, the next, dead. Why so sickening? She had seen death since coming to Sutra; crucifixions, bodies of warriors slain by Zarrus' hordes – it was the sheer disbelief of those young men. The sheer unexpectedness of their demise. And in her world, in her experience, death came softly or suddenly, seldom with callous deliberation. And they were so young – like her.

'Nothing, nothing really.'

'Effie?'

She sighed. 'Tulann, I'm gonna tell you this against my better judgement – because,' she looked at his rapt expression and laughed nervously, 'because you're my friend. So if you laugh at me or think I'm insane, I reserve the right to . . . punch your lights out.'

'Huh?'

'Never mind. Do you believe I'm not going to lie to you?'

'Yes.' This surprised her and she stared closely at his expression, but Tulann was a past master at concealing his inner feelings. His wide blue eyes were unblinking, waiting.

'H . . . okay. Look, I come from . . . somewhere else.'

'Soulis Mor?'

'No listen, another place, another world.'

*

It took about forty minutes to explain; he didn't interrupt or ask any questions which struck Effie as strange – if the situation was reversed, she wasn't sure *she'd* believe her. When she'd finished, she asked the question she'd been leading up to, her heart in her mouth, her palms sweating. 'I was wondering if you might let me take Ferebe Vezul and a few warriors – just a few – through to sort Horza out. Tulann, Zarrus is screwing with my world, too, and Horza is a – a murdering bastard.'

'Such is war, Effie.' His voice was soft, quiet within the confines of the tent. 'But if what you say is true, this world of yours, this amazing world, with guns? and weapons, flying machines, is well capable of destroying Horza. It doesn't *need* you.'

'You're right, Tulann, Horza will be destroyed, eventually. When the snow melts and access back into the canyon is clear, but he could have killed about two hundred people by then. We have to try . . .'

'No,' he said with cool deliberation. 'We do not.'

'But . . .'

'Do you know how many Fine and Shoreth have been picked off on the journey so far? Well I do, almost six hundred – five hundred and seventy-three to be precise – because I have to know these things, Effie, it's my job, my role as emperor.'

'So?' she frowned. 'What's that got to do with me? It's not a competition in suffering. You've been waiting for this all your life – don't give me that "loneliness of power" crap.'

'I need you here,' he snapped.

'Talk to Almasey, why don't you,' she fumed. 'He *has*

to listen to your selfish wittering – I don't.' She stood up to go.

'He's dead. Didn't you hear? Killed last night by Corrannyeid. His quarters were wrecked apparently, blood everywhere.'

'I'm – I'm sorry. He was a good man.'

'Yes. I expect he warned you about me.'

'No,' she lied. 'Look, Tulann, I didn't expect you to be like this when I told you. I thought you might not believe me, or you might laugh at me. I don't understand . . .'

He shook his head. 'Doesn't matter, Effie Morgan. Goodnight.'

'What? Are you dismissing me now?'

He refused to look at her and instead paid close attention to his drink, his eyes obscured by his dark lashes as he stared fixedly into the bottom of his goblet.

'Right, fine . . . goodnight then,' she bristled. As she went out of the door flap a sudden thought occurred to her; a stupid, irrational thought. 'I expect you want your stuff back, now you don't like me any more – now I'm not your accursed favourite.' She hobbled about, pulling off the beautiful kid boots he had given her. 'Well here!' she hurled the first one at his head at the same instant she realised the rashness of her decision – her feet were freezing and soaked within seconds – but she was nothing if not consistent. 'And here!' Both of the boots missed him by inches but it was worth it to see the amazed, unguarded expression on his face. She glanced at the sentry by the door. 'What are you bloody smirking at?' she frowned. Picking up her skirts she fled across the campground to her tent.

*

'Effie, Effie.' She was shaken awake and immediately sat bolt upright, some vague part of her sleepy mind instinctively ready to flee.

'Wha . . . Tulann,' she pulled the blankets up to her chin, 'What are you doing here?'

'I've spoken to Ferebe Vezul and she confirmed what you said about your friends, Talisker and the others. She wants to take the white mammoth, which I'm not so sure about, but at least it won't be endangered fighting in the main battle. It'll be good to have it alive and safe at the end of all this – a symbol of hope for my people, maybe. She's agreed to go with you but wants to wait until nightfall so she can guide the mammoths down the trail into the canyon.'

Effie frowned. 'And that's better because?'

He grinned. 'They're highly visible creatures, Eff, or haven't you noticed? Specially the white one. We don't want Zarrus catching on that you're headed for the gateway – he could panic and have the prisoners slaughtered sooner. Ferebe also seems to think it will keep the mammoths calmer if they aren't so aware of the height. Anyway, it'll give you time to prepare and see me and Sigrid make our joint speeches to the troops.' He was all enthused again, his boyish charm to the fore now he felt he had a plan. 'There's just one thing, Effie,' his smile faded and a look of uncertainty flitted across his face. He reached out and took her hand. 'Promise me you'll come back.'

It's like a dream but he knows it is not. It is something more fundamental – a state of being. He is here – he can

feel the wind in his face, it carries the night scent of
mesquite and the promise of coming rain. He can hear a
man's voice, low soft tones which contain the iron and
strength of the land.

*'Ni'hookaa Diyan Dinéh – Lords of the Earth they
named us. First Man and First Woman came to this
world – the Fourth, or the Glittering World – from the
First World of creation. They came with the animals
and the spirits . . .'*

He sees them – First Man and First Woman – they are
real and they are beautiful; they epitomise the
elemental beauty of the world, giant figures whose
laughter is like clean thunder. All the beasts of the
plains and the mountains are dwarfed by them and run
between their legs, weaving in and out of their striding
feet; buffalo, puma, bears, wolves and, because he is
always there, coyote, the Trickster. Around their heads
fly the creatures of the air, birds of all kinds, bats and
lesser creatures, insects and beetles. The Great Owl and
Golden Eagle twist and glide through the air catching at
the black shining hair of First Woman.

*'The people from the other three worlds were not like
people are today.'*

Around their hands and arms twist roiling eddies of
colourful smoke. Yiska knows that these zephyrs are
spirits; the spirits of the stones, mountains, trees and
water – they are the true essence of the land.

First Man and First Woman are walking towards him
and, at first, they are huge, their footsteps shake the
ground, lakes and canyons are left by the depressions of
their feet. But as they come closer (and Yiska becomes
afraid, their aspect is frightening) they shrink down to a

more natural size, they walk beside the buffalo and the coyote zigzags at their heels. They become the People of the Glittering World and they walk towards the first house, which is a hogan, built precisely as Talking God had instructed.

'Once in the hogan, the people begin to give order to their new world by naming things. They name the four sacred mountains and designate to each symbolic, sacred stones. In such a way, the Glittering World passed from chaos into the natural world that the Gods had gifted to them. But the Gods were still busy making the world.'

It is dark – pitch dark. There are no stars in the sky, only a pale opalescent moon. Yiska can make out the form of the hogan, imagines he hears laughter from within. He can feel the chill kiss of the night breeze. There's something else too, something he cannot identify. A *greenness* is creeping in from the edges of his vision and it worries him greatly; it will destroy them and then, it can never be so . . .

'Yiska. Hold on, hold on,' a woman's voice this time, not the storyteller. He feels the touch of a warm hand slip into his – skin on skin – but he doesn't look down. *'What happens now?'* the voice asks. *'There are no stars in the sky.'*

No. Because the Gods are still making the world, stupid. He has become childlike both in stature and mind. Living in the memory of the land, its lore as *real* to him as it was when he was just a boy.

What happens next is . . .

Ahhh, pain! He did not expect this act of

commitment to be physically painful – *She did not warn him. Melicende? Ahhh* . . . It feels as though his veins, his very bones are being sucked dry; a draining, collapsing sensation. He imagines the weakness which follows is like the moment before death.

'*So, what happens, Yiska?*'

What . . .

'*What happens?*'

The Gods . . . the Gods are placing the stars in the sky.

He can still see them. Wishes he could not, their immensity is frightening. It's as if the world – the Glittering World – is like a stage set to them. He cannot remember all of their names now – *but why can't I? I'm still a boy* – Spider Woman is there and she holds a massive blanket that she has woven from the winds. She rests the blanket on top of a mesa and he can see the stars, their light arcing upwards like a massive crown. Spider Woman is placing the stars into the sky in neat, orderly rows and is so engrossed in her fussy work that she does not see the relatively tiny coyote creeping on his belly to the edges of the mesa. But Yiska sees him, and his young laughter dances out across the coldness of the night.

Coyote, the Trickster – *always knew Dog was* – is impatient, wants the Holy People to make something more interesting than the sky – wants something he can chew, like wood, or something he can roll in. He grabs the corner of the wind-blanket in his teeth and shakes it. As it billows outward, the stars are flung into the heavens, scattering across the velvet dark. It's so beautiful that no one could be angry with the Trickster. Yiska's laughter seems bright music to the new illumination.

'And so, you see, the Holy People did not plan the beauty of the night sky but in fact they were pleased. They continued to make other essentials like rain, clouds, plants, and everything was shaping up just peachy when . . .'

Just peachy?

The greenness is back. And a new surge of sucking pain.

I c-can't. Think I'm dying . . .

'He has to stop. Christ, look at his face!' Different voices now. 'This is sucking him dry.'

'But it is working. Please, just a few more minutes.'

There's a sound which Yiska's beleaguered mind cannot identify at first; a sharp, high hiss. It is the sound of a steel blade being drawn from its scabbard. 'Be warned, Melicende, we will not stand by and watch you kill him.'

The desert of his dreams is in danger of dissolving, eroded by the green. In the distance Yiska can make out dark gashes in the shapes of the mountains and the sounds of voices from within the hogan cease; he is alone and instantly lonely.

Evil appeared in the world in the form of vast destructive monsters. They hunted and killed many of the new people of the Glittering World.

They are the monsters of a child's fevered imagination. Yiska knows he has really seen monsters now – Flays, Shards and Corrannyeid – knows that monsters, like so many other things on the dark edges of his imagination, are real. But these huge, hulking figures which stride across the dreamscape with a kind of easy belligerence are hideous. Because they were imagined by generations of young children they have features which might be considered risible by anyone not actually face-to-face with them – extra limbs, tails, extra eyes all around their heads. Their skin is bright, un-skin-like colours although some are mercifully obscured with matted fur. What is not funny – *no, not at all* – is that Yiska sees them catch and eat many of the First People, who have appeared on the plain as if from nowhere and proceed to flee. The monsters pick them up as if they are scuttling roaches and drop them into their gaping mouths with hardly a pause in their stride. He can hear them crunching, grinding the gristle and bone between their jagged teeth.

He's crying. *No, no, no, make it stop! Make it stop . . .* doing that jiggling little dance that children sometimes do when they cry, stamping his bare feet.

Hush now, Yiska. You know that help is coming. A miracle sent by the Holy People: Changing Woman, Asdzaa Nadleehe has come into the Fourth World. She has two sons, twins whose father is the Sun. Heroes, the first heroes of the Dineh. Their names are 'Child-Born-From-Water' and 'Monster Slayer'. Their father the Sun gives them weapons of lightning bolts.

And it is true. They are coming – the twins. They run from the east where the dawn is rising. They are have the beauty of the mother but the heat and the energy of their father – they laugh scornfully at their quarry.

Ahhhh . . .

The green slices across the scene as if it were the celluloid of a film. The green light burns into the thigh of Child-Born-From-Water but he ignores it and hurls his lightning bolt at the nearest obscene creature. There's a sound, a sudden pulsing roar. It is like the biggest heartbeat in the universe. It is like the sound of all the Holy People, the First People, the creatures and Yiska, little Yiska, all screaming in unison – it is like the birth and death of the People.

'That's it, Melicende. Stop. Stop it now!'

The greenness is everywhere now and the landscape is fading. He can just make out the transparent beauty of Changing Woman as she fades into the West to be with her husband. She turns at the last moment and smiles beneficently – Yiska's heart aches with sadness and longing.

She will remain in the Western ocean but she will make four of the clans from her own skin. In this way, Changing Woman will remain a constant blessing to the Dinéh, those who Walk in Beauty carry her spirit within them. He realises that he has become the voice – or the storyteller – the storyteller has become him, perhaps it was always him.

'Yiska? Yiska? Come on man. Come back to us.'

'Yiska. You done it pal. You kin wake up now. Duncan, he is goin' tae wake up eh no?'

'He will Malcolm. It has just been a great strain on him. On his heart.'

'You'd better hope so, Melicende.'

They had done their best, she knew; but the army of the Alliance looked like shit. No parade-ground shine here, these were men and women who had been rained on, snowed on and marched through the hostile forest while being hunted for sport by creatures from hell.

In total the army was around thirteen thousand strong – minus the recent casualties, of course – and there was no way that Sigrid and Tulann could address them all and be heard. So the forces nearest to where the Thane and the young Emperor would speak were actually generals and commanders who would go back and give their cribbed version of the speeches to rouse their men. Some of the Shoreth leaders had managed to make a show of it – they were disciplined, seasoned warriors and they sat their horses with their backs bolt upright waiting to cheer their Emperor. The Fine however, were more relaxed, waiting to be impressed; they talked to one another in low voices, compared their weapons, even patched their shoes. Many of the rank and file wanted to hear for themselves and had found vantage points in the trees or on any slightly higher ground. There were just people as far as the eye could see, exhausted, muddy, stinking people.

Effie of course would have a privileged position; Tulann had asked her to ride behind him carrying his banner. This had surprised her at first until Ferebe reminded her this was not some easy favour but a public show of her inclusion by Tulann – 'It shows he considers you a warrior, Lady Morgan. Perhaps he is trying to prepare you mentally for our mission.'

'What, by carrying a flag?'

Ferebe had given her a disdainful look. 'Whoever carries his standard protects the Emperor in battle. It means you are his bodyguard – would give your life for him.'

'Really? He thinks so does he?' She had been all ready with some flip comment but then thought better of it. Tulann was doing her a great honour – however misguided – at least she could be gracious about it.

And so they rode out at midday as arranged. It was still raining but at least the drops had turned to fine drizzle. Effie was still uncomfortable on horseback but she had decided to try her hardest not to let Tulann down. Great clouds of steam issued from the horses' mouths and nostrils and Tulann's banner hung limp and wet in the grey air. Effie surreptitiously tried to make it flutter bravely a few times, but it was so wet it was pointless.

She had heard the speech three times already; it was good. Not too arrogantly commanding to the Shoreth and realistic in its approach to the Fine and the alliance. To her surprise though, Tulann started by speaking in a language she didn't know, she guessed it was 'Old' Shoreth, their classic language. It was only a few sentences before she recognised what she had thought was the beginning of the speech.

'. . . Shoreth Usha, hear me. I am your Emperor, chosen by the Gods to lead you. I expect you might be thinking by now that the Gods have a cruel, twisted sense of humour. Well, how d'you think I feel?' There was a ripple of nervous laughter and Effie smiled, she wanted Tulann to win the hearts of his men as much as he wanted it for himself. Perhaps he wouldn't feel so alone when . . .

She wasn't coming back to him. She had known it since he had given her permission to go but she hadn't allowed herself to think it at a conscious level lest he see it in her eyes. Once she was back in her world, she would go home to Scotland just as soon as she could. *Home. There's no place like home,* she thought wryly. Home to her tiny flat, home to her addictions and insecurities. She flinched, dragging her attention back to Tulann. He was addressing the Fine now.

'I know there's little I can say to make you trust me. I besieged your city, almost killed your Thane, who I now consider the wisest, most venerable man I know.' He smiled, genuinely brightly towards Sigrid, who returned his compliment with a regal nod. 'Well, what can I say?' He touched his hand to his chest in a slightly humbled, self-deprecating gesture. 'What a stupid mistake that would have been! But it was a matter of pride – something I know you warriors of the Fine are well familiar with. The Shoreth are a prideful nation also. We share a true bond of nobility. And it is our deepest shame that we have loosed this evil upon Sutra. It's our mess, but with your help . . .'

Effie's attention was wandering again. She was cold, as she knew everyone else was – her hand was numb and wet where she gripped the pole of the banner. Worrying that she might do something really embarrassing like dropping the Emperor's banner, she started looking at the other banners in the crowd – thinking that each man or woman who carried one was charged with the same responsibility as her. As her gaze drifted towards the back of the crowd, she saw something which made her start. Or rather, someone. Shifting her position in the saddle she squinted into the distance, the crowd was parting, making way for someone. Tulann saw it too, and he faltered briefly but continued on.

'With your help, warriors of the Fine, we can wipe Zarrus and his obscene creations off the face of Sutra.' He'd begun to walk his horse up and down the ranks as he spoke and Effie knew that his plan was to stop roughly in the middle and make his rallying cry. However, Tulann could now see clearly what Effie could not. He stopped, a puzzled expression on his face but then he reined his horse back and said something in a low voice to Thane Sigrid.

The old Thane stepped forward to where the crowd was parting, a smile lighting his face, making him appear like his old self once more. It did not last long, though; as the last of the assembly drew back to let the riders through, the smile faded as quickly as it had come.

It was Freya, and behind her a little way, Raco. Both had sustained injuries. Freya was bleeding from a deep gash which ran diagonally across her face from her temple to her chin, she sat her horse unsteadily and it seemed only an act of supreme will kept her in the saddle. She held the reins in her right hand – her left arm held a bundle, wrapped in a thick blue blanket which had been snagged by gorse and thistles. Effie knew immediately it was the bear-cub baby, but she couldn't understand what had brought about Freya's change of heart.

'Tulann,' she whispered urgently. 'Tulann.'

He walked his horse towards her, frowning. 'This could get nasty. Just be careful,' she gestured to the nearby elite bodyguard to stay beside the Emperor. There was no way of telling how the bad omen of Freya's baby might affect Sigrid and, thus, the fragile alliance.

'Daughter, come, we must take care of you,' Sigrid began.

'No Father. I must speak to the warriors of the Fine – and the Sidhe.' Freya's voice was high and clear, cutting through the still grey air with the clarity of needles. She walked her muddied, exhausted horse over to beside her father and turned around to face the hushed crowd. 'I had my baby in Ruannoch Were just before you all set out on this march. His father was a Sidhe, Jevedran, perhaps some of you knew him. He was a great and noble man, tragically killed in an accident. After I gave birth I fled the city thinking that you,' she glanced towards her father, 'you *all* might see my son as an omen – a bad omen for the coming conflict. But as the days and nights passed in the depths of Or Coille and I looked on my newborn I realised that running away was to dishonour the memory of his father and to dishonour the Sidhe – our Fair Folk who have become so much a part of our lives that we take them for granted, indeed, are destroying their history and traditions through our casual assimilation.

'So I have returned. I will help my father to lead us to victory – Fine, Sidhe and Shoreth alike. I will fight beside you because I am proud of you all . . . I do not know what the birth of my child means, if his short existence can be taken to mean our Gods have not abandoned us, or if he is just . . .' She shoved her horse sideways with the thoughtless control of someone who had ridden since childhood – beside where Sigrid and Tulann stood was the remnants of the many trunks which had combined to form *Aon Crann*. Freya placed her baby on the flat surface of a tall stump and pulled away his blanket.

There was an audible gasp from those near enough to see as the bear cub sat up blinking in the sudden light. It really *was* cute, Effie thought, its tawny fur, although dampened by the drizzle, was soft and shiny looking. It missed his mother straight away and began to look around for her, his head bobbing to and fro, his wet black nose snuffling – he let out a cry of complaint at this cold abandonment, a low bleating sound.

As realisation struck home amongst the warriors nearest to the edge of the crowd, three things happened at once; first, everyone began to express an opinion, loudly and excitedly – this upset the tiny cub even more and the sound of his cry underlay the general melee. Secondly, three or four of the Fine commanders reacted on impulse and drew their weapons, fortunately staying their hand long enough to look to Thane Sigrid for orders.

But, most remarkable of all, warriors of the Sidhe, as if with one thought, began to push their way forwards through the mass of animated people. As far as Effie could see none of them spoke to any other, they just seemed to have the same instinct – to protect the baby. A group of around ten of them including Raco, clustered around the trunk of *Aon Crann*, pushing their longspears into the ground to form a protective barrier. There they stood, immovable, with their arms folded in front of them.

It was bedlam; the crowd began to push forward coming perilously closer to the rim of the gorge, the Fine who had drawn their swords and axes were shouting to Sigrid, waving their weapons in the time-honoured way of mobs everywhere; they didn't understand this, so it had to be bad, right? Effie dropped Tulann's standard in order to bring her horse closer to his – if the crowd were to surge now, Tulann, Sigrid and Freya would be amongst the first over the edge. *And Zarrus will just be sitting there laughing his bloody head off.* Effie scowled. She reached over and grabbed the bridle of Tulann's mare which was beginning to sidestep nervously. The mood of the crowd, at least those nearest, had turned as if on a knife edge – fights were breaking out between Fine and Sidhe and a few opportunist Fine needed little provocation to have a tussle with Shoreth warriors. Effie felt her stomach cramp as panic seized her, with inexorable inevitability people were pushing forward; tragedy could be the only outcome. Someone was shouting for order but none was forthcoming.

'Look!' A cry which was immediately repeated by many was taken up by the crowd – people stopped what they were doing and stared towards the stump of *Aon Crann* where Freya's baby boy lay.

Yiska was not a believer in suffering quietly. He always told his patients; 'I'm not gonna bullshit you kid/Mr/Mrs – this is gonna hurt. But you know, if you wanna yell or scream or anything, you just fire on ahead. I'm a good listener.' And usually they *did* give voice to their pain with low groaning or occasionally, actual screams (sometimes the men were worse). He had a theory that articulation of pain was a good, healthy thing, so now, when he felt easily the worst he'd ever felt in his whole entire life, he wasn't about to let his opportunity pass him by. He felt as if his limbs had been twisted and pulled; aches played up and down the length of his arms and legs, bunching and throbbing at the elbow and knees joints as if gathering pain-momentum before coursing into the lower half of the limbs. Also, as his real conscious mind returned he realised that his eyeballs felt funny – and not 'funny ha-ha' either – it was as if they'd been boiled in his skull. He groaned again, partly at his own sick thought.

'Ahhh. Jeez, Melicende, you could've warned me.' He opened his eyes as he spoke, which immediately resulted in a flood of strained tears. 'Godammit, my eyes feel like . . .' he rubbed at his eyes, whilst realising that was probably the wrong thing to do '. . .boiled grapes. Wha . . .' He looked around the chamber which appeared as a seething mass of browns and darkness and began to settle down into fractured images of people. He could still see the green light and as the vestiges of his dreamstate clung to him, the green worried him slightly. There was something wrong though . . . something . . . They were *moving*.

'Who the hell are all these people?' He strained his eyes in an effort to make the images come into sharper focus but, as he turned his face towards the fire, the orange blur only resulted in further tears. 'C-cold,' he added, 'I'm cold.'

'It is the Council, Yiska.' He felt Melicende wrap a warming blanket around him and then the pressure of her hand squeezing his shoulder, a warm hand which brought the sense-memory of his dreamstate back to him.

'Could you see, Melicende? Could you see what I saw?'

'Yes,' she said quietly. 'I saw. You did it, Yiska – your dreams, your lore, gave Braznnair enough energy to awaken the Council of Tema.' He couldn't see her face, just a shadowy outline, but Yiska could tell that Melicende was beaming with joy. 'Here,' she reached out and pressed a cold cloth to his eyes; it was instantly soothing. 'It had to be you, the power had to come from outside Sutra, untainted by Zarrus.'

He nodded, holding the cloth to his eyes. When he took it away his vision was slightly improved; he could make out the people more clearly although small details were still difficult. There must have been about ten male and female Sidhe in the chamber, they all wore ornate robes which had faded under the coating of limestone water and had beads and feathers plaited into their hair. For the most part they were old, certainly Melicende was the youngest. Yiska felt sure he could have identified which Sidhe clan they came from. For some reason, that similarity in their features with their totem creatures seemed more remarkable than he had noticed before. On the floor of the cave, though, were the shattered remains of those whose transfiguration had gone too far – a couple of the women councillors were picking up the pieces of their fellows, mercifully still rock rather than remade flesh, and placing them in an alcove at the edges of the room.

'Yiska, Michael,' one of the elders walked over and for a moment, Yiska expected him to shake his hand, such was his enthusiasm. 'Our thanks are boundless,' the man beamed. 'I cannot imagine the act of will required to rejuvenate Braznnair. Remarkable, truly.'

Yiska smiled. 'Don't mention it,' he mumbled. 'Hey, where's Duncan and Malky?'

Melicende and the councillor exchanged a swift glance that spoke volumes. Alarm caught Yiska unawares – just as his body was recovering from his ordeal a surge of adrenalin coursed through him. 'Where are they?' he frowned, his voice louder and more demanding than he intended.

Melicende reached forward and touched his forearm in a gesture that was intended to reassure him but only worried him further. 'Are . . . are they dead?'

'Good grief, no,' she smiled but it was merely placatory. 'But I'm afraid they . . . well . . .'

'Spit it out, Melicende.'

'They've been arrested, Yiska – for the theft of Braznnair and threatening the Council. It's possible they could be executed.'

Chapter Seventeen

Effie couldn't see at first; she was more enthralled by the sudden hush which had fallen on the crowd. People who had been descending into brawling and the mindless surge forward, stopped everything they were doing to look over to the stump of Aon Crann.

When she did look, her view was blocked by one of the Sidhe who had come forward to protect Freya's baby, but after a moment, he moved aside. Effie gasped.

The little bear cub had stood up on its four paws as its crying for his mother had continued – it seemed the baby was short-sighted, his black bead-like eyes looked weak and myopic in the glare of the daylight but his wet nose still snuffled and quested, sampling the wet fecund air. It did a strange shuffling dance from foot to foot as its head rocked in a movement which was recognisable as self-comfort – he continued to cry. But what had attracted so much attention was that the bear cub baby was being enveloped in tiny, dancing motes of green light. They had appeared from nowhere and were wrapping themselves around his body, forming a latticework of green. Soon, the baby would disappear from view.

Effie glanced at Freya, but it seemed Freya was transfixed by the lights; mesmerised, as so many of the onlookers were. 'What should we do? Do you think the child . . . thing is in danger?' Tulann had leaned in towards Effie and spoke in a low voice. He seemed to be one of the few people able to draw his gaze away.

'No, I don't think so,' she replied. 'Look at the Sidhe. They're not doing anything.' She nodded towards Raco who was as tired and bloodied as Freya – Effie was sure they had had at least one encounter with Shards or somesuch – but he was equally as mesmerised. He stared towards the babe, his eyes shining through the mud and gore on his face.

Finally after long seconds, which seemed to stretch on for minutes, the bear cub was obscured by the lights. It appeared as if a little cub composed entirely of green radiance sat on the stump. The sounds of its crying had ceased and, during the process of whatever it was that was happening, the cub had sat back down. After a few moments the lights began to diminish, unravelling their beautiful web as swiftly as they had come – a chorus of wondering gasps and exclamations rippled through the crowd, but still, no one moved towards the baby.

And when it was finished, Freya's baby sat in full view of the assembled Fine, Sidhe and Shoreth. A baby; its skin still with that pink newborn blush, its only hair now a red flash of fuzz on its head. His eyes were green and he was undoubtedly a Fine. He stared around, wide-eyed, at the onlookers and then screwed up his chubby face in an uncomprehending wail. As remarkable as he was, like babies everywhere, he just wanted his mother.

'Could it be residual magic from the bridge?' Tulann whispered to Effie.

She shook her head, 'I don't think so. Jeez, what the . . .'

*

The Sidhe had clustered around the baby, smiling and laughing, their excitement palpable. There must have been twenty or so around the stump and more were pushing their way through the crowd to see the miracle child. The Fine, aware that this was some magic of the 'Fair Folk', had begun to move back, drawing the Shoreth with them, so there was a much larger space between the assembled crowd and the separate cluster of Sidhe.

There was a sudden flash of green – the same green which had enveloped Freya's baby – it spread outwards from the stump of *Aon Crann* like a thing possessed of wild passion, a thing unleashed with the suddenness of wild exaltation. It enveloped the Sidhe within seconds, but none made any attempt to run – it was a welcome fire.

The conflagration was too bright to look at directly; Effie felt her eyes water and she shielded her face with her hands. 'God, that's bright,' she winced. Everyone not involved was doing similarly, shielding their vision with their hands or the back of their arms – horses whinnied in fright and many were hard-pressed to keep control of their mounts. At the edges of the crowd of Fine and Shoreth Effie noted two or three mares bolting off in panic – fortunately away from the light – their riders giving them their head so that their panic was transmuted.

'Onrir's balls,' she heard Tulann curse, in amazement and turned her gaze back without thinking.

It was all right because the lights were fading now. And what was left behind was like nothing Effie had ever seen; *enormous* eagles, bears, wolves and, delicate by comparison, just a few lynxes. Here and there, transformations were still taking place as more Sidhe strode forward from the crowd and, touching their kin, as if by instinct, began to change into their long-denied totems.

A rush of joy swept across the watching Fine – they began to cheer and sing, hugging one another in celebration. Effie heard them laughing incredulously and saying; 'They're back . . . They've come back!'

The Shoreth stood amongst this tumult looking slightly awkward. Many had heard tales of the Sidhe totems but none had been seen in Sutra for a long time. The unabashed joy of the Fine put them at their ease, though, and most were smiling.

'Wow.' Effie stared at the growing crowd of Sidhe animals. 'It's awesome. They're *huge*, man – I mean, *huge*.' She was talking as much to herself as anything but she glanced over at Tulann. To her surprise he was grinning his massive, Cheshire cat grin – she frowned, momentarily confused. 'What?' she said. 'What's so funny?'

Tulann nodded across the distance of Cerne's Gorge. 'Reckon those huge eagles can fly?'

'Zarrus, Zarrus . . . Zarrus!'

'Wha . . . what's going on?'

'We have a problem. The power is draining away – the Sidhe have found some way of reclaiming their magics. Soon, we will be unable to create more Shards or Flays.'

'I – I don't care. Why are you telling me this anyway? You don't need me now. You have control of our body – don't bother to deny it. I'm – I'm fading.'

'*But don't you see? We are this close! Only a hundred more khetourit . . . perhaps as few as sixty. We need corpses, fast.*'

'*Go away. Tell Horza. Just leave me alone.*'

'*Of course! Horza! He can send me bodies now. Zarrus, when we are Gods, dual aspects of divinity, I will reward you for your patience.*'

'*Jahl, I don't care.*'

'This is ridiculous,' Yiska stormed. 'If it wasn't for Talisker, you'd all still be a heap of limestone.'

'No,' Melicende corrected him, 'if it wasn't for *you*, they'd all be a heap of limestone. If it wasn't for Talisker stealing Braznnair, they could have defended themselves better; perhaps they would never have been in that situation in the first place.'

Yiska glared around the chamber. The Council of Tema had lost little time in getting back to what they were good at, as far as he could see – talking. Debating Talisker's punishment as if it were the most pressing thing in the world rather than the situation with Zarrus. He had not been allowed to see Talisker and Malky yet but, as far as he could tell, Talisker had compounded his supposed iniquity by attacking Melicende and a couple of the Councillors when he thought the process of reanimating Braznnair appeared to be killing Yiska.

Yiska was disgusted by this treatment of his friends. 'All right,' he agreed, 'Talisker made a big mistake taking Braznnair – but need I remind you that it was him who brought it back to Sutra all those years ago. He and his son – Thane Tristan – who led the Sidhe to victory against . . .' He could not remember the name.

'Jahl,' Melicende supplied helpfully.

'Jahl.'

'Yiska. We understand all that, it's our history. It happened almost two hundred years ago. But that does little to negate his most recent actions.' The speaker was an old man – wolf clan, if Yiska was not mistaken. And if he had the qualities of his wolf totem it must have been a smug, fat wolf indeed.

'What is your name, sir?'

'Vedrus.'

'How many remarkable things have you done in your life, Vedrus? How many of us can say we have achieved anything near to what Talisker has? None of us. He is the Worldwalker is he not – the Sidhe respect him, the Fine revere him, they tell tales of his heroism to their children.' He didn't actually know this to be true but it sounded good. 'Have you asked him why he took Braznnair?'

'Yes we have,' Melicende said quietly, 'and he will not tell us the full story. I suspect it is his pride which is stopping him.'

'Pride?'

'It is my feeling that he was cuckolded by a woman but he will not tell it.'

Yiska sighed. 'Did I bring you back here then to kill my friends? Is that my reward?' *Just peachy* . . . the phrase drifted through his mind like some mocking phantom. 'If Talisker had not brought me here and returned Braznnair to you, we would not be having this conversation. I'm not one for calling in favours normally – but you guys *owe me*. You owe me something.'

'The Worldwalker must be punished. If he lives for hundreds more years, how many more times might he cross us.'

Yiska lost it. He leapt up from his seat, grabbed the pompous Vedrus by the neck of his robes and shook him. 'He is your saviour! What part of that don't you understand, you stupid . . .'

'Yiska. Yiska!' Melicende tried to haul him off, digging her sharp cat-like nails into his arm.

'This is ridiculous! The Council has no right to judge him . . .'

'I don't think you really understand, Yiska. What he took from us . . . it was something so essential to the continuation of our Sidhe culture. It was irreplaceable.'

'Oh, I understand, all right. My own people, the Dinéh, have had much stolen from us – our land, artefacts, ceremonial shirts, masks, weavings – all taken. Not for any good reason but to put on display in museums, allegedly so that people might understand us better. Our land, well, they gave it back to us when much of it was polluted and ruined.'

'And did you not seek revenge on those who took these things away from you?' Vedrus asked. 'Did your nation turn to bitterness?'

'Many are bitter, yes . . . there is no denying . . . But you see, it never took away our sense of who we are. The Dinéh will always be Lords of Earth just as the Sidhe will always be what they are. No theft can deny you your spirit and your self.'

Many of the Council were nodding and Yiska hoped his words were getting through. 'The facts remain, Yiska,' Vedrus countered, 'we could have survived the loss of Braznnair as a nation – but when we were attacked, magically attacked by Zarrus, we did not have the power or means to defend ourselves. When the need arises, Braznnair is a weapon of great power and significance.'

'But . . .'

Vedrus held up his hand in a silencing gesture. 'The Council will retire to consider our verdict. Be assured, Yiska, Lorebringer, that we are grateful for your intervention on our behalf. You will always have the gratitude of the Sidhe . . .'

Yiska nodded, a small bow and watched as they walked from the chamber. Melicende did not follow them but stayed beside Yiska. 'Huh, I bet they said that to Talisker once,' he frowned.

'I think you have done enough to save his life,' Melicende said thoughtfully. 'Some of the Council definitely seemed to be on your side. It just remains to be seen what punishment they decide on.'

'Well, they might just let him off.'

She shook her head. 'They have little left them but their pride, Yiska. They will feel the need to make a statement.'

It only took the Council an hour. And when they came back Vedrus was looking sombre which gave Yiska some hope.

'Well?' he said.

'The Worldwalker brought us Braznnair with one hand and took it away with the other. So be it, we of the Council have decided to spare his life but mete out an appropriate punishment.'

'Huh?'

Vedrus looked down his nose at Yiska – a mannerism which brought his wolf totem into sharp focus – as if Yiska were a stupid schoolchild. 'We will remove his right hand.'

'What! No! You cannot be . . . Jeez, Melicende, tell them . . .' Yiska felt his legs shake as he confronted the pain his friend was about to suffer.

'Sit down, Yiska,' Melicende directed him to a stone ledge to sit on.

'They can't, Melicende, they can't . . .' he could not believe it.

'I am afraid it's true,' she said gently. She patted his hand in vague reassurance but she looked fairly pale and shaky herself.

'When? When will they . . .'

A blood-chilling scream ripped across the chamber; there was so much pain and indignation in the sound that everyone reacted to it. Yiska was still weakened from his own ordeal so his gut responded to the sound and he vomited across the floor. As he watched the slimy trail of his stomach contents trickle into the cracks of the limestone his teary gaze caught sight of Vedrus. It seemed the scream had taken the wind from his sails – he looked notably shaken.

Yiska spat a bitter remnant of phlegm which landed near Vedrus' feet. 'Didn't have the nerve to do your own dirty work,' he observed dryly.

There was a tangible air of excitement about the encampment now, a buzz, a sudden belief that the end was not a foregone conclusion. And at dusk, at long last, it stopped raining.

Effie and Ferebe were making final preparations for their mission to the base of the Gorge. Tulann had allowed them to take thirty men and they had chosen a mixed force of Fine, Shoreth and Sidhe. The ten Sidhe were bear and wolf – but only one eagle, Tulann could not spare any more. Ferebe had briefed them about the mission but kept the details of Effie's world necessarily sketchy. She hoped they would be there only a short time and didn't think it appropriate to alarm her men unduly. The Shoreth she had chosen included three *Sanah* as they were taking Storm and three other mammoths.

Tulann came to see Effie just before they left for the head of the trail – she knew he had a thousand and one things to do and was touched at this display of uncharacteristic thoughtfulness. He was in high spirits. 'There's a chance now,' he said. 'And that's all we need.'

His plan was to repair *Aon Crann* under cover of darkness, the Sidhe eagles flying into the gorge and attaching ropes to the ends of the bridge – it appeared it had simply been severed at either end and lay in the base of the gorge almost intact. Winches were already being built on the rim and on the central island halfway across the space which was the central, strengthening point of the bridge. Sidhe eagles had been ferrying men and materials over all afternoon. Once the ropes were in place the winches would be manned by warriors and Sidhe bears whose enormous strength would be required. Of course, the potential problem would be securing the far side of the bridge – from this distance it was difficult to tell the extent of Zarrus' patrols and they would be lucky indeed not to attract unwanted attention. It was a plan of sorts, but even Effie who had no military experience at all could see that it was fraught with potential pitfalls. As Tulann said, at least they had a chance now.

As he tried to speak to her, people kept rushing up to him asking for his orders or discussing logistics with him. Effie watched from where she stood beside the shaggy flanks of Storm; Tulann was truly an emperor now, she felt. Mostly she was glad about this – he had come into his own and the people would come to respect him – but a tiny part of her felt saddened and, she realised with a small shock, slightly jealous. It had been such a short time since their first meeting in the mud of the forest, she smiled at the memory of how Tulann had been unable to contemplate that someone might treat him normally, the expression on his face when she hurled the mud at him. But now, well, he didn't need that reminder any more; he had been right to be secure in his view of the world, he was the emperor after all, it had been Effie who had been finding her way as much as he.

Tulann gestured impatiently at some unfortunate who'd been sent to ask him about ropes. 'Go away,' he scowled. 'I don't want any interruptions for ten minutes.' He walked towards her, shrugging and holding his hands out in a mock-despairing gesture. 'If I ask for ten, I might get five,' he smiled.

Effie smiled back, unexpectedly shy and tongue-tied. Ferebe, who had been standing next to her suddenly decided to busy herself with Storm's harness.

'Effie Morgan. I . . . I'll miss you,' he said awkwardly.

'No you won't,' she said.

'You're always bloody arguing with me . . .' he began.

'I mean, you'll be too busy.' She became minutely interested in the floor. *Christ, look at you – you're like some sixteen year old.*

'I could never be that busy.' To her complete amazement, Tulann stepped in towards her and gave her a hug; it was warm and friendly but for the briefest second before he let her go, his cheek rested against hers and she could not mistake his feelings for her. 'Look after her, Ferebe Vezul,' he said as he stepped back from their embrace.

'I will, sir,' Ferebe smiled.

'I hope that when you get back, you and I can be friends, Ferebe – we didn't get off to the best of starts, what with you murdering my father and all.'

'But I . . .'

'Joke. Something else Effie taught me. You'll have to explain those "knock-knock" things to Ferebe.' Effie giggled, partly through continued embarrassment.

'She has taught me about friendship,' he said, suddenly slightly pensive. 'About letting your friends go – so they'll come back to you.'

'Yes sir,' Ferebe said, slightly mystified.

'Bye then.'

'Goodbye, sir. Oh, sir? What should we do with Horza? Should we bring him back for questioning or trial?'

'Nah. Kill the bastard if you can.' He began to walk away and was immediately swamped by anxious looking clerks and commanders. Just as Effie began to relax, he called back to her. 'Oh, Effie?'

'Huh?'

'Catch.' He threw something towards her; it caught the light, spinning like a golden penny through the space between them. Effie caught it, plucking it from the air as it reached the nadir of its arc. She frowned questioningly to Tulann but he just smiled and gave the briefest of winks.

It was a ring, fashioned from heavy, pinkish gold. In the centre was a huge ruby and wrapped around it was a stylised dragon which appeared to be sleeping on its treasure. 'Jeez,' she breathed, 'It must be worth a fortune.'

Ferebe was sitting atop Storm now but she bent down as low as she could to peer over Effie's shoulder. 'Hmm, I'd say he wants you to bring it back to him, Effie Morgan.'

'He's in shock, Malk.'

'What does that mean?'

'His body is reacting to the injury. His heartbeat is irregular, his system full of adrenalin and endorphins.' Yiska glanced at Malky who continued to look mystified. It was plain to see the Highlander had actually been crying – not something he'd expect from Malky. 'We have to keep him warm, can you get Melicende to get him a warm drink?'

'Aye,' Malky said gruffly. 'I tried tae stop them, ye ken, Yiska. I tried ma best but they held me back. I hope Duncan remembers that . . . I tried . . .' His voice trailed off and he scrubbed his eyes roughly with his knuckles making them even redder against his permanent deathly pallor.

Yiska patted him on the shoulder reassuringly. 'He'll know that, Malk – there's nothing you could have done. It wasn't as if they gave you guys any warning.'

'Nah. But in a way, I s'pose that wiz better – fer Duncan, I mean.'

'Yeah.' Yiska stared down at Talisker who was lying curled up in foetal position on a heap of blankets. Talisker's skin was almost the same shade as Malky's – fortunately this appeared also to be from shock rather than blood-loss – he had to admit the Sidhe were efficient in their barbarism. He was pretty sure now that the scream which had been heard in the main chamber was not the moment when they took Talisker's hand but rather, when they sealed the stump by sticking it in the fire. He could still smell the seared flesh – not an unpleasant smell in itself. Only the knowledge of what it was made his stomach churn.

'Talisker.' He leaned in closely and stared into Talisker's face; his eyes were open, still bulging in fright, but unseeing. He had retreated within himself in denial of the pain and shock. 'Listen to me. It's Yiska – you're going to be all right.'

Talisker moved his position slightly but his eyes remained unfocussed. Yiska took the opportunity to look at the wound, the amputation itself was as clean as any he'd seen performed in the real world.

Malky came back with a mug of hazel tea. 'Melicende says the Council are goin' tae scry usin' Braznnair as a focus.'

It was Yiska's turn to be mystified. 'What's scrying, Malk?'

'It's where they kin look somewhere, like conjure

images o' the present or the future. Ah think it's pretty difficult. Melicende is helpin' them – reckon Duncan was right no tae trust her. She's a sorceress and nae doubt . . .'

'But that's not necessarily bad, right? She's helped us and . . .'

'Aye, but they've always got their ain agenda,' Malky said.

'Hmm. Well we've only got one agenda, Malk, and that's making sure Duncan survives the next few hours. Shock can kill as surely as a sword. Here, help me prop him up so we can get a drink down him.'

It was hours before Talisker began to come back to the world. And when he did, the pain was there waiting for him – his face acquired the etched deliberation of those people who have to deal with such agonies and get past them moment by moment in order to function. Melicende brought him some herbal concoction for the pain but he knocked it from her hand, snarling at her. She was stoic about his attitude although she seemed saddened. 'I understand,' she said as she left the chamber. 'I have let you all down. I'm sorry.'

Talisker said nothing in reply, just watched her go. 'I've had enough,' he said in a small, tight voice.

Malky glanced at Yiska nervously. 'What d'you mean, Duncan? You'll get ower this . . . it just takes time.'

'No, Malk. I'm a hundred and ten years old. My bones ache when there's rain coming, I have little or no immunity left to disease from crossing back and forth between worlds,' he glanced down at the stump of his wrist as he said this, his thoughts plainly written on his face – in Sutra, infection killed many. 'And this was never my fight. Seems the frigging-Council-of-fucking-Tema have everything under control. No, I'm going home, and I hope to die there in a haze of alcohol.'

Malky grinned. 'Count me in, Talisker – we should look up Alessandro when we get back, have a few drams.'

Talisker stood up – this required some effort as his legs were still weak and shaky – but Malky was instantly at his side. 'Are you coming, Yiska?' Talisker asked.

'Well . . . I kinda wanted to see how it all pans out.'

Talisker nodded, 'Yeah, I used to feel like that. And you should feel rightly proud of what you did, Yiska, you've probably saved the Sidhe's arrogant necks. And the Fine and Shoreth of course. You should be proud.' He began to hobble over to the entrance of the chamber. 'Me?' he laughed bitterly. 'Frankly my dear, I don't give a damn.'

Tulann had never been so tired. Not even when his father had insisted he train with the elite guard, and he knew without doubt that this exhaustion was unique, that he would never feel this way again; because this tiredness was as much mental as physical and that was because this *mattered* to him.

All through the night the operation to rebuild *Aon Crann* continued; the first section gave little trouble – Tulann watched as the eagles dove into the gorge, folding their massive wings and dropping into a steep dive. In the darkness they were like shadow-birds, something dredged from the imagination of the Fine, made real by their desire and passion. He didn't understand the relationship between the Fine and the Sidhe but it appeared the Fine were as joyful about the return of the Sidhe's totem animals as they were themselves.

Later, as the winches began their slow inexorable task, he marvelled at the bear Sidhe, at their strength and willingness. And for most of the night it seemed, hope held sway in the encampment.

All that was to change however. As the first light of dawn crept unremarked from the east, Tulann and Sigrid had decided to fly across the Gorge and see for themselves the state of Zarrus' defences. Initially exhilarated by the flight, Tulann's spirit was crushed by what he saw. Thousands upon thousands of creatures – not exactly camped on the narrow plane between Durghanti and the gorge, just *there*. Milling around slowly, directionless; waiting for something to present itself for them to attack. Waiting for them . . . Nearer to Durghanti itself, Tulann saw a few figures wearing Shoreth uniforms – those of Zarrus' elite guard. It was impossible to guess how many Shoreth had remained loyal to the general, but Tulann knew they would be his own men, seasoned warriors whose nature demanded they follow their general zealously and unquestioningly. Those who followed the 'Warrior Path' because they could not imagine anything other. Even when *Aon Crann* was ready, all the opposing army would have to do was pick them off as they crossed over.

He spoke to Sigrid about it on their return – the old Thane's expression was as tight and grim as Tulann's own. 'It will be a slaughter, a massacre. We cannot send our troops across the bridge.'

Sigrid sighed. 'What choice do we have, Tulann? We cannot go back – the forest is teeming with Zarrus' scum. We might lose as many men attempting to return. I do have a suggestion, though.'

He outlined his plan and Tulann agreed with it. It was a desperate, half-baked idea, but perhaps would allow time for sufficient forces to cross the bridge to put up a decent fight. But there was no getting away from the fact that many of the alliance warriors were doomed to die in the attempt.

It was dawn when Talisker, Malky and Yiska emerged from the caverns where the Council had been entombed. It had been frosty overnight and a low har-frost clung to the hillocks and ridges of the moor. Weak rays of sunshine touched upon the landscape but there would not be enough warmth to chase the chill away until past midday.

They walked in silence for the first two hours; Talisker was extremely weak and progress was slow, but he strode out with grim determination using a long hazel wood staff that Malky had 'acquired' from someone in the Council chamber. They stopped mid-morning for a break, Talisker breathing hard, the pallor of his face still worryingly pale.

'How are you feeling, Talisker?' Yiska asked. Not for the first time he wished he had his medical bag with him, but then Talisker had been the one who'd insisted there was no place in Sutra for chemical drugs.

'I'm okay. Just want to get home now.'

Yiska nodded. It was a wholly natural reaction to trauma, to want to retreat from the world or, in Talisker's case, both worlds, to be safe within ones own sanctuary.

'At least I achieved what I set out to do – I gave the Sidhe back Braznnair. I couldn't have died peacefully in my bed otherwise.'

'That's enough talk o' dyin', Duncan,' Malky tutted. 'You'll get ower this, you'll see.'

'Maybe I don't want to, Malk. Maybe I'm past caring – or just too fucking tired. Who says dying is always defeat, anyway? There's always a time when a person is *ready*. And I am. I am ready.'

Malky said nothing, merely looked saddened.

'Talisker. That may be true – but you'd better be sure,' Yiska cautioned. 'My feeling is that if you cross the void again, your immune system will finally give up. You will probably be dead within weeks, months at the most.'

'Okay.' Talisker stared at the stump of his wrist. 'You know, it's true what they say about amputations – you can still feel the missing part. Not just feel it in a vague way either – it's like I can still waggle my fingers. It itches, burns.'

'It's the nerve endings, Talisker,'

'Aye, you'll never play the piano again,' Malky said gravely.

Yiska gasped at the Highlander's sheer lack of sensitivity but, to his amazement, Talisker managed a wry chuckle and then a shaky laugh. 'Stupid bastard, I could never play the piano.'

'Aye,' Malky rolled his eyes, 'Ah ken that . . .'

*

They had walked for another hour before Malky spotted the rider following them. Whoever it was, was making no effort at stealth but rather was galloping hard, whipping the horse to sustain its charge. Shading his eyes against the glare of the sun, Malky studied the rider for a moment. 'Ah think it's Melicende,' he muttered.

'Ah Christ, now what?' Talisker groaned.

They stopped and waited for her but, as an afterthought, Malky drew his sword. After a moment's thought, Talisker tried to draw his weapon but ended up fumbling uselessly with the leather sheath of his sword, cursing weakly.

It was Melicende. She reined in as she came closer and walked her mare up to the group with a bemused expression on her face. 'Really, there is no need for weapons,' she said. 'I am carrying none myself.'

'Aye, but mebbe, you dinnae need real weapons,' Malky frowned. 'We ken you're a sorceress, Melicende. Talisker didn'ae trust you tae start wi' and he wiz right.'

'I am sorry. Truly. I did not think it through. I should have known the Council would demand retribution for the theft of Braznnair. But, to be honest, I don't know what we could have done differently.'

'What do you want?' Talisker asked. There was a long pause as Melicende had the grace to look embarrassed. Her nervousness transmitted itself to her mount which began jig-jogging and swishing its tail in an agitated fashion.

'I . . . we still need your help,' she said.

*

'You've got to be joking, right?' Talisker scowled. 'I'm going home, Melicende. I have earned the right already to die peacefully in my bed. What the hell gives you the idea I'll *ever* willingly help the Sidhe again?'

'Please, Worldwalker, just hear me. It is not for us – not for the sake of the Sidhe – we know we would have no right to ask you if it were. It is for the Fine. They are in danger of obliteration. Zarrus has created enough forces to wipe them from the face of Sutra. He has taught his monsters to create more of their kind.'

They had made a camp of sorts; Malky had fudged a windbreak from a couple of poles and his riding cloak. A weak but determined little fire was heating some water for tea. 'What's he doing it fer?' Malky frowned. 'I mean, he's no goin' tae have anybody left tae rule ower. What's the point o' that?'

'We really don't know, Malcolm,' Melicende sighed. 'But we do suspect that he might be in the sway of dark magics and is attempting to achieve . . .'

'He wants to be a God?'

'Yes, we fear so. What made you think so?'

Talisker was propped up on some blankets, a sheen of sweat still coated his face as his body fought the pain. His laughter cut across the moors like a humourless whiplash. 'Lucky damned guess . . . It's what they all want, those whose egos are too big for this world. Jahl was the same, he nearly destroyed my home city in his attempt.'

'All the creatures which he has made – the Shards and the Flays – and those he has summoned, they have one thing in common. They have been implanted with something called *khetourit*. It represents a prayer.'

'A *prayer*?'

'A kind of living prayer which has energy and power. When he has enough, he will transcend, become such a dark God that we fear our world will be irredeemable.'

'But you've got a plan, right? A plan which probably involves me suffering pain, torture, maybe some insanity. In fact, it might even be impossible for me to survive it.' Melicende did not understand Talisker's sarcasm. She looked towards Yiska in confusion.

'Tell us what you propose, Melicende,' he said.

This was it. The bridge was up and the attack had to start soon before Zarrus' forces made any efforts to destroy it again. Tulann sat on the back of a Sidhe eagle once more, Sigrid only a few feet away.

'Warriors . . . allies. May our Gods look down on us and protect us this day,' he called. At his signal, the eagle began to rise into the clear skies of the dawn. At first they spiralled round and round with dizzying ease, gaining height – the Sidhe who carried him, Hemarch, had explained what would happen – but even so, as they reached the top of their ascent Tulann felt his stomach lurch. He glanced off to one side and saw Sigrid's eagle nearby, while five more would be taking off immediately after.

The wind shrieked past as Hemarch dropped into a steep dive towards his target; a massive bag of flaming pitch which was positioned in a row with the others along the edge of the gorge. The plan was for the eagles to drop their firebombs amongst the massed army on the other side, causing destruction and panic, allowing precious minutes for the allies to stream across *Aon*

Crann. It was a high risk tactic, if the flames took hold of the ropes too fast the whole thing would drop too soon into the floor of the gorge, or if the ropes were not calculated to be long enough, Hemarch could be in jeopardy – Tulann had instructed him to release his burden early if necessary but he doubted that any of the Sidhe eagles would do that, they seemed a proud race.

Tulann could feel the heat of the flames below them, one moment flaring up dangerously towards the feathers of Hemarch's legs and cooling the next, as the wind caught the fire and buffeted it in the other direction. It took only moments to cross the gorge but Hemarch wanted to cause maximum damage so he held on for precious seconds more – just as Tulann lost his nerve and was about to shout to the eagle to drop it, Hemarch released the ropes. In mere seconds the bomb fell as Tulann and Hemarch pulled away to circle back across the gorge. Tulann watched as well as he was able. With a lurch of despair he realised the wind might extinguish the flames before it landed but then, in the same moment it seemed, impact was made.

There had never been anything like it in Sutra before; a *huge* splash of fire which rippled outwards, destroying everything in its path. Even from this height Tulann could hear the strange howling and yammering of the creatures below, he yelled with pleasure and exaltation. This could work!

'Hemarch, can you circle round again?' he asked. He wasn't sure if the eagle had heard him at first but then Hemarch dipped his wings, banking into a turn so Tulann could see the fray.

One eagle had dropped its fire too early, the ropes had

been quickly eaten through – Cerne's Gorge was burning but only sporadically amongst the rivulets and streams which were heavy with rain. The others had found their targets easily, separating Zarrus' forces with a ragged line of fire. The creatures did themselves no favours, running aimlessly as they burned, carrying the swathe of destruction wider.

'*Yes*!' Tulann crowed. Beneath him the allies were running full pelt across *Aon Crann*, fanning out as soon as they reached the other side so as not to cause a bottleneck. Their lines were thin, only one or two deep, and it was difficult to see how they could prevail, even with the panic and pandemonium in the enemy ranks.

Tulann and Hemarch landed on the opposite side of the gorge – the allies were queuing to get over *Aon Crann* and there was certainly an obstruction on their own side. 'Can we go again?' he yelled to Sigrid above the din of the soldiers. 'Can we drop more pitch?'

Sigrid shook his head, 'That's all we had, Tulann. It was Ruannoch Were's whole supplies – about a year's worth.' He was about to continue, but suddenly there was an almighty noise from across the gorge. Tulann realised belatedly that it was the sound they had heard before on the night *Aon Crann* had been destroyed.

'Get back!' he yelled. 'Get those men off the bridge!' Panic ensued as the shout ran down the lines – some soldiers turned immediately only to find their path blocked by some still moving forwards.

But this time, Zarrus' target was not the bridge. Massive tentacles of green light whipped out of the highest towers of Durghanti – their reach more than a mile – the accompanying sound was like a taut whiplash, and where their tips earthed in the ground, men burned. Instant conflagration took hold of the opposite side of the gorge. Zarrus, uncaring whether or not he destroyed his own forces – the ferocious lights wreaked equal havoc to all – sought only to destroy, scorching the earth with such power that Durghanti would never recover.

The arcs sought out the end of the bridge and the fire caught hold of the men there – there was nothing anyone could do. Even at the distance at which he stood Tulann could hear the screaming. Many pitched over the sides of *Aon Crann* into the river below, still others were leaping from the rim of the gorge, almost all of them to certain death. He watched the frenzied terror of their fall with a sickness churning his stomach, they were all ablaze and he would never look into the depths of a fire after this day with anything approaching peace of mind.

The retreat had been sounded and those who were still able streamed back across the bridge; many were scorched, their hair and eyebrows gone, many wounded were trampled in the crush, many fell as the mindless surge of the crowd took hold.

When the bridge was cleared of the living, Tulann's horrified reverie was broken. Someone was speaking to him, he knew, probably telling him how many casualties they estimated. He ignored the voice. He walked to the end of *Aon Crann* on shaking legs and stared across.

The lights were gone, their work done; fires were still burning over there, flesh charring. Smoke drifted over the rim like a torpid waterfall. There were still sounds coming from *Aon Crann* beyond the halfway island, amongst the dead the living crawled in hideous pain, groans and gasps which grew weaker by the second. Tulann could see the black pile of corpses, mercifully blanketed by the smoke of their own pyre. He fell to his knees and retched, tears and snot streaming down his face which was becoming blackened by the smoke. This is what it really meant to be Emperor, then. He had sent these men to their deaths with such blithe naivety.

The army of the Alliance was decimated, burnt, destroyed. It had taken less than an hour.

'We must get there quickly,' Melicende urged. 'They do not know the extent of Zarrus' power. He is almost transfigured.'

'I just have to say goodbye, Melicende,' Yiska said. He walked over to where Talisker and Malky stood watching. True to form the rain had begun again, and the skies were heavy with black, roiling clouds. 'One day the sun will shine here,' he smiled ruefully.

Talisker smiled back, 'Yeah well, it does sometimes, honest.'

'We'll see you in, well, mebbe in Durghanti. But if no, Ruannoch Were,' Malky nodded. 'Mind yersel' on thon eagle. They dinnae really like havin' passengers.'

'Yeah. Okay.' Yiska walked back towards the Sidhe eagle and prepared to sit up behind Melicende who was just getting herself anchored by the ropes the Sidhe had organised.

'Hey, Yiska,' Malky called. 'If ye see Effie, tell her tae stay put – we'll come and get her.' Yiska gave the thumbs up but had to question whether or not Malky was in denial about the threat Zarrus posed – mind you, the Highlander was ever the optimist.

Just before they took off, Yiska glanced back at his friends; Talisker seemed stronger now – his recovery truly remarkable and quite probably, magical in origin – because, in his remaining hand, once again, he held Braznnair.

'I only need a few more. Horza has begun to send them through but it is so slow! Too slow. Now the well is gone and the Sidhe reclaimed their birthright, it is now or never, I cannot sustain the magic for more than a short while. Stupid, stupid Alliance army – that took some energy but they won't try anything else for a while.

'Much as it grieves me, I think I'm going to have to kill the servants.'

Chapter Eighteen

It was about midnight when they came to take the next lot of people. They *knew* now and that made it much harder. Lake, Rodney, Renee and Millie were lucky; by chance they were at the far end of the shelter. When the warriors came there was panic, women screamed and sobbed, clutching onto their sons and husbands. The crowd – Lake estimated about a hundred and fifty people – surged back as if trying to make themselves miraculously insignificant and those against the far end were in danger of being crushed against the walls which, given enough pressure, would react and kill them anyway. Bizarrely, it reminded Lake of people's reaction to audience participation – some even looked the other way at first as if in denial that the soldiers had come again – but this was a much starker, more fundamental fear.

There were children amongst the captives and by unspoken consensus they were hidden behind adult backs and passed behind from hand to hand. Their parents need not have worried however, the soldiers chose the biggest, strongest men, most of whom went stoically, kissing their wives, or mouthing silent declarations through their tears.

The soldiers had made a barrier from Shards and Flays who walked forwards, pressing the crowd back through fear. There was nowhere to go, and the soldiers made their selection as if the captives were meat.

There was a stench in the shelter; Lake was suddenly overwhelmed by it, it oppressed him. One corner had been used as a latrine but that smell was low-key, natural compared to this. Lake realised that 'the smell of fear' was not just some pulp fiction cliché; it was real. A potent mix of adrenaline and pheromones, surprisingly asexual.

Once they took the men away, many sat on the floor and wept, disconsolately. Renee was weeping silently, having seen her friend's husband taken. Lake was glad it was dark outside, realising that if it had happened in the daytime people would watch the path of the prisoners through the transparent gaps of the walls. Although he stared fixedly into the darkness he could not see more than a few feet away.

'*Sicheii, Sicheii*,' he whispered urgently to Rodney – but the old man was still chanting, in fact he had not stopped even during the last few terrifying minutes. Lake was infuriated. 'For chrissakes, *Sicheii*,' he grabbed the old man by the blanket he had wrapped about him and shook him. 'We have got to get out of here . . . stop that!' But Rodney did not stop, his lips continued to move, his face so close that Lake could smell the sweetness of his breath.

'Son,' Renee put her hand on his shoulder and pulled him away. 'He is doing what makes sense to him – don't judge him for it.'

'Why not?' Lake was furious at Rodney's intransigence. 'It's what he's done to me all my life because he doesn't understand me, ma . . . well, I don't understand how we can just sit back and do nothing.'

'And what do you suggest?' Renee regarded her son calmly.

'I don't know.' Lake stared around the shelter trying to count how many able-bodied men and women were left. 'But next time they come, we'd better be ready for them.'

Something was wrong in the void. The many crossings Talisker had made of this place had been characterised by its nothingness, its silence, the space which seemed to stretch on into relentless infinity – enough to drive men insane. But now, there was colour and sound; the colour was jagged arcs of sheet lightning and the sound – the most frightening part – was like nothing Talisker had ever heard before and the only words he could find to describe it to himself were: a shrinking noise. A warping, twisting sound. There was no echo because there was nowhere for the noise to earth itself but it didn't matter, it was so crushingly loud that Talisker's ears rang with pain for moments after each fresh assault was finished. Distantly, he considered that the void might be in danger of imploding, that something was causing so much damage to the status quo that the delicate equilibrium of the time-between-times could not be sustained. Just what the result of such a catastrophe might be he didn't even want to consider. Of course he shared none of this with Malk, who for some reason was twitchy.

'So, we just wander roond the void till we bump intae them do we?' Malky said somewhat peevishly. 'Disnae sound like much o' a plan tae me.'

'Shut up, Malk, will you?'

'And when we find them, what are we s'posed tae say? If I remember right, they're no exactly in possession o' all their faculties shall we say. Or is there another legion o' the dead wanderin' aroond here what still ken how tae talk an' listen? They canny even see us, just kinda jostle ye and bump intae ye, how're we gonna . . .'

'Malk, will you just shut up!'

'Sorry. It's thon bloody noise . . . makes mah skin crawl.'

'Yeah, I know.' Talisker walked slowly, holding Braznnair as if it were a lantern. And it did illuminate the void for some distance although the featureless grey nothing was almost more disconcerting than the dark. 'Melicende thinks they'll be attracted to Braznnair, well, the Sidhe might be, and they'll all kind of swarm together.'

'Yeah. It's what they're like, a swarm of insects.'

'Hmm.'

'But, Duncan, ah've been thinking about this, right? We've said in the past that the void is infy . . . infinite, yeah? That means it like, goes on forever?'

'Uh-huh.'

'Well then, we might never find them, even though there's thousands o' them! They could be a thousand miles away – they're no gonna sense Braznnair.'

Talisker stopped and turned to look at his friend; the pale features which Talisker was used to looking at by now were illuminated by the green glow of Braznnair, giving Malky an even more sickly pallor. He looked tired, exhaustion bleached the features of his face making the *normally genial expression gaunt – it reminded Talisker of a Venetian mask which would be smiling until it was turned upside down, when those same lines would become a heart-stopping frown. 'It's a good point, Malk,'* he sighed. *'But my theory is that the void is defined by those souls within it at any one time – it's always a personal, and relevant, journey. If we're destined to find the Lost, we'll find them. What's really bugging you?'*

'Nothing,' Malky looked instantly defensive. *'Well, it's jist what Yiska said about if you pass through here again, you'll die.'*

'I told you, I've no problem with that.'

'I have. It seems like such a waste after everything you've done fer Sutra and Edinburgh – mind o' them dragons!'

Talisker smiled. *'Yeah . . .'*

'Yeah. Wished I'd been with you – I'd have liked tae see dragons . . . If you die Duncan, that's it ower fer me anall,' he looked fidgety and embarrassed. *'Ah ken it's bloody selfish o' me tae be thinking like that, but . . .'*

'Is that so bad, Malk? How many lifetimes does a man need? Most only get one, y'know.'

'Aye. That's true. But ah've been deid – it's no what it's cracked up tae be – peaceful right enough.'

Talisker looked bemused – he was just about to answer when the sound and lightning came again. But this time the void moved as if an earthquake were happening beneath it. *'Shit, let's go, Malk. We'd better keep moving.'*

And when he saw them again – the Lost Souls – he was immediately struck with the thought: *it's them, they're unbalancing the void somehow. There must have been thousands of them and it seemed, at first, as if they were all blind. He'd forgotten the shocking whiteness of them, not just their ripped, defiled bodies but the tatters that remained of their clothes, their hair and their weapons – all a clammy, unnatural white which reeked of the sweet sense memory of their corpses.*

Melicende had said that somehow, Talisker must get them to come with him – to follow him back to Durghanti. The reclamation of their earthly flesh could only be done by the Lost themselves and was the only sure way to defeat Zarrus' forces. But she had given no indication as to how this could be done. It had taken her all of her time to convince the Council to hand Braznnair back to Talisker, who had taken it with an uncooperative snarl from the hands of Vedrus.

They came silently towards Talisker and Malky like some inexorable white swarm. Malky growled uneasily and drew his sword.

'What are you doing?' Talisker hissed. 'You can't attack them!'

'I'm jist ready tae defend myself. Say something.'

'What?'

'Talk tae them!'

'Warriors. Lost Souls of the Fine, Sidhe and . . .' he glanced around, trying to pick out the details of the armour '. . .the Shoreth. Hear me!' he shouted. The sound of his voice was swallowed up by the void, but the crowd did stop.

'Good,' Malky encouraged. 'They're listening to you.'

'You think? I'm not convinced they can hear me. You might know by now that Sutra's very existence is

threatened. Not by the Shoreth – not even by the divisions of the Shoreth and the Fine but actually by one man. The man who has condemned your souls to this endless journey by the theft of your mortal flesh. That man is Zarrus.'

No reaction. None. Not a flicker.

Talisker decided to try a different tack. 'Melicende sent me. She says you must follow me back to Durghanti and reclaim your bodies so that you might find peace.' The void shuddered again, a double crack of purple lightning lit the sky – or what passed for the sky – behind the Lost, for a second illuminating the rows and rows of pained, dazed faces, giving shadow and definition to their stark white forms. Talisker felt his stomach lurch but he couldn't decide if his physical response was pity or revulsion.

Just as he was composing something else to say, the crowd parted, shuffling aside as if someone had told them to although there was no sign of anyone to give such a command. It was the swarm-mind, Talisker thought, Malky was more correct when he knew when he described them as a swarm of insects. Through the middle of the crowd one of their number walked forward – he moved outwith the body of the Lost to stand directly in front of Talisker. He was hideous, had died of some particularly vicious blows to the collarbone which had sliced through his neck – his head could only be balanced on his torso. Talisker's eyes were unwillingly drawn to the gouges which were rendered even more ghastly by the white gore which oozed from them. The side of the unfortunate man's face was staved in above his cheekbone, his eyeball resting in a ruined socket. When he spoke, his voice was cracked and agonising but – after his initial shock at this representative of the Lost's appearance – it was what he said that stunned Talisker.

'We don't want to go back,' he said. 'We don't want to rest.'

It was almost dawn. The children and old folk were at the back of the shelter, while Lake was at the front with the men and women who had decided to fight. He was trying to decide if he was more like Mel Gibson or Arnie. His arrogance didn't stop just because he was about to do something potentially noble – or stupid. In fact, as ever, his half-baked imagination was the only thing getting him by – from moment to gut-wrenching moment in this case.

They had no weapons, in a conventional sense but one of the older women had suggested they scoop up all the stones and rocks from the floor to hurl at the soldiers. They had agreed that this was a good idea but Lake wasn't holding any rocks, the younger boys and teenagers had volunteered for the task and looked set to launch a blistering barrage. The ground of the shelter was now a mini-canyon of its own as people had frantically dug the wet mud with their bare hands. Lake and some of the other men had broken up the two small tables; Lake was quite pleased with himself as he was now holding a six foot long pole which he'd con-structed by screwing together two of the legs from the poker table. While all this was going on, people stood around the sides of the shelter so that their captors did not guess their purpose. Some of the children, led by

Millie, started to sing a song which Lake dimly remembered from his childhood; it was about an eagle who fell in love with the Sun and when she flew too close, the Sun scorched her feathers which turned her head to white.

It was shortly after they stopped singing that Rodney stopped his chanting – which was great, because it was *really, really* bugging Lake. No one else seemed to mind it, though. Renee asked Rodney why he had stopped and he said the children were right about the eagle. *And what the fuck was that supposed to mean?*

Lake wanted to say something meaningful to his mother about how things would be different if they came through this, but he could not seem to get the words out. Stupid thing was, he could have done it if he'd been pretending to be someone else – briefly, he flirted with the idea of doing his Brando – but it didn't seem appropriate somehow. Instead he gave Renee a tight little hug and kissed her noisily on the top of her head, she had smiled at him but equally had found little to say.

'They're coming,' someone whispered. 'Looks like four blue-light-people and three skinless men.'

'How many soldiers?'

'Lots more, maybe six. D'you think they're planning to take more?'

It was a rhetorical question that no one saw fit to answer as an expectant hush fell on the prisoners. In the corner, one of the youngest girls sniffled quietly.

'Remember, wait till they're all in,' Lake muttered.

They walked in. The Shoreth had drawn their swords – they looked nervy, indeed they'd have to be stupid not to sense the tension in the shelter but then, they probably thought that it was purely through fear.

'*Go!*' Lake yelled.

Absolute pandemonium breaks loose. The stone-throwers fling their rocks and mud at the Shoreth who instinctively fling their arms up to try to protect their face and heads. The crowd surges forward too quickly and Lake is almost knocked off his feet but rights himself by pulling on someone's jacket. He runs towards the nearest skinless man and begins to jab at it with the staff – it's a good tactic – the creatures are light and relatively defenceless apart from their fatal touch. He knows at least four of the other men should be attempting the same thing but he has no time to focus on anyone else. The Shoreth are taken by surprise and Lake hears a cheer go up as one of the blue-light-people is toppled by sheer weight of numbers. There's the kind of tussle that seems to go on for hours as time appears to slow; the fight bursts out of the door of the shelter into the snowy landscape.

Lake is still in the shelter when someone fires a gun. It happens at the same moment he manages to impale the skinless man on the end of his pole; he's hoisting it into the air, a cry of triumph on his lips when the gun goes off – the sound is deafening within the confines of their prison, the sharp smell of cordite fills the air and one of the Shoreth is on his knees clutching at the gaping wound in his chest, an expression of disbelief on his features. For long moments Lake cannot hear a thing except a high-pitched whine in his ears; he stares around at the combatants who now seem to be fighting in some bizarre silent movie, their faces twisted in a violent rage.

It seems there is hope. They will not die without a fight. Lake feels a surge of adrenaline rush through him, his hands have stopped shaking now. Rushing outside to rejoin the fray, he takes in the scene in moments. It is snowing again and there are dead people lying amongst the snow, dead blue-light-people and two dead skinless men. The Shoreth are outnumbered and they are afraid. As his hearing returns, fragments of sounds such as he never wants to hear again blast into his consciousness; agonising screams, desperate curses. The dying . . . the dying are all around him.

He notices in the corner of his vision that Rodney has climbed one of the rocks near the Mummy Cave and is dancing – *crazy old bastard* – Lake knows it is the dance of the bald eagle, the old man's arms are widespread and he moves slowly, his movements describing the flight of the eagle as it rides the high thermals, *yeah that's a real big help*, Lake thinks to himself. He runs towards a small group of people who have cornered a skinless man – their weapons are not long enough to keep the creature at a safe distance.

Afterwards, all he will remember is the bodies, the blood on the snow.

'Stop.'

There's a crashing sound, like every thunderstorm in the desert has focussed on their fight. Everyone stops what they're doing – even the Shoreth. It's not a voluntary cessation, rather that the sound is so goddamned *huge*, it hurts to hear it; it hurts ears and eyes and ribs where it reverberates like some echoing

421

bruise. All eyes turn towards the source of the sound. In the centre of the wrecked campsite one man is sitting on his horse – Lake thinks it's the leader at first, but then it can't be because this guy looks different – he looks different to all of them, he's dark skinned and has black hair, he's more like the Dinéh than the Shoreth. But he must be one of them because he is wearing their armour, and also, he's definitely magical. Lake doesn't believe in magic *per se* but it's difficult to deny when someone is only ten feet away with crackling white light flaring upwards from his hand. The light-energy whooshes up into the sky and then arcs outwards into a huge dome shape which covers the whole of the campsite. He's not sure if doing this magic is actually causing the rider pain because he has a strange, almost panicked expression on his face but his eyes are bright with the reflection of the light – it seems there is a conflict there, but Lake and the others have neither the time nor the inclination to worry about it because he has the children, clustered around the horse, bound by blue light tendrils and thrown in a careless heap of squirming misery.

'We are too late,' Melicende's words were driven back to Yiska by virtue of the freezing wind, her anguish understandable. Below them the shattered army of the Alliance was licking its wounds and burying its dead. A swathe of blackened ash extended from the Durghanti side of the gorge for half a mile to the north and south and out across the first section of *Aon Crann*. As they flew closer Yiska could make out the shapes of burnt – in some cases still burning – bodies caught in the tangle

422

of charred undergrowth on the cliffsides of the gorge, although this high up the smell of burnt corpses was a mere taint on the breeze, it was still bad enough to make him gag.

As they descended he was struck by the strange silence which blanketed the encampment. The smoke muffled everything but there would be little noise anyway, only those whose duty it was to bury or dispose of the dead were busy. Shoreth crucifixions loomed amongst the smoke as their generals and commanders were paid their due, the sound of the hammering rang out like a lost, disconsolate gunshot.

'We were meant to tell them help is coming,' Melicende murmured. 'We are too late. The fight has gone out of them.'

No one moves. It reminds Lake of a scene from a movie – some western or other – but such is the state of his dazed mind he cannot remember which one. But as if the reality of the movie is asserting itself on real life, a voice rings out from the entrance to the Mummy Cave.

'Let them go, Horza.' It is a woman's voice. Despite everything he's seen, Lake gasps as he glances towards the cave.

Firstly he notices that Rodney is still dancing – in fact, he has the distinct impression that *Sicheii* cannot stop. His movements are slower now as if his wings are tiring, as if he's flown too close to the sun, but he only notices that in a kind of residual way, because the woman who has spoken is one of *them* and she is riding an elephant. No, not an elephant, a hairy, woolly . . . yes, a woolly mammoth! A white woolly mammoth.

Horza laughs – and that's definitely like a movie – *hahaha* – he throws his head back in disdain as he does so. 'Ferebe Vezul. What are you doing here? This is not your battle. Go home.'

'Only if you come with me, you murdering bastard.' She is walking the mammoth down the slope now as she talks – at first, Lake thinks it's really slow, but then he realises the beast is covering a huge amount of ground with each stride. It strikes him that it doesn't like the snow much, like some horses. All eyes are fixed on Ferebe Vezul.

Then, it gets real, *real* weird. There's a sound of rushing wings, except these wings are impossibly large and the backdraft from them fans the snow away from the centre of the encampment where it is buffeted and trapped by the magical barrier Horza has created. It looks like some strange snow-globe; Horza's hair and clothes are whipped in the air, his horse whinnies nervously and, like everyone else, he looks up.

It's an eagle – *Sicheii*'s eagle. And it's in a full dive towards the mounted figure of Horza, at the same moment he opens his mouth to scream so does the massive bird, so that the canyon echoes to its shrill, frightening call. There is a burst of light as the eagle pierces the dome although it seems to suffer no ill-effect. Horza is plucked from his horse as if he were a wriggling silver fish, the eagle's talons closing about his chest with the speed and precision of a beautiful machine. But Horza is not finished, as he is pulled into the air he screams: 'Kill them!' and there is little time to watch what becomes of him because the battle begins again in earnest.

Only this time it's different. The spirits of the Dinéh world have taken form to save them – there can be little other explanation, even to Lake. As he fends off the skinless man once more with his pole, it snaps apart, halving the distance between them. The creature lunges forward, reaching out its spindly arms towards him. Lake screams in fright, but then, the bear appears. It grabs the skinless man, apparently impervious to its poison, and just pulls its head off, dropping the still squirming corpse on the ground. It's horrible, disgusting. Lake grins at the bear before running off towards the children. As he runs he sees other guardian spirits – wolves, running amongst the melee, bringing down blue-light-people and skinless men as if they are natural prey.

The Shoreth soldiers rush towards the bound captives, it seems some are intent on following Horza's orders no matter how distasteful. A few have drawn swords although a couple look less than convinced that killing children should figure anywhere in their plans. Fortunately, Lake isn't the only one rushing to their defence: two of the bears are lumbering across the snow and the woman riding the mammoth – Ferebe – is also headed that way. Smaller fights are in progress and the Dinéh are suffering badly. Lake runs past the body of an old school friend of his, whose chest is bleeding out as the life is fading from his eyes. He pauses, 'Eugene? Eui?'

'Dave. Help Sharee . . . my kid . . . help.'

So he doesn't stop. He reaches the group of soldiers just as the first one raises his sword against the children.

But he's too late for the first. She dies with a helpless, high-pitched scream which is cut short. Despite everything, he almost *cannot believe* someone might do such a thing. 'Bastard!' he screeches. He runs into the fray brandishing the now shortened pole and vowing to do maximum damage. But other have arrived, the bears, Ferebe, other Dinéh.

It's all a blur after that point. A bloody, gut wrenching blur. And even though ultimately they win, Lake understands how even the triumphant are broken by such an experience. He'll wake up in the small hours of the morning remembering his own feral grin as he drives a borrowed sword into the intestines of a Shoreth warrior. He'll wash in the shower each morning as if the blood is still there, scrubbing until his skin is red and sore. Worst of all, he'll see that child forever; her tight little plaits and her sneakers that light up when she walks. His heart is broken – he just doesn't know it yet.

And when a silence of sorts falls on the canyon Lake is still looking for something to kill. A girl walks up to him and takes him by the arm – she's speaking to him gently (he must look crazed, he thinks) and she's got a funny accent. She walks him over to Renee and Millie Talloak who both rush to embrace him as if he's been away somewhere. But he hasn't been anywhere.

They're fussing over him, and if he's honest he doesn't mind. His mother is wiping him down with a big towel, getting the blood off – it's a rather rough towel but something about the sensation is bringing him back to himself – as the adrenaline leaves him and he feels the first tight tremors of reaction pull his tired muscles, the strange haze of battle leaves him. He looks over towards the middle of the campsite; all of the guardians are there and those parents and children who are lucky enough to be reunited are walking amongst them; the children, still with that expression of blank shock, are touching the fur and the feathers. One little boy is being cradled by a massive bear while his mother sits weeping beside them. As they are distracted, relatives and friends clear away the bodies of the fallen . . .

'Ma, where's *Sicheii*?' It is his first truly conscious thought.

Melicende and Yiska were shocked by the desolation of the Alliance. When they landed no one challenged them. They both stood in the mud staring into the smoke-laden gloom for a few minutes.

'Do you suppose the Emperor or the Thane have been killed?' Yiska suggested.

Melicende shrugged. 'It would not surprise me. Come on, let's see if we can find either of them.'

It did not take long to find Tulann's voluminous tent and despite the laxity which seemed to have overcome the camp, there was a sentry outside.

'Ah, that's better,' Melicende muttered. 'You there. We have come to see the Emperor. It is of the utmost importance – I am an emissary of the Council of Tema.'

This obviously meant little or nothing to the sentry who was almost asleep on his feet anyway. 'He's not to be disturbed, Ma'am,' he said.

'Send them in, you cretin,' a reedy voice snapped from inside the tent. This was followed by a spasm of coughing. Melicende smiled slightly apologetically at the sentry and they walked into the gloom of the tent.

In the middle of the floor-space a man was sitting on a reclining chair. He was propped up by cushions and he held a large goblet of alcohol in one hand, whilst the other clutched blankets around himself. It was his face which was the most shocking thing, because he had been scorched. His hair, eyebrows and lashes were mostly gone and, although some patches of tinder-dry fuzz still adhered to his scalp, it appeared as though once touched it would just rub away. His eyes were red-rimmed and streaming and his face still covered in ash and mire. As he smoothed down his blankets Yiska noted his hands were not just scorched but severely burnt. It seemed he noted Yiska's interest because he looked at his hands as if seeing them for the first time.

'I tried to dig them out,' he said.

With a shock, Yiska realised who he was looking at. *'Tulann*?' he gasped. 'I mean, Emperor Tulann?'

'Expecting someone prettier, perhaps?' Tulann replied. Tipping up his goblet he took a long draught of his drink and Yiska was close enough to smell that it was straight spirit rather than wine or mead. 'What do you want?'

Melicende pulled a stool over to where Tulann sat and she positioned herself directly opposite him. Yiska was somewhat surprised at her presumption and chose to remain standing.

'My name is Melicende and this is Yiska. We have come from the Council of Tema to tell you that . . .' she seemed to lose her nerve slightly and it didn't help that

Tulann was scowling at her. '. . . that help is on the way.'

It was difficult to tell at first that Tulann was laughing; the sound was so much like a gurgling, retching cough. And it wasn't as if his face lit up with humour either. 'Help?' he gasped, his tone completely incredulous. 'Help is on the way? What . . . eagles, bears, wolves? We have those, Melicende . . . we had more but they . . .' his eyes dulled and he took another slug of his drink. '. . .they caught fire, y'see.'

'Sir?'

Tulann looked towards Yiska, his eyes slightly unfocussed. 'Hmm?'

'I am a healer, Sir. Would you let me dress your wounds? Your hands are very bad – you must be in terrible pain.'

'Oh yeah. Hurts.' Tulann thrust out his hand as if to show Yiska his wounds but he forgot he was clutching a goblet of spirit. The liquid sloshed out onto his hand – probably a good thing, Yiska thought, should stop infection – and Tulann let out a yelp.

Melicende looked slightly impatient and it was clear to Yiska that she did not feel Tulann was treating the Council with adequate respect. 'Melicende, could you get someone to bring in fresh water and clean linen?' he said. He glanced back at Tulann only to realise the Emperor had lapsed into unconsciousness. 'Look, we'll get more sense out of him when he's sobered up and had his wounds dressed.'

'What about Sigrid? Perhaps I should speak to him . . . the Fine will give more respect to the words of the Council.'

'Okay, fine, do that. If you can find him and he's in any better state than this. But send some dressings first.'

Melicende shot Tulann a disdainful look which Yiska felt was somewhat harsh given the circumstances. She stopped by the door and sighed. 'I am sorry, Yiska, but time is pressing. Help *is* coming whether they are ready or not.'

He was still on the rock where he had danced, face down in the snow, his arms outstretched as though he imagined he was the eagle. 'Oh no,' Lake groaned. '*Sicheii*, Rodney . . .' He turned the limp body over and propped him up against his knee, brushing the wet hair aside from his face. Rodney gave a small groan. 'That's good *Sicheii*, wake up.'

Renee came bustling over with a mug of warm coffee and Lake pressed it into Rodney's hands. The old man was shaking violently and Lake was relieved that perhaps it was just that the cold had gotten into him. He watched as Rodney gulped down the coffee, exhaustion making his relief almost overwhelming.

'Did they come?' Rodney asked when he'd finished. 'Did help come?'

'Yes. Yes it did.'

Rodney smiled. 'Sometimes the magic works.'

'*Sicheii* – that's from a movie,' Lake laughed shakily.

'Really? Huh, waddya know. Kinda thought I'd be dead after all this.'

'Many are dead, but not as many as there might have been.'

'What happened to their leader?'

'Dunno really. Reckon the eagle took him and threw him into the Sun.'

Rodney laughed. 'Don't be a galoot, Dave . . . Lake.'

'After today, I'd believe it. By the way, *Sicheii*, there's an eagle – a big, big eagle – over there who's waiting to meet you.'

Chapter Nineteen

It's not as if I am being unreasonable. It is my birthright. Why, why does he seek to thwart me again?

Time is precious; my Godhood could be snatched from my grasp. The instant of opportunity may be much, much less than I anticipated. I have killed the servants – it grieved me to have to do it myself, I seem to have retained none of Zarrus' brute instinct for killing so I poisoned those I could but there were a couple I had to resort to my blade with.

I am so . . . so close. I feel it. I reach out my hand and tiny sparks and eddies of power play around it. But the balance will be so fine in the last moments. If the Lost are truly coming as my sources in the void tell me they are, and they begin to destroy my creations, power will be being lost at the same moment I am making the final Khetourit. And, someone else is coming with them – if I am correct he will be here to see my ascension and that's as it should be I suppose: my father.

Wait, perhaps there is something I can do to slow his progress – while my vanity would have him attend me, practicality demands I try to stop them all. Such is our bloody dance.

'What do you mean, you *don't want to come?*' Talisker was aghast. They were ghosts, aimless spirits denied their rest by Zarrus' necromancy, it stood to reason that they would want to find peace, didn't it?

'Duncan,' Malky said in a low voice. 'Ah think I might ken what's goin' on here.'

'What?'

'Well, somehow they ken their physical bodies are still alive – and while that's true they still have the instinct tae survive.'

'But just look at them Malk – they're in agonies. There's nothing here for them, nothing. Are you telling me they don't care if they wander here forever?'

Malky shrugged. 'Dunno if they've thought about it like that. D'you want me tae talk tae them?'

'Can't hurt, I suppose.'

'Right. Listen you lot. Mah name's Malcolm McLeod and I've been where you are, I've been a man, a ghost, a disembodied spirit. And then, at rest again. And I can tell ye what I know,' he swallowed and glanced towards Talisker as if he realised the truth of his own words before they even found form in his mouth. 'And what I know is this – there's a natural order tae these things. There comes a time when it's right tae be at rest. It's even something that you've earned. Ah know ye might be sad aboot it if ye think ye weren'ae ready, but that's how it is sometimes. That's just what dyin' is . . . letting go. Ye've got tae unnerstand yer confused cos your instinct is tellin' ye that your bodies are still alive. Well, they're no, no really.' As he said this, there was the first sign of reaction from the Lost, a mute shuffling, like a wave passing through the crowd. 'Yer bodies,' Malky glanced nervously towards Talisker who nodded his encouragement. 'They've been stolen by

Zarrus and anim . . . anim . . . brought tae life by taking
a demon soul fae here! Aye! And the worst thing is,
he's using your very bodies tae kill mair of your
people!' Malky looked straight at the spokesperson of
the Lost. 'It's no right what he's doin'. Ye've got tae
help us.'

'I will speak with them,' the spirit garbled in his
strange, painful voice. He walked back into the crowd
and seemed to be swallowed up by it as they
surrounded him. There was no apparent discussion, at
least none that could be heard and Talisker and Malky
turned away to leave them to it.

'Thanks, Malk,' Talisker said. 'That was really quite
moving.'

'Yeah well . . . hope it made a difference.'

The void shook and roared its pain once more. 'I
think they'd better hurry up and decide,' Talisker
frowned. 'I don't think we should be hanging around
here too long.' They turned back to the Lost just as their
spokesperson was walking out of the crowd again. He
spoke without expression or inflection but it was still
enough to make Talisker's skin crawl.

'We will come,' he said. 'For revenge.' As he spoke
there was a strange ripping noise and Talisker and
Malky were thrown from their feet as the void
shuddered again. Perversely, the Lost just stood their
ground as if riding some invisible wave. *It's them,*
Talisker thought, *they're like a paradox, they injure the
internal logic of the time-between-time. We've got to get
them out of here, and quick.*

He held Braznnair aloft again and the gem surprised
him by giving off a single ray of light. 'Think we should

follow it, Duncan?' Malky had to yell over the tortuous rending sound.

'Yeah. I think we'd better run.'

They were quite possibly the most dismal looking army ever to be assembled. They were wet, dirty, many were injured from the previous conflict and were sporting a similar hairstyle to the young Emperor's. Whole teams of men had been sent to clear the bridge and in the end, for expediency, they had tossed many of the remains into the river below. The bodies were rendered unrecognisable by the fire, so hot it had been that bone had fused to bone – Shoreth, Fine and Sidhe truly levelled, indistinguishable in their horrific death. Those men who had been given such duty were to be excused the next assault if they desired, being given support duties instead – but incredibly, many turned up, their faces so grimly determined that none would deny them.

The rain was heavy now, the sound of the river below making a background roar even at this distance. Tulann was glad, despite the discomfort; the rain was cleansing, the smell of burned flesh was clearing away and he knew that smell had been affecting the men as well as himself. In the grey blur of the weather and the mud, one thing stood out in a pristine white glow and that was Tulann's horse. It was a grey, gifted to him by Sigrid that morning along with a magnificent Fine saddle, but Tulann was riding bareback as his father had taught him. Sigrid sat beside him on a red roan and just behind him were Freya, Raco, Yiska and Melicende. For the moment, there was complete silence. No one moved and no one dared approach Tulann. He had decided that, once the Legions of the Lost arrived, he would walk his horse across the bridge and, this time, lead from the front. If they *did not* arrive, and soon, he would have Yiska and Melicende thrown into the gorge. They had been standing waiting for almost forty minutes already.

'Tulann,' Sigrid leaned towards him, 'perhaps we should have waited until they arrived before assembling the men – they're going to die of the chills at this rate.'

Tulann scowled back from beneath his bandaged brows. 'No, Sigrid, we must be ready.'

They're running now, although in the darkness it seems that they cover little or no ground. It makes Talisker think of all the times he's crossed the void before – makes him think about his perception that the void is somehow a space between worlds. The void shakes and lurches again . . . and what if it is destroyed? Do the twin worlds somehow collide?

Behind him the Lost are running also, silently, but the silence of three thousand men is loud in the starkness of this place. He's panting, his breathing laboured in the thin air.

'Duncan, up ahead. Aw naw.'

Talisker steels himself – it's fire again. They will come through fire.

'What if they don't come?' Sigrid spoke as quietly as possible lest his doubt spread to his men. 'What if the Sidhe witch is wrong?'

'Then she will die . . . Anyway Sigrid, Talisker is the hero of your people – to come again at your time of need – somesuch bullshit. You Fine are so romantic . . . have some faith, why don't you.' Sigrid said nothing in response, just pulled a wry expression.

Tulann stared stubbornly ahead and so he was perhaps amongst the last to notice when flames began to flicker in the sky above the northern end of the gorge and the air began to waver as if some foreign heat was issuing outwards.

'Tulann. Sir, look!'

'About time,' he muttered. He glanced back to where Melicende was sitting and gave a small nod. She looked as frozen as everyone else, her long hair was plastered to her face and neck by the rain, but she appeared calm, calmer than he felt.

Tulann had never met Talisker but he was sure it could only be the Fine's legendary hero – he was running inside the portal as it widened and crackled with energy, although he wore a short-sword fastened behind his back he did not brandish a weapon. He was running fast . . .

Behind Talisker, Tulann could see the grisly forms of the Lost, and as the portal widened he gasped at their number – there must have been thousands of them! They also ran, following Talisker with grim purpose.

As Talisker neared the exit of the void there was a grinding, contracting sound and the shape of the portal wavered and buckled. It seemed to Tulann to be a kind a gathering of energy, a readying for an explosion.

'Get back!' he yelled to his men. 'Move back!'

*

Flinging himself forward, Talisker burst through the flames and was still burning as he leapt onto the wet ground, the momentum of his speed rolling him over and over. The image of the Lost flickered. Talisker turned back to check the portal remained open and Melicende galloped her horse towards him.

'Talisker, give me Braznnair,' she called. 'Quickly!'

It seemed to Tulann that Talisker hesitated a moment longer than he might have expected, but then he threw the gem to Melicende who caught it deftly. Leaping from her horse she positioned herself in the space of the portal, Braznnair burning and glowing with a curious urgency. She held it high and the arcs of light from its glow seemed to push the gash in Sutra's reality apart once more. The warriors of the Lost streamed out past Melicende.

Talisker walked up to Tulann and Sigrid and gave a small bow whilst absently wiping the mud from the sash of his plaid; beside him stood another clansman – and now he was closer Tulann realised he was not the same as the Lost, it was difficult to know whether he was dead or alive. On Talisker's other side was the spokesman for the dead warriors and it was he who addressed them.

'Thane and Emperor,' he said – his burbling voice was horrible to listen to – 'as we were in life so are we in death, your loyal servants. We seek only the return of our flesh and the solitude of the grave.' As he spoke the warriors continued to file out of the portal and line up in grim silence. Tulann heard someone behind him gasp as they recognised one of the ghosts.

'You must not touch us,' the spokesman said. 'Never touch us.' Tulann felt his flesh creep as he realised that the ghosts had a somehow *unnatural* solidity – the man was being rained on and this made the whiteness of his form brighter, more luminescent, when rational thought told him he should be *melting*.

'The way I see it, Tulann, we are still presented with the same problem,' Sigrid nodded towards *Aon Crann*, 'getting everyone across the bridge . . .'

'Oh no,' the spokesman said. 'We do not need the bridge.'

Even though they were still running it took some time for the Lost to exit the void. As the final hundred or so rushed towards the portal Melicende noticed something in the distance racing towards the Lost.

'Hurry,' she yelled. 'Something's coming . . . Corrannyeid!'

There must have been a thousand – they carried firebrands and this lit up the void like a tide of flame. They were closing fast.

'Come on!'

Tulann glared into the portal unable to assimilate what he was seeing. He had never seen that many Corrannyeid, no one had.

'Melicende. Come out, come out. We must close the portal.'

She ignored him. There were only thirty or so of the Lost to go . . .

'Come out!' Tulann yelled. The watchers on the rim of the gorge were helpless to do anything, but the warriors of both the Lost and the Alliance readied their blades.

439

But they were through. Melicende leapt away just as the void let out another crushing roar. The Corrannyeid were so close she could smell their brimstone stink. There was an explosion of flame which shot outward for fifty feet or more – fortunately she had leapt aside.

The Alliance let up a huge cheer, clapping one another on the back as if the victory had already been won. The Lost just stood there in the deluge of the rain; waiting.

Tulann's expression was grave. He was relieved to have new intervention but this time there could be no retreat, no surrender. He listened to the roar of the cheering men knowing he was sending many to their doom, that despite any victory, many would not return to Ruannoch Were. It was a lesson he had learned in the ashes of *Aon Crann* the day before, the lesson which made him an emperor . . .

This time there would be no rousing speeches – it was all crap. He held up his hand for silence and waited until he could hear the sound of his banner whipping in the breeze, then he began to walk his horse forward. 'Let's go,' he said.

'I can see them coming. They are like a wave, a roaring, screaming wave of retribution; Shoreth, Fine, Sidhe eagles, bears, wolves, lynx and, like a crest of malignant white foam, the Lost. The Lost are coming to reclaim their flesh.

'I am afraid. I would be stupid to be otherwise – but my vulnerability will only last a short while longer. Still, I must stop watching.'

*

'Stay close, Duncan,' Malky yelled. 'Stay close tae me.'

Talisker nodded but continued running across the bridge – beside him were Malk, Raco and Melicende. He'd been surprised to see the sorceress gird her skirts with a shortsword and dagger.

'You've done enough, Melicende,' he'd said gruffly.

'This is my fight,' she replied. 'I am like them,' she'd gestured to the Lost souls coursing across the gorge – they ran through the air as if it were solid ground, 'my flesh and my peaceful rest is over there.'

And so they ran into battle through the driving rain, swept up in a maelstrom of energy that coursed across the gorge like a living incarnation of fury.

Talisker had seen battle many times now and it never got any easier, but this was different. As soon as they were over *Aon Crann* and he saw the Lost souls method of reclaiming their flesh he groaned and cursed, hot saliva rushing into his mouth as he fought the urge to vomit.

They grabbed the nearest Shard or Flay and attempted to embrace them in a deadly hug, but if they were unable to embrace them it mattered little, the process began from the point of contact – but it was slower, they were eaten away a piece at a time; it was like looking a slugs being coated in salt – the Lost *corroded* them away – the flesh fizzed and disintegrated. The Shards in particular seemed to feel the agonies of this dissolution, screaming and yammering incoherently. And as they died, melding together into a pool of acid, a stink of decayed flesh filled the air.

Fortunately, Talisker had little time to watch the hypnotic horror of it. He was beset by Corrannyeid which seemed to be concentrating on human prey. Raco and Malky fought either side of him, Melicende and Yiska behind them. It was difficult with only one hand but Talisker kicked and lashed out with the *targe* he had strapped to his other arm knowing the Corrannyeid had to be kept at arm's length as much as the Flays. They were harder to kill than he remembered – or perhaps it was that he was getting old – by the time he and Malky had despatched three or four between them he was winded and the tell-tale warm tracery of blood on his wet skin told him something had injured him. It couldn't be too serious because he couldn't feel it, his body sending a rush of endorphins to deal with the pain.

He heard Melicende scream and turned back around. A huge Corrannyeid had her in its grasp, already its shape was changing, a filthy shadow in the grey of the rain, twisting, becoming sinuous and absurdly female. Yiska had already engaged it with the longspear he was using but the creature's movement had twisted the wooden haft, causing the wood to splinter and break. Discarding the longspear Yiska was in the process of drawing his sword – something which Talisker knew he was nervous of as he had no experience of the weapon. Lashing out with his own sword Talisker got lucky and severed the connection between the creature and its prey by lopping off its wrist, a spray of insects and maggots falling onto Melicende's body. Once released, she, Talisker and Yiska targeted the creature and, it went down when Talisker managed to skewer it through the throat – Melicende delivering the *coup de grâce* with a strong thrust through the chest where its heart might have been, if indeed it had one.

Talisker was about to turn back towards Durghanti's walls, determined to forge forward, knowing that in battle such progress, mere feet and inches, made the difference by the end of the day. His ears were buzzing with the noise of his own heartbeat and he had given himself over to the fray.

'Talisker.' He didn't hear her at first – they had come to an empty space in the crowd and he cast around for his next prey. 'Talisker.' Melicende came up behind him and he almost lashed out as she grabbed his wrist.

'What?' he scowled.

'Here. Take this.' She held out Braznnair and he blinked at it somewhat stupidly until she realised he could not take it as he was gripping his sword. 'Oh,' she mumbled. She tucked it in his pouch and he pulled away impatient to get back into action, knowing that should he stop and his energy rush were to fade, he would become fatally slow. She pulled him back by his wrist.

'For chrissakes, Melicende . . .'

'Listen to me. You have to get to Zarrus. Soon. He must be destroyed and the time to do it is limited. Very limited. Don't fight. Take your friends and run – Zarrus is in the dungeons.' As she spoke, Melicende began to fade, first becoming transparent and ghost-like so that Talisker could see the silver rainlight through her form.

'What the . . .?'

'One of the Lost has found my mortal flesh,' her voice was almost too quiet to hear above the din and Talisker moved in as near to her as he could.

'You're dying?' He knew it was a stupid thing to say with dead and dying people all around, but up until a second ago Melicende had seemed so real.

'Talisker . . .' he heard Malky yell but he was unable to tear his gaze from Melicende's vanishing for long seconds.

She smiled. 'I was always dead, Talisker. I am sorry about . . .' she nodded towards his hand.

'No, no it's all right. I mean, it wasn't your fault. Melicende . . . th-thankyou . . . you . . .' But she had gone; faded from sight. As Talisker turned away towards Malky and Raco he saw Yiska staring at the spot where she had been, mesmerised it seemed.

'Yiska! Move it! You heard what she said! We've gotta get to Zarrus.'

But getting to Zarrus – even getting into Durghanti – seemed unlikely. As they raced forward, making good progress for all of two minutes, Talisker heard a chorus of yells from the Alliance soldiers and glanced up to where some of them were pointing. A crackle of energy was flickering out from the main building of the keep. He had not been there when Zarrus' fire had consumed the troops before but he had heard enough to know that the men feared it more than any creature the necromancer had devised. There was *nothing* anyone could do against the lightning and the ensuing flames. In the distance to his left he saw Tulann, the young Emperor, yelling at his men to raise their shields. They had prepared in as much as they could, soaking the leather of their *targes* in the rainwater. No one was kidding themselves that it could deflect a sustained burst of the magical energy but it was all they could do.

Those around the Emperor raised their shields just as

the flames struck and the reaction spread outwards – of course many were unable to defend themselves in such a way as they struggled with Corrannyeid. The lights arced out from Durghanti keep with a sound like a giant whiplash and, holding his shield above his head, Talisker flung himself face forward into the mud screaming; 'Get down! Get down!'

Fiery explosions rocked the battlefield and the sound of people screaming and burning was all around. Peering out, Talisker saw that Yiska was unprotected having lost his shield in the previous encounter and lay quailing in the mud, his arms around his head in the futile hope of self-protection – there was little he could do for his friend but he crawled towards him holding his own *targe* before him.

The lightning ceased after only thirty seconds but its damage was already huge. Talisker stared about at the chaos, after-images of the flashes he had seen fragmenting his view – men, Corrannyeid, Sidhe animals, bears and wolves, all were burning, many running aimlessly, panic robbing them of the wit to roll in the wet mud. Battles were still being fought regardless, some whose combatants were aflame – the sounds and the stench were unbearable.

'Come on,' Talisker urged Yiska and Malky. 'This is as near a lull as there's gonna be. We need to run for it.'

'Run?' Malky frowned. He had not heard Melicende's instructions to Talisker and misunderstood his intention. He would never flee the field, Talisker knew.

'We've got to get to Zarrus,' Talisker yelled as he started to run across through the mire. He was coated in mud, his hair plastered to his head and shoulders –

only his eyes and the whiteness of his teeth in a feral rictus shone out from this slimy coating.

'Oh, aye,' Malky began to run alongside him and Yiska ran also.

'Where's Raco?'

'Dunno.'

No one spoke for a few moments but it was clear they had lost another comrade. As they ran it seemed the battle tried to draw them back; people and demons alike crashed against them – a flailing blade caught Malk across the arm – Yiska stopped momentarily, his eyes full of new horror as a burning Sidhe bear lurched past them bellowing in agony and fear. 'Get down,' he yelled after it, 'in the mud,' but it was mercifully lost from view as Malky yanked him into motion again.

And so they stood at the gates of Durghanti. Fighting for breath, bleeding and gently steaming as their body heat had risen due to the exertion.

'How do we get in?' Malky frowned. The gates were locked and barred, Zarrus' creatures were apparently issuing from some other entrance.

'C'mon, I'll give you a leg up,' Yiska said. There was enough room to go through the space at the top. Malky went first, then Yiska – Talisker was about to take a run up so they could try grabbing his arms when he heard a voice behind him.

'Hey, You there.' He turned around to see Emperor Tulann watching him. It was obvious Tulann didn't recognise Talisker due to the mud. 'Are you deserting?' Tulann looked incredulous and drew his blade.

'N-no.' Talisker tried to wipe the mud from his face.

446

'It's me, sir, Talisker. I'm going for Zarrus.'

'Really? I think it could be too late. The Sidhe tell me he's doing some spell, trying for Godhood. Seems he already has a lot of power . . .'

'With respect Tulann, I haven't got time to talk about it.'

Tulann nodded. 'Where's your sword?'

'I . . .' It seemed Talisker had lost his weapon somewhere in the race to the gates.

'Here.' Tulann tossed him a blade – it was beautiful, folded steel with the lineage of Tulann's royal house picked out in hieroglyphs along its edge. 'I reckon we have another half an hour's fight in us – then we're in trouble. Make it count, Talisker.'

'Thank you.' Talisker was astounded, this didn't tally with what he'd been told about the Emperor.

Tulann grinned, although, given the circumstances his smile had something of a broken quality to it. 'Effie spoke highly of you.' He turned his horse and headed back towards the battle lines.

'Duncan – are ye coming?' Malky yelled.

'Yeah.' Talisker swished the blade experimentally. It moved with an easy balance, light and fast enough even in his fatigued swordarm to become a bright blur of silver. 'Yeah . . . I'm coming.'

'Well, what do we do now?' Malky was scowling at a wall which, it seemed, was a vertical pool of shimmering, liquid blackness. 'You dinny think it's another entrance tae the void, do you, Duncan? Cos, ah'm no too keen tae go back in there.'

'No. I think Zarrus must be shielding his lair, but we've got to go through. We've got no choice.'

Malky nodded. Although they had met little opposition once inside Durghanti – the servants all seemed to have fled – their urgency had been compounded both by the sound of further bolts of flame issuing from the keep and the fact that Zarrus had, presumably accidentally, set the city on fire.

Durghanti was predominantly wood within the stone shell of its city walls and the fire coursed unchecked first through the upper levels and then inwards towards the level where Talisker, Malky and Yiska now stood. Smoke was streaming down the passageway towards them even though they'd shut the heavy oak doors behind them.

'Okay.' Talisker reached into his pouch and took out Braznnair. 'Take hold of me,' he instructed the others, 'Braznnair might protect us . . . after three. One, two, three . . .'

They had taken a few steps back instinctively wishing to gain momentum so now they ran towards the barrier. Just before they made contact Malky let out a battle-cry and they leapt into the space, their grim determination ablaze on their faces, their mud-crusted plaids swinging with the momentum. A leap into the unknown, possibly more frightening than anything they had faced that day.

But only Talisker landed. Clattering ungraciously onto the stone floor he instantly realised his companions were missing. Turning back he saw them – they were caught, held like flies in amber; they did not struggle or fight against the viscous trap, they were frozen. He stared at their fixed expressions for long moments –

there was little sign that they were suffering. Malky's face was still contorted with the yell, his left hand brandishing his sword ready to do battle, should he ever land. Yiska was more composed, his fear and hesitation unmistakable on his features.

Talisker felt sure they were not dead, but if Zarrus was not stopped soon it would be immaterial. He glanced around the dimly lit corridor, a cold breeze was blowing from somewhere and it carried bright echoes of a stench which was worrying. 'I'll come back for you guys, promise.' He had no idea if they could hear him, but it helped him to articulate his promise.

As he passed down the corridor he realised that this place could not physically be inside Durghanti – the ceilings stretched so far up into the distance their pinnacles were obscured by wisps of mist or cloud like some vast gothic cathedral.

'Talisker.' He jumped when he heard the voice; it was mocking and cruel – and he could not help but think it faintly familiar. It echoed around the empty space, the sound dying away in the distance like a sigh.

'Zarrus,' he growled. 'Come out, show yourself.' He knew that was another pointless thing to say but the situation had an intrinsic inevitability to it. Zarrus was watching him for sure.

As he turned the corner Talisker entered the charnel house of Zarrus. He let out a low, sickened groan when he saw the defiled corpses stretching away into the distance on their stone slabs. On some of the slabs there were merely bits of bodies left, unidentifiable scraps of bloody anatomy. But there were more slabs than bodies; only the first three rows were full, behind them the empty spaces marked the birthplace of Zarrus' unwitting army. Talisker walked down the line trying to tear his fascinated gaze away from the dead, swearing to himself that he would not allow Zarrus to meddle with any more souls.

As he neared possibly the hundredth slab, something made him gasp with fright; a sound issued from one of the bodies. Not any ghostly sound but something equally unexpected – the high beeping pulse of a watch alarm.

'Huh?'

He raced towards the source of the sound – the body there was not Sidhe or Fine, or even Shoreth. It was a young man, a Navajo, he was wearing jeans and sturdy desert boots, a silver Kopelli on a chain is around his neck. It seemed he was killed quickly, looked almost as if he was sleeping. How had he got there?

Talisker moved to the next slab and the next; there were about twenty or so Navajo, mostly young men, a few older. He was completely aghast. He stared around the vastness of the chamber, his eyes round with shock.

'You – you've been to my world?' he yelled. 'You've friggin' well been to *my* world!'

A burst of laughter echoed through the space, sending a flight of black birds coursing and wheeling through the buttresses and arches high above. Talisker tried to calm himself, but he was shaking with fear and indignation. If Zarrus had been killing the Navajo it meant he had used the gateway in the Mummy Cave – and that meant this was *his fault*, except that the dreams of Rodney had brought them there in the first place.

'Self-fulfilling-fucking-prophecy,' he cursed. He looked at the final slab, a young boy, couldn't have been more than fifteen. '*Zarrus*! I'm coming for you, you bastard.'

There was a doorway just to one side of a column, it was kind of insignificant looking but Talisker knew of old that this meant nothing. Running towards it he kicked it open sending it crashing back against the wall. The room was in relative darkness and Talisker drew his new silver blade before going in.

It was a tiny room – an antechamber, he guessed – and there was little in the way of furniture or decoration, except for a Spartan wooden bench against the wall. Although it was in darkness, light spilled out across the floor coming from underneath yet another doorway in the far wall. That was where Zarrus would be, he was sure. Somewhere deep down he felt faintly surprised that the General had not sent his forces against him, that his inner sanctum should be so ill guarded – but then, why did it matter if the time of his ascension was really as close as it seemed?

Talisker stepped into the room, his eyes adjusting to the low light. As he did so, a figure seemed to detach itself from the shadows and walked, slowly and confidently, towards him.

As the light spilled onto the Shard – for such it was, its blue light scars strangely muted – Talisker gave an anguished yell of despair.

'Noooooo . . . Zarrus! Zarrus, you . . . you . . .' He fell to his knees, tears coursing unchecked down his face. 'I can't . . .' he cried. 'I can't . . .'

It was Sandro.

Chapter Twenty

It's taller than most Shards; blue light issues from rents in its ripped flesh across the torso and around the thigh of one leg as if it had been pulled off and re-attached. It doesn't attempt to speak and this is a blessing to Talisker whose sanity could not have stood the sound of his best friend's voice. It's definitely Sandro though, even death has not robbed him of the olive gold of his skin; his hairline has receded in the last couple of years but he still wears his trade-mark ponytail low against the nape of his neck.

Perhaps most importantly of all, he is carrying a battleaxe.

It's not him, Talisker thinks. He almost yells it at himself to have his rational thoughts heard above the chaotic screaming of his mind. *It's not really him. If he's here like this, he's dead already. Christ, he's dead. Sandro . . .*

The Shard (*because that's how he has to think of it*) unexpectedly smiles. Probably a convulsion of the dead muscles in his face. But it's Sandro's smile – like he's gonna say '*Ciao bella,*' any moment now.

Talisker stands up and takes an involuntary step backwards into the doorway. He wants to say something but he knows it's stupid, pointless. 'Zarrus did this to you,' he hisses through gritted teeth. His throat is constricted as if someone has tied a noose around it and the words escape him as an agonised sound. Tears are coursing down his face but even so, he feels his fingers tighten around his blade. '. . .gonna have to kill you.'

He ducks just in time as the battleaxe crashes into the side of the doorframe. He's shocked by the speed of the thing but then, Sandro was always deceptively fast for a man of his size. There's no room to sidestep and wield his sword while the Shard tugs the axe from where it's lodged in the wood so Talisker steps back into the larger room.

'Come on, Sandro,' he yells. A strangled sound escapes his throat as he realises his intent has to be deadly serious or he will not survive. He must do the deed and do it quickly – only then will he have the opportunity to make Zarrus pay.

The Shard steps out through the doorway and walks swiftly over to Talisker, drawing its arm back to swing the axe again. Talisker has never liked battleaxes, thinks they are clumsy, artless weapons, and Sandro had agreed with him. For some absurd reason this thought cheers him. It cannot have been Sandro's decision to take the axe, therefore, *it's not him . . . it's not him . . .*

Talisker whirls away at the last moment and the axe hits the column, knocking a chunk from the marble. He's behind the Shard now, to its right side and he should aim to drive his blade into its neck – he knows that's their most vulnerable part. But he hesitates, feeling awkward and clumsy with the sword in his left hand, missing the opportunity as the creature turns to face him and, feigning with his left arm which holds the axe, lashes out a tight fist and punches Talisker hard between the ribs. Talisker is winded, staggers back against the nearest slab, his mutilated arm, flailing in his quest for balance, crashes into the stone sending shockwaves of pain up through his shoulder. He glances back towards the slab on which lies the cold body of the young Navajo; anger flares in him again – which is a good thing, it gives him perspective.

'See, look what he's done, Sandro. I gotta get him, just let me . . .' Although he knows reasoning with the walking corpse of his dead friend is pointless, it's like he has to justify it to himself – what he has to do.

'Sandro. It's not you. I'd never – I'd never . . .' he doesn't even really hear what he's saying, the stream of words only a vocalisation of something he knew that Sandro would have known anyway. It's as if his mind is distracting him, racing away from the moment . . . as he lunges in with the sword Tulann has given him and – slipping beneath the lumbering swing of the axe – jabs the blade through the throat of the Shard, severing the dead jugular, the magic, the *Khetourit,* the . . . whatever it is that animates and possesses the body of Alessandro Chaplin.

Just before the Shard drops soundlessly to the ground, the blue lights pulsing its distress, Talisker tries to back-step away as the shard makes a compulsive movement, swinging the axe loosely back, its momentum dying as the creature dies. The swing catches Talisker unaware and the steel bites through the top of his thigh, fortunately not contacting bone – it is a flesh wound, but bad enough and it bleeds ferociously.

Talisker just stands and watches the creature, his sword hanging loosely from his hand, warm blood coursing down his leg. After a few moments, the lights begin to obscure the body and maybe, just for a tiny second, Talisker sees something of his old friend in the eyes. But then, that's not possible because Sandro's soul must be like the Lost, wandering the void forever.

'Shit, shit, shit. That was too easy . . . he didn't fight me much. He was my friend.' He's still talking nonsense, watching the blue lights do the vanishing.

And when he's gone, there's something left on the ground. Talisker sheaths his blade and bends down to retrieve the object, knowing before his hand closes over it that it will be Sandro's crucifix. He had worn it all his life – his father gave it to him. Talisker crushes the gold cross in his palm, wishing it was warm.

'*Zarrus!*' He tips his head back and screams the name aloud again watching the birds or bats way up there wheel across the roofspace.

The door, he thinks. He's behind that door Sandro was protecting.

Suddenly the urgency of the situation grabs him once more and he knows there will be time to mourn later. Vaguely, he hopes that his leg wound will stop bleeding of its own accord – he knows the blow did not hit an artery or he would not be standing. He draws his sword and begins to run as best he can, crossing the darkened antechamber in seconds, on reaching the door he turns and puts his shoulder to it and it falls open with surprising ease, catapulting Talisker forward onto the floor with his own momentum.

*

Inside, the room is lit with perhaps a thousand candles, they give a flickering white light to the scene. There are more bodies, freshly killed by the look of them, and he realises with no surprise where all the servants have gone. Zarrus is ignoring him, leaning over one of them with a knife; he has removed the corpse's heart and severed a main artery in the process, there is blood everywhere.

This could be the last one, Talisker thinks, *the last soul he needs.* He glances at the others. Nearest him is a young woman and she is wearing a Khetourit stone around her neck.

'Zarrus,' he fidgets with his blade, suspicious of Zarrus' feigned ease. There must be a reason he thinks he can ignore an armed man, Talisker glances around looking for Shards, but nothing else is moving in the chamber – perhaps he's bluffing, Generals would be good at that, he guesses. Talisker's never seen the general before and he's smaller than he had imagined, also in the low light of the chamber his hair at the back looks dark, which is most unusual for a Shoreth.

Zarrus turns around and walks into the lighter area in the centre of the room where he sits with arrogant nonchalance on a low stool. His hands, face and clothes are smeared with blood but that does not stop Talisker from recognising him.

'Hello, father,' he says.

'*Jahl?*' Talisker feels his legs begin to shake, from muscle fatigue, blood-loss and shock. 'How in the hell did you . . .?'

'Oh, in hell is right. That's where my darling sister sent me. It took me years to claw my way back up and out to the edges of the void. By the time I had, I didn't look like this any more . . . I looked like this.'

There's a sudden flicker, like a magician's trick of the light, and sitting on the chair in Jahl's stead is a hideous slimy brown demon, a small, chittering thing with bat-like arms and stick thin limbs. It's so horrible Talisker recoils but then it's gone and Jahl is back.

'Not very attractive, I'm sure you'll agree.'

'Where's Zarrus?'

'Oh, he's right here,' Jahl waves his hands theatrically, 'I used him as raw material. Promised him power, eternal life. Well,' he grinned nastily, 'you know the drill.'

As Jahl spoke, Talisker noted that in the corner of the room was something that looked like a font or a well. Tendrils of light were emerging from it, tentatively questing over the rim. The longest strand was approaching the nearest corpse.

He's stalling me.

Without any warning Talisker runs towards where Jahl is sitting and aims his blade straight for his heart. But at the last moment, Jahl vanishes. Talisker hears his laughter from the other side of the room.

'I do believe you've become slower in your old age. I see my creation has added to the damage done by the Sidhe.'

'How many, Jahl?'

'Huh?'

'How many more souls do you have to steal?'

'Oh, only one.'

The light tendrils are snaking out of the well, the first is almost at the wrist of the nearest corpse. With a yell

Talisker stumbles towards it and hacks at the light. He is amazed when it works, the light is severed and recoils back as if injured. But there is no time to congratulate himself, the other lights twist towards him with deadly purpose and begin to wrap themselves around his ankles and waist. He curses and hacks at them, but for each he severs, another two appear. They are holding him back and he is weakening now; he glances at the corpse again and sees the thickest strand begin to twist itself around the wrist.

'No!' he tries to hack out with his blade once more but his wrist is caught, held tightly by the snake-like soul.

'It's over, father,' Jahl says.

He watches in horror and time seems to stretch into miserable minutes as the light progresses up the arm, towards the neck where Jahl has fastened the *Khetourit*.

There's a bang, like something collapsing and Jahl's sanctum is shaken. The fire in Durghanti has reached the physical boundary of Jahl's space. At the same instant Malky and Yiska rush in.

'Malky! Kill that light thing! Hurry!'

Malky casts around to see what Talisker is yelling about. 'What? That . . .'

'Yeah, do it, chop his arm off, anything.'

Without further question Malky slashes the light apart, severing it far enough down that it will take minutes to recoup its loss.

Jahl curses and runs towards one off the corpses intent on dragging it nearer to the well. Malky who is helping Talisker to sever the bonds which hold him, sees Jahl for the first time.

458

'Frickin' hell! That's . . .'

But Yiska has no previous knowledge of Talisker's bastard son and perhaps, for that reason he is less intimidated than he might otherwise be. He runs forward, drawing his dagger and stabs Jahl in the only area he can reach, his shoulder.

The wound is deep and Jahl drops the corpse he holds and staggers to his knees. Malky and Talisker are almost free of the lights but not quite. 'Finish him,' Malky shouts. 'Don't wait . . .'

But Yiska cannot. He has never killed another human being – Shards, Flays, Corrannyeid during the battle, but fortunately for his continued survival has not come face to face with a human foe before. He hesitates.

Talisker is free. He lurches across the room leaving Malky to hold the lights at bay – which he does with his usual scurrilous curses. Jahl is just standing up as Talisker reaches him. Father or not, he has no hesitation and plunges his blade so deep into Jahl's chest it emerges from his back. He looks him straight in the eye as he does so.

'For Regan,' he growls.

Jahl falls back soundlessly, his dead weight crashing against the chair which leaves him propped up, graceless in death. Talisker grins nastily, knowing how that would grieve his vanity.

There's another crashing sound from outside and the smell of smoke permeates the room. 'We've got to get out of here,' Yiska says.

'Aye, but how come these bloody things are no stoppin'?' Malky yelps, hacking at another of the light tendrils. 'Should his spell no jist stop?'

Yiska races over to help and Talisker is just about to say something when a movement near Jahl's body catches his eye. 'Aw yuck,' he mutters. It's the thing – the demon that Jahl had become whilst languishing in hell. It is breaking out of the corpse.

He cannot conceive of the idea that it could have been physically inside the body, but somehow it has reformed itself. It is covered in the hot blood of its host and the light in its eyes is sheer demonic fury. No sooner is it free of the chest cavity than it hurls itself towards Talisker – a bloodied, chittering ball of hate.

But Talisker is ready; he has his sword in an overhand grip and he stabs the thing through just as he has its host – skewering it in mid-air. It doesn't die though and this compounds his nausea. 'Ah jeezuzchrist,' he breathes. It begins to pull itself along the length of the blade and Talisker does not want to even think about what will happen if it reaches his hand.

'Duncan, ower here!' Malky shouts.

Of course. Running across the room, praying his bloody leg will not fail him yet, Talisker casts the thing into the well, sword and all. The creature, so focussed on the object of its hate, does not realise his intent until too late. The last he sees of it is its furious little face as the weight of the sword makes it plummet back towards where it came from.

Talisker watches for long moments to make sure the thing is really gone. 'Bye, son,' he says quietly. The lights have stopped this time and he feels that's as good an indication as any that his son is finally, irrevocably, dead.

*

Outside, the battlefield had fallen into a stupefied silence. Zarrus' creatures had vanished – even those who had yet to be reclaimed by the Lost. The Lost had also gone, disappeared in that same instant. Only the dead and the living of the Alliance army were left on the field; those who had survived this day were too shell-shocked by it to know they have had any kind of victory.

Durghanti was burning. Tulann was watching the walls intently, surprised by how few people were fleeing the city, chilled to realise how few were left alive. Durghanti had become a symbol to the Fine – the place of their glorious last stand against the Shoreth – but to the Shoreth, it was merely another conquered city. Now it would be ashes.

Sigrid rode up beside him to watch the conflagration. He said nothing at first, merely clapped Tulann on the back in muted celebration. After long moments he said, 'Are you watching for someone?'

Tulann nodded. 'Talisker and his friends. They must have killed Zarrus, it's the only reason the creatures would have vanished. But they haven't come out.'

'Ah. Then they have died gloriously, like every other man on this field.'

Tulann scowled at the Thane. 'Gloriously? I saw nothing glorious about it. Do you really believe that?'

Sigrid sighed. 'No lad,' he said quietly. 'It's just something we say to make ourselves feel better.'

Tulann turned his horse away, not relishing the thought of picking his way through the still smouldering corpses. 'Tulann?' Sigrid called. 'Look.'

*

They staggered out of the smoking remains of the western wall; covered in ashes, their faces blackened by soot and mire, beating the embers which had blown onto their clothes. Tulann grinned, inordinately pleased to see the heroes.

'Ho there, Talisker,' he called. 'Can I have my sword back now?'

Chapter Twenty-One

They had been singing a song since daybreak. The Blessing Way – or part of it – Rodney explained. Ferebe and the Sidhe were preparing to leave, the remaining eleven men of Horza's force trussed up and ready to face Tulann's justice. Effie sat in the circle beside Renee and Aunt Millie as some of the older men passed a pipe around – they offered it to Ferebe because she was seen to be the leader and they all politely tried not to laugh as she nearly choked on the strength of the tobacco.

The snow had stopped at last and the sun was peering over the rim of Canyon De Chelly – over towards the cave the black cold of the wetness and the snow still held sway, but here, in the middle of the campsite, it was good to feel the warming touch of the sun. The children were playing around Storm and the other mammoths and the air was punctuated by squeals of delight as the *Sanah* commanded their charges to pick up the children and put them on their backs. The Sidhe had all transformed to their human form and this caused some consternation amongst the Dineh. Rodney had to remind them all that, had they truly been Skinwalkers, the Sidhe would not have come to their aid.

Effie felt herself nodding. She was exhausted like everyone else, her belly full of a delicious chicken stew and, despite the strange mixture of her company the

463

world felt normal again. She had no thought of purging and knew deep within herself that something had changed in her, that something broken inside felt whole again. She wished she could explain it to Tulann.

She jerked awake as Renee nudged her. Rodney had stood up and seemed to be about to make some speech.

'I just want to say, first, how all we people of the Dinéh will mourn your dead as we mourn our own. How we owe a debt which can never be repaid. Because if the Gods sent you from the First World we know you must return.'

Return. Effie stared at the ring Tulann had given her, Rodney's voice fading into the background, joining the quiet harmony of the sing. Ferebe had told her they were leaving soon. They had agreed they must not be found by anyone once the canyon reopened; their time was limited by the melting of the snow. And that was all the time Effie had in which to make her decision.

She must have fallen asleep because when she next jolted into wakefulness many of the people around the circle had gone. The sun was blazing brightly overhead, the snow melting fast. Aunt Millie and Renee had moved to speak to Rodney and his nephew – he was called Lake, or something strange – she had seen him fight and protect the children, though, he might have had a funny name but he was pretty damned impressive.

As she walked over to them, smiling apologetically for falling asleep, she saw Rodney reach out and snatch at the air as if he were catching a fly.

'Here,' he said to Lake. 'We can't have you being Mr Hollywood forever.' He held out his clenched fist to Lake who reached out his hand tentatively, a puzzled expression on his face. When Rodney opened his hand as if to pass something to him, there was nothing there.

'What?' Lake looked perplexed. Millie and Renee were smiling as if they already knew the secret.

'I am giving you your name,' Rodney said solemnly. 'Lake "First Eagle" Talloak of the Black Water People.'

Effie had seldom seen anyone look so overwhelmed. 'What . . . really . . . ah, *Sicheii, Sicheii*, that's fantastic. Fantastic! I don't know what to say. Thank you, thank you.' He crushed the old man into a sudden embrace and Millie and Renee laughed at Rodney's abashed expression.

Effie frowned her puzzlement towards Renee who shrugged. 'It meant nothing before,' she explained. 'An elder is meant to give you such a name.'

'Like Yiska,' she said.

'Yes.'

'What does Yiska mean?'

Renee smiled. 'It means, "the darkness is over".'

'I've changed my mind. I'm staying in Sutra.' Talisker said to Yiska. They were all scorched; Talisker had so little hair left on the sides of his head he had shaved it into a kind of Mohawk, his hand was burned and he had a red weal on the side of his face which would make a long scar. Yiska too had lost some of his hair but he didn't look as bad as Talisker – there was a burn on his leg and because of it, he now wore a plaid which Thane Sigrid had gifted him since his jeans were in tatters. It suited him and he assured Sigrid he would wear it often. Malk was relatively unscathed, perhaps his strange skin was more difficult to burn.

'Me and Malk are gonna retire to the country,' Talisker joked.

'Aye. Ah'm gonna teach Duncan how to brew beer,' Malk looked animated and pleased at the prospect.

'Well, it's been . . .' Yiska was lost for words. ' . . .real. Yeah. It's been real.'

They laughed and embraced one another and he turned towards the gateway alone. A small group of people had come to see him off and this included Emperor Tulann. 'Yiska,' he called.

'Yes?' Yiska stopped and looked back. Tulann hesitated.

'Give Effie Morgan my love,' he said.

'Are you coming, Effie?' Ferebe was mounted on Storm and was impatient to be going. Despite the gratitude and hospitality of the Dinéh, this world made her uneasy. She didn't understand the strange alchemy of things like cars and had – if she were honest – been afraid when she had seen someone start up the engine of one of the trucks. Lake had assured her it was something other than magic but she could not see what else it could be and she'd had a bellyful of magic.

'No . . . I . . . don't think so, Ferebe. This is my world. I belong here.'

Ferebe arched her brows in surprise. 'Emperor Tulann will miss you,' she said. 'In my opinion, Effie Morgan, he is a better man for knowing you.'

Effie laughed at this strange idea. 'Goodbye, Ferebe. I would promise to visit but then it's not very likely.' She stared down at Tulann's ring, tears welling unbidden into her eyes.

Ferebe urged Storm onwards and the group of Shoreth and Sidhe walked towards the gateway and vanished into the enveloping dark.

It was hours after Yiska had gone. Ferebe had arrived back shortly afterwards – without Effie Morgan. Tulann had not belittled his pride by asking after her but Ferebe seemed to know and had shaken her head sadly as if in answer to his unspoken question.

Almost everyone had left the gorge now and Tulann could hear disjointed sounds drifting down from the feasting which had begun on the rim. Tomorrow, he and Sigrid would decide a course for the rebuilding of Durghanti and plans for the first free-trade city in Sutra. It would be his legacy and Tulann liked to think that finally, he might have made his father proud.

He stared disconsolately at the point where the gateway had been. It was probably closed now and, he had no idea how it could ever be reopened. He mounted his horse to begin the ride up the trail. The rain had stopped at last but the trees still dripped each time the wind caught them and he expected to be pretty wet by the time he emerged at the top of the trail. Still, he reflected, at least he was alive to drown his sorrows. He felt his spirits lift slightly; dusk was falling and it promised to be a beautiful night.

There was a bang on his back. Perhaps a heavy droplet of water . . .

'Tulann!'

He turned around in his saddle and was hit square in

the face by a soft ball of mud and leaves. This was followed by the sound of slightly nervous giggling.

'Effie?' he spluttered, 'Effie, is that you?'

A lithe shadow detached itself from a nearby tree. Effie Morgan was smiling mischievously. 'Hey, a girl can change her mind, can't she?' Her expression softened, became more serious as she noted the scars of Tulann's recent battles. 'Oh no,' she breathed, 'Ohmigod, Tulann, are you all right? Cripes, you've got no hair . . .'

Tulann dismounted from his horse making a great show of wiping the mud from his face and shoulders. 'Well, we are alive, are we not?' He seemed unsure what she wanted him to say for a moment and she walked towards him through the gathering dusk and took his tattered hands. 'Scars fade, Effie Morgan.'

'I know . . . I know that . . .'

He kissed her then through the mud and her tears.

Weeks later. Talisker is sitting outside the cabin he and Malky are building. He's been burning twigs and wood shavings in a small bonfire. Although his scar is healing he can feel a slight nipping tightness in his cheek if he gets too near the heat. His hair is growing back, a slightly depressing silver-grey, but it's a good indicator that his body is repairing itself once more. More than this, he senses within his body that the malaise which afflicted him in the other world – which had eventually found physical manifestation – was gone. The night is beautiful, blessed by a million stars and a faint southern wind. He is almost peaceful, his thoughts calm but saddened; he is staring down at Sandro's crucifix.

'Hey, Duncan,' Malky wanders over with a mug of warmed wine. 'Ah've been thinking.'

'Hmm?'

'Aboot Sandro.'

'Yeah?'

'Well, I reckon he didn'ae deserve tae be killed like that – by Zarrus, I mean. And . . . and the land needs *Seanachaidhs* right?' Talisker frowned, not quite sure where Malky's thoughts were going. 'Yiska's help is no goin tae last forever – the land needs it's, what's it called? *Hozro* back, and the way Sutra gets it is by its *Seanachaidhs*.'

'But Sandro's dead, Malk.'

'Well aye, kinda. But his spirit might be like those Lost folk, wandering the void. He could be like me, Duncan.'

'Wait a minute, are you saying . . . ?'

'Aye. I reckon we should go and get him.'

'Go and . . . Are you crazy?'

'Listen, it's no like the Gods dinny owe you a favour, big man. They just sat on their fat arses and did nothing through aw this. Nae doubt they'll show up again once the Fine are aw settled and the land is recovered.'

Talisker is laughing. The sound mingles with the tiny sparks of the fire and is carried heavenward.

'Well, ah'm right, am I no?'

'You've really thought about this, haven't you?' He stares into the flames for long, considered moments before he finally smiles and says, 'Yeah. Reckon you could be, Malk.'

Malky beams. 'So, shall we go an' get the big lummox then?'